My Lady Mage

A WARRIORS OF THE MIST NOVEL

Alexis Morgan

A SIGNET ECLIPSE BOOK

SIGNET ECLIPSE
Published by New American Library, a division of
Penguin Group (USA) Inc., 375 Hudson Street,
New York, New York 10014, USA
Penguin Group (Canada), 90 Eglinton Avenue East, Suite 700, Toronto,
Ontario M4P 2Y3, Canada (a division of Pearson Penguin Canada Inc.)
Penguin Books Ltd., 80 Strand, London WC2R 0RL, England
Penguin Ireland, 25 St. Stephen's Green, Dublin 2,
Ireland (a division of Penguin Books Ltd.)
Penguin Group (Australia), 250 Camberwell Road, Camberwell, Victoria 3124,
Australia (a division of Pearson Australia Group Pty. Ltd.)
Penguin Books India Pvt. Ltd., 11 Community Centre, Panchsheel Park,
New Delhi - 110 017, India
Penguin Group (NZ), 67 Apollo Drive, Rosedale, Auckland 0632,
New Zealand (a division of Pearson New Zealand Ltd.)
Penguin Books (South Africa) (Pty.) Ltd., 24 Sturdee Avenue,
Rosebank, Johannesburg 2196, South Africa

Penguin Books Ltd., Registered Offices:
80 Strand, London WC2R 0RL, England

First published by Signet Eclipse, an imprint of New American Library,
a division of Penguin Group (USA) Inc.

First Printing, July 2012
10 9 8 7 6 5 4 3 2 1

SIGNET ECLIPSE and logo are trademarks of Penguin Group (USA) Inc.

Printed in the United States of America

PUBLISHER'S NOTE
This is a work of fiction. Names, characters, places, and incidents either are the
product of the author's imagination or are used fictitiously, and any resemblance
to actual persons, living or dead, business establishments, events, or locales is
entirely coincidental.

The publisher does not have any control over and does not assume any responsibility for author or third-party Web sites or their content.

ALWAYS LEARNING   PEARSON

Acknowledgments

Books are always a collaborative effort, with so many talented people playing a role in bringing a story to life. I so appreciate everyone's hard work to help polish *My Lady Mage* to its shiny best! A great big thank-you to all of you!

There are few people I need to thank individually:

To my friend Janice Kay Johnson, for always being there when I need to bounce around ideas. Your gift for storytelling always helps me bring my own nebulous thoughts into sharper focus. Your friendship means everything.

To Michelle Grajkowski, my fabulous agent. As I've said before, I can't imagine doing this without you. Thank you for your friendship, your support, the constant encouragement, and all the laughter.

To Kerry Donovan, my amazing editor. Your enthusiasm and support for the Warriors of the Mist has been a real gift, something I am truly grateful for.

And finally, a special thanks to my husband, Bob. I do know how lucky I am.

River of the Damned

*T*he Warriors of the Mist are a legend, their origins lost in the shadows of the past. In dark times, it is whispered, the warriors can be summoned from beneath the roiling currents when a champion is needed and if the cause is just.

However, the cost will be high and the risks great, for if the battle is won, the champion faces judgment by the same gods who had once condemned him to the cold chill of the mountain river. If his performance is found worthy and valiant, at long last the warrior will make the final journey to the great hall where the noble knights of the past dwell for all eternity. However, if the champion is found lacking still, he returns with his brothers to the river.

If the battle is lost, regardless of fault, both the champion and the supplicant will be condemned to the netherworld. Together they will wander without hope and without light, lost in cold darkness until the ages have passed and all that exists ceases to be. Only the powerless and the desperate dare approach the Warriors of the Mist to plead for their cause.

Many years have passed since last a worthy supplicant journeyed to the river's edge, but times are dark and desperation has once again come to the people of Agathia. There is a disturbance in the mists, and the waters grow restless. Someone comes, bringing either disaster or redemption.

The Warriors of the Mist ready their weapons and prepare to meet the enemy.

Chapter 1

Merewen tripped over a twisted knot of tree root jutting up in the narrow game trail and pitched headfirst to the ground. It wasn't the first tumble she'd taken racing through the night to reach the river. This time, though, she didn't—in fact couldn't—immediately push herself back to her feet. As she waited for her pulse to ease and her lungs to fill, she leaned back against the tree for support and used the hem of her cloak to wipe away the trickle of blood on her knee.

If it hurt, she didn't notice. Lately, pain and fear were her constant companions, her chest aching from more than just breathing the thin air of the mountains.

"A few seconds' rest," she whispered into the darkness. Whether the words were a prayer for a respite or a promise that she wouldn't give up, she didn't know. Probably both were true.

All too aware that time was quickly passing, she settled her cloak back over her shoulders and started upward again. If her enemies had discovered her absence, they would've already sent the hounds racing after her, hungry for a chase and the taste of fresh blood. The deep blue of her cloak might hide her presence among the deep shadows of the woods, but nothing would hide her scent from the pack, especially given the traces of blood she'd left behind.

She hurried her steps, well aware that if she didn't reach the river before the moon rose, all would be lost.

At times it seemed as if the very woods themselves conspired against her. Low branches blocked her way. Roots and rocks tripped her. The undergrowth sprouted vicious thorns just to tear at her clothing.

At the crest of the next rise, her hem became entangled in brambles as she brushed past them. Pausing to yank her cloak free, she heard a distant sound, one that gave her hope for the first time since sneaking past the sentries to run toward the woods.

Merewen closed her eyes and listened with everything she had as she sorted through the sounds of the night. She ignored the soft rustle of a small creature dashing through the underbrush, the whisper of an owl riding the air currents, and the breeze dancing its way through the leaves overhead. One by one, she acknowledged the sounds and discarded each of them, until all she heard was the distant rush of water down the mountainside.

Her destination was close by. With renewed vigor, she ripped her hem free and hurried forward, fighting the urge to run. She'd come too far to risk another fall that might prevent her from reaching the water's edge.

Ahead, the trees thinned out and the path widened. The roar of the water drowned out all other noise as, at last, she cleared the forest, stepping out on a rocky shoreline blanketed in a heavy mist. As she waited and watched, the mists swirled and parted, revealing the river at last. Merewen compared the reality of the scene before her to the descriptions in the ancient text she'd found buried on a back shelf of her late father's library.

As if it were burned into her memory, she pictured the faded script, the words blurred with age and difficult to decipher. It had taken her hours, days, and even weeks to work her way through the worn pages. At first, she read to keep her mind occupied and off her father's illness. Once he passed into the afterlife, she read to ease her grief. And finally, she read with desperation, hoping to find a way to save her people.

The words, written by an unknown hand, spoke of a narrow path up the mountains that led to the far edge of the forest. Beyond the trees lay a clearing surrounding a deep pool. Its waters fed the river right where it began a long tumble down the mountainside.

The rising moon outlined everything before her in stark shades of black and white and silver. Merewen took a cautious step forward and then another until at last she reached the edge of the wide pool. For a moment, she averted her eyes, not yet prepared to see if the text had been fabricated from truth or lies.

With shaking hands, Merewen drew a piece of paper from her pocket and gently unfolded it. She'd carefully copied the words written there directly from the old text. Even though she had them committed to memory, she couldn't risk any mistakes, not when there would be only this one chance to get them right.

For on this one night, all things rested in balance as spring was reborn into the world. On this vernal equinox, twelve hours of light would be followed by an equal number spent in darkness. The full moon would add its special powers to her plea. All these things promised her hope of success, something she'd had very little of for a long time.

There was no time for delays. She had to look; she had to know if she'd come to the right place. Edging closer yet to the damp rocks where the water lapped at the edges of its boundaries, she took a deep breath and looked down, gradually moving her gaze outward from the shore to the deepest part of the river.

The water was mirror smooth and midnight black, the moonlight reflecting back only her darkest thoughts. Had she journeyed this far, risked so much, on a fool's mission? No, she wouldn't believe it. Now wasn't the time for doubts that would weaken her resolve and her words.

It was almost time to begin, but standing on the edge, so far from the center of the water, didn't feel right. She studied her surroundings, noticing for the first time a stone outcropping that jutted out over the pool off to her left. Her feet were already moving in that direction before she made a conscious decision to go.

The mist had left the rocks damp and slippery, making it difficult to walk. Her heart climbed into her throat as she slowly made her way, sidestepping across the narrow ledge to where the rock widened out over the pool below. There she hung her cloak on a branch of a tree that twisted up and out from between the rocks above. With the crumpled paper in hand, she drew a deep breath and walked out to the very edge.

She ignored the queasy knot of fear in her stomach. With a deep sigh, she cleared her throat before reading the words, at first in a soft whisper, then stronger, offering her plea to the darkness. As she reached the end of the first line, she became aware of the heavy silence surrounding her. Gone were the normal sounds of the night, leaving behind only the muted burbling of the river itself. It was as if the entire world held its breath in anticipation of what was to come.

The words, awkward at first, now poured from her mouth as she raised her hands upward toward the full moon directly overhead. The black sheen of the water swirled into silver, reflecting only the night sky above and giving no clue what lay beneath the surface.

"Mighty warriors, dwellers of the deep, hear my plea and awake from sleep. Darkness and fell deeds now haunt this land. Lift your swords for my people. This I command."

They were daring words, she knew, as she repeated them for the third and final time. When the last one died away, she held her breath, waiting and watching for some sign that the Lord and Lady of the River had heard and would release the warriors from their hold.

Nothing. Silence, at first, but then slowly the normal sounds of the night returned. The nearby call of an owl startled her, almost causing her to lose her balance. She quickly backed away from the edge of the drop-off, retreating to where she'd left her cloak. Disappointment tasted bitter.

Given the late hour, there was little chance that her absence had gone unnoticed. She had no choice now but to return to the keep and face the consequences of her follies. She shuddered at the thought of her uncle's wrath, well aware that he would likely order her beaten for disobeying his orders. She still bore the bruises from her last attempt to defy him, but someone had to stand up to his tyranny.

She looked to the moon's cool face one last time before leaving the river's edge. Oddly enough, she felt comforted by the pure silver light that streamed down from above, less lonely, less desperate.

"Thank you for listening," she whispered in the cool night air, feeling a little foolish.

No sooner had the words left her mouth than a ripple slithered across the surface of the pool. She froze, uncertain that she'd really seen anything at all. Then it happened again and again until the water churned and frothed with a deepening roar.

Fear mixed with wonder at the sight unfolding before her. Could it be that her plea for help had indeed reached the ears of the gods? Just as abruptly, the river stilled but thrummed like that last moment of peace before a storm exploded over the keep, bringing with it a flash of lightning and the crash of thunder as if the gods themselves were at war.

Then, an arm brandishing a sword burst forth from the

deepest part of the river. Merewen wanted to run, but her feet remained frozen in place. A second sword appeared, this one oddly curved but just as deadly. Within a handful of heartbeats, three more joined in, bringing the total to five. With the appearance of the last one, all started moving in her direction.

The manuscript had been vague on the details of what Merewen should expect, other than to say the warriors known as the Damned should not be called upon lightly. Now she knew why. One by one, five men strode from the river. Not a single drop of water fell to the ground from either their weapons or their clothing. How could that be?

And their eyes were a horror to behold—pale to the point of having no color and glowing with the cold chill of death. They spread out, leaving her no avenue of retreat if she'd been foolish enough to think she could outrun even one of them, much less all five.

The middle warrior took one step closer to her, his sword held up in challenge. "Woman, why have you called us?"

Merewen met his hard, pale gaze head-on, holding it for what seemed like an eternity. Then she did what seemed the sensible thing.

She fainted.

"Captain?"

Gideon tore his eyes away from the woman sprawled at his feet to look at his four companions, nodding at each one in turn. How long had it been since they'd last stood together, free from the deep chill of the river? Too long by far, and all too short would be the days that they walked free under the sun and moon.

The woman stirred, drawing all of their attention back to her. Who was she that the gods granted her demand when they had denied so many before her? He'd heard each and every call for help over the centuries. Most had done little more than briefly disturb his sleep; yet this woman had called out, and the gods had answered. He sheathed his sword, confident that the others would guard his back while he dealt with her. Gideon knelt down and slid his hand under her head to check for injuries.

"Is she well?"

Gideon frowned at Averel, the youngest of the warriors. "No, she's not. She's unconscious, but there are no lumps or blood."

At least she was breathing. He took in the details of her appearance at the same time he ran his hands over her in search of further injuries. Her hair was a rich, deep brown, and he was willing to bet it sparkled with red in the noonday sun. Her hands were surprisingly calloused for a female of quality. Styles might have changed since he'd last walked the land, but he recognized expensive cloth when he saw it. Who was she to wear the clothing of a high-ranking woman and yet have the hands of a commoner?

Rather than ponder more questions for which he had no answers, he rubbed her hands, hoping to awaken her without frightening her any more than they already had. Why was it that petitioners asked the warriors to appear and then panicked when they did? Even after all the times he'd answered their calls, he'd yet to have one stand his ground. At least this woman hadn't gone screaming back down the trail, forcing Gideon to send one of his men pelting after her.

"Someone wet a cloth in the river and bring it here."

He would've done it but found himself reluctant to leave the woman's side. It didn't surprise him that it was Duncan who immediately headed back to the water's edge. Murdoch's sense of duty wouldn't allow him to leave Gideon's back undefended while he was kneeling and unable to draw his sword. Young Averel was too busy staring at the woman to do anything else. And Kane avoided all contact with outsiders. Whether the woman lived or died was of no importance to the dark warrior.

"Here, Captain."

Duncan thrust a dripping scrap of cloth into Gideon's hand and then stepped back. Gideon squeezed the excess water out of the rag before laying it across the woman's forehead. She moaned softly, and her eyes fluttered as she tried to wake up. He didn't want to frighten her, so he eased his hand from beneath her head and moved back slightly.

As soon as he did, her eyes popped open and stared directly into his, a wild, fey look in their dark depths. When she struggled to sit up, he reluctantly offered her his hand. She ignored the gesture, instead pushing herself upright after dropping the wet rag back into his palm. He didn't know whether to be relieved or insulted that she'd avoided his touch.

"Who are you?" she demanded now that she had gathered her wits about her. Then she answered her own question. "The Warriors of the River, the Damned."

He flinched, hating that description even though it was true. He rose to his feet, towering over her. "Just warriors will do, my lady, or, as the one whose petition was granted by the gods, you may use our given names."

When Duncan offered her his hand to help her stand, she accepted. It shouldn't matter, but the slight fed Gideon's temper. It wasn't as if she knew any of them well enough to know who was the most trustworthy.

"I regret my unseemly reaction to your sudden appearance. I don't know what came over me."

Her smile was a bit uncertain, but she offered it to each of them in turn, even Kane, which spoke to her courage. "If you would be willing to share the gift of your names, I would know them. Mine is Merewen."

So she knew enough of the old ways to know that there was power in the exchange of names, especially when the gods were involved. He nodded toward Averel, wordlessly ordering him to provide the necessary introductions. It was amazing to realize that the young knight still had the tendency to blush after all these centuries.

"I am Averel, my lady, and this noble warrior next to me is Duncan." He pointed toward the other side of their ragged line. "That is Murdoch on the right, and Kane on the left."

Each man responded to the introduction according to his own nature: Duncan smiled and bowed slightly, Murdoch jerked his head in a quick nod, and Kane stood back and ignored everyone.

Merewen acknowledged each introduction before turning in Gideon's direction. His four friends joined her in staring at him as Averel came to attention and spoke one more time.

"And this, my lady, is Gideon, our captain and Avatar of the Gods."

The power of her gaze held weight, as if she dared to judge him and perhaps found him lacking.

"That is quite a title, my lord. It must be a heavy burden to carry," she said, a teasing smile tipping up the corners of her mouth.

He was too old and too tired to put up with audacity from one such as she. He allowed his temper to show in his reply. "The night grows short, Lady Merewen. We have much to do before dawn. Please explain yourself."

She remained quiet for another few seconds. Was she having trouble accepting what she'd set in motion here tonight? Second-guessing her decision would accomplish nothing. Even if she did have regrets, it was far too late for that. The gods themselves had weighed and judged her petition and found it worthy.

For the next three months until the summer solstice,

she had five warriors to fight her battles for her. Did she think they were any happier about the situation? Granted, whatever her difficulties were, he was sure they were dire or else he'd still be sleeping beneath the heavy chill of the river. But did she think the existence that he and his men had been condemned to was any better?

If at long last he managed to balance the scales with the gods, he and his men would finally find peace in the halls of their fathers. If he failed yet again, they would count themselves lucky to end up back in the darkness under the river's mirrored surface where not even a glimmer of sunshine penetrated. The alternative didn't bear thinking about. Perhaps he deserved to wander in the eternal black night of the afterworld alone and lost, but the others were guilty only of being his friends.

He stepped forward, deliberately crowding Merewen and taking small pleasure when she immediately retreated. Then her chin snapped up, and her eyes narrowed in anger. He smiled, but the expression had very little to do with being friendly.

"You're keeping me waiting, Lady Merewen. You'll do well to remember that I am not a patient man."

Chapter 2

$\mathcal{M}$erewen flinched as the five men crowded closer. Despite their varied appearance, there was no mistaking them for anything but seasoned warriors, the shimmer of barely controlled violence there for anyone to see. One even bore the mark of a dark mage on his right cheek.

She suspected it wouldn't take much to provoke their tempers, especially that of Captain Gideon. That would not deter her, not when the lives of her people depended on her ability to convince him to lead his men against her uncle and perhaps against even Duke Keirthan himself.

In truth, all of the citizens of Agathia had suffered under Duke Keirthan's cruel iron-fisted rule. Her own people bore the second burden of Uncle Fagan's selfish neglect.

Gideon arched an eyebrow and glanced skyward. Merewen followed his gaze and gasped. The moon was already fading as the world prepared to welcome the sun again. A chill that had nothing to do with the cool of the night washed over her. There was little possibility she would be able to return to the keep before sunrise.

"I must leave now. I'll return to explain everything when I can."

Meaning when she could escape the confines of the keep again, which would prove far more difficult to do if her uncle had discovered her absence. She started to retreat when the dark one, Kane, blocked her path. She spun to the right, only to find another warrior in her way.

"Please, there's no knowing what my uncle will do if I don't return before sunrise."

Captain Gideon gave her a considering look. When she realized he was staring at her hands, she clenched them in fists to hide the trembling. She had good reason to fear her uncle's temper.

"How far a journey is it?" Gideon asked.

"An hour's walk, perhaps longer." Especially when the long trek up the mountain had already left her exhausted.

He nodded as if reaching a decision. "I will escort you to within sight of your home. You will explain your need of us on the way." After looking at the others, he added, "Kane, accompany us."

But she was already shaking her head. "I appreciate your offer, Captain, but it will be disastrous if we encounter my uncle or his men with only the two of you."

Kane's answering laugh was chilling. "For them, not us. It's been a long time since my sword dined well on the blood of an enemy."

"Kane, we will not provoke a fight." The words were spoken softly, but Gideon's rebuke was clear. Then he added, "Yet. If there is to be a battle, it will be at a time of our choosing."

Merewen shuddered. What had she unleashed by calling upon such cold killers? But then, her uncle had left her no choice. If someone didn't stop Fagan, the legacy of countless generations past would be destroyed and everything, including her, sold off to the highest bidder.

Gideon turned his attention to the other men again. "Expect us shortly after dawn. Duncan, set up camp in the usual place. Kane and I will retrieve our shields from the cave on the way down the mountain."

"Don't worry, Captain. I'll see to it that young Averel

here gets right on that." Duncan smiled as he cuffed the younger warrior. "What about the saddles and tack? Should we leave it all in the cave until we have time to purchase horses?"

"For now." Gideon nodded. "Finding mounts for all of us will be the first priority or we'll be fighting afoot."

For the first time, Merewen knew she had something to offer to the warriors. "My lord, you can leave that to me. I will provide horses for the five of you before we reach the keep."

Gideon looked skeptical. "We don't have time to haggle prices if we're to get you home ere dawn, Lady Merewen. Besides, farmers aren't likely to have war steeds readily at hand."

Under the circumstances, she couldn't blame them for their doubtful looks. Perhaps she should have kept quiet until they reached the valley below. Proving the quality of the horses she had to offer would be more easily shown than explained.

She reluctantly followed Gideon down the rough mountain trail. Very much aware of Kane's silent menace right behind her, she crowded too close to Gideon in the darkness. When she stumbled into him a second time, he came to an abrupt halt.

What could she do but apologize? "I am sorry, Captain, but I lost sight of you in the shadows."

His voice made his irritation more than clear. "If you were any closer, Lady Merewen, I'd be carrying you on my back. Is that what you want?" He sounded much put upon.

"Of course not!" At least the night hid her embarrassment.

Kane's voice came from right over her shoulder, making her jump. "I believe the lady is more afraid of me getting too close than she is of crowding you, Gideon. Mayhap she's cleverer than she first appears."

She would not stand for his insults. "I'm not afraid, Lord Kane, but it's difficult to see in such darkness. Can we please move on?"

Gideon reached for her hand. "Hold the back of my belt. That will allow you to keep better track of me."

The offer was made grudgingly, but she accepted it anyway. It felt strange to be towed down the mountainside by a man she barely knew, but once they fell into a rhythm, they made far better time. About halfway down the trail, Gideon suddenly veered off into the trees.

"Lady Merewen, wait here while I retrieve our shields. I won't be gone long. Kane, stand guard."

Before she could protest, Gideon faded into the trees, leaving her alone with the silent warrior. Kane moved farther down the trail, giving her some much-needed space. She was glad for the opportunity to rest for a few minutes, even if it allowed her far too much time to worry about the fate awaiting her at home.

She had no doubt that if her uncle could figure out a way to manage the herds without her talent, he would have seen her banished or dead long before now. He already used every possible excuse to make her life miserable. Tonight she had openly defied his orders, providing him with the perfect opportunity to punish her. She'd survive. For the sake of her people, she had to. That didn't mean she didn't quake at the thought of what she had yet to endure this night.

Gideon made enough noise to alert her to his return. She suspected he did so deliberately to avoid frightening her, but perhaps not. The man had shown little regard for her feelings since he'd first walked out of the river. He held a pair of shields, passing one off to Kane when he rejoined them.

It was a sign of how tired she was that she hadn't thought beyond reaching the bottom of the trail. "I should have told you to bring bridles with you."

"I've already said . . ." Gideon stopped speaking mid-sentence, tilting his head in the direction of the trail below.

The three of them froze as the sound of dogs baying echoed in the night air. Merewen's heart raced as she recognized the distinctive call of hunting dogs hot on the trail of their prey. They were drawing close.

"My uncle has unleashed the hounds." She turned to her two companions. "It's me they want. Go back up the mountain to your men. Once they run me to ground, it should be safe for you and your men. I will return to you as soon as I am able."

Before she'd gone two steps, Gideon grabbed her arm. "You have a low opinion of us to think that we would abandon a woman to be hunted like a rabbit."

She fought to free herself from his iron grip. "Captain Gideon, I don't want them to kill either of you just to get their hands on me. Please let me go."

He ignored her. "Kane, can you distract them?"

The taller warrior's smile gleamed bright in the darkness. "My friend and I haven't hunted together for far too long. We will lead them on a merry chase."

Gideon gave his man a hard look. "Avoid bloodshed for now."

Kane met his gaze, his smile chilling. "You would deny us the true joy of the hunt?"

"It is too soon. We need to learn more before we go on a rampage."

"Fine, but my friend will not be pleased." Kane set his shield against a tree and stepped back.

Evidently satisfied that his friend would obey, Gideon turned his attention back to her. "Come with me, Lady Merewen."

Before she could protest, he swung her up in his arms and carried her off the trail. She could barely catch her breath, much less rail at him for his outrageous behavior.

Then she realized he was attempting to break her scent trail in hopes of further confusing the dogs. As Gideon loped through the trees, she caught one last glimpse of Kane's pale eyes watching them before he turned away.

The deep murmur of his rough voice carried through the night, although she couldn't make sense of the words. Then, the shadows shimmered as an unholy roar shattered the silence of the woods.

"By the gods, what was that?" she managed to gasp out as Gideon finally set her back down.

He ignored the question as he drew his sword and then wrapped his cloak around the two of them, preventing her from seeing any more. His strength surrounded her, shutting out everything except the warmth of Gideon's body and the mixed scent of wool and warrior.

Odd how much comfort she drew from the combination of sensations.

He leaned in close, sending a shiver through her as he whispered near her ear. "Quiet now. They draw close. If we remain still, Kane will make sure they take no notice of us. Once they're gone, we'll continue down the mountain."

Merewen nodded, shivering as the eerie howl rang out again. She wasn't sure which was worse—the awful baying of the strange beast or the bark of Kane's laughter as he joined in.

The woman had a stubborn streak and an unfortunate tendency to argue, but she knew when to hold her tongue. Gideon sensed the fierce pounding of her heart, but she was no coward. Lady Merewen might fear what would happen to her at the hands of her would-be captors, but her determination to protect him and Kane from the same threat had rung true.

When was the last time another had given thought to his welfare? The passing centuries all tended to run together, but he would have remembered something like that. Even Kane, who had never cared for anyone outside their close-knit group of five, had looked at her with a fair measure of respect.

The dogs were almost upon the little surprise that Kane had waiting for them. The poor beasties were about to face something they'd never seen before. He had no doubt the pack would break and run in panic after one look at Kane's companion. Their human masters wouldn't fare any better, but then they deserved the nightmares they'd gain from their encounter with Kane.

The dogs' barking intensified as soon as they reached Lady Merewen's fresh scent on the trail. That didn't last long. He knew the instant they realized that something other than a lone human woman awaited them. The taint in Kane's blood might confuse their sensitive noses, but his predatory nature was nothing compared to that of his companion.

Voices could now be heard over the din of the dogs. Kane's battle cry rang out over the mountainside, his native language harsh and raw to the ear. An eerie howl sang counterpoint to his words. Shouts of success turned to cries of confusion and then terror. Men and dogs alike scattered like a covey of quail in a flurry of noise and fear as the hunt disintegrated into chaos.

Merewen gasped, leaning in to close the small gap of distance that separated them. Gideon didn't blame her for seeking the comfort of his protection. Kane's full-throated battle scream was enough to leave the bravest of warriors badly shaken. Gideon knew well the terror the pair caused when they fought side by side with blade and claws. Their human quarry was in for a rough night.

The bastards deserved it.

As he waited for the din to die away, Gideon became aware of the nearly forgotten sensation of holding a woman at his side. Merewen's hair had a fresh scent; lavender, if he remembered correctly. Her body was curved and womanly, although she was hardly built along the lush lines he usually preferred. Not that he could remember when he'd last taken pleasure in a woman's bed. It was doubtful Lady Merewen would appreciate the direction his thoughts had taken. He felt a moment of regret that he was not free to act on those thoughts.

For the moment, the night air soothed him. Here in the darkness, for a few minutes, he was but a simple man with simple needs. This peace wouldn't last for long, not with the burden of battles to come never far from his mind. But while he could, he savored the opportunity to feel the night, to breathe pine-scented air, to simply *be*.

Then the woman stirred, shifting her weight away from him now that the hunters were no longer close by. With luck, the stampede Kane had started would continue until well after Gideon returned Lady Merewen safely home. Ignoring how sharply he missed the soft press of her hip and shoulder, he removed his cloak from around the two of them. The cloth held no magic, naught but its darkness concealing them in the fading shadows.

Gideon sheathed his sword. "We must be off. Eventually they'll begin to doubt the truth of what their eyes told them, and return."

He allowed himself a small smile. "Of course, Kane will be waiting to remind them. Let's make use of the time he has bought us."

Telling himself it was for the sake of speed and not to prolong the chance to touch her, he took Merewen's hand in his much larger one and set out again. Aware dawn was coming, he set a brutal pace. It would be a close race to return Merewen to her home before the sun crested the horizon.

He liked that she didn't complain, but then she likely needed all of her breath just to keep moving. If it came to that, he would carry her again, although that would slow them down considerably. It always took a few days of life out of the river to regain his full strength. Fortunately, the trail before them was already flattening out. Once they reached the valley floor, the path should grow easier.

Merewen tugged on his hand to get his attention.

"What?"

"Can we stop here? There is something I need to do." She looked him straight in the eye, something even most men were reluctant to do. "I promise it will not take long."

Something in her demeanor made it clear that she wasn't simply wanting to take care of private needs behind a handy clump of bushes. It was insanity to stop here or anywhere, but he nodded. "Make haste."

She immediately scrambled atop a nearby boulder. Once she found her balance, she raised her hands above her head and began to chant. Even without understanding their meaning, Gideon sensed the sharp tang of power in her words. Unsure of his duty, he laid his hand warily on the pommel of his sword. Slowly, the sweet sound of her voice soothed his mind. Whatever she was doing, it lacked the sharp edges and sick feel of words spoken for ill purpose.

Even so, what kind of woman wielded power with such casual ease? The gods he served did not tolerate those who dabbled in the darker magics and commanded the Damned to stand against it. The matter would bear careful watching. For now, with time growing short, he could but wait and watch.

She stopped as abruptly as she'd started, holding her head tilted as if listening to the wind. Finally, she smiled. Climbing down, she immediately took his hand again.

"Hurry, Captain. My friends will be waiting close by."

Anger burned hot in his veins. "Are you a fool, woman? I can keep you safe from your uncle's men, but

I am not yet at full strength and cannot guarantee the safety of anyone else. You put your friends at risk needlessly."

Rather than cower, she giggled—at him. Had she really gone daft? No one dared laugh at him—ever. He closed his eyes and prayed for patience. Why had the gods granted the petition of someone who was clearly not in her right mind?

As if realizing that her merriment wasn't appreciated, Merewen instantly sobered. "I'm sorry, Captain. I should not have laughed. You have no way of knowing that my friends have four feet, not two. They'll join us near the shoals below."

He had no choice but to follow her. Her earlier exhaustion had obviously faded, because he had to hurry his pace to keep up with her. They were nearing the river again, its song a cheerful one as it tumbled over the last drop-off to the valley floor. The water had been his home for so long that he thought he'd known its every mood. But here, far from where he slept in the black depths of its beginnings, the river babbled and chortled happily as it flowed over the rocks.

The trail took a sharp turn to the right and then back again before leading them beyond the edge of the forest. The moon still held sway here, showering the rippling grasslands of the valley floor in its dim glow. He was grateful for even that much light; else he might not have believed the amazing scene before him.

Merewen left him behind to greet her friends. Horses! She had called horses with her song of enchantment, and such horses they were! However she had commanded them to attend her, it was obvious from the way they took turns nuzzling her hand and woofing their greetings that they had been happy to come.

"Here, Captain Gideon. Let me introduce you."

Her simple joy at their presence wiped away all of the

tension that had shadowed her face and eyes, letting her true youth and beauty shine through. It was all he could do to tear his gaze from her to study the horses that had turned their attention to him.

He approached slowly, not wanting to startle them. The horses might trust Merewen, but if he were to spook them into bolting, she could easily be trampled. On the other hand, she seemed blissfully unaware of how small she was in comparison as she stood in their midst.

For these were warhorses, well-muscled and sleek, and the most impressive of their kind he'd ever encountered in all the long centuries of his existence. Why were horses of this quality running loose with neither halter nor groomsmen riding in attendance? He'd known kings who'd ridden lesser animals and been proud to do so. As he studied them, the tallest took two cautious steps toward him.

"Who owns these beauties?" Gideon asked as he ran his hand down the stallion's neck, enjoying the play of smooth muscle under the sleek coat.

The horse tossed its head and sidled closer, encouraging Gideon to give it a good scratch. The big animal stretched out its neck and leaned into Gideon's hand when he hit just the right spot. The stallion was heavily muscled and had a jet-black coat with only one white mark peeking out from under the long fringe on its neck.

"They decide their own master, Captain. However, I maintain the strength of their bloodlines and see to their training." She looked from him to the horse and back, nodding as she did so.

"I see that you two have chosen each other," she said. "I call him Kestrel because he flies across the plains. That, and the shape of that mark tucked beneath his mane."

"What's special about it?" Gideon asked as he brushed the mane out of the way. One glance at the mark had Gideon's heart stuttering as he stared at the horse and then back at Merewen. How could this be?

His reaction caught Merewen's attention. "What's wrong, Captain? You look as if you'd seen a ghost."

Still not able to explain, he pointed toward the pale shape on Kestrel's neck and then held up his shield with the image of a white gyrfalcon emblazoned on its surface. The two were nearly identical in shape. When he traced Kestrel's mark with his finger, a shiver of power slid through his senses.

The woman had no way of knowing the power and sight of the raptor were Gideon's to command. If he had needed one last sign that the gods supported Lady Merewen's quest, he had it.

Chapter 3

"*I* know not what kind of magic you wield, Lady Merewen, but it is powerful."

Once again, he wondered how he should react. The gods would not have sent him and his men to defend a practitioner of the dark arts. Lady Merewen didn't seem to notice his discomfort.

"It's not magic but merely a gift for working with horses."

"Then it is a gift blessed by the gods. But enough talk."

He turned away from the horse, wishing he didn't have to. "We've wasted far too much time. We'll never get you back before dawn now."

"Kestrel and one of the others will carry us there in no time." She grabbed a handful of mane and swung herself up on the back of a pale-colored mare. "He will also return in the morning with horses for your men."

Another man might have questioned her sanity in speaking of the horses making their own decisions about whom they would serve. But like each of the Damned, he'd been blessed with a loyal companion whose soul wasn't human but possessed the heart of a warrior.

When he swung up on the stallion's broad back, the horse danced in place briefly before settling again. After only a few steps, Gideon knew that he and Kestrel would do well together. If they'd had more time, he would have enjoyed putting the big fellow through his paces. From the way the stallion kept tossing his head and high stepping, Gideon knew he wasn't the only one who wanted a long run. They galloped for a few minutes before he next spoke.

"How far to your home?" Gideon kept his voice low, knowing how words could carry on the wind.

Merewen's pleased expression quickly faded into something edged in fear. "Once we pass through that rocky passage up ahead, we will be in sight of the keep. You should turn back now while I walk on ahead from here. The mare will follow Kestrel."

Something still didn't feel right. What wasn't she telling him? "When will you return to us?"

She immediately looked away before replying. "As soon as I am able."

"That's not much of an answer."

"Well, it's the best I can give." She kept her eyes focused on the trail ahead.

Her refusal to give him a direct answer was infuriating, but he let it pass for the moment because they'd reached the turn. The open grasslands lay behind them, but the path narrowed down between a series of rocky outcroppings. Beyond that lay a large cluster of gray stone buildings peeking up over a wooden palisade. At this distance it was difficult to note much detail without invoking the power of his shield companion. For now, he'd settle for studying the general layout. On the far side of the keep, trees marched down the hillside to end just shy of the timber wall surrounding the keep. The land on the near side had been cultivated with large pastures beyond.

He realized Merewen had already dismounted. She gave her horse a gentle slap on the backside to send the mare on her way. Then she drew a deep breath before taking the first step down the path, evidently planning on walking straight toward the front gate.

Gideon didn't like this at all. The Damned had been called forth from the river to help this woman. He would try one more time.

"Merewen, if your uncle finds proof that you've disobeyed him, what will he do?"

When she looked back at him, her mouth was a straight slash, her lips edged in white. "Captain Gideon, please let it be. I will be fine. Go back and get your men settled."

"Merewen, that's not what I asked."

This time she answered him, her words choked out one by one, full of both fear and determination. "He'll beat me or order one of his men to do so. Again."

Gideon bit back his rage. Right now it would serve no purpose, but there would be a reckoning for such abuse. "That is what you meant when you said you'd come when you were able? And the brute has done this before?"

Merewen flinched. "Yes."

"And you expect me to let you walk in there, knowing what awaits you?"

"Please, Captain, I must go," Merewen whispered. "Others will suffer in my place if I don't return to face my uncle. I will not allow that to happen. Not again. My people have already endured too much under his rule. His evil is why I called you from the river."

She walked away, leaving Gideon staring at her back and muttering a stream of curses. She was a most stubborn woman. Allowing Merewen to face the wrath of her uncle alone went against everything Gideon believed in.

If he rode forward, anyone maintaining watch from the keep would be able to see him. Deciding he'd be better off afoot, he slid down off Kestrel's back. "Stay here, boy. We'll be right back."

At least they would if he had anything to say about it. With his longer stride, he caught up with Merewen quickly. She wheeled around to face him.

"What now, Captain? You're only delaying the inevitable and making it worse for me."

"I cannot allow you do this."

"It is not your decision to make." She sounded weary beyond endurance. "Please, Gideon, I have to go."

He glared down into her face. "I am your defender, Lady Merewen. Let me do my duty by keeping you safe."

She didn't back down. "No! I won't allow Fagan to harm others in my stead. Would you let Kane or the others suffer because you feared a little pain?"

No, he wouldn't, and they both knew it. He had his water-soaked mind to thank for not figuring out sooner what fate awaited her inside those wooden walls.

"What will happen if you don't return?"

"He'll throw more of my servants out with nothing but the clothes on their backs. No one will take them in for fear of his retribution, so it is little better than a death sentence."

She shivered. "He's done it before, Gideon. Long has my uncle coveted all that my father owned, especially because he was the elder of the two. By both law and custom, the land and all it holds goes to the son in our clan who has the gift for bonding with the horses. Seeing all my uncle wanted go to his younger brother made Uncle Fagan a cold, bitter man."

"And you inherited this gift from your father?"

"Yes, but because I am a female, my uncle petitioned the duke to appoint him my guardian until I marry a man of their choosing."

"Why hasn't Fagan married you off already if he doesn't want you under his roof?"

"Because if I were blessed with a son who inherited the gift, the land will pass directly to him. My uncle won't risk that happening. If he sends me away, the horses will leave as well because there will be no one with the power to hold them here."

She looked back toward the stallion. "They sense my uncle's cruelty and reject his control. Kestrel almost killed Fagan when the fool tried to master him."

Her smile was understandably vindictive. "It is evil of me to think this way, but I almost wish Kestrel had succeeded."

Gideon thought better of her for her honesty. "There must be some way to smuggle you back into your rooms without his knowledge."

She shook her head. "Even if there were another way through the palisade, my room is on the second floor. The only approach is the staircase from inside the great hall."

He gauged her weight as he studied the buildings in the distance. "Is there a balcony in your quarters?"

"Yes, not that it matters. Fagan's men patrol the keep at all hours. They'd see me even if I had a way to reach the balcony from outside."

Once again she simply walked away.

He knew that Kane would pay a steep price for the magic he'd wielded on the mountainside, as would Gideon if he were to follow suit. This soon after awakening, he would be all but defenseless for hours afterward. So be it. He could do no less for Merewen than she would do for those she was trying to protect.

His decision made, he hurried after her. "Lady Merewen, if you will do exactly as I say, there is another choice."

She pointed toward the horizon. "The sun is almost upon us. There is no way you can get me inside the gate without someone seeing."

"Yes, that much is true. However, I can distract them while a friend smuggles you in from the trees on the hillside."

To prevent any further arguments, he wrapped one arm around her head and covered her eyes. Ignoring her struggles to get free, he used his other hand to reach for his shield and quickly chanted the words the gods had given him to call forth his avatar.

A flash of blinding light was followed by the familiar and welcome sound of wings catching the air. He released Merewen as they both watched the enormous white gyrfalcon gracefully rise into the sky above them. After circling overhead, the bird screamed out a greeting and swooped down to land on Gideon's outstretched arm.

"Lady Merewen, meet my friend and ally. His full name is Scimitar, for the shape of the weapons he bears. I call him Scim."

After her initial surprise faded, she held out her hand in greeting. "Hello, Scim. You're a handsome fellow, aren't you?"

The bird immediately stretched out his head to gently nibble on her fingers, startling a giggle out of Merewen. She repaid the falcon's courtesy by scratching the feathers under his throat.

Gideon found her reaction amazing. Most people were afraid of the gods' magic. "You're handling his sudden appearance rather well."

"Don't forget, I call horses myself. What I don't understand is how he is going to help me."

Gideon stroked Scim's chest. "I will draw the guards' attention to the front gate. While they are investigating, my friend here will carry you up to your window."

She now knew that Gideon's long sleep in the river had affected his mind. It wasn't obvious at first, but his claim that his gyrfalcon could support her weight up to her window was proof enough.

"For once don't argue. Just accept. He can't carry you over long distances, but up and over the palisade to your window is within his power. Wrap the ends of your belt around your hands and stretch it tight between them. Hold your arms over your head so he can grab it in his claws."

"You two have done this before?"

Gideon's grin took years off his face. "No, but there's always a first time."

The bird stared at her with a surprising amount of intelligence glimmering in his predator's eyes. It took considerable effort for her to return her attention to Gideon. So far he'd risked both himself and his men to help her. Either she trusted him or she didn't. Which was it?

"Tell him to find me on the far side of the keep near the palisade. I'll wait for him there."

"I would prefer that you return to the mountain with me, but Scim will be there to offer you aid." Gideon lifted his other hand toward her as if to touch her face, only to jerk it back at the last second.

She was surprised by how strongly she regretted his change of mind. "If this works, I will find you just after midday tomorrow. I'm due to check the herds, so my uncle will not question my absence. Kestrel will bring you to me."

He nodded. "After today, we'll need to set up camp where we can keep horses. Our usual one is too high on the mountain."

Merewen gave the matter some thought. "There's a deserted crofter's hut on the far side of the grasslands, no more than half a day's ride from the keep. I'll take you there when next we meet. It will need some repair, but it's big enough for the five of you."

"We don't mind doing a little work if it means sleeping under a roof."

Instead of under the river. She shivered at the thought. "I need to go."

"We'll see you tomorrow, then."

As she started for the keep, taking care to stay out of sight, she realized she no longer felt so alone. Perhaps she was crazy for thinking that the gyrfalcon could whisk her over the wall and safely to her room, but she believed Gideon. What was more, she no longer feared her uncle's retribution, knowing that she had Gideon and his men on her side.

Running full out, she finally reached the palisade, breathless and exhausted from her sleepless night. She leaned against a tree for support as she pulled off her belt and studied the sky, watching for Gideon's falcon. A soft cry above and behind caught her attention. The falcon sat high in the tree, his beak open as if laughing at her. How long had Scim been watching her?

"All right, feathery one, you won the race. Now what?"

Just as she spoke, she heard the sound of shouting coming from inside the keep. At first she feared that she'd been discovered, but then she realized they were reacting to the distraction Gideon had created at the front gate.

Immediately the bird spread his wings and silently swept down out of the tree right at her. Merewen managed to stand her ground and position herself as Gideon had directed. When the bird latched onto the leather with his talons, he pumped hard with his powerful wings. Suddenly Merewen found herself flying over the high wall surrounding the keep, praying she didn't fall atop the pointed ends of the logs that made up the palisade.

The ride put painful stress on her shoulders, but she'd experienced far worse. Gritting her teeth as they cleared the wall, she held on as the bird headed straight for the small balcony off her room. How had he known which one was hers? This was no time for questions even if the bird had a way to answer them. The building was coming at her too fast. She could but hope the bird's aim was true.

At the last second, he veered off to the right and let go of the belt, dropping Merewen on the balcony. Her hands scrabbled to get a hold to keep from teetering back over the edge. It took the last bit of strength she had, but finally she caught her balance and tumbled into her room.

The impact had knocked the breath out of her, but at least she was safely home. Now, only time would tell whether she'd managed to fool her uncle. It would all depend on how thoroughly he'd searched for her.

But right now her head was still spinning from the amazing experience. Would anyone believe her if she told them she'd actually flown? She pushed herself to her feet and took one last look out the window. The gyrfalcon was circling high overhead. Feeling a bit foolish, Merewen waved at the bird in case he was watching for a signal that she was safe. As soon as she did, Scim broke away, flying back in the direction they'd come. At least Gideon would know she'd made it this far.

Stepping inside, Merewen looked at her bed longingly, but there was no time for that. She had early-morning responsibilities. After quickly stripping off her filthy clothes, she washed her face and hands before putting on a fresh tunic. Her hair was a tangled mess. It was a wonder that Gideon and his men hadn't been repulsed by her appearance.

Merewen combed out the worst of the tangles and braided her hair. After pinching some color into her cheeks, she made her way to the kitchen to oversee the preparation of the first meal of the day.

If anyone was surprised to see her, he hid it well. Most were too busy with morning chores and chattering about the mysterious warrior who had appeared at the front gate. Gideon had created quite a stir.

According to one of the men-at-arms, the man had

simply stared up to where they stood on the wall, saying and doing nothing until he'd held out his arm to serve as a perch for an enormous falcon. Then his horse, blacker than the night, reared up on its hind feet to paw at the air for several seconds. At the man's command, the horse then wheeled about and tore off toward the south.

Merewen had to hide a smile. She could picture Gideon doing just that as she joined the cook in slicing fresh bread and arranging it for the servants to carry it out to the tables. It wasn't until she followed them out to make sure everything was proceeding normally that anyone took notice of her.

One of her uncle's men was just walking into the hall when he spotted her. Olaf blinked as if to clear his vision before charging across the room. He started bellowing at Merewen before he was halfway to where she stood.

"I hadn't heard that your uncle had returned." Olaf never treated her with the respect due her station, but then none of her uncle's men did.

She kept her voice level when she replied. "I'm sorry. I overslept a little and only just came down from my room a few minutes ago. No one told me he'd been called away. I had better go make sure Cook knows we'll have fewer for breakfast."

Before she had gone two steps, Olaf grabbed her arm, squeezing it hard enough to leave bruises. "Oh, he wasn't called away, Merewen. He rode out with the hounds to drag you back here to the keep. You're to be punished in front of everyone for your disobedience."

"How could he drag me back if I'm here? Mayhap you misunderstood his mission." She ignored the pain in her arm when he released her. She had to get back to the kitchen before she made the mistake of laughing at the man's obvious confusion.

But he wasn't done with her, and once again he blocked her way into the kitchen. "Where were you,

Merewen? Your uncle will want to know how you managed to sneak back in through the gate without being seen and who helped you. He knows you were not in your room last night."

"And why would he think that?" Although she could guess.

The brute was enjoying this. "Because I told him. He sent me to check on you. Your bed was empty."

"Did you check in the garderobes? Last night's stew didn't settle well with me, and I was up several times."

The man blanched, answering her question without words. No, he hadn't checked and now believed he was responsible for sending her uncle and his men on a wild chase through the mountains for no reason.

Perhaps she should feel some guilt that Olaf might bear the brunt of her uncle's temper, but she couldn't bring herself to feel much regret. The man was cruel and picked on anyone he saw as his inferior in either strength or station.

"You weren't to be found, Lady Merewen. Admit that you were outside of the keep for the night, and I will try to convince your uncle to show mercy when he punishes you."

That was an obvious lie. Olaf would never have the courage to interfere with her uncle's plans. "But if you were on duty, Olaf, you know I didn't come through the gate, and it would be impossible for me to climb the walls."

All of which was true. She gave him a sympathetic look. "I'm sure my uncle will overlook your mistake, Olaf. We both know what a forgiving man he is. Now, if you'll excuse me, I believe I just heard the gate swing open. If he and his men have been out riding all night, they will be hungry."

She left Olaf standing there, his face pale beneath his shaggy red beard. Once she was safely out of his sight, she stopped to take some calming breaths. This wasn't over yet. Her uncle was not the fool his man Olaf was. It wouldn't be easy to convince him that she hadn't disobeyed his orders if he was of a mind to torment her. That he'd spent the night in his saddle rather than his bed wouldn't help his already unpredictable temper.

It wouldn't take Fagan long to send for her once he learned she was there. It would be better to confront him directly than to be dragged into his presence, if for no other reason than her pride. She stopped in the kitchen long enough to pick up a ewer of fresh water and a basket of apples before returning to the great hall.

The first of the riders had just arrived. Merewen joined the rest of the household in watching them file into the hall. They looked exhausted, and a couple wore rough bandages on their arms or heads. Had her uncle been one of the casualties? Had Kane disobeyed Gideon's orders and gone on the attack?

With a sick feeling, she waited and watched. Two more men limped in to sit down at the first table they reached. The tension in the hall thrummed in the air as everyone waited for their leader to make an appearance.

Finally, the dogs poured through the door, heading straight for the warmth of the fireplace. A few were favoring a leg or had cuts to show for their efforts; the night had been rough for both man and beast. Right behind them came her uncle. He paused inside the doorway and scanned the room, enjoying his power to bring all work to a halt with a single glance.

From a distance, Fagan was a comely man, his appearance reflecting all the wealth and power her inheritance could purchase. It was a shame he didn't see the need to invest some of that same money back into the lands that provided it. It was only up close that one could see the cruelty in his eyes and in the angry slant of his mouth.

At first, his eyes passed Merewen by and then

whipped right back to stare at her. Everyone who stood between them wisely scrambled to get out of the way.

"You!" he snapped. "Attend to me now."

She didn't play coy by pretending to misunderstand. "Yes, Uncle."

As soon as she was in reach, he snagged a fistful of her hair, bringing tears to her eyes. "How did you slip past us?"

"I don't understand, sir. I've been in the kitchen helping prepare the meal, but I came out as soon as I heard you'd returned."

"My dogs tracked you to the mountain, but you somehow managed to return to the keep before us." He looked around for Olaf. "I left you on guard. What time did she return?"

"I don't know," Olaf said, although he clearly hated to admit it. "For certain, she didn't come through the gate, sir. I was stationed there myself until just after the sun came up. I left orders she was to be brought to me whenever she appeared. I questioned all the men myself, but no one actually saw her leave or return. Cook says Lady Merewen arrived at the usual time to help her with the meal."

Her uncle might rule the keep, but he was still reluctant to alienate everyone. Her people had been known to take revenge in small and irritating ways. Certainly, he was too fond of well-prepared meals to risk angering Ellie, the cook, by calling her a liar without proof.

Merewen stood still as he struggled to figure out if she'd fooled him and if so, how. Finally, he dragged her a few inches closer to inflict just that much more pain and humiliation.

"If I find out that you disobeyed me, Niece, you will be damned sorry you did."

He gave her a hard shove, almost sending her to the floor. "Now, fetch my breakfast."

As she walked away to do his bidding, she heard him snarling to the guards that he'd heard enough about strange warriors and monsters for one night. She hid her smile as she slipped through the throng to the kitchen.

As she walked, she sent a silent prayer skyward, thanking the gods for sending Captain Gideon and his men to her aid. For the first time since the onset of her father's long illness, she remembered the sweet taste of hope.

Chapter 4

Gideon dismounted at the foot of the mountainside, his very bones aching from fatigue. He would've liked to ride Kestrel to their camp to show the others the quality of horse that Lady Merewen had provided. However, the path was little better than a game trail, and he wouldn't risk the stallion for so selfish a reason.

Odd as it was to find himself talking to a horse, he felt obligated to express his gratitude. He patted the stallion's thick neck and traced the hawk-shaped mark with his fingertips. "Thank you for your aid today. I pray our efforts saved Lady Merewen from the wrath of her guardian."

The big horse shook his head and snorted as he stomped his heavy hoof, his opinion of Merewen's uncle clear. Even without ever meeting the man, Gideon shared the horse's opinion. Using his link with Scim's vision, Gideon had traced Merewen's movements until she was safely inside her room. He'd have to wait until they were reunited to learn how she'd fared beyond that point.

"I will do everything within my power to see that man face a day of reckoning. Only the worst kind of monster mistreats those who are in his care."

He patted the horse one last time. "Now, I must return to my friends."

After shouldering his shield, considerably lighter with Scim flying free, Gideon started up the path but turned back, feeling a bit foolish for doing so. "We will rest to-day. Will you meet us here tomorrow after sunrise? If I am to serve Lady Merewen, we will need to relearn the lay of the land."

Kestrel stared back at Gideon, his ears forward and listening. Finally, the stallion nickered softly before spinning away and cantering back down the trail toward the grasslands below. Gideon watched until the horse disappeared from sight, taking pleasure in the animal's sleek beauty in motion.

Fighting the burn of exhaustion, he climbed toward the cavern where he and the others always set up their initial camp. All things considered, this had definitely been an eventful start to their campaign. In the past, they'd most often walked out of the river and right into an impending battle because Gideon and his men were most valued for their strong sword arms.

This was the first time that they'd been greeted by a beautiful woman with a measure of her own magic. Until he better understood the source of that magic, it would bear watching.

Right now he knew too little about the situation to know what would be required of them. The gods wouldn't have granted Lady Merewen's demand for assistance lightly. Was there more trouble afflicting this land than one selfish uncle who resented his niece's gift for working with horses?

For now, all Gideon could do was rejoin his men and tell them what little he had learned. Knowing Murdoch and Duncan, they would have set the camp up first and then gone hunting. The thought of fresh-roasted game gave him a new burst of energy.

What had Kane learned about Merewen's uncle and his men?

On the way back from the keep, Gideon had watched as Fagan's men and hounds straggled by on their way home. More than one wore a bloody bandage as a reward for their night's work. No doubt the injuries were the result of panic and fear. Did they realize they were actually lucky? Men who faced Kane and his companion in battle rarely lived to tell the tale.

A shadow passed overhead as Scim soared through the trees to land on a branch just over Gideon's head. The bird held a small squirrel in his beak.

"Eat hearty, my friend. You've earned it."

Scim didn't hesitate, immediately ripping into the animal as Gideon continued on. As he walked, he caught the slightest hint of smoke in the breeze, giving him hope that a hot meal would be waiting up ahead.

He was in need of food to restore his body's balance. Over the centuries, they had all learned not to rush calling on the magic that brought forth their avatars until they'd had time to adjust to life on dry land again.

Using too much magic too quickly meant it would take that much longer for Gideon to regain his full strength. The same would be true for Kane as well since the warrior had played chase with Merewen's uncle and his men.

As the path turned, Gideon sensed he was no longer alone. He paused briefly but then continued on. If danger was afoot, Scim would have screamed out a warning. The man waiting up ahead offered no threat.

"Murdoch, a smarter man would be taking his rest near the fire."

His friend stepped away from the thick trunk of the oak tree he'd been leaning against. He held up a brace of rabbits. "I was headed there but stopped when I heard you stomping up the mountain."

His teasing grin was short-lived. "We waited until Kane returned before going out to hunt to make sure we weren't needed."

"How much did he tell you?"

Murdoch frowned. "Only that Lady Merewen was being hunted with dogs. What kind of scum would do such a vile thing?"

"Her uncle. I'll tell you and the others everything that I've learned after we reach the camp rather than tell the tale twice. I'll be very interested to hear what Kane has to say."

Murdoch looked disgusted. "He brought that miserable creature back to camp with him. I was hoping for one day of peace before he brought Hob out to play."

None of the other warriors had ever felt comfortable around Kane's companion. Gideon understood their feelings, but the two were inseparable and had been for far longer than even Gideon had known Kane. Perhaps it was because each was the last of his lineage.

The scent of roasted meat now hung heavily in the air. Good. Someone else must have had a successful hunt. Based on past experience, they would all crave extra food as if making up for the years without eating a single meal.

Today they would sleep in shifts and then begin training at sunrise even though the time spent in the river did little to dull their fighting skills. In fact, the five of them remained unchanged from one awakening until the next. As far as Gideon could discern, none of them had aged a day since they first were banished to sleep beneath the river.

Instead, it was the world itself that moved on, ever changing as they slept. In order to cope, they'd learned to find strength and comfort in the familiar, which helped them to accept the things that were new and different.

The trees grew sparser, letting through more of the sunshine from above. Gideon paused to hold his face up to the light, taking pleasure in its warmth. When a man spent decades upon decades sleeping in the damp chill of the river's darkness, he learned to appreciate the light.

As always, Murdoch stood at Gideon's shoulder, his patience infinite.

Mindful that he wasn't the only one in need of a meal and sleep, Gideon moved on. A few minutes later they reached the campsite. There was no written rule that they always had to start off in the same spot, but it provided them with another familiar anchor to this world.

When they entered the clearing, Averel was seated by the fire, turning a sizable piece of meat on a spit. The young warrior looked up with a smile. "Captain, just in time. We were about to go looking for you."

Duncan came out of the cavern carrying several bedrolls. He dumped them in a haphazard pile. "Gideon, I am glad you have returned. I've had a hard time keeping our young friend here from eating your share of the meal."

"Well, then dressing these will keep him busy and out of trouble." Murdoch dropped his own catch at Averel's feet. "Get those cleaned and ready to cook. Once they're on the spit, we'll eat."

As usual, Averel did exactly as he was told without complaining. They all treated him as a favored younger brother but never underestimated him as a fellow warrior. Despite his good nature, he was as fierce in battle as any of them.

He quickly cleaned the hares and set them to cooking. Meanwhile, Duncan carved the venison and passed out portions to each of them. Kane walked out of the cave just in time to join them.

Gideon didn't want to think about how long it had been since he'd last eaten a meal. How he and his men survived the centuries with neither food nor drink was a mystery only the gods could answer. He chewed the first few bites slowly to give his body a chance to adjust to having all the usual human needs again.

They ate in silence, relishing the moment of peace sitting in the sunshine. Even Kane, whose nature made him more attuned to the darkness, seemed content in the moment. Maybe the night's adventure had eased his inborn need for violence.

After they finished their meal, Averel carried the bones out into the woods to provide a meal for the local scavengers. When he returned, he joined the others in staring at Gideon expectantly. He'd rather be sleeping, but he'd get no rest until such time as he satisfied their curiosity. Not that he blamed them. It was difficult to guard against danger without knowing what it was.

He quickly repeated what little Merewen had told him about the situation and then added his own grim conclusions. "Her uncle is determined to destroy what he cannot possess. His younger brother inherited the family wealth along with the talent with horses that made that possible. Under the current laws, Merewen herself cannot inherit because she is a woman."

He paused to sip some water before continuing. "Her uncle knows that her ability to work with horses will pass through her direct bloodline, not his. If she were to give birth to a son with her talent, Fagan's control over the manor and all of its wealth and land would end."

Duncan, always the first to follow facts to their logical end, spoke next. "Then I'm surprised he hasn't already arranged for her to die in a fatal accident. If she were out of his way, would he not inherit anyway?"

Gideon shook his head. "Not according to Merewen. Their clan's true wealth lies in the quality of the horses they breed. She claims the herds will leave if there is no one with the gift to hold them. Then the duke who now rules Agathia would be free to award the manor to one of his own followers or even take it for himself."

Murdoch joined the conversation. "On our past campaigns in this area, we heard nothing of this gift. You speak as if this were more than a talent for judging horse flesh and choosing the strongest stallions and mares for breeding."

Gideon had really wished to hold this particular part of the conversation when he'd had more time to come to terms with the truth of what he'd seen with his own eyes. Of course, like him, his men had their own abilities that were beyond human understanding.

"She believes it a simple gift given and blessed by her gods, but I definitely sensed a powerful magic. I don't know the truth of how it came to be, but Lady Merewen says it goes back generations."

He looked at each man in turn as he sought the right words to explain what he'd seen. "You all heard Lady Merewen offer to provide us with horses."

Kane sneered. "I can only imagine the quality of horses she had in mind. Being able to pull a plow is not the same as carrying a warrior into battle."

Gideon shook his head. "After our ways parted on the trail, I watched as Lady Merewen used her gift to summon her horses."

He closed his eyes and tried to recall the exact flavor of spell she had used. It had tasted wholesome, even sweet. He still didn't trust it.

"Our gods do not tolerate dark magic of any kind, but they made no protest when she began to chant. Truly, I found the music of her words soothing with no hint of darkness or evil as she called out to the horses. That doesn't mean I like it. Too often we have seen that even the purest magic can be twisted to ill purpose. Long have we fought against it."

He paused again. "We all know well that magic is both seductive and dangerous."

"And the outcome of this calling?" Duncan asked as he poked the fire and checked on the hares. He pulled them farther from the flames as he waited for Gideon to answer.

"When we reached the bottom of the trail, a small band of mares and their stallion stood waiting for us."

Averel's eyes were wide with wonder. "Truly? They came when she called?"

One of Gideon's favorite things about Averel was his ability to take pleasure in the simplest of things. It was a reminder of better days in Gideon's own life, days of innocence that he had squandered at such a terrible cost. Rather than dwell on that which he could not change, he simply nodded.

"That they did."

Kane was still skeptical. "Assuming these beasts are willing enough to carry us, my question would be whether they are battle trained."

Although his friend was asking for all of them, Gideon suspected that what Kane really wanted to know was if any of Merewen's horses would tolerate him on their back. Thanks to the taint of his bloodline, few horses would. Gideon allowed himself a small smile before answering.

"She says the horses themselves decide who they will or will not accept. I was chosen by a war stallion, one that almost killed her uncle for daring to ride him."

He waited for the laughter to come. It didn't take long. Even Murdoch joined in. "You almost had us believing you, Gideon. Since when do the four-legged pick their own riders?"

"Doubt my words, but you will learn the truth soon enough. The horses will meet us tomorrow just after sunrise at the bottom of the trail."

He accepted the haunch of rabbit that Duncan offered him. "Now, enough talking. I plan to seek my bedroll as soon as I finish this."

When they were all finished eating, Murdoch stood up. "I'll stand guard while the rest of you sleep."

Once again Averel gathered up the scraps. "I'll take the next shift, Murdoch. Wake me when it's time."

Gideon stretched out a short distance from the fire in the dappled shade of the trees. While the quiet murmur of his friends' voices lulled him to sleep, he found himself thinking of Merewen and praying to his gods to keep her safe until he found a way to free her people from the tyranny of her uncle. And if his last conscious thought was the memory of how sweet it had been to hold Merewen's body next to his as they'd shared his cloak in the darkness, well, that was his secret to keep.

Merewen's back ached, and her head was pounding from near exhaustion. She counted the minutes until the evening meal would be over and she could safely retreat to her room. Her uncle hated it when she disappeared too early, but sometimes he also grew angry if she lingered overlong. She'd learned to wait until he was well into his nightly pitcher of wine before trying to escape from his odious presence. Right now she was waiting for him to appear before signaling the servers to start bringing out the food.

A movement across the great hall drew her eye. Fagan's wife, Lady Alina, was making one of her rare appearances for the evening meal. Although Alina was near to Merewen in age, the two of them weren't particularly close. That was her uncle's doing rather than any fault of the two women.

Alina was moving slowly and with great care, as if each step caused her pain. Although Alina never complained, Merewen was well aware that she was not the only one who lived in fear of her uncle's unpredictable temper. All too often Alina's delicate skin carried the marks of Fagan's hand or fist.

It was tempting to rush to her aunt's aid, but Fagan had followed her into the hall. Alina would not appreciate Merewen making a fuss, and both women would likely suffer later for the gesture.

Rather than stare, Merewen turned her attention to ensuring the flow of food from the kitchen to the hall continued smoothly. Then a small ruckus in the middle of the hall caught her attention. Olaf held young Edric, one of the pages, by the collar and shook him as a terrier did a rat. Then with a curse, he flung the small boy to the floor, laughing as he did so.

The boy scrambled backward until he was out of Olaf's reach. He was careful to avoid the two other men-at-arms, knowing he'd get no sympathy from them. He hobbled toward the kitchen as fast as he could. Her heart hurt for him. Edric had been born with one leg shorter than the other, making it unlikely he'd ever be strong enough to train with weapons. That made him worthless in the eyes of her uncle and his cronies.

When he walked into the kitchen, Edric wiped his face clean of tears and immediately picked up a pitcher of wine to carry out to her uncle's table. The boy never complained or asked for easier duty. For tonight, at least, she wasn't about to send him back out there to be abused again.

"Edric, Jarod needs your help out in the stable."

The boy's mood improved instantly, but his smile quickly faded. "But what of Lord Fagan's wine?"

"I'll take it myself."

She relieved him of the pitcher he was carrying. Later she'd speak to the stable master about assigning Edric to work out there permanently. The boy would be happier caring for horses, and his willingness to work hard would stand him in good stead with Jarod.

Out in the hall, she carried the pitcher to the head table. By rights, she should be seated with her uncle and his close friends, but he enjoyed seeing her play the role of servant.

In truth, she secretly preferred it as well because it kept her from having to sit with the rough lot he surrounded himself with, and Olaf in particular. He'd yet to forgive her for making him appear the fool to her uncle. She'd overheard several of the men whispering about how Fagan had beaten Olaf to the ground during weapons practice earlier in the afternoon. If that was true, it would only add to the man's grudge against her.

If Olaf ever figured out how she'd managed to escape and return undetected, he would immediately report her to her uncle and claim the right to punish her himself. She feared for her life if that were to happen.

As she moved to refill her uncle's drink, she used the moment to meet Alina's gaze, asking without words whether she was badly hurt. Her aunt shook her head before returning her attention back to her bowl of soup. As she turned her head, the candlelight illuminated a large bruise on her jaw. The sight caused Merewen to flinch, slopping some of the wine out of the pitcher and onto the table. From there a few drops fell on her uncle's lap.

"Must you always be so clumsy?" Fagan snapped. "Clean up this mess."

She averted her gaze so that he wouldn't see the fury there. "I will fetch a cloth and a fresh pitcher immediately."

He gave her a disgusted look. "Never mind. Just go before you do more damage."

She nodded and backed away, forcing her anger back under control. He waited until she'd gone a few steps before speaking again, making sure his voice carried across the hall for all to hear.

"And, Merewen, don't think I have forgotten about your disappearance last night. Once I discern how you evaded my guards, you will be severely punished."

Then he smiled. "However, if you were to confess, I might be persuaded to show mercy."

He would do no such thing. Fagan knew nothing of

mercy and took far too much pleasure in making the weak suffer. He might see her that way right now, but things would change soon. Just the memory of Captain Gideon and his men gave her the courage to stand up to him, at least a little.

"But, Uncle, you saw with your own eyes that I was right where I was supposed to be when you returned."

Then she shot a glance in Olaf's direction. "Your own man testified there was no way I could have escaped or returned through the gate while he stood guard."

The room grew quiet. Perhaps she would've been better off to simply walk away, but she had grown tired of cowering before her uncle and his men. Before she could say so, she noticed how pale her aunt was. Alina's eyes silently pleaded with Merewen as she slowly shook her head, obviously trying not to draw her husband's attention.

The bruise that marred Alina's beauty served as a harsh reminder that Merewen wouldn't be the only one to suffer were she to further provoke her uncle. She immediately backed away.

"Before I leave, is there something I can bring you, Uncle Fagan?"

Fagan stared at her for several seconds before answering, as if wondering at her sudden change in behavior. Finally, he shook his head.

"Just go. I grow weary of your presence."

Relieved that the confrontation was over, Merewen headed for the kitchen and from there to the stables, her one haven within the keep walls.

Inside, the earthy scents of hay and horses soothed her soul. A chorus of soft nickers greeted her, bringing a smile to her face. She moved from stall to stall, checking each of her friends as she patted noses and slipped a few favorites a treat. These beauties were the broodmares who now carried the next generation of saddle horses and therefore the future of her people.

"Ah, Lady Merewen, I shoulda knowed it was you. These ladies don't talk to just anyone."

A small wizened man poked his head around the corner from the tack room. He looked past her as if making sure she was alone. She didn't blame Jarod. On the rare occasion her uncle took it upon himself to pretend some interest in their breeding program, he left the whole stable in an uproar. It sometimes took the stable master hours to calm the horses.

She smiled at him. "While the others were finishing their evening meal, I thought I would come see how your ladies were doing."

There was no mistaking her elderly friend's relief or the anger in his voice when he continued. "They be doing fine exceptin' when them that knows nothing about horses decide to go poking their nose where it don't belong."

Merewen gritted her teeth. She couldn't ban either her uncle or his men without causing herself even greater trouble. However, if their presence did adversely affect the mares, she'd have to find a way to prevent them from entering this part of the stables.

She paused to stroke the nose of one of her favorites, a mare who had already given her two handsome foals that showed tremendous potential. "I'll try to keep them away, Jarod, but I cannot promise."

"I know, my lady." He sighed and moved on down to the next stall. "I swear, horses have more sense than most men, and they definitely are better judges of character. If a horse takes to someone, I figure that's a man I can trust."

"I agree."

Merewen looked around. "Did young Edric find you? I would like him to work here in the stable. He's a hard worker, and I think the two of you would get along."

Jarod's old eyes always did see too much. "I'll keep him busy and out of sight."

"Thank you." She patted her friend on the shoulder. One less person she needed to worry about.

As they continued on through the stable, she thought back to the look on Captain Gideon's face when he first saw her horses. Not only had he immediately sensed their beauty and their quality, but the strongest stallion on the estate had chosen to bear the warrior himself.

She'd never admit it to anyone, but her heart had leapt in her chest at the sight of the powerful warrior astride Kestrel. It was as if the two had been born to race the wind together.

She truly hoped Jarod was right about that meaning Captain Gideon could be trusted. The lives and welfare of her people depended on it.

Chapter 5

Gideon led the small procession down the path after they had spent an hour at weapons practice. Already he could feel his strength returning, and the others had clearly enjoyed the workout as well. Kane, especially, had taken pleasure in crossing swords with him, and they both sported bruises to prove it. The injuries would fade within the day, another gift from the gods.

Gideon had actually considered hiking down the trail by himself and only returning to fetch the others after he made sure the horses were actually waiting for them. However, fear of embarrassment did not justify wasting the time or the energy. The day had dawned hot and threatened to get more so as the sun rose higher in the sky. It was only prudent to guard their strength for the meeting with Merewen on the chance that her uncle and his men were to happen upon them.

One trip down would be difficult enough, especially burdened with more than just his sword and shield. At about the halfway point as they made their way along the rugged path, they ran into a heavy blanket of mist, which cut their visibility to just a few strides in any direction.

As they'd prepared to set out, no one had complained about the long hike until Gideon announced his decision that they should also fetch their saddles and tack from the cavern to take with them. By now, even Averel was grumbling whenever he didn't think Gideon would hear him.

He didn't blame his young friend, but they all knew how little time they had to end the threats against Merewen. Three months might sound like a long time, but not when it represented the total number of days they would walk the earth. They couldn't afford to waste a single hour.

He shifted his saddle to his other shoulder as he neared the bottom of the trail, close to where Merewen had stopped to call the horses. His pace quickened as he once again heard the happy babble of the river and knew they'd reached the last stretch before the mountains gave way to the grasslands below.

After setting his saddle and bridle down on the grass, he waited for the others to catch up with him.

"Wait here while I scout ahead. If the horses are already there, I'll whistle."

"If?" Kane snapped as he tossed his own equipment to the ground. "They'd better be here after I hauled this down the mountain."

Gideon ignored his friend's bad temper, understanding its true source had nothing to do with Gideon at all. Every time they'd been called from the river, finding a suitable mount for Kane had posed a serious plight. If the animal was calm enough to accept one who carried the mark of dark magic on his face and in his blood, then it was likely to be worthless as a war steed. Fighting to control the fear of a more high-spirited horse carried with it a whole different set of difficulties for Kane.

Bracing himself, Gideon marched forward. As soon as he turned the last bend in the trail, the mists parted and he came to an abrupt stop. Not only was Kestrel there, but a small herd of horses stood clustered behind him. The sight was beyond Gideon's wildest imaginings, for no two of the animals looked the same; yet each was a beauty in its own right.

It was time to share the spectacle. He put two fingers

to his lips and let loose with a shrill whistle, causing the horses to stir restlessly. One by one, Gideon's men joined him as they all stared in stunned silence. He couldn't help but grin at the expressions of total wonder on their faces.

Duncan was the first to break the silence. "What do we do now?"

"In truth, I'm not sure."

After giving it some thought, he added, "As strange as this might sound, I'd suggest spreading out and let the horses come to us. That black one is Kestrel. I'll go to him."

As soon as he stood beside the stallion, the big horse nudged Gideon, hinting for some attention. Gideon scratched his neck as the two of them watched his men study the horses. The mares seemed to weigh and value each of the men in turn. Finally, a sorrel with a sweet face stepped away from the herd to approach Averel, obviously her chosen warrior.

His face lit up with obvious pleasure as he reached out to stroke her nose. "Hello there. I am called Averel."

Then he blushed and looked around to see if the other men were going to tease him for introducing himself to a horse. No one said a word, as each man waited to see if he would be the next one to be matched with a steed.

A dappled gray mare whickered and pranced forward to stop in front of Duncan. Always the most chivalrous of their group, he immediately bowed his head. "My lady, I am honored. My name is Duncan."

It was no surprise that the next to be selected was Murdoch. A powerfully built blood bay with a white blaze and feathered legs slowly approached him. She rivaled Gideon's stallion in size, which made her a fitting mount for Murdoch, the largest of the five men. Tall with broad shoulders, he carried more muscle on his bones than any of the others.

Though Murdoch was usually slow to smile, his face lit up with a big grin as he and the mare studied each other. "She's perfect."

That left Kane. He crossed his arms over his chest and waited impatiently as they all looked on. Gideon hurt for him, knowing the truth about the man's worth both as a friend and as a warrior. The remaining mares shifted uneasily, their eyes wide and worried. After a few seconds, Kestrel stamped his foot and whickered.

Finally, one of the horses took a tentative step forward and then another, her eyes wild and her breathing ragged. Before the mare reached Kane, though, another horse bugled in challenge. Everyone turned to face the intruder's approach. With stone gray coloring and a face that had weathered to white, another stallion materialized out of the fog.

The big gray stopped a short distance away to rear up on his back legs and paw the air. Kestrel immediately answered in kind, determined to defend his mares.

The intruder charged down the slope, heading straight for the mare who'd been about to choose Kane. The big gray gently shouldered her aside, snorting and pawing the ground, but otherwise making no move toward the other horses.

Even so, Kestrel clearly perceived his presence as a threat. He sidled away from Gideon, his ears back and tail high. Before Kestrel could charge, Kane launched himself up onto the gray's broad back, and the two tore off at a dead run.

Gideon blocked Kestrel's path, praying the stallion wouldn't run him down to give chase. Slowly, the horse calmed down, still snorting and prancing in place.

Keeping his voice low and soothing, Gideon approached the horse. "They're gone. Everything is fine, and we have business to attend to."

Kestrel let out a deep breath and shook from head to

tail but gradually calmed and turned his attention to his mares. Evidently satisfied with the choices they'd made, he whickered softly. The rest of the small band immediately retreated and trotted off in the opposite direction from the one Kane had taken.

For the moment, the crisis appeared to be over. Gideon could only hope that Kestrel would learn to tolerate the presence of the other stallion, because it would appear that Kane had found a kindred spirit. The mists had lifted enough that he could see the two of them running in the distance, moving as one.

He checked the sun's position overhead. The appointed time they were to meet with Merewen was growing close. Having no idea how far they'd have to ride, they needed to get moving.

"Let's see how our friends here take to saddle and bridle."

After retrieving his tack from where he'd left it, he slowly approached Kestrel. Obviously the stallion was willing to accept a rider on his back. That didn't necessarily mean he was accustomed to wearing a saddle.

But in truth, it took little time to have all four horses saddled and ready to ride. As they were about to mount up, Kane returned. He kept a wary eye on Kestrel as he and the gray skirted the edge of the group to stop a short distance away.

Kane slid down off the horse's back and disappeared into the trees to fetch his saddle. As he adjusted the cinch, he murmured under his breath to the horse in what sounded like Kane's native language. He rarely used it except in battle or times of high emotion, making it clear that he and the gray had bonded quickly. While everyone waited for him to finish, Gideon studied the horse and decided he was a good match for his friend.

Certainly, the stallion would never take a prize for beauty, but something about him drew the eye. He was a behemoth of a horse. Muscular and powerful, he'd carry his rider for hours and still have enough left in him to charge into battle.

His coat bore the faint scars of past fights. How many of those were from confrontations with Kestrel? Gideon suspected that today wasn't the first time the two stallions had crossed paths. As if sensing Gideon's interest, the horse turned to face him, revealing yet another set of scars on his right shoulder. The deep claw marks looked to be from an encounter with one of the reclusive mountain cats. If so, it was a miracle the horse had survived such a vicious attack.

Once Kane finished, all five men mounted up. Once again, it was odd to let Kestrel choose their path. Duncan urged his mount forward to keep pace with Gideon and asked, "So, do we know where we're headed?"

He could only shrug, wishing they didn't have to trust to magic they didn't understand. "No, Lady Merewen only said that Kestrel would know where to take us."

His friend blinked twice and then chuckled. "I guess that makes sense in a land where the horses pick their own riders."

They both glanced in Kane's direction. He was deliberately maintaining some distance between his stallion and the other horses. Gideon noted all three mares made sure to say on Kestrel's other side. He had to assume that was deliberate and probably accounted for why the two stallions seemed to have declared a momentary truce.

For now, Gideon concentrated on refreshing his memory of the lay of the land. This area seemed familiar, although he was fairly sure that the last time he and the others had passed through, it had still been heavily forested. If he was right, then they should come to a river crossing just ahead. Unless things there had changed drastically, it was shallow enough to make crossing easy.

Just as he expected, a short time later he heard the

sound of water, and the grassland quickly gave way to a rocky shoreline. Kane and his mount immediately waded out into the river, the water barely coming to the horse's knees. The gray paused midstream long enough to drink before moving on. The other horses followed suit. Kestrel then led them the rest of the way across the river to a small meadow on the other side.

Upon reaching the center of the clearing, the stallion stopped and refused to go another step. In fact, none of the horses would budge.

"It appears that we have arrived," Murdoch said as he looked around. "I find it most strange to move at the whim of horses."

A feminine voice responded. "Ah, but these are not your usual horses, Sir Murdoch."

All five men drew their weapons but sheathed them again when Lady Merewen stepped out of a stand of trees, leading the same horse she'd ridden the previous day. When her eyes first sought out Gideon, he nodded by way of greeting as he studied her face for any sign that her uncle had further abused her. But no, she looked rested and far less haunted than she had when he'd last seen her.

Good. The man could live for another day.

Her gaze had moved on as she offered each man a smile, but it faded as soon as she spotted Kane. Her eyes widened in obvious shock, although Gideon could detect no fear in her expression. As usual, Kane's first reactions were suspicion and anger.

"Is something wrong?" the testy warrior demanded as he dismounted.

Gideon started forward, not about to let his friend take his usual bad temper out on Merewen. He'd intervene if necessary, but it would be better for everyone involved if she learned to deal with all five of the warriors on her own.

For now, her expression had slowly brightened again, and she actually smiled directly at Kane. "Not at all, my lord. I apologize for staring, but seeing you on Rogue caught me by surprise."

"And why is that? Am I not good enough for one of your horses?" Kane sounded defensive, but he'd had good reason to question people's motives in the past.

Merewen dropped her mare's reins and headed directly toward Kane. "Forgive me, but I truly meant no insult to you. It is just that to my knowledge, Rogue here has never before had a rider on his back, not even me. I had no idea that he would accept a bridle, much less a saddle and rider."

She walked right up to the gray and patted him on his scarred shoulder. The horse sidled away from her, but she only laughed. "Go on and pretend you don't like me, you big baby, but I know better."

Then she pulled out a small apple from the pouch at her side and held it out to the huge horse. Rather than chase after him, she waited patiently. After only a brief hesitation, the horse stepped closer and delicately accepted the apple from the palm of her hand.

Then she took out several more and offered them to Kane. "He has a strong fondness for these."

The warrior accepted the gift and immediately offered the horse another. "Rogue seems a fitting name for him. Is there a story behind it?"

Although Kane rarely talked to anyone outside their close-knit group, Gideon liked that he made the effort with Merewen. He also admired her courage as she stood next to the warrior without any sign of fear or hesitation. Both of them focused their attention on the horse.

"My father had a true talent for seeing the potential in a horse. He said Rogue shared not just the color of the rock that forms the backbone of the mountains, but also its strength. While Rogue might never appeal to those who look only for surface beauty, he would be an excellent mount for the right person, one who appreciates heart and strength more than looks."

She shot a quick glance at Kane before continuing. "When Rogue here was but a two-year-old, he'd already grown to his full height but had yet to fill out to match his bones. Winter that year was a bad one, and the snows lasted well into the spring after the mares had already foaled. A hungry mountain cat ventured down to our winter pastures looking for an easy kill."

She traced the deep scars on Rogue's side. "I was there when the cat went after the new foals. The mares were screaming in fear and doing their best to save their young. The cat got past their guard and was closing in on a foal that had barely found its legs when Rogue jumped the fence and charged to drive the beast back. Before the guards could draw their bows, the cat attacked Rogue and buried its claws deep in his shoulder, shredding these muscles."

Her voice thickened with emotion. "Somehow Rogue managed to dislodge the cat and stomp it to death, saving who knows how many of our other horses. Unfortunately, when the stable master attempted to treat the wounds, Rogue was out of his mind with pain and terror. He struck out, breaking one man's arm and another's leg."

Kane fed the horse another apple. "I'm surprised they didn't put him down."

Merewen nodded. "Most of them wanted to, hoping to offer him a kinder death than what he'd face from the infection that was sure to follow. I begged my father to spare him. He finally agreed, but only if Jarod and I could coax Rogue into letting us treat his wounds."

Gideon joined the conversation. "I'm guessing that was an uphill battle."

"It was, but Rogue eventually let us care for him. Even though his wounds healed, the experience taught him that it hurt when people touched him. That spoiled him for any kind of normal training."

Rogue snorted loudly and shook his head, as if he'd been following the entire conversation and agreed with her conclusion. Even Kane's mouth quirked up in a small smile.

She gave him a considering look. "I am exceedingly glad that you and Rogue found each other, Kane."

The warrior seemed at a loss how to respond. In fact, if Gideon had to guess, he suspected his friend was actually embarrassed by all the attention, and so intervened.

"Lady Merewen, perhaps it is time we make plans."

She looked up to the sky, probably to guess how much time had passed. "Yes, we should. My uncle knows that this is my usual day to check on the outlying herds, but he expects me to return in time to serve the evening meal."

Gideon frowned. In his experience, the lady of the manor had the duty of choosing the menu and overseeing its preparation. She certainly wasn't expected to do a servant's work. It was obviously just one more way her uncle had found to humiliate Merewen in front of his men and any visitors to the keep.

His men knew it, too. They had crowded close, their expressions fierce enough to have Merewen looking apprehensive. He felt an unexpected urge to plant himself firmly between her and his friends, and even took a step in that direction despite knowing full well they would never lift a hand to harm her.

Duncan shot him a questioning look. "Lady, perhaps you'd like to sit down."

He offered her his arm and gestured toward a downed log near the water. She allowed Duncan to lead her in that direction, leaving Gideon no choice but to follow. He wasn't particularly happy with Duncan right now, but it was for the best. They'd all learned a long time ago to maintain a certain distance when it came to the people they were called forth to serve.

Emotions only clouded judgment. Besides, their time was limited, and friendships made it that much harder to return to the cold loneliness of the river. Anyone they'd met would be long dead by the time Gideon and his men returned to walk once again among the living. He knew better, but something about Merewen was bringing out every protective instinct he had.

All five men arranged themselves around her, each keeping a wary eye on their surroundings lest someone had been sent to spy on her actions. Even the horses stood facing outward, watching both the river and the woods with their ears pricked forward and listening. They didn't seem anxious, merely vigilant.

Although he suspected he knew the answer, Gideon asked the question anyway. "Did your uncle learn that you'd been out of the keep when he returned?"

Merewen shook her head, but as she did, her hand immediately started rubbing her other arm as if soothing a sudden pain. Her uncle might not have beaten her, but either he or someone else had treated her roughly. Gideon noticed Kane's hand had strayed toward his sword, as if ready to defend her.

"He suspected I was lying to him but couldn't prove it. I did learn why he thought I had disobeyed him and left the keep. One of his men, Olaf, had checked my bed during the night and reported me missing."

Murdoch joined the conversation. "Your uncle sent one of his men unchaperoned into your bedchamber?"

Merewen blushed as she stared down at her lap. "Yes, and it wasn't the first time. I've only ever left the keep during the night once before. He'd turned out one of my servants, and I was trying to bring him enough food and coin to find a new home."

Gideon hated the remembered pain in her expression as she continued speaking. "I don't know what my uncle suspects me of doing now or how often he has someone check. When Olaf saw that my bed was empty, my uncle immediately unleashed the dogs to hunt me down."

Gideon's temper was fraying around the edges. "What happened after you returned?"

His question brought out a small smile on her face as she quickly described her confrontation with her uncle.

Once again she was rubbing her arm. "Although I did not witness it, I heard that Uncle Fagan beat Olaf badly in weapons practice. Certainly, the man was moving slowly when I last saw him. I would be glad of that, except Olaf already hates me. This will likely only make matters worse."

Kane, always the first to seek battle, drew his sword and snarled, "I say we ride in and kill both Olaf and her uncle and end this."

Gideon shared the sentiment, but there was too much they didn't know. If all the trouble could be solved with a simple stroke of a sword, the gods would not have responded to Merewen's plea, no matter how heartfelt or justified. Past history had taught him that the Damned were called to do battle under only the most dire of situations.

He placed his hand on Kane's sword arm. "Not yet."

Merewen was now staring at both of them with that same fearful look she'd worn at their first meeting when he and the others were fresh from the river. Clearly she was wondering what horrors she'd unleashed on the world. It was too late to turn back the tide of events that were now in motion.

Her fear scented the very air, leaving a bitter taste upon his tongue. In the past, he had cared little or not at all what the people he had to champion thought of him and his men. For whatever reason, Merewen's opinion mattered.

"Why not, Captain? It's a simple-enough matter," Kane continued, crowding closer to Gideon. "But wait. You also chose to hide from her uncle and his men in the woods. Why? Has the river washed away your courage?"

Gideon snarled back. "Would the gods have answered her call if it were that simple? Think beyond your taste for killing."

The warrior's expression turned to stone. "Killing is what I was bred for. If you no longer have the stomach for bloodshed, then stand back and let me do what we were sent here to do."

Gideon drew his own sword with one hand and shoved Kane back a step with the other. "Do you wish to challenge me? Is that truly what you want?"

The air around them shimmered with a cold energy as if lightning were about to strike. The image was all too appropriate if the gods took offense at their actions.

Murdoch pushed his way into the discussion, planting his considerable bulk firmly between them. Rarely did the big man let his temper show, but right now he was furious.

"Stand down, both of you. Now." He glared first at Kane and then back over his shoulder at Gideon himself. "Not only do you risk offending the gods with your actions; you are frightening Lady Merewen."

Gideon's anger drained away slowly, and he kept his eyes locked on Kane's until the other man blinked and lowered his weapon. Fine. They'd reestablished the order of things. That left Lady Merewen to make peace with. Gideon sheathed his weapon, but when he moved to walk around Murdoch, his friend sidestepped to block him.

Gideon arched an eyebrow and stared into the other man's eyes. "You have something to say?"

"No, but if you scare her again like that, we will have words."

His words were spoken softly, even calmly, but the threat was still there. Gideon flexed his hands, praying for patience.

"Murdoch, step aside. I know my duty and will see it done."

When the warrior retreated, giving Gideon room to move, room to breathe, Gideon made eye contact with Duncan and Averel as well. Both nodded, acknowledging his leadership. With that settled, he approached Merewen. She had left her seat on the log to stand next to her mare, the two of them clearly on the verge of bolting.

He moved slowly, not wanting to spook either the woman or her horse. Both stood their ground, but their uncertainty showed in the way they shifted from foot to foot and the tight grip that Merewen had on the reins.

Pretty words always came more easily to Duncan, but Gideon gave it his best effort, striving to keep his voice low and calm. "My apologies, Lady Merewen. Perhaps we can take a walk and discuss our plans."

Then he offered her his arm and waited to see what her decision would be.

Chapter 6

Merewen studied the man in front of her, his handsome face set in such harsh lines. Common sense said she should be wary of him even if the gods had sent him and his friends to aid her. There was such violence in all of these men, and Gideon was clearly more at home with a weapon in his grip than with a lady's hand on his arm. Yet the same instincts that told her that Rogue would never hurt her said Gideon would lay down his own life before he'd see her harmed.

Odd that in the face of such potential violence she felt so safe.

As soon as she rested her fingers on the sleeve of his tunic, feeling the warm flex of muscles between the soft fabric, it was if the air around them breathed a sigh of relief. Certainly all six horses relaxed their stances and dropped their noses down into the soft grass to graze.

The other four warriors spread out over the clearing, each taking a direction to watch and standing guard as their leader escorted Merewen down to the river's edge. Neither of them spoke as they strolled along the shore.

If her predicament had not been so grim, she would have taken some pleasure in the experience. Not since her father's death had a man come courting. Even before that, she'd had little time for such things while she'd struggled to perform her father's duties when he no longer had the strength to carry them out.

At the time, her uncle's arrival had seemed fortuitous.

Although he lacked the ability to commune with the horses, he'd certainly been trained to oversee the more mundane duties of managing the clan's land and wealth.

Unfortunately, his real gift was for spending the family's fortune on his own selfish needs. In truth, she often feared he wouldn't even provide the basic provisions for the keep if he didn't need her people to farm the land, prepare his meals, and wash his clothes.

I truly hate Uncle Fagan and the suffering he has caused.

"I'm not surprised. He has certainly earned your enmity."

"What?"

Gideon's deep voice startled her. Had he actually read her thoughts?

He gave her an amused look. "You were saying that you hate your uncle. I said that, all things considered, I'm not surprised. The man is clearly a villain."

Her skin flushed hot. She would need to watch herself when she was with this man. Since her uncle's appearance in her life, she'd had to learn to school her tongue, parceling out words carefully so as not to draw his wrath. How odd that she didn't feel the need to be so cautious around this fierce warrior.

"Yes, he is that, and his men as well."

She stopped to stare at the water, enjoying the soothing sound it made as it flowed over and around the rocks.

"I'm almost glad my father didn't live to see the man his brother has become. When they were younger, they were quite close. Then Fagan left to live in the city for years, visiting only rarely. He returned to stay when I sent news of my father's illness, a decision I regret. He is no longer the man I remembered from my childhood."

She didn't want to make excuses for Fagan, but she had some sympathy for him. After all, she was in a similar position herself solely because of her gender. "I'm sure it was painful for my uncle to see all of the family's holdings pass to a younger brother simply because the gods chose not to bless him with the same gifts my father received."

Gideon stared out at the surrounding land, his expression difficult to decipher. Finally, he spoke. "A man chooses his own path in this life, Lady Merewen, for good or for ill. At the end of his days, he will stand judgment for those decisions."

What choices had Gideon made that etched such stark pain in his expression? Now wasn't the time to ask, not when he seemed lost in the shadows of his past. She gently took his hand in hers and tried to tug him along the path.

"Shall we walk a little farther? I know you must have questions to ask of me, Captain. I would answer what I can and then show you the cottage I spoke to you about. Soon I must return to the keep."

He glanced down at her small hand touching his and let himself be led. She was conscious of the fact that they were now beyond the sight of his men. Perhaps it would be wiser to turn back, but she knew he would distance himself from her were they to do that. At this moment, she wanted to savor the few minutes of being alone with this man.

His pale eyes stood out in sharp contrast to his dark hair and sun-browned skin. When first she'd met him, his eyes had appeared as cold as death. Now they reflected the warmth of the summer sky. "Kane was right, you know. It would be a simple matter to eliminate your uncle and even his men."

Merewen wanted to deny it, to make it clear that she didn't want their deaths on her conscience. But in truth, she would bear that burden willingly if it meant that both her people and the herds would no longer suffer from her uncle's callous neglect and abuse.

"Yet you seem hesitant to do that, Captain, at least for now."

She was careful with the words she used, making sure to question his motives but not his courage. As they walked, she had once again placed her hand on the crook of his right arm. After a few seconds, he had covered her hand with his left one. The warmth of that connection spread throughout her body, the sensation heightening her awareness of him as a man.

Seemingly unaware of the reaction his touch had upon her, Gideon responded to her comment. "This is not the time for me to tell you of our history, my lady. Suffice it to say that the gods do not wield their weapons recklessly. They would not use a hammer to kill a fly."

She considered the meaning of his words. "So you fear there is more wrong than just my uncle's greed."

Gideon nodded. "I do, although my first duty is to protect you, my lady. If it becomes necessary to kill your uncle in order to keep you safe, know that I will not hesitate. However, I believe it is best not to act in haste, not until we know more. I do promise you that before our time is at an end, your uncle will die."

She stared up into Gideon's eyes, once again the color of ice, and shivered. He noted her reaction and immediately retreated, putting more distance between them. Merewen started to follow him, but he held up his hand to stop her.

"I apologize again, Lady Merewen. I'm a warrior and more used to the rough company of men, and so I speak too bluntly. I fear I lack Duncan's courtly manners."

Although his expression hadn't changed, her reaction had inadvertently hurt him in some small measure. Rather than let that stand, she resolutely stepped forward and placed the palm of her hand against his, hoping her touch would show him the truth of her words.

"No apologies are necessary, Captain . . . Gideon. I

may fear what I have put into motion and for my people, but I do not regret the decision to do so. And I do not fear you or your men."

For the second time that day, the air around them thickened, and time slowed as they both stared at the joining of their hands. She eased nearer, or perhaps it was Gideon who closed the gap. This time, when she lifted her eyes, his eyes no longer held the chill of the river. The heat reflected there drew her even closer.

His fingers gently twined with hers as his other hand lifted to cradle the side of her face so very gently, the pad of his thumb brushing across her lips. She smiled and closed her eyes, savoring his touch and wanting more. When a shadow passed over her face, her eyes flew open just as Gideon's mouth followed the path his thumb had only seconds before.

The sensation stunned her, the touch of that stern mouth so soft and the moment so fleeting. She held still, fearful if she were to move too quickly, he would once again withdraw. But no, he settled in to kiss her, tempt her, taste her. It was as if the warmth of the sun had entered her veins and settled deep within her body.

Gideon pulled back slightly, enough that she could see him smile. "And I thought the magic of the gods was potent, my lady."

What could she say to that? Before she could think of a reply, Gideon stiffened, staring past her, back down the river.

He immediately stepped in front of her, once again protecting her from a perceived threat. What had he heard?

When his man Murdoch stepped into sight, some of the captain's tension eased, but not all.

"What is wrong?"

"We're not sure. The horses were all growing restive, but both stallions stared at the woods as if sensing a threat."

Gideon glanced at Merewen, his eyes back to their iciest. "Any idea whether the danger is human or animal?"

"No, but Kane and Duncan are investigating. Averel stayed with the other horses while I came to fetch you."

"Well done," said Gideon, nodding. "My lady, we should return to the others."

By the time they reached the horses, Merewen was out of breath from trying to keep pace with the two warriors. Although both men made an effort to adjust their strides to better suit her shorter stature, their concern about what was afoot quickly had them picking up speed.

At least her tunic worn over trousers afforded her more ease of movement than a dress would have. When they reached the clearing, the three mares stood clustered around Averel with their eyes trained on the trees. At the moment, they appeared attentive but not on the near edge of panic.

Gideon strode forward, for the moment leaving Merewen to follow in his wake. Murdoch brought up the rear.

"Any word from Kane?"

"No, he and Duncan rode out with Kestrel at their side." Averel smiled. "For the moment, the two stallions have united against a common foe."

Gideon didn't look amused, but then with his horse out scouting, that left him afoot. "We should be prepared to ride in haste when they return. The rest of you mount up."

Merewen led her horse over to stand near Gideon. She waited until he looked in her direction before speaking. "My mare can bear both of us, should it become necessary."

He acknowledged her offer with a jerk of his head but kept his gaze focused on the woods. She appreciated his

fierce determination to defend her safety. At the same
time, she missed the brief moment where the world had
disappeared and they'd simply been two people enjoying
a walk—and a kiss.

Rather than dwell on it, she swung up into the saddle,
her mare sidestepping and snorting.

"Steady, steady."

She continued to talk to the restive animal, all the
while infusing her words with the calming warmth that
she used with all of her four-legged charges and even
some of the two-legged ones when the situation called
for it. The mare slowly relaxed and stood still. When
Merewen looked around, all three warriors were staring
at her with rapt attention.

Averel and Murdoch exchanged worried glances and
moved farther away from her, although Gideon remained where he was. Their reaction was puzzling. "Is
something wrong?"

Finally, the captain answered her. "Your words have
power, and the gods have charged us to fight against
dark magic. Yours lacks the sick feel of evil; yet it still
speaks strongly of a powerful magic."

She didn't understand their concern. Turning to face
Averel and Murdoch, she said, "I swear I know nothing
of dark magic."

When neither of them responded, she looked back to
their leader to enlist his support. "Captain Gideon,
you've seen me do this before to call Kestrel and the
others. The gods granted my family a simple gift, nothing
more than that. In each generation, at least one person
in my family is born with it. It's in my blood just as it was
in my father's."

But Gideon was shaking his head. "It is more than
that, Lady Merewen. Many people have a knack for
working with horses, but it doesn't flavor the very air
around them or call horses from long distances. There's

no denying that the heart of your gift is magic. The only question is its source."

She had no answer for that. "I am not working magic. Since I was a small child, I have been able to understand horses just as my father could. We also both studied herbal medicine."

Gideon looked as if he had more to say on the subject, but the sound of approaching horses brought the conversation to an abrupt halt. All three men turned as one to face the woods again, this time with swords at the ready. Kestrel appeared first, quickly followed by Duncan. A short time later, Kane rode back into sight. He paused to rub the right side of his face, but, judging from his relaxed manner, the threat had passed.

Kestrel headed straight for Gideon, who patted the stallion while he waited for his men to dismount and report in. Right now, Merewen was glad for anything that diverted the attention away from her.

They were right, of course. Even if it wasn't accurate to refer to her ability with horses as a gift rather than magic, it definitely was safer. Within the borders of Agathia, true magic was rare and often feared for good reason. It was another kind of power, and power was often abused. Even without the rumors about Duke Keirthan, she'd read enough history in her father's library to know that was true. Still, she believed magic was a tool, one that could be used for good or for evil.

Which brought her right back to Captain Gideon and his men who claimed to stand against the evils of dark magic. Even though she believed that was true, why had the manuscript she'd read described them as the Damned, especially if they were doing the work of the gods? As she considered that thought, a shadow seemed to pass over the sun, dimming the day. She stared up at the sky, seeing nothing but blue and a scattering of clouds. Even so, she found herself dismounting and returning to Gideon's side. As soon as she stood within arm's reach, the shadow passed, leaving her to wonder even more about the magic of the captain of the Damned.

Duncan was talking, saying something about some dead deer, but all Gideon heard was the rapid pulse of the woman standing next to him. Something had left her feeling skittish, although he could perceive no direct threat to her at the moment. Perhaps it was all the talk of magic, but she hadn't hesitated to cast the spell to call them from the river. Granted, the spell to call them forth could be invoked by anyone who knew the correct words. It was up to the gods to decide whether the five warriors should be released from their sleep in the river.

But didn't she realize the power it took to invoke that kind of magic? Each time it washed over him and his men, it left them all edgy and feeling unclean.

He started to wrap his arm around her shoulders but caught himself just in time. It was unlikely Averel or Murdoch would have noticed from where they stood, and Duncan was too focused on describing their scouting expedition.

Kane, on the other hand, was staring at him with a curious expression on his normally impassive face. When he realized Gideon was looking at him, Kane arched an eyebrow as he looked from Gideon toward Merewen and back again.

Cursing himself for a fool, Gideon forced his own attention back to what Duncan was saying. At least his friend could be depended on to keep his mouth shut. If Kane had any questions, he would hold them until he and Gideon were alone.

Duncan had finished.

"So you never saw anything that would have set the horses off? No trace of a predator prowling in the area?"

Kane shook his head. "I studied the ground myself.

The only fresh tracks I found belonged to the deer. None of the dead animals bore any marks or injuries, so I can't explain what killed them. Beyond these woods, the grasslands stretch for miles in all directions. We saw no sign of riders. But—"

Then he paused, once again looking toward Merewen before bringing his gaze back to Gideon, asking without words if he should continue to speak in front of her. Gideon nodded. This was Merewen's home. If there was a threat out there, she should learn of it.

The warrior's hand once again strayed to the mark on his cheek, his fingertips tracing the symbol that had been burned into his skin at his birth. "Something left a taint in the air, one I have encountered before. It was as if a dark power briefly cast its gaze in this direction, but I can tell you nothing more specific than that."

Kane frowned, clearly frustrated. "I wish I could catch the right memory, but it keeps dancing just out of reach. If we had access to the right manuscripts, perhaps Duncan and I would be able to learn its name and more about its nature. For now, all I can say is that we need to be very wary of drawing its attention in our direction. At the moment, the darkness is but a pale shadow of what it could be, but these things have ways of growing stronger."

If anyone else had spoken of taints and shadows, Gideon might have scoffed, but not when it came to Kane. His friend had too much firsthand experience with such things. After all, he'd spent his youth living under the forced tutelage of his dark mage grandfather. Kane had been exposed to the blackest magics from birth.

"You are welcome to make use of my father's library, Kane. His collection of books and manuscripts is one of the largest in Agathia." Then Merewen frowned. "His interests were wide ranging. However, I cannot promise that he owned any books on dark magic."

Kane frowned but didn't dismiss the idea out of hand.

"How would you suggest we do that, Lady Merewen? Your uncle is bound to ask questions if we simply followed you home to rummage through the library."

She gave the matter some thought. "He's always looking to hire more men-at-arms."

Gideon joined in the conversation. "That might work, but not if we all approached him at once. It is likely that he would perceive five heavily armed men arriving at the same time as a threat. We will need to approach him in smaller numbers."

He studied his friends and considered their options. "We'll start with Averel and Murdoch. You can pass for two men-at-arms whose previous employer died, leaving you penniless and in need of a new position. That should make you attractive to a man like Fagan. Once they're safely within the keep, Duncan, you'll be next. You would do well to approach Fagan as a wealthy traveling scholar. I would imagine Fagan would gladly take your money for allowing you the run of his late brother's library."

Duncan nodded. "I would enjoy that. It's been a long while since I had the chance to pursue my studies."

He was serious about that. Gideon had never understood his friend's love of spending hours among dusty books and manuscripts. Duncan's own father had berated his son for his scholarly bent, but Gideon had quickly learned to value his friend's quick mind. His self-taught knowledge of tactics and military history had served them all well over the centuries.

"Well, that leaves me and Kane. We will try to trace the source of this power Kane is sensing. Once the three of you are settled, we'll plan our next move."

Merewen frowned in thought. "When you're ready, Captain, perhaps you could pose as a potential buyer looking for mounts for a mercenary commander. My uncle is always in need of gold. He also delights in sending my horses away from me."

He liked the idea. "Perfect. We'll have to make a trip back to the mountain to obtain enough gold to make my story and Duncan's believable. We'll take care of that tomorrow."

"What about Kane? What is to be his role in all of this?"

Gideon was about to explain that most people and nearly all animals found Kane's company too disturbing to tolerate for long. Instead, his friend abruptly took matters into his own hands.

"Lady Merewen, it is not yet time for my part in this play to begin."

He held up his shield, which was emblazoned with a likeness straight out of a nightmare. The creature pictured there looked to be a cross between a wolf and a reptile, but it also had vestiges of wings. "My companion and I are weapons to be wielded only when it is time for blood to flow and the wicked to die."

Then Kane offered her a mocking bow and walked away.

Merewen started to say something, but Gideon cut her off with a sharp look. "Perhaps it is time for you to show us the cottage you mentioned."

Her eyes were wide with shock mixed with fear as she stared after Kane. After a few seconds, she nodded. "If you'll all follow me, it's not far."

Chapter 7

Neglect had left the cottage in poor repair, but it wouldn't take long to make it habitable. Certainly, the five of them had lived under worse conditions. But then Kane backed away, refusing to step across the threshold.

He turned to Merewen. "What happened to the people who lived here?"

She shrugged. "No one knows. They simply disappeared, leaving many of their belongings behind. One of my men happened to stop by and found the place deserted, their animals wandering loose. He said there were still dishes on the table as if they'd left in a hurry."

Gideon watched Kane's reaction to her words. The warrior slowly nodded as if she'd confirmed what he was sensing. "Has this happened before?"

Merewen sighed, rubbing her arms as if feeling a chill. "I've heard rumors of people disappearing, but the reports were not confirmed. Considering how Uncle Fagan treats our crofters, I'm surprised more haven't moved on, looking for a better life."

Averel and Duncan were already hard at work, sorting the useful items that the previous dwellers had left behind from those that would be better off burned. As they worked, Merewen joined them to make a list of what they would need.

Meanwhile, Gideon followed Kane out to the small

corral. "What's wrong?" he whispered, not wanting to worry Merewen needlessly.

Kane started brushing the dust off Rogue's coat. After a few strokes, he finally answered. "This place reeks of blood magic and death."

Gideon looked around the area. "What did you sense about the people who lived here?"

Kane met his gaze from across Rogue's broad back. "They didn't leave willingly. There's no scent of old blood, so they were most likely alive when they were taken. That's all I can tell you except that this place has the same ill feel to it as those deer we found dead in the woods."

Gideon had feared that was the case. Until they knew more about what was going on, there wasn't much they could do. They had to identify the enemy before they could best decide how to confront him.

While the others were busy setting up their temporary home, Gideon gave in to the temptation to watch Lady Merewen as she talked to his men. Just as he'd first suspected, her dark hair sparkled with red highlights in the sun, and a few freckles dusted her fair skin. Her looks were striking, especially with that lush mouth that smiled so easily and tasted so sweet.

Neither of them had mentioned the kiss they had shared. She might have her own reasons for remaining silent on the subject, and he was truly at a loss as to what he should say, if anything. In his youth, a man didn't kiss a woman lightly, but that had been an eon ago in a time and place lost to the ages. Manners had no doubt changed during that time, but Merewen didn't strike him as a woman who would lightly share her favors.

With only three cycles of three moons to walk upon solid ground, only a knave of the worst sort would pursue a lady, especially one of quality such as Lady Merewen. Looking back across all the centuries since

Gideon had first stood before the gods waiting for them to render their judgment, he could not recall a single time he'd felt such a powerful draw to a woman.

Were the gods testing him to see if he would risk his hard-won honor for the sake of a few nights of pleasure in a woman's arms? Surely they would not be so petty, but he could not risk it. That he had imperiled his own soul was bad enough. He would not further endanger his friends, who had walked into the river with him out of loyalty and friendship.

"Captain, I've been meaning to ask where you have been keeping Scim. I would think it difficult to hide a bird of his size."

Lost in the dark turn his thoughts had taken, he hadn't noticed Merewen's approach. He drew a slow breath to clear his head and then pointed toward the row of five shields. They were lined up along the outer wall of the cottage where they could be grabbed quickly should the need arise.

"He is resting in my shield, my lady, as is Kane's friend. It draws a great deal of our strength to call them forth until we have once again grown used to walking in the world."

Merewen came to an abrupt halt, immediately turning to stare back toward the cottage. After giving him a puzzled look back over her shoulder, she headed right back to stand in front of the shields. As each of his men took note of her interest, they joined her, even Kane.

She looked a bit bewildered. "So that's what I sensed. I mean, the other day when you covered my eyes. One minute Scim wasn't there, and then he was. I'd almost convinced myself it had been part of a dream and that he'd simply followed us down off the mountain."

If Gideon was correctly following the confusing trail left by her words, she'd felt the magic he'd used to call for his avatar. "Believe me, my lady, when I tell you that is more than a picture of a gyrfalcon. That is Scim himself. When he flies, my shield is plain but for the outline of his shape."

Her eyebrows were riding low over her eyes as she considered his words. By now Averel and Duncan were grinning. Even Murdoch and Kane looked amused as she tried to decide if he was telling the truth. At last she reached out to caress the glossy, smooth surface of his shield. Before touching any of the others, she looked at their owners and waited for them to nod.

Kane hesitated and then agreed. "You heard my companion the other night on the mountain. I'm sure your uncle and his men had something to say about the nature of what pursued them in the darkness."

Gideon thought her hand might have been trembling a little when she touched the dark warrior's shield, but then there had been plenty of warriors who had cowered in the presence of Kane and Hob. When she finished her examination of all five, she stepped back.

"The magic of your gods is powerful indeed." Looking a bit shaky and her eyes wide with wonder, she slowly smiled. "It has been a day of amazing surprises."

Was she thinking of the kiss they'd shared or just the avatars? Gideon answered for all of them. "Indeed it has."

"I must go now, but I will return in two days with more supplies."

Her mare was already heading straight for her. As Merewen mounted up, she asked, "When do you plan to approach my uncle?"

"We will do some scouting tomorrow to grow familiar with the area as it is now, and then wait until your visit the day after. We should be at full strength by then."

Gideon caught the mare's reins. "Would you like me to ride with you?"

He didn't know whether to be relieved or disappointed when she shook her head. "We shouldn't risk it. I'm safe enough on my own, and my uncle's men sometimes patrol the areas closer to the keep. Things could go badly if they were to spot us together."

"Then, until we meet again." Before releasing the mare, he added, "And if you feel that you are in any danger from your uncle or his men, return to us immediately. If you cannot break free yourself, send your mare to us, and we will come."

Her smile was sunshine bright. "I will."

Then she was off, she and the mare flying across the grasslands and out of his sight. That bothered him far more than it should have, enough that he returned to the wall to pick up his shield and called out the words that would send Scim soaring high up in the sky. Once the bird took flight, Gideon reached out with his mind to join with Scim's.

Through the bird's eyes, Gideon would be able to follow Merewen all the way to the keep and even after she rode through the gate. He hated knowing beyond that point she would be at the mercy of her uncle and his men.

Murdoch caught Gideon's arm, helping to anchor him in one spot while he grew accustomed to seeing the world through Scim's eyes rather than his own. His friend murmured, "She really is quite amazing."

Gideon could only agree. "That she is."

His friend stared out over the grasslands in the direction Merewen had gone. "I fear our mission involves far more than merely eliminating her uncle."

Murdoch's grim prediction mirrored Gideon's own thinking. Something was terribly wrong here in Agathia, something so dire that the gods had chosen to send their most fell warriors against the gathering evil.

Lady Alina kept her head down and her needle moving in and out of the linen she was embroidering. Her husband approached, his voice growing closer and setting her pulse to racing.

Please, gods, let him pass her by. Let him have business elsewhere. Let him—

Her silent prayer was cut off by the sound of his bellowed command. "Wife! Attend me now."

She shuddered at the thought of what that might mean, but delaying only increased the chance of setting off his always precarious temper. After setting her needlework aside, she followed Fagan into his room.

"Did you order my bath?"

"Yes, my husband. The servants should be arriving shortly. Shall I also have a tray brought up from the kitchen?"

He was already pouring himself a drink. "Yes. Order enough for two."

Her breath caught in her chest. "Are you expecting company?"

His answering smile was both cruel and cold. "Only yours, my lady wife. The gods know you do little enough to earn your keep around here. It has been too long since you last graced my bed."

Not long enough for the last set of bruises to have faded completely. The very thought of him touching her body had Alina's stomach roiling, but she was careful to hide her reaction. Past experience had taught her that he loved inflicting both pain and fear far more than he'd ever loved her.

She was saved for the moment by the arrival of a line of servants. Fagan left it to her to ensure the bathwater was the proper temperature while he stripped off his clothes, carelessly tossing them on the floor.

All too soon, the bath was ready, and the servants filed out of the room. More than one glanced in her direction with sympathy or, worse yet, pity. Alina hated knowing that although everyone in the keep knew what went on in the privacy of her husband's room, none would lift a hand to help her.

He was a bully in his dealings with anyone he perceived as weak or his inferior. Merewen was the only one who dared stand up to him, and she had paid terribly for it. Alina wished the younger woman would learn to hold her tongue and her temper, but at the same time she admired Merewen's courage.

She sighed, disgusted and ashamed that she lived in such a continuous state of fear. There had been a time in her life when she'd been happy. She was sure of it.

"Come here, Alina." Fagan's voice was soft when he added, "Please."

She turned to face him, wishing she had the courage to run, but things only went harder for her if she resisted. She reluctantly took the hand he held out, knowing that, whenever he made the effort to coax her, she would hate whatever he had in mind for her. There was nothing gentle in Fagan, especially when he was rutting away on top of her and spilling his seed deep in her body.

That she'd failed to conceive was just one more excuse he used for abusing her. Each month when her courses came, she felt a profound mix of both relief and regret. As much as she'd love a babe to call her own, she despaired of how a child would fare at the hands of her husband.

He pulled her in close to his nude body, his anticipation for the afternoon's activities obvious. "I've decided to share my bath with you, my dear. I will watch you disrobe."

After pressing a gentle kiss to her forehead, he whispered, "Now, Alina. If the water grows cold, I will not be pleased."

His expression avid, he stepped back to sprawl back in a chair, watching for the least sign of disobedience. In fact, he was hoping for it and relishing the idea of pun-

ishing her. How could a man so fair to look upon have
such a black soul? It was a question she'd been asking
since her wedding night. Before that, he'd been as charm-
ing and attentive as any maiden could hope for.

But now, knowing she was trapped, Alina resigned
herself to an afternoon spent in hell. One way or another, Fagan would have his pleasure of her. She began
the arduous process of trying to please her husband,
knowing full well she was doomed to fail.

Merewen hurried into the kitchen, relieved to see that
all was in good order. She trusted Ellie, the cook, to do
her job and manage everyone else around her, but acci-
dents happened. On the rare occasion Fagan's meal was
delayed, everyone suffered.

For some reason, the first person to cross her mind
was his wife. Alina had yet to appear, and here it was
nearly nightfall. Two nights ago, when Merewen returned
from taking Captain Gideon and his men to the crofter's
hut, Olaf had met her at the door.

He'd smirked as he'd informed that her uncle had
chosen to dine in his room with his lady wife. At that
moment, Merewen had sorely wished she had the
strength of the captain or one of his men so she could
beat that expression off Olaf's face. Only a monster
would find the way Lady Alina suffered at her husband's
hands amusing.

Merewen would not be the only one relieved if Fagan
were to disappear from her life. As much as she hated
the thought of losing her last blood relative, the world
would certainly be a better place without him in it.

But back to Alina. Early that morning, Merewen had
made a quick trip out to the cottage with supplies for the
warriors. She'd returned to spend most of the day helping Jarod out in the stables and studying the plans they'd
been making for the next year's crop of foals.

She'd also been counting down the hours until Averel and Murdoch would approach the keep, the first to seek employment with her uncle. As preoccupied as she'd been, it was possible she'd simply missed seeing her aunt over the past two days, but she doubted it.

The cook came bustling over, her face red and sweaty from standing over the fire. "Is he out there? Shall we serve?"

Ellie made a point of never uttering Fagan's name if she could help it. She'd been the previous cook's assistant when Merewen's father and Fagan were small boys. He'd been a much different person back then, and she refused to acknowledge that the man who'd returned to the manor was even the same man.

"I will check."

When she stepped out into the great hall, Fagan was just then coming down the steps. Alina was right behind him, once again moving slowly. Obviously the bastard had hurt her again.

"If your uncle sees you looking at him like that, he will not be pleased. Perhaps I should go tell him and of-fer to teach you to show some respect."

The threat in Olaf's deep voice was all too real, but Merewen did not bother to ask him to hold his tongue. He was just as likely to agree and then tell Fagan anyway. Olaf had learned from a master all the ways to torment those around him.

Rather than respond, she returned to the kitchen to order the food brought out. By the time Fagan had reached his seat, she already had the first course served and his drink poured.

Everything seemed to be going smoothly, when Alina lost her balance and stumbled into her husband.

When Fagan's soup spilled down the front of his tunic, he immediately lurched to his feet and dragged his wife back up off the floor. "I'll teach you to be so clumsy."

He backhanded her across her face. Before he could strike her again, Merewen had circled the table to latch onto his arm. She wouldn't stand by and watch Alina further abused even if it brought her uncle's wrath down on her own head.

He froze midmotion, staring at her white-knuckled grip on his wrist. "Merewen, I warned you what would happen the next time you interfered."

But before he could carry out his promise, one of the guards entered the hall at a run. He skidded to a halt in front of the high table and executed a rough bow. "Forgive me for disturbing you, my lord, but two riders are at the gate, seeking work as men-at-arms. You asked to be notified if any likely prospects came seeking jobs."

Merewen didn't blame the poor man for reminding her uncle that he had issued the orders, because Fagan was never happy to have his meal interrupted. He immediately released his wife, not caring at all that she slumped to the floor in a boneless heap. As soon as he did, Merewen let go of his wrist and stepped back. She would see to her aunt as soon as her uncle left.

Unfortunately, he had other plans. "Have them brought before me immediately."

Then he gave Merewen a look that froze her to the bone. "Get her up off the floor, and then stand right there. I have had enough of your insolence and will deal with you myself after I talk to these two."

Alina had managed to push herself upright, but it took most of Merewen's strength to keep her aunt standing. Merewen motioned for one of the servants to bring a damp cloth so she could wipe the trickle of blood off her aunt's cut lip. She was still tending to Alina's injuries when the guards escorted Murdoch and Averel into the hall.

She delayed looking in their direction until they were standing before the high table. Her great worry was that if they realized what was going on, one or both would feel obligated to intercede on her behalf. While she had no doubt that each in his own right was a fearsome warrior, they were greatly outnumbered in the hall.

It was unlikely that they would be able to rescue both her and Alina and still defend themselves long enough to escape. Sure enough, when she finally glanced toward Murdoch, she could feel his fury. A quick peek in Averel's direction confirmed that he, too, was fighting the need to draw his sword.

She hoped her uncle would assume their edginess was due to being brought before the lord of the manor and being surrounded by heavily armed men.

"I have been given to believe that you are both seeking employment."

As the elder of the two, Murdoch answered. "Yes, my lord. My name is Sir Murdoch, and my companion is Sir Averel."

"Let me see your weapons." When both men hesitated, he gave them a disgusted look. "I hope you are normally better at taking orders. I find you can tell a lot about a man by the quality of his weapons."

Both men drew their swords and held them out for Fagan's inspection. He gave them a cursory study. "Those are exceptionally fine weapons for two such as you. Are you any good with them?"

Murdoch's smile didn't reach his eyes. "I have some talent with swords, sir. I've done my share of teaching others how to fight, including my young friend here."

"Very well, you may put your weapons away for now. I'm a fair hand with a blade myself. I'll see how you do in the morning during weapons practice before I make my final decision.

Fagan next turned his attention toward the younger man. "And what do you have to offer me besides your ability to fight?"

Rather than answer directly, Averel let loose with a loud whistle.

"What are you about?" Fagan demanded, but the warrior simply cocked his head to one side as if listening. A noise near the door signaled the arrival of a pair of immense dogs that headed straight for Averel.

Merewen could scarce believe her eyes, but she wasn't the only one in the hall staring in wide-eyed wonder at the dogs making their way to their owner. One was black and the other white, but otherwise they were almost identical in height and build. She'd never seen such beasts in all of her life.

Fagan studied the dogs with a greedy light in his eyes. He prided himself in breeding some of the best hunting dogs in the duke's realm. Was he already trying to decide which of his bitches to mate with this pair? What would Averel have to say about that?

The dogs calmly flanked their owner. Averel patted each one on the head as Fagan moved in closer to study them.

"I've never seen their kind before. What are they good for?"

"Running. Hunting." The young warrior's eyes took on a definite chill. "Fighting, too, if I ask it of them."

As if to illustrate that point, both dogs yawned loudly, flashing two impressive sets of teeth. Her uncle had been about to reach toward the white dog, but quickly pulled his hand back.

Meanwhile, Murdoch was still studying Alina, his pale eyes clearly taking note of the fresh handprint on her cheek. Luckily, Fagan was too entranced with the dogs to notice the warrior's attention was focused elsewhere.

Fagan retreated out of reach of the dogs. "I will talk with you both about your duties in the morning. Until then, you may join us for the evening meal. Olaf here will show you where to sleep."

"Thank you, my lord. That is most generous of you."

Murdoch backed away but had to tug on Averel's sleeve to get him to do the same. Clearly he understood the danger they'd all be in if they were to attack her uncle at the moment. She could only hope that he'd manage to hold back should her uncle decide to punish her in front of everyone.

Fagan had done it before.

But, to her surprise, he seemed to have forgotten about it. "Merewen, where are your manners? Please let the cook know that we have guests."

Alina had recovered enough to stand on her own. After she had quietly taken her seat, this time without mishap, Merewen left to do her uncle's bidding.

Regardless of what the night brought, the battle to free her people had started even if her uncle had no idea that he was under attack. She took great comfort from that notion.

Chapter 8

Gideon's patience was at an end. When he'd sent Scim to follow after Murdoch and Averel, all he learned was that they had made it safely to Merewen's family keep. Nothing more. That Murdoch and Averel would be able to defend themselves went without question, even if it became necessary to fight their way clear of Fagan and his men.

No, it was their ability to protect Merewen that had Gideon all tied up in knots. Feeling this way was ridiculous. His men had never failed him in all the long years of their service together.

Early this morning he'd sent Scim winging toward Merewen's home a second time, hoping he would spot his friends so they could send back news with his avatar. Ever since the previous evening, he'd had this powerful compulsion to reassure himself that Merewen was safe.

He'd been resting when the strangest sensation that Merewen was in danger had washed over him. The feeling had passed as quickly as it had come but left him unsettled. He'd always felt a connection with the person the gods had sent him to serve, but this time was different. Stronger. More personal.

So far, all he'd been able to see through Scim's eyes was a distant view of Fagan's men at weapons practice in the bailey. Frustrated, he'd finally broken off the link, leaving Scim free to hunt if he so desired.

Right now Gideon could use some practice himself,

anything to work off the burn of worry. Duncan had gone hunting, so that left Gideon one potential partner. "Get your sword, Kane."

His friend was brushing Rogue again, leaving the gray's coat gleaming in the bright sun. Gideon would have cheerfully done the same for Kestrel, but the stallion had disappeared earlier in the morning. Before charging off, he'd come to an abrupt halt in front of Gideon, stomping his forefoot and shaking his head.

On some level, Gideon knew the horse was promising to return. No doubt he needed to check on his mares. All things considered, he had a newfound sympathy for the stallion. They both were away from the women in their lives, and the not knowing was worrisome.

Not that Merewen was Gideon's, not in the same sense. However, she was his responsibility. That much was true, or at least as much of the truth as he was willing to admit right now.

Meanwhile, Kane continued polishing that damned horse's hide. "I said for you to get your sword."

Kane finally stopped to look at Gideon, his eyes seeing far too much. "Any reason I should let you take your temper out on me? It is not my fault that Lady Merewen is there and you are not. Murdoch and Averel will watch over her."

The man knew Gideon all too well. And leave it to his friend to be blunt. "I know they will, but there is far more wrong than just her uncle's greed. Until I learn more about what it is that you sense, I cannot plan how to fight against it."

Kane joined him in leaning against the side of the cottage to stare up at the morning sun, as if the answers were all written up there in the blue sky. Gideon endured the silence, knowing he wasn't going to much like whatever Kane was struggling to put into words.

Finally, he spoke, his accent rougher than usual. "This

calling feels strange to me. Certainly you're different this time."

Gideon did not argue the point. He was more interested in what Kane was thinking.

"Explain."

"In the past, you've shown little interest in those we were called to protect. You assessed the situation and then used us as your weapons to put the evil to rest. It mattered not for whom we fought but only that we fought."

Gideon felt obliged to point out the obvious. "That is the duty given to us by the gods. That is why we are called from the river—to fight evil and protect the weak."

In his head, he added, *And why we then stand side by side to face judgment again, each time hoping, praying it will be the final time. That at long last my friends and I will know peace.*

Even though he didn't utter the words, Kane knew what he was thinking. They'd been friends far too long for Gideon to hide much from him. Although Gideon wanted this unending damnation to end for all four of his friends, he wanted it most for Kane, whose life had never been easy. That Gideon's thoughtless actions had only made it worse was a guilt he would carry to the grave.

If he ever had one.

Once again Kane read him as easily as Duncan did all of those manuscripts he loved to pore over. "I made the choice to stand beside you, Gideon. I have had far too few friends in my lifetime to allow you to face this curse alone."

Then Kane grinned, the resulting sight never exactly reassuring. "Besides, my friend and I have always loved a good fight. This one promises to be worthy of a warrior's blood."

Gideon was about to order Kane one last time to fetch his sword when he spotted something high in the sky. Scim was soaring high overhead, slowly making his way down and waiting for Gideon to take notice. He stepped away from Kane and held his arm out at shoulder height, bracing himself to take the bird's weight.

That was all the encouragement Scim needed, and he immediately went into a sharp dive. He'd dropped only a short distance when a bright flash of light streaked across the sky to hit the bird. Scim screamed as he pulled up and tried to wing his way back up into the sky.

"What just happened?" Gideon asked, not expecting an answer.

A second flash of light followed the second. Both men watched in horror as, between one heartbeat and the next, the falcon crumpled in the air and plummeted back toward the ground. Gideon took off running, at the same time reaching out to Scim with his thoughts and hoping to share his strength with his avatar.

Down and down Scim fell, fighting to regain control. His movements were far too sluggish to slow his descent. Bound as he was to the bird, Gideon could feel Scim's fear and taste his pain, slowing his own movements and making it hard to put one foot in front of the other as he struggled to reach the injured bird.

Kane caught Gideon's arm when he stumbled and almost plunged headfirst to the ground. He managed to keep them both upright, but just barely. Kane jerked Gideon to a stop and forced him to look in his direction instead of at the impending tragedy in the sky.

"Captain, cut off your tie with Scim. Now, before it is too late."

Gideon fought to break free of Kane's grasp, needing to reach the falcon. "He's hurt. He could die."

"And if he does, he'll take you with him unless you break the link between your minds right now. The gods have given you a job to do. Your duty to them comes first."

"I don't care."

"Then care about Lady Merewen and what will happen to her if we fail—if you fail. Would you condemn her to wander in the darkness with us?"

His words were getting through as much as Gideon wanted to deny their truth. It took some effort, but he closed his mind to Scim, barely managing to break free from the tangle of their thoughts. Echoes of the bird's fury faded in Gideon's head. Kane released him to charge toward where Scim was about to hit the ground.

At the last second, the big bird burned the last of his strength to catch just enough air under his wings to slow his fall. He still hit the ground hard, but even from a distance Gideon could see Scim struggling to stand up.

That didn't mean he would survive. An injured bird couldn't hunt. Gideon could provide game for Scim to eat, but what if he could no longer fly? It would be far kinder to put Scim down now before he suffered such a fate, even if it would destroy a part of Gideon he would never get back.

Both men slowed down, Kane stopping short of reaching their destination. Gideon appreciated his friend's forethought. Although Scim was well acquainted with the warrior, he tolerated others only because Gideon asked it of him. Right now, in pain and hurt, Kane's presence would only add another layer of strain.

"I'll fetch your shield."

Gideon managed to nod as he crooned soothing words full of promises of comfort and prayers for the healing touch of the gods. As he chanted, he eased closer to his feathered companion, not wanting to startle the bird. Scim had managed to stand, but he was holding his right wing at an awkward angle, dragging it on the ground as he half limped and half hopped toward Gideon.

Rather than guess at the full nature of the injuries, Gideon cautiously reopened the link that would join their minds. The first wave of pain almost knocked him out. How could Scim remain standing in the face of such agony?

Finally, the gyrfalcon stopped struggling, instead waiting for Gideon to come to him. Already Scim's eyes looked dull. Whether it was due to the pain or to death's stealing the spark from his gaze was impossible to say.

If only the bird could hold on until Kane returned, Gideon would chant the simple spell that would return Scim to the shield. With luck, the act of returning the falcon to the sanctuary of the shield would keep him stable until nightfall. Both the Damned and their avatars healed faster after sundown, a gift from their gods. As they waited, Gideon knelt on the ground and pulled the bird gently into his arms.

Scim struggled against the embrace, using up even more of his waning strength.

"Hush, boy. Stay calm."

But Scim continued to fight, finally snapping at Gideon's fingers with his beak, but not with his full strength. It was as if he were trying to convey a message. Once again, Gideon linked with the bird's thoughts, this time fighting through the waves of pain to see what it was Scim was trying to show Gideon.

His leg—was it broken, too? Gideon slid his hands gently over Scim's body, keeping his touch light as he felt for wounds. Instead, he found a note tied to Scim's leg. He located the end of the string and worked it free. A small scrap of paper dropped into his hand. As soon as Gideon had it in his grasp, Scim fell against him, his mission complete.

If Gideon hadn't been able to feel the bird's every breath, the collapse would have scared him far beyond the terror he was already feeling. Kane was coming. A second set of footsteps meant that Duncan had returned from the hunt and was headed right for them.

The sun had barely reached its zenith, weakening Gideon's ability to call Scim back to the shield. If he failed ...

No, he would not allow thoughts of failure to lessen Scim's chances for survival. Kane set the shield down next to Gideon and started to back away to where Duncan had come to a stop.

"Stay close, both of you. I will need your strength."

They knelt down on the grass beside him and placed their hands on his shoulders. He closed his eyes and drew in the comfort of their touch. Even Scim seemed to breathe more easily. Gideon forced his mind beyond the immediate moment, seeking instead the calm of the river, the soothing flow of the water.

Slowly, then with more speed, he chanted the words that would call Scimitar back to rest within the shelter of the shield. Over and over again, he repeated the spell, pouring every hope, every prayer he had within his heart into the words. Nothing. Scim still lay in his arms, his life force slowly ebbing away.

Gideon opened his mind to the bird, ignoring his friends' protests. As he and the falcon linked, he told Scim of his love for him. He promised to ensure the bird would not suffer and thanked him for his service and friendship.

Within seconds, Scim's heartbeat sped up again, matching Gideon's heart in rhythm; his breathing grew stronger as well. After a flash of hot light, Gideon's arms were empty. Once again, the bird's image was emblazoned on the shield although faded and dull. Obviously the war was not over even if the first battle had been won. Gideon could only maintain a vigil until he learned whether the gods' magic would allow Scim to heal.

His own strength was at low tide at the moment. Kane

forcibly dragged him up off the ground and aimed them both back in the direction of the cottage.

Duncan held out his hands. "Let me carry the shield for you."

Gideon waved him off. He needed that small connection with Scim right now. When they reached the cottage, Kane led Gideon inside and shoved him down on the bench. "Stay there."

The shadowy interior felt cool and soothing. He didn't know if getting the shield inside and out of the sun would help, but it wouldn't hurt. Already, his own tolerance for the bright light of day had increased substantially since leaving the river behind, but the night remained more comfortable.

"Drink this."

Duncan shoved a dripping cup of water into Gideon's hands. The cool liquid tasted sweet, helping to cleanse away the taste of worry and fear for his feathered friend. When he finished, he held the cup out. Instead of taking it away, Duncan filled it a second time.

Gideon managed a small laugh. "Has anyone ever told you two that you'd make a fine pair of nursemaids?"

Kane looked particularly disgusted by the suggestion, which went a long way toward improving Gideon's mood. He closed his eyes and continued to sip the water as he contemplated what had happened outside. Logically, he knew the entire episode had taken but a handful of minutes. Even so, it was as if everything had seemed to happen slowly, each image vivid in his head. Scim soaring in lazy loops up high in the sky, then starting down when he realized Gideon had seen him. Then something happened. But what? A flash of light followed by a second one. He remembered the pain in Scim's scream as he tumbled from the sky.

"Kane, what did you see?"

His friend sank down on the floor, stretching out his

long legs in front of him. Gideon noted that he kept his sword within arm's reach. Did he sense a threat to more than just Scim?

"We were talking, but then you spotted Scimitar returning from the keep. The bird began his dive when you held out your arm, but then there was a bolt of lightning."

He frowned. "But with no answering thunder. How could that be? And if Scim was close enough to the flash to be hurt, why was he not burned? None of this makes sense."

No, no, it didn't. And now that he'd had time to catch his breath, Gideon's temper was stirring again. He nodded in the direction of Kane's sword. "What are you sensing that you feel the need to keep your weapon drawn?"

Rather than answer, Kane closed his eyes, and the mark on his cheek darkened briefly. His upper lip curled, revealing the longer-than-normal pointed tips of his canine teeth, another gift from his grandfather's magic.

"A faint echo of that same feeling I had two days ago. I might not have noticed it at all if I hadn't been looking for it." He wiped his hands on the hem of his tunic as if he'd touched something foul. "I have yet to recall the nature of this threat, but I will."

Gideon studied his two friends. "And you, Duncan. Did you see anything while you were out riding this morning?"

"Grass. Horses. More grass. No sign of anyone in the area." He smiled. "I did see Kestrel out there running with his band, leading them farther away from Lady Merewen's keep, toward the mountains, although the grazing there would not be nearly as good. It now occurs to me to wonder if he, too, senses that something evil moves upon the plains."

It was just as Gideon had feared. The evil they were

sent to challenge existed beyond the keep itself. He considered their choices. Until they had more information, they were flying in the dark. He glanced toward his shield and thought perhaps the colors were growing brighter. He hoped that was true; he would need Scim in the days ahead.

The plan had been for Duncan to wait a few more days before approaching the keep to avoid any suspicion that he was acquainted with Murdoch and Averel. Unexpected visitors had to be rare at such an isolated manor. Too many arrivals so close together might draw unwanted suspicion.

They were going to have to take that risk. "Duncan, we need you to explore Merewen's library. Can you be ready to ride later this afternoon?"

Duncan cut up the rabbit he'd brought back and put it on the fire to simmer. "Are you sure changing our plans is wise?"

Gideon looked to Kane for support. "I do not see that we have a choice. Today's attack is the second time we have encountered this same presence on the plains. We cannot fight what we do not know."

Kane stared at the shield propped in the corner. "If Duncan leaves today, what about you? Will you be able to stay away from the keep if you no longer have Scim's eyes to watch for trouble for you?"

Crowding Fagan too soon might make the situation worse. It would be best to wait until the appointed time to approach the man. If only Gideon knew more about the situation, especially about what had been happening the night before when he'd sensed that Merewen was in jeopardy. He had no proof, but he'd learned to trust his instincts. He could trust Murdoch to send word if there was trouble. Scim's image popped into Gideon's head, especially the bird's insistence that Gideon pay attention to his leg.

The message! In his rush to save his friend, he'd forgotten all about the note the falcon had been carrying.

When he lurched to his feet and headed for the door, Duncan blocked his way. "Where are you going?"

"Scim had a note tied to his leg. I must have dropped it."

All three charged back to where Scim had plummeted to the ground, fanning out to search the area for the paper. Gideon found the bit of string that had held the note in place, but the paper was nowhere in sight. They widened the search, allowing for the slight breeze.

Kane pounced. "Found it!"

Duncan and Gideon crowded close as he unfolded the small paper and read it aloud.

" 'Success, but know that Warwick dwells within. Murdoch.' "

Kane pointed to the paper. "Who is Warwick? Why does he think we'd know that name?"

Duncan also looked confused by Murdoch's comment, but Gideon needed no explanations. The terse message confirmed his belief that Lady Merewen had been in danger last evening. His friend's wording had been clever. If anyone other than Gideon had found the message, its meaning would have been lost on him.

The name Warwick was a link to their shared past, one that only Gideon and Murdoch knew the truth about. The memory also made Gideon's blood run cold. As a small boy, Murdoch had been fostered by a brutal knight, one who used his fists on anyone he perceived as weaker. When Murdoch grew big enough, he'd fought back, almost killing the man. To prevent Warwick's sons from seeking retribution, Gideon had helped Murdoch escape by bribing the guards. The two of them had been inseparable ever since.

But now Murdoch's message was clear. He'd already known that Fagan mistreated Merewen and her people, but Murdoch had been there less than a day and had already seen evidence of the man's vile nature firsthand.

Under most circumstances, Murdoch could be depended on to maintain control, to follow directions, to play his part. However, like all of the Damned, he had his own demons that drove him, even after all these centuries. This was the warrior's declaration that if Fagan lifted a hand to harm someone weaker, especially a woman or a child, Murdoch would kill him or die in the attempt.

All five of them had their own secrets, and Gideon had left it up to each individual how much to share with the others. If Murdoch had chosen to keep the nightmares of his youth to himself, Gideon wouldn't betray him now.

He pointed to the name on the note. "This is Murdoch's way of telling us that Fagan is even worse than Merewen had indicated."

Kane growled something harsh in his native tongue. Gideon didn't ask him to translate but agreed with the sentiment. He briefly considered making his approach to the keep rather than sending Duncan, but he needed to wait until Scim was back to full strength before risking entering into battle.

"Duncan, I do think you should ride for the keep this afternoon. You can always have Averel send messages with his dogs. They'll be able to track their way back to me."

"That makes sense, although my friend hates when I don't use him."

Duncan had his own avatar, but it wasn't suitable for delivering messages during the daylight hours.

"Blame it on me." Gideon had the same difficulty with Scim, whereas Kane's avatar wouldn't stoop to being a messenger.

"I'll wait until after the midday meal before leaving,

but I'll pack now." Duncan started to walk away but then paused briefly to point toward the horizon. "It appears your stallion is returning."

Gideon and Kane remained where they were. For his part, Gideon should take pleasure in watching the simple beauty of the stallion in motion, his black coat gleaming in the bright sunshine. Instead, he wanted to jump on Kestrel's back and ride for the keep with no more plan than to force his way inside to cross swords with Fagan and his men.

As the horse closed the remaining distance, Kane spoke, his words intruding on the gloom of Gideon's thoughts. "Hold steady, Gideon. The man will pay for his abuses. The gods will have it no other way."

Kane was right. One way or the other, a battle was quickly approaching. But rather than respond, Gideon launched himself up on Kestrel's back and urged the stallion into a gallop. Maybe with the wind ripping through his hair and the pounding of Kestrel's powerful hooves, he could find some brief moments of peace.

Chapter 9

$\mathcal{M}$erewen needed to be careful if she was to approach Sir Murdoch without drawing unwanted attention to the men her uncle had hired last night. She had a reputation for ignoring Fagan's men. Most of them looked to Olaf for leadership, making it wise to keep as much distance from them as possible. However, Murdoch and Averel were different, even if her uncle was too blind to see it.

She waited until they were in the stables. There, no one would question if she acted more interested in the horses than she was in the men.

When she walked into the stable, Murdoch was checking his mare's feet. "Is there something wrong with your mare, Sir Murdoch?"

This time she managed to hide her shivers when he turned those cold pale eyes in her direction. Earlier she'd heard some of the servants muttering about the two men, but she'd shushed them.

Murdoch lowered the hoof to the ground. "Just making sure she hadn't picked up a rock. We've done some hard riding the past few days, and she was limping a bit."

Merewen nodded and ran her hand down the big mare's leg, opening herself up to the mare's thoughts. "It feels a bit hot, but she's not in any pain. Still, if you'll come with me, I'll fix you a poultice to put on it."

"Thank you, my lady."

"I'm glad to help. We pride ourselves on the care we give our horses."

No, here it was the people who suffered from neglect. She led him toward the small workshop she'd had built nearby. Several of her treatments required the use of boiling water, and the risk of fire prevented her from preparing them in the stable itself.

Murdoch stood close by while she steeped the herbs in hot water and then wrapped the mixture in a piece of cloth that would enable him to tie the poultice in place. As she worked, he stared out the door, his silence becoming heavy like a storm about to break.

Finally, he spoke, his voice filled with the chill of the river. "The lady, who is she?"

Merewen looked around to see which woman Murdoch was talking about, but there was no one in sight.

"Which lady?" she asked, although she had her suspicions. Both Murdoch and Averel had had a clear view of Alina while they were speaking with her uncle the previous evening.

"The one with your uncle's handprint on her face."

The cold fury in Murdoch's voice had Merewen shivering despite the heat of the fire. "Alina is my uncle's wife."

To her relief, Murdoch merely nodded as if she'd confirmed his suspicions, and then he changed the subject. "I told Captain Gideon that we've been hired on."

"He was here and I missed him?" As soon as the words slipped out, Merewen regretted them.

If her companion found anything odd about her distress, he gave no sign of it. "No, he wouldn't risk coming close to the keep yet. He sent the gyrfalcon in his stead. Scim carried the message back to him."

What had Murdoch told Gideon? It couldn't have been a very long letter if it had to fit around a gyrfalcon's leg. Of course, she knew from personal experience that

Scim was capable of carrying far more weight than the average bird, not that there was anything average about him. Averel's avatars, too, were outside the normal size for dogs.

What symbol was painted on Murdoch's shield? She couldn't remember. Was it out of bounds for her to ask? He could always refuse to answer.

As she squeezed the excess water from the bandage, she asked, "Who is your special companion?"

At first she thought he was going to ignore her, but the big man's stern mouth softened almost into a smile. "A mountain cat. It is unlikely that you'll meet her anytime soon. She wouldn't attack except at my command, but people and horses are skittish around big cats. Besides, it is difficult to explain to people why she's with me in the first place. Mountain cats are known to be reclusive."

The only such cat she'd ever seen firsthand was the one that had attacked Rogue. She had no desire to meet another one. Those sharp fangs had haunted her dreams long after Rogue had healed from his wounds.

"Here's the poultice. The herbs should draw out the heat and relieve any swelling. Leave it in place for several hours. If her leg is not better by tomorrow, send for me so we can try something else."

Murdoch accepted the bandage with a small nod. "Thank you, my lady. I'll apply it and then join the other men for sword practice."

Averel was waiting for them as they walked outside. She cautioned them both. "Sir Averel, Sir Murdoch, please be careful if you cross blades with Fagan or his captain. The others are only average, but my uncle prides himself on his skill with a sword. Olaf is almost as good. They take pleasure in besting anyone new to the keep. Most men require stitches after they are introduced to my uncle's style of practice."

Averel bowed his head as they withdrew. "We appreciate your concern, Lady Merewen, but have no worry. We can defend ourselves."

She hoped so. She really did.

Alina didn't know what had brought the two strangers to the manor, but blessings to the gods who guided their footsteps. She hadn't spoken a word to either of them and couldn't imagine an occasion where she would have need to, but nonetheless she was glad for their presence. Their arrival last evening had been enough to distract her husband from his displeasure with both her and Merewen.

For that, she would be grateful. One night without new pain was a gift to be cherished. She'd slept undisturbed in her own bed and felt much better when she rose to face the day. When she'd peeked in her husband's room to see if he had need of her, she was relieved to find him gone.

His servant said he was outside observing the young warrior's dogs. She shuddered at the thought. Both of the animals stood nearly waist-high to a grown man with teeth strong enough to crack bones. Still, they had been well behaved during dinner, and the other dogs had stayed clear of them—a good thing. Fagan would not have easily forgiven an injury to one of his precious pack. After all, he cared more about the dogs than he did about her.

Oddly enough, it was the older of the two new men who had drawn her attention during the meal. More than once she'd noticed him staring at the high table. When he'd been looking in Fagan's direction, the warrior's expression had been rock hard and cold, typical of the men her husband liked to surround himself with. However, when the man's gaze had turned toward her, she'd thought those oddly pale eyes were sympathetic.

That was probably only wishful thinking. Other than Merewen, no one was willing to risk Fagan's fury by befriending his lonely wife. Alina didn't blame them, but she missed the days spent in her mother's bower surrounded by other women.

But that was then. Rather than dwell on the past, she hurried down the stairs to the hall. She'd slept through the early meal, but she was certain Ellie would give her bread and cheese to break her fast.

Before she made it to the kitchen, a movement near the door caught her eye. The two new men were entering the hall, the younger one holding a bloody bandage on his friend's arm.

She couldn't hear what the older warrior was saying, but from the way he was snarling, she suspected the words were not ones a lady was supposed to hear. She'd no doubt heard far worse from her own husband, but that didn't mean she liked it.

As soon as they spotted her, both men stopped walking. Even from where she stood, it was obvious that the injured man was in pain. She hesitated and then changed directions. If he was bleeding that badly, he likely needed the wound sewn closed. Such injuries were common enough when her husband was out to show his prowess with weapons. Ordinarily, the men treated their own minor wounds with Merewen handling only the most serious ones. However, at this time of day she'd be out tending to the horses.

That left Alina. Most of the men-at-arms thought she was cold and unwilling to lift a finger to help them. Preferring to maintain her distance, she was content to let them think ill of her. However, she felt compelled to ease this warrior's pain. Rather than think too hard about the reasons, she stopped just short of where the two men stood.

Both bowed their heads as she approached, another

sign that they were different from the usual type Fagan hired. It made her wonder why they would seek employment at such a remote estate.

"Please be seated and let me see the wound."

The younger man answered for the pair. "I can take care of his arm, my lady, if you can tell me where to get a needle and thread."

She tried to remember how to smile. "It is no bother. I will take care of it if you'll just fetch my sewing basket from my bower. Go up the stairs and to the right."

The two men looked at each other before acceding to her request. The wounded man finally spoke, his deep voice sending shivers through her. How odd that he didn't inspire the fear that a man his size usually did.

"If you are sure, my lady."

He sank down onto a nearby bench while his younger friend ran for the steps, taking them two at a time. Meanwhile, Alina caught the eye of a servant. "Meg, please bring a basin of hot water and some clean cloths."

The silence that settled between her and the warrior bothered her. Considering she never knew how Fagan would react to the most innocent of statements, she'd long ago lost the art of simple conversation. She settled for lifting the edge of the makeshift bandage, wincing when she saw the gleam of bone. Whoever had swung the blade had done so with great force.

He pulled his arm back. "Lady Alina, you don't have to do this if the sight of blood bothers you overly much. Averel is well practiced in treating wounds."

She caught his wrist before he could withdraw it completely. "No, I was only imagining how much it must hurt."

He stared at her hand for the longest time. When she realized what he was doing, she blushed and jerked her hand back. Still, she intended to stand by her offer.

Luckily, the servant had returned with the water and

rags. She'd also thought to bring some of the soap that Merewen insisted on using to cleanse all wounds. Since few of the injured her niece treated developed infections, Alina had learned to follow her advice.

"I'll try to be gentle, Sir—"

Alina stopped, realizing she didn't remember his name from when he'd introduced himself to her husband the previous evening.

"I am called Murdoch, my lady."

She liked the deep rumble of his voice and found smiling came a little easier this time. "Well, Sir Murdoch, shall we get started?"

Murdoch sat still, biting his lip to keep from flinching as Lady Alina carefully washed away the dried blood and dirt. The wound was bad, but it would be nearly healed come morning. However, if he didn't go through the motions of having it treated, it would draw far more attention than he could risk right now.

He'd planned to have Averel put a few stitches in it and then cover it with a bandage, one he wouldn't remove for several days. By then, no one would remember how deeply the late blow from Fagan's sword had cut into Murdoch's forearm.

No, that wasn't true. Averel would remember and so would Murdoch. They had both immediately added it to the growing list of crimes that Merewen's uncle would pay for, not the least of which was the fading bruise on Lady Alina's cheek. For that alone, the bastard would bleed.

Murdoch struggled to keep his fury hidden from the lady herself. Thanks to the monster she was wed to, she was as skittish as a young mountain cat. How would she react if she were to meet Shadow? When he'd first found the mountain cat, she'd been shot by a hunter's arrow. It had taken Murdoch hours of tracking to finally corner her long enough to dress her wounds. Once she'd decided he wasn't going to hurt her, she'd taken to following him whenever he hunted in the woods.

They were both solitary by nature, but their partnership had suited them. Now they'd been together for centuries because Shadow had chosen to follow him when Murdoch had thrown his lot in with Gideon. It was a decision he'd never regretted. He'd always hoped Shadow felt the same.

"There, it is all clean."

Lady Alina rinsed away the last bit of the soap and wiped his arm dry before dropping the bloody cloth into the basin. The servant girl had hovered nearby. "Please bring me a fresh basin. He may bleed again while I stitch the wound closed."

The girl picked up the bowl and retreated as fast as she could without slopping the water out onto the floor. Obviously Lady Alina wasn't the only one who had learned to be cautious around the men of the keep.

Murdoch heard Averel running down the stairs and cursed his friend's speed. That boy never did anything at a normal pace. Perhaps in this case it was a good thing. Murdoch was all too conscious of Lady Alina's womanly presence as she fussed over his arm.

The fact that she was wed to a vicious fool didn't change the fact that she was married. His honor recognized that fact even as certain parts of his body stirred to life for the first time since he'd first slept beneath the river. He shifted uncomfortably on the bench, grateful that his tunic would hide any unwanted evidence of the effect Alina's touch was having.

Averel held out the basket. "Here, my lady."

"Thank you."

She quickly threaded a needle. "Brace yourself."

"I've survived worse."

For some reason his gruff reply made her smile. It was

a shy, fleeting expression but one that warmed him through. Then she bent her head down and began the arduous process of closing the wound, her stitches neat and careful. He closed his eyes to keep from staring, but there was no way to avoid the perfume of roses that scented her hair. Nor could he ignore the soft touch of her fingers as she worked her needle in and out of his skin.

When she was finished, she studied her work with a critical eye as she gently wiped away the last few droplets of blood. "I don't think the scar will be too noticeable."

Actually, within days it would disappear altogether, but he couldn't tell her that. He settled for thanking her.

"I'm in your debt, my lady."

Averel joined the conversation. "Truly, we both are, Lady Alina. You saved me from having to listen to Murdoch holler while I stitched him. He has no tolerance for pain."

He meant it in jest, but Alina took him seriously and glared at him. "You malign Sir Murdoch! He has not uttered a single complaint."

Murdoch warmed at her adamant defense. "Averel was but teasing, Lady Alina. The young dolt does not realize that not everyone appreciates his humor."

She blushed. "I apologize then."

Clearly flustered, she gathered up her thread and needle and stuffed them into the basket Averel had brought down from her room. He hated that her hands were shaking, but he knew she would not appreciate it if he were to comment. Instead, he laid his hand over hers briefly.

"Thank you again for your kindness."

She stared down at their joined hands and then looked up at him. For the first time, her true beauty shone through the fading bruises and the haunted look in her silvery gray eyes.

"It was nothing."

"I would argue, but my mother taught me not to contradict a beautiful woman."

Then, realizing he'd said too much, especially in front of Averel, Murdoch rose to his feet. "If you will excuse us, we should rejoin your husband and the other men."

Just the mention of Fagan made her go pale. "Yes, of course. I should return to my rooms now."

She started to walk away but then turned back. "Sir Murdoch, if your wound reddens or becomes more painful, seek out my niece, Lady Merewen. She has far more skill as a healer than I do."

"Yes, Lady Alina. Thank you again for attending to my wound."

Bowing briefly, Murdoch grabbed Averel's arm and dragged his friend back out of the hall.

As soon as they were out of the lady's hearing, his friend mumbled, "That was certainly interesting."

"Shut up, Averel."

Never one to take a hint, the young fool tried again. "But in all these years I've never seen you—"

Murdoch normally was slow to anger and prided himself on his sense of fairness. Right now, though, his emotions were a tangled mess. Taking his foul mood out on Averel would be wrong, but that didn't keep him from grabbing his friend by the throat and shoving him up against the nearest wall. He put enough strength into his grip to cut off Averel's breath as well as the words Murdoch had no interest in hearing.

Well aware they weren't alone, he stared into Averel's eyes as he slowly relaxed his hand. "I said for you to stop talking. Are you going to?"

Even as the young warrior nodded, his mouth opened to say something. Clearly, he was not understanding what Murdoch was telling him. He tightened his grip again.

"Whatever it is, I do not want to hear it. Not now. Not ever. Understand?"

When he once again allowed him to draw a breath, Averel had the good sense to remain quiet. Murdoch released his friend and stepped back, only to realize he'd been flanked by Averel's two dogs with their ears back and lips drawn over their teeth. The dogs were normally good-natured but not when their master was being threatened.

Averel intervened, his voice rough with pain. "Down, both of you."

They backed away but kept a wary eye on Murdoch. He tried to shake off some of his temper.

"I'm sorry."

He directed his words to the dogs but hoped their owner accepted the apology, too. Evidently, he did, because Averel immediately clapped Murdoch on his shoulder.

"You mentioned something about returning to arms practice." He glanced at the bandage on Murdoch's arm. "How's the wound?"

"Better."

Averel grinned. "Good, because I don't want you to use that as an excuse when I beat you bloody."

All things considered, Murdoch might even let him. "Better yet, mayhap we can entice Fagan and his friend Olaf into a match. I would hate to be the only one who bleeds today."

With that happy thought, they headed for the bailey with the dogs trailing behind.

Chapter 10

"*H*ob and I need a run in the mountains."

Gideon looked up from honing his knife to where Kane stood silhouetted in the doorway.

"Why?"

Kane tilted his head to the side. "Because we grow restless. Do we need a better reason?"

From where Gideon sat, he couldn't make out the expression on Kane's face, but it didn't matter. Sometimes a restlessness rode his friend hard, driving him out into the night. With Hob at Kane's side, it was unlikely that anyone—or anything—would get the best of him.

Gideon went back to stroking his knife on the stone. "Enjoy the night. If you feel the need to make a kill, make it something edible. Meat for tomorrow's dinner wouldn't go amiss."

Kane didn't comment. They both knew what happened when his dark side was on the ascendance. "We'll be back by morning."

"Are you taking Rogue, too?"

"Only to the foot of the mountain. I'll send him back before I release Hob."

Ordinary horses were terrified of Kane's avatar, but Gideon suspected Rogue might react differently. "They have to meet sometime, Kane. Better now than in battle."

"I'll consider it." Kane picked up his shield. "Get some rest, Gideon. Duncan and Murdoch will ensure the woman is safe."

There was nothing to be said to that. "Go. I'll be fine."

A few minutes after Kane left, Gideon ventured out into the gathering darkness himself. It suited his mood.

The long ride he'd taken earlier had done little to ease his mind. Kane was right. He worried about Merewen, but it was more than that. He'd never liked dividing his forces.

Nothing about this situation was normal. There were battles to come, he was sure of it. But until he had a clearer vision of the true nature of the danger, he was hunting on a circular trail and tracking a ghost. He preferred his enemies standing within easy reach of his sword and ready to die.

A noise disturbed the soft rustle of the breeze. He stopped walking to listen, noting that Kestrel was on alert as well. The stallion stood his head up and nostrils flared wide to catch a scent on the breeze. Perhaps his band of mares was seeking him out. Lucky horse.

This time the sound was closer. He finally spotted a single horse approaching and at speed, as yet too far distant to pick out any details. Drawing his sword just in case, Gideon faded back into the gray shadows along the cottage and stood watch.

The rider was too small to be one of his men. That left only one person it could be: Lady Merewen.

He slid his sword back into its scabbard. If something was seriously wrong, Averel would have sent one of the dogs with a message. What crisis would warrant Merewen's risking her uncle's wrath by coming herself?

Only one way to find out. He walked out to meet her, telling himself his pulse was racing out of concern for her safety. It had nothing to do with the way she and the horse moved as one, all grace and feminine beauty. For a woman of such slight build, there was a great deal of strength in her. He shifted restlessly from foot to foot, the realization that she had the power to affect him so strongly making him edgy.

He cursed his lack of control. Granted, he was still a man with a man's needs. However, with so few weeks to walk in the world and do the work ordained by the gods, the last thing he should be thinking about was how sweet it would be to be the one Merewen rode with such abandon.

He crossed his arms over his chest, waiting not so patiently to find out why the lady had come to visit.

Merewen slowed her mare to a walk. Did Gideon realize how much he and Kestrel resembled each other at the moment? Both males were tense, both staring at her and the mare in stony silence.

So much for a warm welcome, but then her visit was unexpected. She had a strong suspicion that the good captain didn't much enjoy surprises. He obviously wasn't going out of his way to make her feel welcome. Fine. He wasn't the one she'd ridden out to see.

Rather than approach him directly, she dismounted near the small corral next to the cottage. After turning the mare loose and closing the gate, she took the time to greet Kestrel, petting his nose and slipping him a carrot from her pouch. As she waited for him to finish crunching it before offering another, she felt a warmth at her back and turned to face Gideon.

"Captain."

He didn't bother with a polite greeting, growling instead, "Why are you here?"

"Your man Duncan arrived late this afternoon. After some negotiations, my uncle has granted him access to my father's library at a steep price. I'm sure no one will benefit from the gold that exchanged hands except Fagan himself."

She let her disgust show in her voice. "While I showed Duncan around, he told me that Scim had been hurt. I came to see if there was anything I could do. Although I mainly work with horses, I have some experience in treating injured hunting birds."

The words poured out all in one breath, leaving her feeling a bit winded by the time she reached the end of her explanation. Or maybe it was the fact that Gideon was standing so close to her that was leaving her breathless.

If anything, that stern mouth was frowning even harder. "Did he also tell you that I called Scim back into my shield?"

"He did, but—"

Gideon let out a sigh, as if her being there sorely tried his temper. "Lady Merewen, Scim is not an ordinary bird. None of our avatars are exactly how they appear, not even that pair of idiot dogs that follow Averel everywhere he goes. All of them were ensorcelled by the gods, just as my men and I were. You should never forget that."

As if she could. The memory of the five warriors marching out of the water, the river's chill in their gaze, was never far from her mind. Still, it was hard to reconcile that image of the captain with the man who had kissed her with such hunger. Did he regret that moment? Did he even remember? Most assuredly, he didn't act as though he kept it close to mind.

She couldn't find the words to ask and wasn't sure she wanted to know the answer anyway. It was better to leave the memory untarnished by second thoughts.

"I have not forgotten what you are, Captain, or your purpose for being here. You and the other warriors came to end my uncle's tyranny."

"That's right, my lady. The gods heard your plea and sent us here to kill your uncle and his men. They will die upon our swords, leaving them wandering in darkness of the netherworld, lost and soulless for eternity."

His words hung sharp and jagged in the evening air, a barrier between them as solid as a stone wall. It was

Gideon's truth as he knew it, but there was more to him than just a sword arm to be used at her bidding or on a whim by the gods. He was still a man, one who could feel lonely, who could need. She was sure of it.

If he were as cold as he pretended to be, he wouldn't inspire such loyalty in his men. She loved his fiercely protective nature as well. She knew firsthand how people suffered under the rule of a man who was both brutal and selfish. Gideon's touch was gentle even when his temper ran hot.

And she was drawn to the flash of heat in his gaze whenever he looked at her. Perhaps if she couldn't find a way through that wall he was determined to build, she might find a way around it.

"Since I am here anyway, why don't you let me check Scim to make sure there isn't anything I can do. If nothing else, I brought him some delicacies from the kitchen."

It was difficult to tell in the dim light, but she thought the harsh lines carved in Gideon's face softened just slightly. He might not take any comfort she might offer him, but he had a harder time denying the same to Scim.

"Come with me. Now that the sun is almost down, it is probably safe to call him forth again. I won't do so, though, if tarrying here will cause you difficulties with your uncle. Does he know that you left the keep?"

"I told him I'd received word about an injured animal." She fought to keep a straight face. "He'll be happy enough if I bring him payment for my services."

Gideon definitely looked angrier. "He sells your services to his own people?"

She nodded. "He sees it as another way to tax them. I usually bring home a chicken."

"Something most of your crofters can ill afford to lose."

"Yes, that would be true." She finally let a sly smile slip loose, hoping Gideon would enjoy the joke. "But you see, he's never noticed that I always bring back the same one."

At first she thought he misunderstood her, but then finally he rewarded her with a small smile. "My lady, you are dangerous indeed. Remind me never to thwart you."

She grinned up at him, totally unrepentant. "You would never be so foolish. Now, let's go check on Scim."

"Come inside."

Looking far more resigned, Gideon headed back to the cottage while she fetched her medicine bag as well as the food she'd brought for both the gyrfalcon and his owner.

He should have made her leave immediately, but it was fast becoming clear that he would have better luck trying to force the river to run upstream than to make Merewen change course. Right now, letting her see for herself that Scim was on the mend was the only way to make her leave.

And he needed her to go before he weakened and begged her to stay.

Ordinarily, it would have been better to carry the shield outside, but Scim had already drawn the attention of the hidden evil haunting the grasslands. The bird had barely survived the first encounter. It was unlikely he would a second time.

Gideon lifted the shield and held it close, hoping Scim would be able to draw extra strength from him. Merewen walked in as he finished the chant. The entire cottage lit up with a flash of light as the gyrfalcon left the sanctuary of the shield. No matter how many times Gideon had seen the miracle, he never failed to be dazzled by the gift the gods had seen fit to give him.

This time, rather than taking to the sky, Scim flapped down to the ground, the awkward movement due to the limited room rather than to his injuries. The bird ruffled his feathers and fluttered his wings one last time before settling down to watch the two humans.

Seeing his companion whole and in no obvious pain was an enormous relief. Gideon offered a silent prayer of thanks as he knelt down to offer his arm to the falcon.

He carried him over to the small table and let him hop off while Gideon took a seat on the bench. He patted the space beside him and said, "Approach slowly. He should remember you, but I'd rather not startle him when he's been hurt."

Merewen inched forward, crooning softly. Obviously, she did have experience in working with skittish birds of prey. After she was seated, she offered the bird a smile. "Scim, we meet again."

The falcon tilted his head to the side to study her. Satisfied that she offered no threat, he walked toward the edge of the table and leaned out to nibble her hair. Merewen laughed softly and let the bird do as he pleased.

Gideon watched the woman win over his avatar with nothing more than a smile. It should have come as no surprise that she'd do so. After all, she'd had a similar effect on all of his men, even Kane. Did she have any idea how amazing that was?

She was talking to the falcon again. "Scim, I'm going to touch you now. If I hit a tender spot, be patient with me. I need to see how badly you were hurt. Behave like a gentleman, and I'll have a special treat for you."

Once again Scim stared at her as if weighing the meaning of her words. He actually bobbed his head and held out his injured wing. Gideon couldn't believe what he was seeing, but the now-familiar warmth of Merewen's magic flowed through the room as she gently traced each of Scim's wings, his legs, and then his entire body, beak to claws.

Gideon found himself leaning toward her, wanting some of that sweetness for himself. As soon as the thought crossed his mind, he jerked back. That was the seduction of magic calling to him, making him hunger for it. He would need to be more vigilant in the future. Merewen might not practice the dark arts, but magic was magic, addictive and lethal.

Right now, whatever she was sensing had her looking pleased. "He's fine, Gideon. The bones have mended smoothly, and his pain has greatly eased."

When she was finished, Scim stepped farther back from the edge and ruffled his feathers again. Merewen's magic gradually dissipated, leaving a fresh scent in the air, and a new warmth in the room.

She pulled a pouch out of her bag and unwrapped a small bowl, which she placed in front of Scim. Gideon leaned forward to see what she'd brought for the bird. Giblets—lots of them. Not his own favorite food, but the gyrfalcon definitely perked up at the sight.

She gently scratched Scim's head. "I'd tell you to eat slowly, but I know better. I'm betting those will be gone all too quickly."

Scim immediately set about proving her right. She'd already cut the meat into small pieces, so all he had to do was gulp them down. When they were gone, he stretched his neck toward her bag and gave her an expectant look.

Merewen's laughter brightened the darkness in Gideon's world as she gave in and offered the bird a second bowl of the bloody tidbits. Scim's lack of table manners only seemed to amuse her.

Then she dug into the bag a third time and held out another small package wrapped in cloth. "I figured you had used up a lot of your own strength in helping Scim. Duncan said he'd left you stew simmering on the fire. Since he took care of your dinner, I brought dessert for you and Kane. That is if either of you like sweets."

Gideon accepted the gift and gently unwrapped it. Inside was a plate piled with a stack of pastries. The scent of apples and spices wafted up, setting his mouth to watering.

"Thank you, my lady. I assure you that I like sweets, and Kane does as well, although he's likely to deny it. This was most thoughtful of you."

For the first time, Merewen was looking a little nervous. "I baked them myself."

He picked one up with his fingers and took a bite and then another, wolfing down the flaky crust and tart apples. He was tempted to lick his fingers, but they'd only get sticky again when he ate the next one.

After the third one, he pushed the plate back and covered it with the cloth. "I'll save those for Kane when he returns."

Then he winked at Merewen. "Or at least I'll try to. If he stays gone too long, I'm not sure I'll be able to resist them. Besides, I wouldn't want them to get stale."

His words obviously pleased her. As much as he was enjoying her company, it was time for her to go. Night had fallen, and riding in the dark was hazardous.

"Thank you for both your care of Scim and for the pastries, but now you must return to the keep. The moon should provide enough light for you to make the trip safely, if you're careful." Not that she was always careful when it came to her own well-being.

Merewen picked up her bag and started for the door. She paused briefly to glance toward the rafters where Scim had taken roost. "I'll be fine. It is a relief that your friend up there is doing so well."

Gideon followed her out to the corral, knowing his next words would not make her happy. "Merewen, you should not return here."

She hung the strap of her bag on the saddle and turned back to face him. "But—"

He hushed her protest with a finger across her lips. "There is evil loose on the grasslands. This time it attacked Scim. I would not risk the same thing happening to you."

She looked up him, her pretty face bathed in the silver light of the moon overhead. "When will I see you again?"

"Not until I arrive at your gate, which will likely be a few days at least. Unless my men send word that I am needed sooner, Kane and I will try to track the source of the attack on Scim."

Not that he wanted to remain at the cottage. It was getting harder each time he had to send her back into peril. Although he was glad to have his friends in place, he had to wonder why Fagan felt the need to surround himself with so many armed men.

"For now, try to stay out of your uncle's way. You can depend on Duncan and the others to see to the safety of your people."

"I'm not worried about myself, Gideon." Her chin came up. "I will not cower in a corner and let someone else suffer. They are my responsibility."

Her driving desire to protect her people from her uncle's viciousness rang true in every word. She would willingly sacrifice herself to save them. As much as Gideon admired Merewen's warrior spirit, he wanted to shake some sense into her.

Instead, he cupped the side of her face with his hand, unable to deny himself that small touch. "What if the next time he doesn't just beat you? What if he loses control or decides you've become too much of a thorn in his side and kills you instead? What then? If you sacrifice yourself, Merewen, there will be no one left with your gift to care for the horses. Without them, your people will have nothing."

That she started to protest again had him gritting his teeth. This woman took stubbornness to new heights. Once again he hushed her, this time with his lips. May the gods forgive him, but he couldn't resist another taste of this woman. He teased her lips apart, then swept in with his tongue to claim possession.

If he couldn't convince her with his words, well, there were other ways to impose his will. He swept her up in his arms and carried her deeper into the shadows. He briefly considered taking her back inside the cottage but wasn't ready to cross that threshold—literally. Inside, it would be all too easy to lay her down upon his pallet. If he were to do that, there would be no turning back. He wouldn't be satisfied until he uncovered and explored every inch of her silken skin.

Despite her bravado, Merewen was an innocent, one he was sworn to protect—even from himself. Maybe especially from himself.

When he started to set her back down on her feet, she protested and wrapped her legs around his hips. This was going too far and too fast, but he couldn't remember anything ever feeling so right. He kept his hands firmly anchored on her narrow waist, but he savored the sweet press of her body against his.

One more kiss—surely they deserved that much. A few seconds later, with his blood racing and his need for her throbbing in his head, in his heart, in his body, he eased back. Slowed down. Stepped away. Hated the breath of cool night air that filled the emptiness between them.

"Gideon, I want—"

It didn't matter what she wanted; what he needed. Duty came first. It had to, for both their sakes. He shook his head and backed away another step. "The hour grows late. Leave, Merewen. Now."

Her lips were swollen from his kisses, her dark eyes shining bright with the sheen of tears.

She brushed past him and mounted her horse. From there, she looked down into his face. "I'll wait for you to come to me, Captain, but don't keep me waiting for long."

Then she spurred her mare forward in a headlong gallop back toward the keep. So much for her being careful. He could only hope that the mare had more sense than her rider did. Aching and alone, he watched Merewen disappear into the night.

Chapter 11

*T*o avoid drawing attention to himself, Murdoch waited but a minute or two after Merewen rode back into the keep before following her into the stable. It didn't appear that her uncle had noticed her absence at dinner, but Murdoch could be wrong about that.

Right now he was more concerned about why Olaf had been watching for her. The man hadn't actually said that was his purpose in pacing along the walk near the top of the palisade and observing the approach to the gate. However, he wasn't on duty, and as soon as she'd been spotted, he'd immediately disappeared. Murdoch's instincts warned him that the man was on the hunt and Merewen was his intended prey.

Murdoch had no intention of letting Olaf anywhere near her for long, especially alone. And if the bastard touched the lady, he would bleed, although Murdoch really hoped that it wouldn't come to that—not yet. Luckily, he had a perfect excuse for seeking her out himself. After all, Lady Alina had told him to present himself to Merewen if his arm bothered him.

The stable was dim and quiet. Tired from their day out in the sun, the horses stood dozing in their stalls. Murdoch closed his eyes to focus on listening. If there were any humans in the massive stable, he couldn't sense their presence. He walked toward the stall reserved for Merewen's horse. The mare was there, but she still bore both her saddle and bridle.

Murdoch suspected Lady Merewen's first concern would always be for her mount. Unless something was wrong, she would never neglect the mare's care no matter how tired she was herself. His hand on his sword, he started back through the stable, checking each stall as he went. Despite his hope that Merewen had been called to see to another horse whose needs were more pressing, he found no sign of her anywhere.

That left her workshop and the great hall. He started with the first one simply because it was closer. As soon as he turned the corner toward the small building, he heard voices—one female, one male. He recognized both, which had him hurrying his steps. Although Merewen sounded irritated, her voice held a hint of fear as well.

The belligerent male voice belonged to Olaf. If he was attempting to bully Merewen, Murdoch would teach the man some manners. He stopped outside the door in a spot that afforded him a clear view inside the workshop. Just as he expected, Olaf was crowding Merewen.

"If I tell your uncle that you disobeyed my orders again, you will suffer for your willful behavior either at his hand or mine." His smile made it clear which of those choices he was hoping for.

Merewen stood her ground. "Tell him anything you want to, but Fagan knows that I only go when someone needs my aid in treating an injured animal. I returned as soon as I was able."

Her voice remained calm, but her clenched fists told the real story. She was afraid, but Murdoch couldn't tell whether it was Olaf who caused that tremor in her hands or the fear of facing her uncle. Either way, it was time to intervene.

Acting as if he hadn't heard the prior discussion, Murdoch entered the workroom. "Lady Merewen, I'm sorry to bother you, but your lady aunt suggested I see you if my wound worsened."

He held out his bandaged arm as proof of his claim.

Olaf didn't appreciate the interruption. "Take care of it yourself. Lady Merewen isn't here to tend to the likes of you. It is hardly her fault that you were clumsy enough to get yourself cut in arms practice."

Merewen immediately turned to her worktable and started gathering supplies. "Please be seated, Sir Murdoch."

He was reluctant to sit down because it would leave him at a disadvantage if Olaf went on the attack. He was still debating the issue when Averel appeared in the doorway, flanked by both of his dogs.

He ignored Olaf, looking instead at Murdoch. "I see you found Lady Merewen. What did she say about your arm?"

Confident his friend could handle any confrontations with Olaf, Murdoch continued the charade of needing medical attention and took a seat on the bench. "She was just about to look at it."

The dogs crowded into the room, leaving their master standing in the doorway. With her love of animals, it came as no surprise that Merewen had small treats to offer the beasts. With that one gesture, she won their hearts forever.

Olaf still hadn't given up. "I told you to take your wound elsewhere. Lord Fagan will be displeased that you bothered his wife with the injury as well."

Enough was enough. Murdoch was about to teach the bastard some manners, but the dogs decided to take charge. Both of them shoved their way between Olaf and Merewen, their ears back and deep growls rumbling in their chests. It would take a far braver man than Fagan's captain to face them down.

He was smart enough to retreat even as he made one last threat. "I'll be talking to your uncle about all of this, Merewen."

Averel, always the last to lose his temper, joined his coursers in facing down Olaf. "Lady Merewen has done nothing wrong, Olaf. It has been my experience that the lady of the keep often serves as the healer. Either way, it is none of your business."

"Her uncle—"

Averel's knife appeared in his hand as if by magic. He began flipping it over and over, drawing Olaf's attention in his direction. "Her uncle has more important business to attend to, Olaf. Right now he's trying to decide how best to convince me to allow him to introduce my dogs' bloodlines to his pack. If I were to refuse, he would be most unhappy to find out that it was you who convinced me I shouldn't allow that to happen."

Recognizing he was well and truly outnumbered, Olaf muttered a curse and stormed out into the night. At a signal from Averel, the dogs took up position right outside the door to make sure he didn't return unnoticed.

Merewen let out a shaky breath and leaned back against her worktable. "Gentlemen, I am in your debt. Olaf gets worse every day. He's always been volatile, but that wild look in his eyes is new. Perhaps it is my uncle's influence over him, and some of the other men are almost as bad."

Interesting. "So it is not just your uncle whose actions have changed?"

She ran her hands up and down her arms as if warding off a chill despite the warmth of the fire burning in the brazier. "No, the few remaining men who served my father are as they always were. It is only the ones who owe their first loyalty to Fagan who grow more violent and unpredictable."

Averel looked to Murdoch. "This sounds like something we should report back to the captain."

He agreed. "About the men who were loyal to your father. How many are there, and do you think they would take up arms against your uncle if you were to give such orders?"

He liked that she didn't immediately respond, clearly giving the matter some thought. The price for a wrong answer would most likely be paid in blood. Finally, she nodded.

"Most would, I believe. For certain, none of them have any fondness for Fagan and his men. I think the only reason they have stayed this long is many have family here. Otherwise, I fear they would all be gone."

The hour was growing late, and the lady looked as if a stiff wind would scatter her across the ground like a pile of dried leaves.

Even so, she offered Murdoch a weary smile. "Now, let's see your arm."

He stood up. "My arm is fine. It was only an excuse to walk in without drawing Olaf's suspicion. Give me a fresh bandage and Averel will tend to it. You should retire for the night. We'll also see to your mare for you."

That she didn't protest only gave evidence to how tired she really was. She banked the fire in the brazier. "I was going to come find you both to let you know that Scim is nearly recovered from his injuries."

So that was where she'd been. "That is indeed good news."

As they walked out into the night air, Averel stepped in front of Merewen. "Let me go first to see if Olaf intends to cause you trouble with your uncle. If it is safe for you to enter the hall, I'll send my dogs to fetch you. If it isn't, we will all come."

While they waited to hear, a movement in one of the narrow windows on the second floor caught Murdoch's attention. A woman was watching them from above. Although she was too far away for him to see any real detail, he knew it was Lady Alina. When she raised her hand, no doubt she was acknowledging her niece, not him.

But perhaps not. Truly, however, he had no right to be wishing that she were as aware of him as he was of her. The woman was married, even if the man she was wed to was a monster. Murdoch's own honor would not allow him to admit how powerfully their few minutes together had affected him. Certainly, he would do nothing that would call the lady's honor into question.

"The dogs are coming. Sir Averel must think it is safe for me to return."

Murdoch had been so caught up in staring at Alina that he'd forgotten Lady Merewen. To make up for his brief neglect, he looked down at her. "Would you like me to walk in with you?"

"I'll be fine. Averel is inside, and I suspect the dogs will act as escorts as well."

Then she softly brushed her fingers across his bandaged arm. "Are you sure that you don't want me to check your wound?"

"It's fine. Your lady aunt did an excellent job stitching it closed, and she cleaned it well beforehand using the soap you recommend. Either Averel or I will remove the thread. We've done it before."

"I'm sure you have." Merewen's deep brown eyes saw far too much. "I suspect the five of you have borne far more pain and injuries than any of you would admit or deserved."

Their story was not his to tell. If Gideon chose to share his truth with the lady, that was up to him. "We serve the gods, my lady. Now go before Averel thinks something is amiss and comes looking for you. I'll see to the mare."

"Thank you for that. I hated to turn her into the stall that way. When I realized Olaf was hunting for me, I had hoped to avoid him by escaping to the workshop. Obviously he found me there."

"He will learn to keep his distance."

If Murdoch had to kill the fool to make sure of it. Certainly if the bastard ever laid a hand on her again in violence, Olaf had better hope it was Murdoch who came after him. He would make the man's passing swift. Gideon would kill him, too, but without such mercy.

"Good night, Lady Merewen."

He waited until she reached the door of the great hall before heading toward the stable. Once he took care of the horse, he'd seek out his own bed. Just before he walked through the door, he allowed himself one last look toward the window.

It was empty. He tried not to think about how much that disappointed him.

A boot in the ribs was never Gideon's favorite way to wake up. He glared up at Kane and tried to decide whether the man had outlived his usefulness, because right now Gideon wanted to kill him.

He rolled onto his back, shading his eyes from the sun. "What do you want?"

When Kane smiled, Gideon grimaced. Smiles were also something he didn't like to see so early in the day. "I was just curious why you're sleeping out here in the grass when you could have a roof over your head."

"It was a nice night."

Not to mention once he'd pictured Merewen sharing his pallet, Gideon hadn't been able to face sleeping there alone. He gave up on getting any more rest and threw his blanket aside. At least standing up, he didn't feel at such a disadvantage. Kane followed him over to the well where Gideon drew a bucket of water to splash on his face to vanquish the last vestiges of sleep from his mind.

Kane waited until he was finished to ask, "So, how long was the lady here last evening?"

Gideon ignored the question, preferring to ask a few of his own. "Was your hunt successful?"

His friend looked toward the mountains, his face settling into grim lines. "Hob enjoyed it."

"But you didn't?"

Kane dropped down on the bench by the door and stretched his legs out to look down at his dusty boots. "Not as much as I'd hoped to. We ran the trails together. Hunted some, enough to keep us fed."

"That's good, but I take it there is something you're not saying."

Kane seemed to be staring at something only he could see. Whatever it was, it haunted him. Finally he looked up again, his pale eyes tinged with a bloodred sheen. "That foulness in this land watches and waits."

He finally glanced up. "Its song calls to my blood."

Kane looked back at the mountains again. "I fear we've disturbed it somehow, drawing its attention in our direction. I've grown certain that Lady Merewen's uncle is only a small part of why the gods have called upon us again."

Kane's dark words came as no surprise. Gideon sat down beside his friend. "Have you remembered when you've encountered this before?"

Kane's hand touched the black stone imbedded in the hilt of his sword, the one he'd inherited from his grandfather. "No, not specifically, but eventually I will. Let us hope Duncan has better luck with his search. This evil grows in strength."

His somber words hung heavily in the air, a shadow that dimmed the day and sent a chill through Gideon. How were they to fight an invisible enemy?

Perhaps there was one way. "If it becomes necessary, I will return to the river and ask for guidance."

Not that he would do so except as a last resort. Sometimes the price for asking the gods for gifts could be too high to pay. If Gideon alone would incur the debt, he wouldn't hesitate. But his life was linked too closely to his friends; he would not risk causing them any further pain if he could avoid it.

Kane sighed. "We are not yet that desperate."

Then he cast a sly look in Gideon's direction. "You never answered my question earlier. How long was the lady here? At least tell me why."

Gideon didn't bother asking Kane how he knew that Merewen had paid another visit to the cottage. To him. No one was a better tracker than Kane. He would have spotted her footprints in the dust and tasted her scent on the wind.

"She came to tend to Scim's injuries."

Kane might not believe that was the whole truth, but for the moment he accepted the change in subjects. "How is that feathered scavenger, anyway?"

The gyrfalcon and Kane had an interesting relationship, one that wasn't always peaceful. Over the years, Scim had been known to swoop in and rob Kane of his kills. The bird also took great delight in harassing Hob. Although Kane had his own ways of getting even with the falcon, Gideon knew his friend had been genuinely worried about the bird.

"By the time the lady arrived, his colors were already almost back to full strength on the shield, but she insisted on checking him over herself. It turns out she has the same talent for working with birds as she does with horses. She soothed away the last of his pain."

He smiled. "Certainly Scim's appetite hadn't suffered. She brought him a mess of chicken entrails that he devoured with his usual lack of table manners. The last I saw of him, he was inside, sleeping off his meal up in the rafters."

"And how long did Lady Merewen linger after she'd seen to Scim's injuries?"

Always a dogged hunter, Kane obviously wasn't going

to stop until Gideon answered him. "Long enough to watch me eat the apple pastries she brought for us."

"That doesn't explain why her scent clings to you."

The attempted distraction didn't work. "No, it doesn't."

He decided to share some of his frustrations. "She confounds me, Kane. First, she rides out here, knowing full well her uncle does not like her to wander at will. When I told her to let Murdoch and Duncan handle any abuses of her people by her uncle, she told me it was her duty to interfere because they are her responsibility. I lost my temper. That's as much as you need to know."

It came as no surprise that Kane still had more to say on the subject. "The lady has a strong gift for tying you up in knots. I wish I'd been here to see it."

Gideon has mixed feelings about that. If Kane had been there, things would not have gotten so far out of hand. Still, he preferred not to lie to himself. He could not bring himself to regret kissing her again.

Well aware that Kane was still waiting, Gideon finally turned to face him. "I have no control around her. I'm not sure what I'm going to do about that. Now, unless you want me to have the rest of the apple pastries for my morning meal, I suggest you go eat them now and then get some rest. I think we should both ride the plains this afternoon to see what we can learn."

Kane rarely touched anyone, but he put his hand on Gideon's shoulder. "The river has made us all cold. Perhaps putting the lady in your path is the gods' way of reminding us all of what it feels like to be human."

His smile wasn't a happy one. "Or at least mostly human. My darker half is never far from my mind."

There wasn't much Gideon could say to that, so he said nothing. Kane left him sitting in the sunshine and disappeared into the cottage.

* * *

When the sun was directly overhead, the two of them rode out onto the grasslands. Gideon had no particular destination in mind other than to avoid Merewen's keep. He needed to give Fagan time to adjust to the three new additions to the keep before making his own approach. Too many visitors to the remote estate in such a short time could make the man suspicious. Besides, Gideon couldn't risk any of Fagan's men seeing Kane. The warrior, marked as he was by dark magic, was too distinctive to be easily forgotten.

Kane's grandfather had been a dark mage of the worst kind, greedy and violent. He'd been dead for untold centuries, yet his name was still whispered in fear. That Kane had foresworn anything but the magic wielded by the Damned never seemed to matter. He carried the taint in his blood and the mage mark on his face, and so was shunned.

He pretended not to care, simply ignoring the insults and the whispers that often followed his footsteps. Gideon hurt for his friend, knowing Kane to be an honorable warrior, one who had fought at his side for far too long. And even if Kane's blood did carry his grandfather's gift for magic in his veins, he still hurt and bled like any other man.

They rode on in silence. The two stallions weren't happy to be so close together but soon settled down. It probably helped that none of Kestrel's mares were there, but for everyone's sake, Gideon hoped they'd make peace with one another.

Which brought another thought to his mind. "Kane, did you introduce Hob to Rogue last night?"

The rough sound of Kane's laughter rang out as he leaned forward to pat the big gray on the neck. "Yes, I did. Rogue trembled, but he stood his ground as Hob circled around him. I was worried that if Hob got too close, Rogue might kick him."

As he described the event, there was a lightness in Kane's mood that had been absent earlier in the day. "They finally ended up standing nose to nose for the longest time before turning to look at me. Rogue shook his head and snorted while Hob growled a bit. I think they were saying they'd better stand together since they both share the burden of putting up with me."

Gideon could picture that in his head. Hob's fierce loyalty to Kane also extended to those Kane cared about. Rogue was just contrary enough to like the beast.

They'd reached a low rise that afforded them a view of the grasslands in several directions. If something was out there, Gideon couldn't sense it, but then the attack on Scim had come out of nowhere.

He turned to ask Kane if he was having better luck, but the words died unspoken. His friend sat stone-still, staring off into the distance toward the east. The muscles in his neck stood out in stark relief as if he were in pain. Worse yet, the symbol on Kane's face had darkened to nearly black, a warning that evil magic was in the air.

"Kane?"

Rogue stirred restlessly, pawing the ground with his forefoot. Still no response from the warrior on his back. Gideon guided Kestrel closer to the other horse, and for once neither stallion objected. They seemed to realize that right now there was something more important than their usual bickering.

Gideon hesitated to touch his friend. But if Kane had been ensorcelled, he had to do something. Grabbing Kane's arm, he squeezed it hard enough to bruise. "Kane, what is it? What's wrong?"

The day was not hot, but a heavy sheen of sweat gleamed on Kane's face, and his eyes were unfocused and unblinking. Gideon tried again, this time punching Kane's arm—anything to break him free from whatever it was that held him in its grip.

Abruptly, the tension was gone, and Kane slumped forward in the saddle. He swallowed hard and breathed deeply several times as though struggling to fill his lungs.

"Kane, what is it?" Gideon asked, keeping his voice to a whisper, fearful of drawing the danger back to them.

Over the centuries, Gideon had seen plenty of expressions on Kane's face—from anger to bloodlust to amusement. Together they had faced enemy armies, overwhelming numbers, and even the judgment of the gods. Fear was the one thing that Gideon had never expected to see in Kane's eyes.

Sometimes there were questions that a man never wanted to learn the answer to; yet they had to be asked. "What was it?"

At first he thought his friend would refuse to answer. Finally, he spoke, his words colder than the river in midwinter.

"There are magics that even my grandfather knew better than to invoke, the kind that destroy a man's soul." His hand gripped his sword, the black stone flashing bright with the power of his blood. "Someone has been foolish enough to unleash one such evil upon this land."

Now at least they knew why Merewen's call for the warriors' help had been granted. Gideon offered his hand to Kane, once again to swear a solemn vow to do the work of the gods.

"So we are charged with rooting out the source of this evil and destroying it."

Kane took Gideon's hand; his grip had a desperate feel that had never been there before. "Captain, know this. I know not who the true enemy is, but I can tell you this much. A bargain has been struck, and the price was paid in innocent blood."

Then once again he looked into the distance. "Even now I sense it hungers for more."

Chapter 12

"Niece! Attend to me."

Merewen's footsteps faltered to a stop. She'd hoped to reach her room without attracting her uncle's notice. Knowing she was trapped, she started across the hall to where Fagan waited with his wife. Alina stood at his side, her hands clasped at her waist, her eyes focused somewhere in the distance. Clearly she was hoping that, by remaining motionless, she wouldn't draw her husband's attention.

"Yes, Uncle."

He looked at her in disapproval. "Must you always reek of the stables?"

His hand shot out toward her head. She ducked back, sure that he was about to hit her. Instead, he snatched a piece of straw from her hair. Despite his supposed disgust with her appearance, he obviously enjoyed seeing her flinch.

Fagan nodded in his wife's direction. "Alina might not be good for much, in my bed or out of it, but at least she looks the part of a lady. You would do well to learn from her example."

Alina paled at her husband's cruel remarks but remained statue-still. Merewen understood why the woman didn't defend herself. She had good reason to fear Fagan far more than Merewen did. If he had so little regard for his wife as to insult her in front of others, how badly must he treat her in the privacy of their bedroom?

It wasn't in Merewen's nature to always back down or to cower in fear. She knew in her heart that were she forced to marry such a man, she would likely provoke him to the point of murder—either his or hers. Gideon's image filled her mind, his strength incredible but his touch so gentle. With the blessings of the gods, he would end Fagan's tyranny. Would Alina rejoice or mourn her husband's death? For it was coming, even if the man himself was unaware that his actions would lead to his own destruction.

Back to the moment. Now wasn't the time to be thinking that way lest she make Fagan suspicious.

"Did you have need of me, Uncle?"

"Yes. Duke Keirthan has requested my presence at court. I will depart at first light with most of the men. Olaf will be in charge in my absence. You will answer directly to him. Not that you'll listen, but my advice is to do exactly as he says."

She couldn't help but protest. "But—"

Olaf appeared at her side. "But nothing, Merewen. Your uncle trusts me to see that things are handled properly while he is gone. It is not your place to argue."

His eyes glittered with the hope that she would, though. Fagan knew exactly what he was doing by leaving Olaf in charge. Merewen would need to tread carefully every minute to avoid giving Olaf the excuse to lash out at her. The best she could hope for was that if he did attack her, one of three Damned would be close enough to prevent him from killing her.

What if her uncle ordered Murdoch and Averel to accompany him? The thought didn't bear thinking about. If he did force them to go, at least Averel might be able to send word to Gideon with one of his dogs.

For now, she needed to get away from both Olaf and her uncle. "It has been a long day, Uncle, and I would like to retire for the night. I wish you safe travel."

He nodded his permission as he turned his attention to his captain. "Olaf, see that arrangements are complete for my journey."

"Yes, my lord." Olaf bowed slightly and walked away, brushing past Merewen, close enough to make her step aside to avoid his touch. She hated showing even that much weakness.

As usual, Fagan didn't miss the small interaction. "Merewen, do not cross him. He has my explicit permission to act as he sees fit. Do you understand what that means?"

Yes, she did. "How long will you be gone?"

"As long as the duke has need of me." Fagan held out his arm. "Wife, you will accompany me now. I have plans for you. For us."

Alina couldn't quite disguise the shiver that ran through her as she silently set her hand upon his arm. Even so, she offered Merewen a small nod.

"Sleep well, Merewen."

They both knew it was unlikely Alina would. At least she would have a few days of peace once Fagan rode out in the morning. Merewen hoped that brought her some measure of comfort.

As they walked away, she noticed Duncan watching from the corner. He jerked his head in the direction of the stairs. Was he telling her to disappear? Or that he needed to talk?

The man had been a ghost since arriving at the keep. After she introduced Duncan to her father's collection of books and manuscripts, he'd settled in to hunt for information, coming down only for meals. Had he already found what he was searching for?

At the top of the stairs, she made sure that no one was following her before she veered away from her bedroom toward the library. She'd wait there to see if Duncan had indeed been signaling that he wanted to speak to her. If so, she hoped he wouldn't be long, because she hadn't been lying to her uncle. It had been a long day, and she was tired to the bone.

Inside the library, she dropped into her father's old chair, drawing comfort from the memory of happy hours spent with him, sharing his love of knowledge with her as together they pored over some new book he'd found. She picked up a small book of poetry and started to read out a favorite verse aloud. Her voice cracked as she recalled the day her father had first read it to her. She struggled to blink back the tears that burned her eyes.

Their love of books was one more thing the two of them had shared. Gods, she missed her father so much. His passing had left a gaping hole in her heart that nothing seemed to fill.

A footstep outside the library dragged her thoughts back from the past. She held her breath and hoped it was Duncan, not Olaf, who had followed her.

"Lady Merewen?"

She sighed with relief. "I'm here, Sir Duncan."

He came straight to her, a worried look on his face. "Are you well?"

Not really, but he wasn't there to hear her complaints.

"I am merely tired. I've been meaning to tell you that Scim is fine. His injuries are nearly healed, and he's no longer in pain."

The handsome warrior smiled, clearly pleased. "And Gideon, how did you find him yesterday evening?"

She gave him a narrow-eyed look. "You last saw him only yesterday morning. Were you expecting a big change in that amount of time?"

He chuckled. "No, but I'm sure your visit was unexpected. Our captain doesn't always enjoy surprises."

For the first time since leaving Gideon, she grinned. "No, he doesn't. He does, however, like giving orders."

Duncan cocked his hip to lean against the table, his arms crossed over his chest. "That he does. In fact, I suspect he likes giving orders as much as you enjoy ignoring them."

There was no use in denying the truth. "I don't ignore all orders, just the ones I don't agree with."

Such as the ones her uncle issued. Her smile faded, the fun gone out of the conversation. Duncan saw too much.

He straightened up, once again the grim-faced warrior who'd walked out of the river at his captain's side. "You were having trouble with your uncle and his man, Olaf, down in the hall a few minutes ago."

It wasn't a question. "Uncle Fagan has been called to Duke Keirthan's court again. He'll be leaving at dawn with a company of his men. As captain of the guard, Olaf will be in charge while he is gone."

The thought set her stomach to churning. Someday, when he slipped into her bedroom at night, he would do more than watch her sleep. The one time she'd barred her door to keep him out had been the first time her uncle had raised his hand to her.

"We will endeavor to see you come to no harm, my lady."

Duncan meant it, she knew, but fear had become her constant shadow, and it was hard to let it go. Besides, if Fagan were to order Duncan to leave, he'd have no choice but to depart. Rather than think about what she could not control, she gestured toward the books strewn about the table. It would appear that Duncan had been following a thread of information.

"Have you had any luck in finding what you seek?"

"Not as yet." He picked up the volume closest to him and ran his fingertips over the cover, a sad smile on his face. "I wish I could have met your father, Lady Merewen. I'm sure he and I would have had much to talk about.

This is an impressive library for one man to have collected. It has been far too long since I had the opportunity to spend time on my studies."

He looked around the room, his expression hungry. "It would take me a lifetime to catch up on all that I have missed while we've been . . . gone from the world."

She had so many questions but suspected Duncan would not welcome them any more than his captain would have. The Warriors from the River of the Damned definitely had their secrets. As much as she wanted to know Gideon's truth, she wanted to hear it from him, not peck at his men for the few tidbits they might share.

Back to why Duncan had asked to see her. "Is there something that requires my help?"

"Yes. I've barely begun to search through the books. I was wondering if you could point me in the direction where you found the volume that allowed you to call us from the river. I'm thinking that would be where your father kept the oldest of the manuscripts."

"I have that particular one hidden in my room, but I will bring it to you. I found it on this shelf back here."

She picked up the candle and carried it over to the farthest corner. "I didn't notice anything else similar to it in content, but perhaps you'll have more success. I'm not familiar with the old languages."

"And I grew up speaking several of them." Duncan's smile no longer reached his eyes. "Thank you, my lady. I'll let you know if I find anything."

"I'll go fetch that book for you."

He shook his head. "It can wait until tomorrow. I'll be retiring soon myself. Would you like me to escort you to your room?"

She appreciated the offer, but it would be better if they weren't seen together. "I'll be fine."

For tonight, that was probably true. Olaf had been given his orders to carry out, and her uncle was otherwise occupied. With that thought, she offered up a silent prayer to the gods for her lady aunt's well-being.

Gideon studied the message that had arrived during the night. He'd been asleep when Scim had raised the alarm. Kiva, the great owl that was bonded with Duncan, had swooped in on silent wings to land on the fence outside. The huge bird, rivaling Scim for size, sat quietly while waiting for Gideon to pick up the leather pouch he'd dropped on the ground.

"Thanks, boy," Gideon murmured as he pulled out the piece of paper inside.

Kane joined him outside, carrying a candle and cupping the flame with his hand to keep it burning. "What's wrong?"

Gideon quickly scanned the brief note and then handed it off to Kane. After he finished, they stared at each other for several seconds. The decision wasn't a difficult one.

"With Fagan gone, the keep will be at its most vulnerable. Unless Duncan and Averel are ordered to accompany him, we'll be able to take control with a minimum of bloodshed."

Kane, always the first to point out complications, looked toward the grasslands. "We already know that Lord Fagan is not the true reason we returned to walk the land this time. Will this divide our efforts?"

Gideon wanted to deny it. "I think the two problems are opposite sides of the same coin. I cannot imagine the gods would have answered Merewen's call if her welfare wasn't necessary to our purpose."

He waited to see if his friend would argue the point. When he didn't, Gideon considered the possibilities.

"If we take possession of her keep, we will be in a position of strength rather than skulking about in the mountains or living here in this crofter's cottage where we would be vulnerable to attack. At the same time, we will weaken her uncle's hold on her people."

Kane weighed his words before nodding. "We'll need to send a reply to Duncan to forewarn Averel and Murdoch that we'll be coming."

Gideon returned to the cabin. He had no ink or pen, but the end of a burned stick would work well enough. When he'd scratched out the message, he returned to where the owl waited. He tucked the note inside the leather pouch and then offered the bird a chunk of meat for his efforts.

The owl blinked his amber eyes and delicately took the treat from Gideon's hand with his beak. When it was gone, he took the proffered pouch and took off with a powerful downstroke of his wings.

As Kiva disappeared into the night sky, Gideon held his breath. The bird had made it to the cottage well enough, but there was always the possibility he would be attacked on the return flight. There was nothing they could do to prevent it—another reminder that they could ill afford to waste a moment of their limited time.

"Let's get some sleep. It will be dawn soon enough, and tomorrow we ride."

The sound of angry voices woke Merewen out of a deep sleep. Grasping the dagger under her pillow, she remained still. She'd started keeping the weapon within reach soon after her uncle had returned to take charge of the family lands. Once she'd noted the type of men he surrounded himself with, she no longer felt she could trust him.

Now, the worst of those men was right outside her door—Olaf. He was the one talking now. She strained to hear what was being said. It came as no surprise that her name was part of the conversation, especially when it was her uncle who spoke next.

"Yes, I understand, but return to the hall. You have no business here tonight."

For once Olaf was speaking to Fagan as an equal. "I remind you that you promised your niece to me in return for my services. I grow tired of waiting."

Her uncle's voice carried all too clearly. "I know I did, but that was before I suspected the duke might have plans for her."

Olaf wasn't ready to back down. "There are many ways I can enjoy her without completely destroying her value."

She was shocked to hear as much fear as anger in Fagan's response. "And if you lose control? What then? Do you want to face Duke Keirthan and tell him what you have cost him? Cost us? I, for one, am not willing to thwart him, not when he grows stronger with each passing day. We both know what happens to those who cross him."

Her blankets did nothing to ward off the chill his words sent coursing through her. If only she were dreaming, but this nightmare was only too real. She prayed the two villains would simply walk away.

Finally, their voices faded into the distance, still arguing, but at least they were gone. She remained frozen in place, fighting against the panic beating in her chest. She wanted to believe that Fagan had convinced Olaf to leave her alone for this night.

But what of tomorrow night and the one after? With Fagan gone, no one would be holding Olaf's reins. Would she even be safe during the daylight hours? Murdoch and Averel would do their best to protect her, but only if they weren't ordered to accompany her uncle.

That left Duncan. She didn't doubt his prowess with a sword, but one man couldn't stand alone against Olaf and his men. She sat up in bed, the knife still clutched in her hand. What should she do? Run? Hide?

"Lady Merewen?"

Gods, please, save her!

She leapt to her feet, knife in hand, and waited. Olaf might be too strong for her to stop, but he would bleed.

The whisper came again. "Lady, are you unharmed? Will you open the door?"

She didn't immediately recognize the voice, but it was clearly not Olaf. He would never ask permission. Duncan—it had to be Duncan.

"I'm coming," she promised as she hurried across the floor.

Pausing to light a single candle, she opened the door just far enough to ensure that it was indeed Sir Duncan. As soon as she recognized the tall blond warrior, she stepped back and motioned him inside.

His discomfiture at being alone with her in her bedroom was clear, which spoke well of his honorable nature. Even though she was covered from chin to toes, she was far from comfortable having a man in her private quarters.

With his gaze firmly directed over her head at the wall beyond, Duncan started talking. "I heard voices as I was leaving the library."

He risked a glimpse in her direction. "I didn't want to get close enough to be seen, but it was your uncle and his man."

She nodded. Where was he going with this?

"Rest assured that had either of them made a move toward your door, I would have stopped them." Duncan's pale eyes flashed hard and chilling in the darkness. "On that, you have my word."

"Thank you."

He turned his attention back to the wall. "I also wanted to let you know that I heard from Captain Gideon a few minutes ago. He sent word with my owl that he and Kane plan to join us here tomorrow night after sunset. The five of us should be able to wrest control of the keep while your uncle is gone."

Her heart resumed its pounding, and her knees refused to support her. When she started to sink to the floor, Duncan muttered something under his breath and lunged forward to catch her. He supported her long enough for her to sit down on the trunk at the foot of her bed. He immediately stepped back, his hands at his side.

"I apologize, Sir Duncan. I'm not usually given to such weakness."

"Given the circumstances, my lady, it is most understandable."

She managed to bring herself back under control, but he was right. Within the hour, she'd been threatened with rape and then offered salvation. She could scarce believe that at long last she knew hope, but the terror still lingered. Yes, she'd planned for this, prayed for it long and hard. But now that the moment was upon her, she feared for what she'd unleashed.

Duncan remained close by, his attitude expectant, as if waiting for her to do something—probably even something sensible and coherent.

"What would you have me do to prepare? If there is to be trouble, I want to help protect my people."

Duncan was already shaking his head. "Murdoch and Averel will find a way to let Gideon and Kane through the gate."

There had to be a way to do that without drawing swords. It wouldn't be unusual for her to be called out during the night.

She sat up taller. "I can help with that. Our dairyman lives along the road to the west and is a trusted friend. He's been known to come to the gate when one of his animals is sick or hurt. No one would be suspicious of him. If your captain and Kane wait nearby, they can enter the keep when the gate opens to let me out."

Duncan paced the length of her room and back. "Gideon will not much appreciate my putting you in harm's way, my lady."

"These are my people, Sir Duncan. I will aid you in every way I can."

He offered her another of his quick grins. "I can see why you have Gideon so stirred up."

He gave her a quick bow. "I will send word to the captain of your plans. He will not be pleased, but perhaps it is good for him to not always get his way."

She didn't know how to react to that. Her mind was too busy whirling in circles over what lay ahead over the next day and night.

"Be careful, Sir Duncan. My uncle and Olaf make for very bad enemies." She paused and said, "Please tell me that we are doing the right thing."

Duncan had been about to slip back out of her room. He froze for a heartbeat, staring at her with those feral eyes. "Never forget that the gods granted your plea that we aid your cause. They send the Damned to walk the land only in the direst of times."

At that moment, the warrior side of Duncan's personality outshone his scholarly nature. "Right now someone has unleashed a great evil upon your land. Innocent people have died to feed its hunger. More will die if we don't stop it while we can—if we still can."

Then he disappeared, pulling her door closed. She crawled back under the covers, still clutching her knife and wishing she could somehow make it all go away. Praying she'd made the right decision by calling on the gods to send Gideon and his men to free her people, she closed her eyes and shut out the frightening place her world had become.

Chapter 13

$\mathcal{M}$erewen had not planned on seeing her uncle off, but she'd been unable to sleep more than a handful of minutes at a time after Duncan had left her room. Nightmares combined with fear for what the next day would bring had kept her tossing and turning.

The hall was chaotic as the men gathered their gear for travel while the servants moved among them with trays of drink, bread, and sliced meat. Merewen stopped halfway down the stairs, trying to locate Murdoch and Averel in the crowd. She spotted the younger warrior's two dogs first. They were stretched out in the rushes in the far corner, clearly in no hurry to start their day.

Murdoch strode into sight. He paused only long enough to grab a fistful of bread and meat from a passing server before heading for the door. Rather than follow him directly, Merewen wandered through the hall, helping as she could before slipping into the kitchen. She cut directly through to the door that opened out into the bailey.

As soon as she did, she spotted Averel patrolling up on the walkway that encircled the inside of the palisade. Good. If he'd been assigned guard duty, it was unlikely that he would be among those riding with Fagan.

As she watched, Murdoch entered the stable. She skirted her workshop around to the far end of the stable and found him inside helping Jarod's stable hands saddle the horses.

No one would think anything of her being there, especially if she pitched in to help. When she stopped to adjust the cinch on one of the geldings, Murdoch wandered closer.

She offered him a smile. "Sir Murdoch, I don't see your horse among those being saddled for travel."

"I turned her out to pasture this morning." He led another horse out of a stall. "Your uncle wants to leave soon. I thought I'd be of the most use in here. Once he and his men ride out, I'll join Averel on guard duty."

It was hard to disguise her relief at learning for certain that Gideon's two warriors would remain at the keep.

"Why are you out here?"

At Fagan's question, Merewen patted the gelding and handed off the reins to one of the boys. "I came down to help ready the horses. However, I see they have things well in hand, so I'll return to the hall."

Fagan caught her arm before she could escape. "Make sure our provisions are ready."

She forced herself to stand still and not fight against his hold. "Yes, sir. Does Ellie know how much to prepare?"

Her uncle finally released his hold on her. "She should. I told her myself. We need enough for three days."

All of which meant he would be gone a minimum of six days. In the past, his stays in the capital usually ran three to four days. She couldn't count on that being true this time, but the longer he stayed gone, the more time Gideon and his men would have to establish themselves as the new power in control of her lands.

She realized that Fagan was staring at her with growing impatience. "Sorry. I will go speak with the cook now."

Inside the kitchen, Ellie was in full command of her helpers, reminding Merewen of a military leader planning a campaign. She moved up next to the woman, waiting for a break in the line of people needing direction.

When the woman finally acknowledged her, Merewen gave her an apologetic smile. "Uncle Fagan asked that I ensure that his provisions were ready and adequate for three days of travel."

Her friend shook her head in disgust. "You notice he did not have the courage ask that question himself."

Merewen laughed. "True, he didn't."

Then she dropped her voice. "With fewer men to guard the keep, it would be wise of you to have your helpers sleep in here and to bar the doors tonight."

The cook's eyes widened, but she asked no questions. "Thank you for the wise advice, my lady. I will see to my people."

Merewen gave the woman a quick hug. "As will I."

As soon as she stepped back, Ellie gave her a considering look. "I do not like the way Olaf's eyes follow you. Take care not to be caught alone by him now that your uncle will not be here to interfere."

"I will."

The memory of last night was still fresh and filled her with terror. She drew comfort from the knowledge that Fagan's rule of fear and abuse was about to end, and Olaf's along with it. In but a few hours, Gideon would arrive.

Since her father's passing, the only time she'd felt truly safe was in Gideon's embrace. For the briefest second, it was as if she could still feel his lips against hers, his arms holding her tight.

Feeling better than she had in hours, she smiled at Ellie. "If you don't need me, I'll go see how things are progressing outside."

Kane had been going over his weapons for the past hour. His daggers had come first, followed by his throwing knives. At the moment, he was honing the edges on both of his swords. Gideon had already finished his own preparations and now regretted having begun so early. He never enjoyed empty time, especially before a battle.

The final hours before a fight were always difficult, and each of his men handled them differently.

Kane polished steel. Duncan read a book or studied a map. Murdoch groomed the horses, and Averel played games with those misfit dogs. But right now, with only Gideon and Kane in the cottage, the silence was burdensome.

Kane held his sword up to the light to study the curved blade. Evidently it wasn't quite up to his standards, because he went back to working the edge.

He looked across at Gideon. "Why don't you go for a ride?"

Gideon had already considered the idea and rejected it. "Kestrel will need all his strength for tonight."

"Go for a walk." Kane grinned. "Of course, you'll need all your strength for what we face this night and for after."

Somehow Gideon didn't think Kane was referring to maintaining control over Merewen's people. "After?"

"Your lady will be satisfied once we return control of her lands to her. Do you think she will like knowing that is only the start of our battle?"

Gideon didn't like the idea much better. "Don't you ever grow weary of fighting one battle after another?"

The sunshine outside drew him toward the doorway. "How many times have we routed the evil from this land only to have it return, perhaps in a different form, but otherwise the same?"

Kane's teasing mood disappeared. "Such is all I have ever known, Gideon, even before we two first crossed paths."

He held up his swords. "The only value people have ever seen in me is my talent with these."

They'd had this same discussion before, and Gideon always ended up on the losing end of it. There was no convincing Kane he was worth far more than simply his ability to outfight and outkill his opponents. If nothing else, he was Gideon's friend. That counted for a lot. The gods knew he'd had few enough of those over the centuries.

"Lady Merewen sees beyond your blades, Kane. She would not trust you with one of her horses otherwise. Thanks to her uncle, she has had little cause for happiness in her life, but seeing you and Rogue together definitely brought her joy."

Having had his say, he walked outside. Kestrel and Rogue stood nose to tail, dozing in the afternoon heat. A few seconds later, Kane joined him at the fence to watch the horses.

They stood without speaking for some time. Finally, Kane broke the silence. "I fear this battle will prove the toughest we've ever fought. This calling unsettles me."

"How so?" Gideon asked, although he was not confident he wanted to hear the answer.

"I'm not sure. Normally we've been called by a priest or maybe a clan chieftain. Lady Merewen is the first woman to call the Damned from the river."

Gideon pointed out the obvious. "If she weren't female, she would be the head of her family."

"True enough. Mostly it is because the battle we're to fight is unclear. Despite our best efforts, we have yet to track the source of the attack on Scim or the poor bastards who used to live in this cottage."

Kane stopped talking to stare out toward the grasslands. Gideon followed his line of sight and finally spotted what had caught Kane's attention. Something was headed in their direction. Too small to be a horse and rider, it was most certainly one of Averel's dogs. He tried to be happy about that, telling himself to be relieved that Lady Merewen had heeded his warning to stay away.

Oddly it felt more like disappointment.

He walked out to meet the messenger. As it turned out, it was both dogs. They trotted up to him with their tongues hanging out and plopped down in the dirt, panting from the day's heat.

Gideon patted the white one on the head and unfastened the pouch from around his neck. Kane came with a pan of water. The dogs lumbered back to their feet and slurped it up with lots of noise and splashing. Averel had named them Alabaster and Ebony because of their coloring. Everyone else had a variety of less complimentary names for them.

Kane watched in disgust as they finished drinking and decided to roll in the dirt, sending up a cloud of dust. "Did these misfits bring good news?"

As soon as he read Duncan's message, Gideon started cursing. It didn't help that Kane started laughing.

"Would I be correct to guess it is something Lady Merewen did that has soured your already bad mood?"

There was no use in denying it. "Rather than let Murdoch or Averel open the gate for us tonight, Merewen is most likely going to be right in the middle of things."

Kane's smile faded. "Has that woman no sense at all?"

"Not that I have seen. She's going to have one of her farmers come knocking on the gate when we're ready to enter. He'll tell the guards that he has need of Lady Merewen for an injured animal. They'll send for her and open the gate to let her out."

Gideon headed back inside the cottage to send a reply, asking—no, ordering—his men to come up with a better idea. If all else failed, Murdoch should lock Merewen in her room or, better yet, tie her up and stuff her in a trunk.

How did she expect the five of them to fight Fagan's men and defend her at the same time? With the enhanced strength and abilities of the Damned, common men-at-arms would be no problem for them, but what if they managed to take Merewen hostage?

He understood and even admired her determination to protect her people, but he couldn't let her risk herself. He couldn't bear to see her hurt, not to mention that the gods' retribution against Gideon and his men for failing to protect her would be swift and terrible.

He scratched out a return message to Murdoch. He could only hope Merewen would listen to reason.

The dogs followed their noses into the cottage, no doubt hoping for some of the meat Kane had roasted earlier. He cut off two sizable chunks and tossed them to the dogs.

After they'd finished their treat, he attached the message to the white dog's neck and sent them coursing back to their master. As they disappeared into the long grass, he could only wish that he had run with them. Even with Merewen's uncle gone, she was far from safe.

Come nightfall, though, all of that would change. For the first time in only the gods knew how long, the Damned would fight, but not alone. There were men loyal to both Merewen and her late father who would join their cause.

The avatars were formidable warriors in their own right, joining the battle with fang and tooth and claw. More than one enemy had lost his life while trying to fend off Scim's attacks.

Speaking of Scim . . .

Gideon grinned. Perhaps there was one other way to enter the keep without risking Merewen. He yelled for Kane, who had gone back to honing his weapons.

*   *   *

Merewen spent most of the day visiting the closest farms, dispensing herbs and ointments for any of the livestock that needed it. She'd been tempted to warn her tenants to stay close to home and avoid the keep for the next few days, but she held her tongue. While she trusted most of them, she couldn't trust them all.

If even one person passed along the warning to Olaf or one of his cronies, things could go badly for Gideon and his men. When she finally returned to the keep, Murdoch himself opened the gate to let her inside. His expression was far from welcoming.

She quickly dismounted. "What's wrong?"

"Only that you left without telling any of us where you were going or why."

"I've been tending to the horses and other livestock on my own for years, Sir Murdoch. Today was no different."

But it was. They both knew it.

He led her horse toward the stable. "Olaf has been looking for you for the past hour. It is not wise to provoke him unnecessarily."

"I'll go see what he wants."

"Let's tend to your mare first. Then I'll make sure Averel is inside the hall before you enter. He's been waiting for his dogs to return from Gideon, but they should be back by now. If he's not there, I'll stay, even though I'm supposed to be manning the gate. You shouldn't face Olaf alone, especially not after what Duncan overheard last night."

Merewen's skin burned cold at the memory. She couldn't hide her relief. Her uncle's orders were to leave her untouched. That didn't mean Olaf couldn't punish her if he thought she'd defied him for some reason. He'd even make up an excuse if she didn't provide him with one.

It didn't take the two of them long to strip off her

mare's tack and dry her off with a couple of rags. While Merewen finished up, Murdoch went to check on Averel. He was back all too quickly, giving her no more excuse to linger in the stables.

"Averel has yet to return, and Olaf wasn't anywhere to be seen. Perhaps you should retire to your quarters for the time being."

"If you think that's best."

As they crossed the bailey, Murdoch paused to look up toward one of the windows on the second floor. "It would be best if you stayed out of sight, but I would ask a favor first."

"Anything," she responded, although she was puzzled as to what it could be.

"I would ask that you check on your aunt. I know she rarely leaves her bower except for meals or at your uncle's orders, but I have not seen her at all today."

A sick feeling settled in Merewen's stomach. "I didn't see her this morning before Uncle Fagan left, but that's not unusual. Sometimes she's not able. She doesn't always feel well."

Merewen paused, not sure how much of her aunt's situation she should share.

Murdoch's expression hardened. "I've seen the bruises, my lady. Only a fiend would treat any female in such a brutal manner, especially one as delicate as Lady Alina."

He shifted from foot to foot as if uncomfortable with the direction their conversation had taken. Did he have any idea how much he'd just revealed? Was there something between the rather dour warrior and her aunt? She wouldn't press for answers, not when she had her own secrets to protect.

"Let me know if she needs anything." He looked as if he wanted to say more, but he started toward the door.

She hurried her steps to keep up with his longer strides. "I will."

Inside, the hall was empty except for a few servants setting the tables for the evening meal. It seemed so strange to see all look normal, routine.

Any other time she would have washed up and helped with the preparations. Not today, though. She couldn't risk anyone noticing how tense she was or the way her eyes kept straying to the three men who would be fighting for their lives, and for those of her people, in only a few hours.

How would she ever repay them?

Worse yet, how would she bear it when the gods called her warriors back to the river, knowing she'd never see any of them again? How had they become so dear to her in just a few days? Even Kane was no longer as frightening as he had been that first night.

And she wouldn't let herself give name to what she was feeling for Gideon even if she hungered for his touch, his rare smile, and the safe harbor of his arms. There was no point in it, and she had others who had first claim on her.

She made it upstairs without incident. Murdoch's concern for Alina had Merewen heading for her aunt's room. If all was well, then perhaps she'd lie down for a while to make up for the sleep she had lost during the night.

It was no surprise that her aunt's door was closed. Merewen knocked softly. "Alina?"

No response. She knocked harder this time. Although she respected Alina's privacy, Merewen needed to know she was all right. Finally, she heard the shuffle of footsteps toward the door.

It opened just a crack, but it was enough to see that her aunt was far from well. "Let me in, Alina."

"I'm tired, Merewen."

The two women weren't particularly close, but Merewen wasn't about to walk away until she knew Alina's condition. Tired could mean so many things.

"Please let me see you. Once I know you are truly only weary, I promise I'll leave."

Although he might not appreciate Merewen's using his name, she added, "Sir Murdoch was concerned. I thought you'd prefer that I was the one who came to check on you."

She thought she might have to actually force her way into the room. Finally Alina sighed and opened the door far enough to allow Merewen to slip through.

Once inside, she almost wished she'd taken Alina at her word and walked away. But that was a coward's reaction, and it wasn't in Merewen to let anyone suffer, especially alone.

"Let me send for a bath for you."

Alina turned aside. "That's not necessary."

Merewen wanted to draw the battered woman into her arms, but she was afraid it would only cause Alina more pain. She clenched her fists at her side, wishing her uncle were home right now. If Murdoch were to see what Fagan had done to his wife, her uncle would not live long enough to ever raise his fist against anyone again.

But right now Alina needed her help, not her temper. "A warm bath with some of my special herbs will soothe both your injuries and your spirit. Please let me do that much for you."

Alina's suffering had etched its mark on her pretty face. "If you insist."

"I'll summon servants to bring the bath while I return to my workshop to fetch the herbs. I shan't be gone long."

Before she stepped through the door, she turned back

to face Alina. Maybe she could offer the woman a small bit of hope. "This will not happen to you again. This I swear."

For the first time, Alina showed a spark of emotion, even if it was fear. "Merewen! What have you done?"

"Now is not the time, but take comfort in the knowledge that Fagan will never—never—lay a hand on either of us again."

Rather than risk sharing another word, Merewen left in search of the servant woman who saw to Alina's needs.

"Magda, your mistress has need of you. Have a bath sent up for her and take her something light to eat. I'll return shortly with some of my special herbs for her bath. They'll help to soothe her—her spirit."

Magda's eyes were clouded with age, but still she saw enough. "I'll go see to my lady. And thank you, mistress, for helping her. She's known little enough of kindness in her life for some time now."

Merewen could only nod. Her aunt's suffering had been well-known to everyone within the household, but all had been powerless to stop it.

She hurried down the steps, hoping to make it to her workshop and back to her aunt's room unseen. She made it only halfway through the hall before luck deserted her.

"Where in the gods' names have you been?"

Olaf's roar brought all activity to an immediate halt.

Merewen ignored the stares. "I was out on my rounds, seeing to the livestock and checking on the herds."

Having answered his question, she started past him. She should have known better. He planted himself back in her path, his fists on his hips as he glared down at her.

"Was there something else you needed? I have duties to see to now."

The flicker of unholy heat in his gaze pointed out her

poor choice of words. "Yes, there is something I need of you, but it will have to wait. Soon, though, soon."

But only because her uncle had told him so. She never thought she'd be grateful to Fagan for anything. Of course, he'd only forbidden Olaf to bed her before his return. That didn't mean he couldn't beat her if he so desired.

And he desired. It was there in the gleam of his beady eyes and the way he just licked his lips.

"I apologize for not telling you where I was, and I won't neglect informing you of my plans again."

She tried to look cowed by his displeasure. "If you don't have need of me right now, I promised Lady Alina I would bring her some of that special soap she likes so much."

For a minute, she thought he was going to let her pass unharmed. Instead, as she sought to walk around him, he tangled his fingers in her hair and yanked her up to her toes. He dragged her so close that her head was filled with the stench of unwashed male and garlic.

"You think you are too good for the likes of me, wench, but that's going to change and soon. Considering what your uncle and the duke have planned for you, the day will come when you'll be damned glad to spread your legs for me."

He shoved her, sending her stumbling back into a nearby wall. "I don't care what your aunt wants or needs any more than your uncle does. Fetch my dinner, and maybe I'll reconsider your punishment for leaving the keep without my permission."

She didn't bother to reply. Nothing would change his mind, not if he was determined to humiliate and hurt her again. If the warriors weren't there to stop him, she'd survive. She had before.

Knowing that, she straightened her shoulders and walked away. Olaf's meal would wait until she fetched the herbs from her workshop. One of the servants could take them to Alina.

And rather than dwell on what Olaf had planned for her that evening, she focused on the knowledge that this was the last night he would terrorize her or her people.

Chapter 14

Gideon reined in Kestrel and waited for Kane to catch up. The sun hovered right over the horizon, bathing the world in shades of red and gold. It was beautiful to look at but far too revealing. If they traveled much farther, they risked being seen by the sentries at the keep.

Kestrel didn't protest when Scim swooped down to land on Gideon's arm. After giving the horse a few seconds to accept the bird's presence, Gideon lowered his arm to let the gyrfalcon step off onto the specially designed perch on the front of Gideon's saddle.

Kane had yet to call forth his own companion. Hob didn't do well in sunlight, even at the dimming of the day. They also couldn't risk running into anyone with Hob running loose. While Gideon could easily pass as a nobleman with a penchant for falconry, Kane couldn't. His eyes flared red in times of high emotion, especially right before a battle. Coupled with Hob, the pair would send most humans screaming. As amusing as that might be, it certainly wouldn't help their chances of approaching the keep unnoticed.

Kane stood up in his stirrups to look ahead. "We must be close."

Gideon agreed. "We are. The gate is only a short distance beyond that bend you can see just ahead."

Both men dismounted to rest the horses. Gideon took a long drink of water and then offered the skin to Kane, who shook his head.

Gideon stuck it back in his pack. "It shouldn't be long now. Once the sun touches the horizon, I'll position myself on the far side of the palisade."

Kane's laugh was unexpected. "I can't believe you're really going to attempt to breach the walls that way."

To be truthful, neither could Gideon, but if he succeeded, they'd have four of the warriors within the keep and only Kane left to come through the gate itself. It would be helpful to know how many men Fagan had left behind to guard the keep. They hoped a few would side with Gideon and his men out of loyalty to Merewen's father, but how many? It would be better not to count on any assistance at all.

"If I can slip into the keep early, I can prevent Lady Merewen from getting right into the middle of the fighting." Gods above, he hoped so.

Kane's mouth quirked up in a brief smile. "I've never known you to worry so much about one woman before. But then the others we've championed were content to stand back and let us do all of the fighting."

And the bleeding. That much was true. Most of their applicants had been too beaten down by their oppressors to have the strength to fight back on their own. Merewen was defiantly different to the point of being reckless.

"Our calling has always been to protect those the gods found worthy of saving. I will not allow her to get hurt. She has suffered enough abuse at the hands of one who should have protected her." He looked to the darkening sky. "I sense she is in danger far worse than just Fagan's neglect and abuse."

All trace of humor disappeared in Kane's expression. "You think she might be a target for the dark magic that has been invoked in this land?"

"I think her uncle is hungry enough for power and gold that he would sacrifice her to get it. I suspect he has struck a foul bargain with the duke."

Fear for Merewen made him restless. As he paced, Scim picked up on his tension and drummed his wings. The noise made Kestrel restive as well. Gideon fought down his emotions, struggling to find the cold, unemotional warrior he'd always been.

It was hard. This intense connection to Merewen had him taking risks he wouldn't normally consider. He'd always done as the gods commanded by relentlessly defending those who'd called the Damned from the river. For the first time, he was willing to risk everything, to lay down his life if it meant Merewen could live in peace.

Did this power she had over him strengthen his determination to prevail, or did he risk disaster by letting thoughts of her cloud his thinking? How was he to know?

"Tell me more about what you sense in this magic."

Now Kane's gaze was drawn to the north and east. "Such discussions are better left for the bright light of day. Suffice it to say that once unleashed, it will demand sacrifice of life and blood until it reaches full strength."

"And when that happens?"

His friend turned a bleak smile in his direction. "Then nothing and no one will be safe. The gods themselves will be hard put to contain the damage it will do."

Gideon moved to stand shoulder to shoulder with his friend, a position comforting in its familiarity. "Is this something that can be fought with sword and shield?"

"Perhaps." Kane shrugged. "It's been too long since I last studied the magic my family practiced. The dangers in invoking such power remain clear in my mind, but the details are but dim memories. Our best hope in finding a way to stop it lies with Duncan's search."

Gideon would far rather rely on something solid, like his sword. "Would an ordinary man's library include such lore?"

Kane drew circles in the dust with a stick. "Perhaps

not, but then Lady Merewen's father did own the old text that had the terms of our calling in it. It would seem from what she told Duncan that her father assembled a substantial collection."

He snapped the stick in half and tossed it away. "My grandfather's library would certainly have had the information we needed. I have no idea what became of his spell books after he was killed. Much knowledge was likely destroyed by those who executed him and razed his home to the ground."

The loss of Kane's family was something he rarely talked about. He'd never been one to show the true depths of his feelings, but Gideon knew his friend still mourned the passing of his mother. His grandfather was another matter entirely.

As Gideon stood staring up at the fading sun, an unexpected wave of terror washed over him, strong enough to buckle his knees and to leave him flailing for balance. Kane managed to catch him before he hit the ground.

Kane's second effort jerked Gideon back upright. "What in the name of the gods is wrong with you?"

Gideon drew a ragged breath, searching for control. It was slow in coming. "I'm not sure."

Then he was. As certain as the moon would rise, Merewen was in trouble. This crippling fear he was feeling wasn't his, but hers. Someone was threatening her, hurting her.

He fought for his balance, Then he jerked free from Kane's grasp and took off at a dead run for Kestrel. "It's Lady Merewen. She's in danger."

"How do you know?" Kane asked as he vaulted onto his own mount.

"From the beginning, the gods have forged a connection between us that I cannot explain. Right now, Lady Merewen is beyond scared. She's terrified." He urged Kestrel forward. "We need to ride hard. Now."

Kane moved up beside him, shouting over the sound of pounding hooves and pulses. "I will wait nearby for Murdoch to open the gate."

"I don't see any alternative."

The sun was about to slip out of sight. At least he'd have the cover of darkness. And when he found the bastard who was terrorizing Merewen, blood would run.

Averel strolled slowly along the walkway, his eyes constantly on the grasslands outside the keep. Like Murdoch's, the young warrior's ability to see in the dimmest of light was superior to that of the merely human guards. Only Kane had better vision at night, but that was due to his family's ties to the darkest of magic.

Murdoch reversed directions when he reached the far corner and started back toward the center. He hoped Merewen had taken his advice to stay cloistered in her rooms after checking on Alina.

Unfortunately, that would be out of character for her. His replacement was due to arrive soon. Once he was off duty, he'd check on Merewen and perhaps her aunt. His hand strayed to the dagger in his belt at the thought of Lady Alina.

His instincts were telling him that she'd remained sequestered in her rooms for more sinister reasons. Telling himself that Merewen would have gotten word to him if Alina had been seriously injured, he made the turn again and counted off the steps to the corner.

Back and forth he went, going nowhere, just as he had done for so much of his life, for so long. He never regretted standing at Gideon's side on that day centuries ago when their lives had been turned upside down and inside out. Without Gideon's intervention, Murdoch would have likely died at the hands of Warwick, his liege lord.

He owed Gideon both his life and his sanity. He would stand with the captain as long as the gods decreed the five of them would live in this endless cycle of cold sleep alternating with the brief tastes of life—if three months of walking, talking, breathing air, all accompanied by endless fighting, could be called living.

Each time they answered the call, they all secretly prayed it would be the last time. Surely the gods would eventually grant them peace.

But for now, their purpose was clear, and he needed to remain focused. Averel was coming toward him. He stopped and waited for him to ensure the other guards would not overhear their conversation.

His friend looked puzzled. "Your relief has been here for several minutes. I thought you were in a hurry to make sure all is quiet inside the hall before Gideon and Kane arrive."

For the first time, Murdoch realized how dark it had gotten. "I have been lost in thought. Sorry."

Before Averel could reply, the cry of a raptor stopped them both in their tracks.

"Gideon."

As tempting as it was to rush to the gate and throw it open, they had to stick to the plan. Murdoch kept his movements slow and casual as he peered over the wall toward the narrow road that led to the front gate.

If his friends were out there, he couldn't see them, but then he didn't expect to. Gideon wouldn't reveal his presence until the last possible second, and Kane's very nature was at one with the night itself.

"Go let Duncan know the battle is upon us."

Averel's eyes glittered in the darkness as he squeezed past Murdoch on the narrow walkway, his battle fever already running high. "To our success, Murdoch. Let's pray that the gods guide our swords and our footsteps this night. May the dawn bring a new day for Lady Merewen and her people."

Murdoch could only nod. He'd long ago given up on

the gods making anything easier on Gideon and the others. They weren't called the Damned for no reason.

"Watch your back, pup."

He waited a scattering of minutes before following the young knight. By the time Murdoch started down the circular staircase to the bailey, it was difficult to keep his pace slow and steady. He checked the slide of his sword in its sheath and then his throwing knives.

The rush of blood in his veins left his skin flushed and hot. Unlike Kane, Murdoch had no love of violence, but he did have a talent for it. Right now, with him poised on the edge of a battle, his senses sharpened his awareness of his surroundings—the sounds, the smells, the shadows, and the patches of light.

When he walked into the great hall, he knew where each man sat or stood, who looked tired or drunk, and which men would be most likely to respond to the sound of an alarm with swords drawn and ready to defend the keep. Fagan had taken a fair portion of his men with him, but there were enough left to offer the Damned a good fight for possession of the keep. Murdoch did one last survey of the area.

No sign of Lady Alina or Merewen. With luck they were both safely tucked away in their rooms. He noticed the servants were also absent. It was early for all of them to have disappeared for the night.

But it was certainly all the better for everyone.

The real question was, where had Olaf gone?

Murdoch wheeled around and headed right back out into the night. Fagan's captain liked to prowl around on the walkway at odd times. The last thing they needed was for him to interfere with the plans their captain had put in motion. It would be just like Olaf to send the farmer away and refuse to send word to Merewen that she was needed.

Murdoch charged back up the steps ready to face the enemy.

*   *   *

Merewen hoped she'd made it back from her workshop without Olaf's noticing that she'd delayed in bringing him his meal. She'd handed off the soap and soothing herbs to a servant and sent her to find Magda. Meanwhile, Ellie had piled Olaf's tray high with food and a flagon of his favorite wine. With luck, he'd eat and drink himself into a stupor. Merewen briefly considered adding some special spices to his drink that would help with that, but using her gift to do harm was forbidden. She didn't know who had set down the rules, but at her father's urging she'd sworn to follow them.

Olaf's eyes tracked her progress as she walked across the hall. The smirk on his face boded ill for her, but she kept a steady pace. The man relished the taste of fear, and she refused to feed his appetite for it.

She shouldered the heavy tray and made her way to Olaf's seat at the head table. He watched her every move, much like a mountain cat sat motionless, waiting for its prey to come within striking distance.

The man had never been much more than muscles and a strong sword arm. But the longer Olaf served her uncle, the more cruel and vicious he'd become, taking far too much pleasure in watching others suffer. Her father would never have tolerated anyone given to that kind of behavior to remain in his employ.

Fagan encouraged it.

Merewen set down Olaf's trencher and drink. He leaned back in his chair, his arms crossed over his chest. As soon as she had the food arranged, he struck out, sweeping it off the table onto the floor.

"You defied my orders again. Bring me fresh food, and then wait for me in your room. I'll be along presently to teach you a lesson about what happens to women who don't obey their masters."

Merewen wanted to heave the tray at Olaf's thick

skull, but that would only set him off. As long as he thought she was properly cowed by his threats, he'd savor the moment and stay seated long enough to eat his meal.

Backing away, she was careful to keep her eyes down so he wouldn't see the absolute fury in them. The shaking held off until she reached the kitchen. She leaned against the wall, fighting to breathe. In her head, she knew that to stay safe, all she had to do was find one of the three warriors already within the keep walls. Any of them would fight to protect her from Olaf's fists.

Her heart, though, wanted Gideon—no one else. There was safety to be found within the captain's strong arms where Olaf could never hurt her. If he was there, she would sleep through the night without worrying about who might come charging through her door.

Soon, she reminded herself. The captain would be there soon with his fierce nature and gentle touch. With that thought to hold on to, she could endure anything.

"My lady, is something wrong?"

"I'm fine." Merewen straightened up, drawing on her newly formed resolve, and held up the empty tray. "Olaf didn't think I brought his food fast enough, and he wants fresh."

Ellie snatched the tray out of Merewen's hands. "Give me that tray. I'll show that addlepated fool what fresh is."

As entertaining as it might be to see the older woman take on Olaf, now was not the time, and it would likely only make things worse for Merewen.

Merewen managed a placating smile and held her hand out for the tray. "I promise this will be the last time he makes such demands on you—or on me. Let me refill this and get another pitcher of wine for him as well. After I deliver it to his table, I will retire for the evening."

She gave Ellie a hard look. "You should do the same. Remember to lock the doors."

The other woman stared at Merewen, her eyes narrowed. "If you need help with whatever you have planned, my lady, you need only ask."

"Thank you, Ellie. Your loyalty means much to me, and I need to ensure you and your staff stay safe. Sending you out there would only further provoke Olaf's uncertain temper."

When they had the tray loaded again, Ellie asked, "Do you want me to have one of the boys carry the tray for you?"

"No, Olaf is expecting me."

It would be cowardly to send someone in her place and could endanger her substitute. Bracing herself for whatever might come next, she picked up the heavily laden tray and headed back to where her tormentor waited.

This time Olaf accepted his dinner without comment. Instead, his eyes did all the talking. Despite her being fully clothed, she felt as if he'd stripped her bare right there in the great hall. More and more, she feared that he'd slipped his leash and would ignore her uncle's warnings to leave her unsullied.

It was well past the hour for her to withdraw. If she hurried, she could check on Alina again before retreating to her own room. And if the gods were listening, Gideon would arrive in time to lead his warriors in saving her people.

Chapter 15

*L*ady Alina was sitting near the fire in her room doing needlework when Merewen arrived. She looked up with a small smile when Magda opened the door to let her in.

"Merewen, I didn't expect to see you again tonight."

The warmth from the fire banished a little of the chill that had been haunting Merewen since encountering Olaf. "I wanted to see if you were feeling better."

Alina set her embroidery aside. "Thanks be to you, I am much better. The bath and the herbs you sent up were most soothing."

"I am glad they helped. Most of my patients have four legs, but people are not so different."

To her surprise, Alina laughed. "So you gave me the same soap and herbs that you use on your horses? I shall be sure to let you know if I get any strange urges to eat grass or sleep in the stable."

She returned Alina's smile. "Perhaps I should have had Ellie send up a bag of oats for your dinner."

Seeing her aunt looking decidedly happier made the risk Merewen had taken for her worth any possible cost to herself. She could not remember the last time she'd seen Alina look so content, but then she rarely saw her aunt at all when Fagan was in residence.

His absence had to be a godsend for Alina. Merewen wasn't the only one who rarely had the opportunity to sleep without fear stalking through her dreams. Well, except that tonight would not be peaceful for anyone within the keep.

Merewen would issue one more warning and then return to her rooms. Tonight, despite her uncle's orders, she would barricade her door until the guards at the gate came to say she was needed.

"Alina, when I leave, make sure to bar your door."

As soon as the words were out, her aunt was up and following her to the door. "Merewen, wait."

Alina surprised her by merely hugging her instead of asking questions. "Stay safe."

She returned the embrace, appreciating her aunt's concern. "I'll do my best."

As she slipped out the door, Merewen paused. "You might want to let Magda sleep here with you."

"I will do that. Won't you stay with us as well?"

"No, I'm sorry, but I cannot. In fact, I fear I've tarried too long as it is."

Out in the hallway, Merewen remained close to the door until she heard the bar slide into place. Relieved her aunt had taken her warning seriously, she retreated to her own room.

And she immediately regretted not having accepted Lady Alina's invitation.

Olaf had positioned himself in a doorway down the hall from her room where he couldn't be seen until she was almost within reach.

"It's about time you got here. Once again you have disobeyed me."

And that obviously pleased him. He licked his lips as he stared at her, sending a wave of revulsion flooding through Merewen's veins. The twisted expression on his face was almost inhuman, showing him for the monster he'd become.

He stepped toward her, his hands out with his fingers

curled like talons. She feinted as if to run for the stairs, praying he would lunge after her in that direction instead of blocking the entrance to her room. When he did, she immediately spun back to throw open her door. She dove inside and slammed it shut.

Her uncle had ordered the bar removed the first time she'd tried to avoid his punishment by locking herself inside. All she could do was try to brace her body against the door and hope she could keep Olaf from forcing his way inside.

It was hopeless, considering he outweighed her by nearly double. She screamed for help, hoping to draw Duncan or one of the other warriors to her aid. Even if they were to come running, Olaf would still have time to do her great harm before they arrived.

"Let me in, Merewen. You're only making this worse for yourself."

He gave the door a powerful shove, forcing it open far enough to get his foot in to block it from closing again.

"Get out, Olaf. You will regret your actions if you come in here."

At least he would if she managed to get her hands on her knife. Considering the distance between the door and the pillows on her bed, it was doubtful that she'd make it.

"We both know how this is going to end, Merewen." His voice dropped to a husky whisper. "But to be fair, I'll give you a chance to change the outcome."

"How would I do that?" she asked, more to stall for time than because she actually wanted to hear his offer.

"I usually like my women to have more meat on their bones and to wear dresses rather than those tunics and trousers you prefer. I'm sure you can make me forget about your shortcomings if you try hard enough."

Only sheer stubbornness was keeping her from collapsing in panic. He shoved the door open another few inches. Another push like that one and he'd be inside. Yet it wasn't in her to give up.

"My uncle ordered that I was to remain untouched. We both know he's not a man to be crossed."

"Don't you worry about that." He gave another shove. "There are plenty of ways I can bed you without destroying your value to the duke and your uncle."

He slacked off the door a little and started whispering all the possibilities. Merewen's stomach heaved at the pictures he painted. He'd obviously given this a lot of thought. She reset her feet and waited for the next onslaught, knowing it would be coming as soon as he tired of playing his games.

The next push cost her the small amount of ground she'd regained and then some. It wouldn't take much more effort on his part to break through her defenses. Time was running out, and all hope of a reprieve was fading away.

"Let me in, Merewen, or I'll start my evening's entertainment with your aunt. After all that she has suffered at the hands of your uncle, there's not much chance of her being of much use to the duke. That makes her fair game."

Thank the gods that Alina had barricaded herself in her room. If she had been truly at risk, Merewen would have given up the battle rather than let the woman suffer in her place.

He gave one more mighty heave, and Merewen found herself flying across the floor. The door slammed against the wall as Olaf plunged into the room. Before he could regain full control of his attack, Merewen threw herself on the bed.

She fumbled under the pillows, searching for her knife. She managed to wrap her fingers around the hilt just as Olaf dove on top of her, pushing her down into the blankets hard enough to make it all but impossible to breathe.

His big body was too heavy for her to shove off, but neither would she surrender.

His breath, hot and foul, feathered over the back of her neck and face. "I have waited far too long for this. You always act as if you're too good for me, but you're little better than a stable hand."

He rolled to the side, still keeping her pinned in place with the weight of his leg as his hand roamed free. Her hand holding the knife was trapped underneath her body, but eventually he would make a mistake.

When that happened, she would attack and, by the grace of the gods, he would bleed.

Gideon tasted Merewen's fear, and her pain pounded in his ears, growing worse by the second. Her terror formed a volatile mix with his fury, making it hard to focus long enough to reach her.

With the same technique they'd used to return Merewen to the safety of her room, Gideon slung a coil of rope over his shoulder and then stretched a leather strap between his hands as he held his arms over his head. Because of his larger size, Scim had just enough strength to lift Gideon to the top of the palisade. From there, Gideon repelled down to the ground.

He was about to toss the hook on the end of his rope up to catch the edge of the balcony of her room when she screamed a second time. Even at his fastest, he'd unlikely be able to climb up in time if she was in imminent danger.

"Scim, help her!"

The gyrfalcon shrieked in challenge and dove straight toward her open window. With luck, the bird could position himself to do serious damage to Merewen's attacker with his claws and beak, distracting the bastard long enough for Gideon to join the fray.

A deep bellow came from the room above as Gideon spun the hook in a circle several times, building up speed with each pass. Finally with a flick of his wrist, he sent it soaring up to catch on the low wall surrounding the balcony off Merewen's room.

Hand over hand, his feet braced on the wall, he climbed upward, hoping and praying to the gods to let him get to her in time. When he pulled himself up and over to land on the balcony itself, he drew both his sword and favorite dirk and charged into the room to defend his lady.

Inside was a scene out of the deepest hells of the netherworld. A brute of a man lay sprawled atop Merewen, and their legs and arms were twined in a tangled knot.

Scim's attack had done some damage, but there was little more he could do within the confined space of the canopy that arched over the bed frame. Gideon could only hope the raptor had managed to slow down the assault on Lady Merewen, at least enough to prevent her from being—

No! He couldn't think past that possibility. That this beast would even think of robbing Merewen of her innocence was beyond bearing. The bastard was already dead. Whether his passing would be swift or piece by piece would be determined by how badly he'd hurt her.

Two steps farther into the room, he tasted the scent of blood in the air, taking him from rational to berserk between one heartbeat and the next. Gideon sheathed his knife and grabbed the man by the back of the collar. He used all of his god-enhanced strength to fling the vermin off the bed, sending him bouncing across the floor to land in a broken heap next to the still-open door.

The man was slow to move, but he was already scrambling to his feet. Gideon positioned himself between Merewen and her attacker, his sword up and ready to split his foe from groin to gullet. It didn't take Fagan's man long to assess the situation. He stared past Gideon toward Merewen, his lip curled up in a sneer.

"So this is the reason you spend so much time out on the grasslands. Your uncle will not appreciate knowing you've taken a lover, not when Duke Keirthan has plans for you."

Gideon entered the conversation. "Hold your tongue."

He ignored Gideon's order, focusing instead on Merewen.

"Fagan will kill you himself for your slatternly ways. Your actions will bring ruin down upon us all. Keirthan won't stop until everything you hold dear is dead or destroyed if you've given yourself to this knave."

Gideon wouldn't allow the fool to further berate Merewen, especially when the charges were unfounded. When he started forward, ready to cut out the man's tongue if that was what it took to silence him, the man broke and ran.

He charged down the hall, sounding the alarm.

Rather than give immediate chase, Gideon asked, "Lady Merewen, are you harmed? Did he—?"

Once again Gideon couldn't pull together the words and could only repeat, "Did he?"

Her head wobbled from side to side, but he wasn't sure if she was really answering him or if she was too numb to understand what he was really asking. Her tunic was torn and covered in a spray of blood drops, but otherwise her clothing appeared to be intact.

That gave him hope that he'd arrived in time.

Then he noticed the bloody knife in her hand. He tried to recall her attacker's condition. Yes, Scim had left deep claw marks on the man's face, but there had also been a wound on the side of his shoulder that still dripped blood. For the first time, Gideon could breathe. His lady had put up a good fight of her own.

But now wasn't the time for congratulations. Her attacker almost certainly had to be Olaf, the captain of Fagan's guard. No doubt he'd earned that position by his skill with a blade. That was fine with Gideon. The two of them would definitely cross weapons over Olaf's attack on Merewen. He hoped the man survived the initial clash of swords, because he wanted the villain to see his death reflected in Gideon's eyes.

Already footsteps were approaching. Gideon prepared to face a second foe when he recognized the voice calling Merewen's name. It was Duncan.

"Lady Merewen!"

The other warrior skidded to a stop in the doorway. It didn't take him long to assess the situation or Gideon's mood.

"Captain, how is Lady Merewen?"

"She will be fine." He glanced at her again to reassure himself that was true. "How are things below?"

Duncan's expression was grim. "I was about to fetch Merewen to answer the farmer's call when Olaf charged through the hall, screaming the keep was under attack. I left Murdoch and Averel at the gate and came here to make sure the lady was safe."

Gideon wasn't about to let her out of this room. She'd barely escaped grave injury once already. He would not risk her safety again.

"The plan has changed. She stays here."

With him. Barring that, perhaps he could entrust her care to her aunt while the battle raged below. The bed creaked behind him, warning him that Merewen was on the move. He turned around just as she pushed herself up to her feet.

"Captain, I will decide for myself what I should do or

where I'd best serve my people. If I am not with you, there's almost no chance that those loyal to me will surrender. I won't have them die while I cower in safety."

Merewen drew herself up to her full height as if shrugging off the terror of her attack. "Unless we can convince the guards to open the gate, it will only be harder to get Kane into the keep."

She met each man's gaze head-on as if daring them to argue. When neither one did, she continued. "I'll change clothes first, so they won't think you've harmed me. Duncan, tell my people I will come down shortly."

Duncan knew marching orders when he heard them, but nonetheless said, "Captain?"

Gideon hated to admit it, but she was right. They needed Kane, and perhaps it would actually help her to get past the shock of having been attacked if she took an active role in retaking control of her home.

He shrugged. "Do as she says. I'll remain here to ensure her safety."

Duncan bowed his head to Merewen and disappeared back down the hallway. Gideon closed the door and then held out his arms to Merewen, hoping she would accept the offer. She didn't hesitate, collapsing against his chest and holding on with all her strength.

Gideon stroked her back, pleased that she'd accept his touch when she'd been so recently brutalized by a man. Time was running short, but he'd stand there and hold her as long as she needed him.

"Thank you for coming, Gideon, and for sending your avatar. My knife hand was trapped underneath Olaf. Until Scim attacked him, I couldn't work it free."

He brushed a lock of her hair back from her face. "You're a fighter, my lady. You would have found a way."

She leaned into his touch and sighed. "We must go before Olaf causes even more trouble."

Gideon let her see only a small portion of his fury. "I will avenge your honor, Merewen."

She chewed her lower lip but nodded. "Olaf is my uncle's equal with a sword, Gideon."

He liked that she worried about him. "The gods decreed that I am your champion, Merewen. I almost failed in that duty, but I will not do so again."

She wasn't done arguing. "Even the poorest fighter gets lucky sometimes."

"True, but even if Olaf were to best me, he has never fought the likes of Lord Kane. He will die either way, but if he faces Kane, he will pray for death long before it comes for him."

Perhaps he shouldn't have been so blunt, but it was nothing less than the truth. She eased back, putting a small bit of distance between them. Had he horrified her?

"I believe you."

Then she rose up on her toes to press a soft kiss to his lips. "But now we must go. I am ready for this hell to end."

So was he. "I'll stand guard in the doorway."

Gideon was careful to keep his back turned as Merewen changed clothes. He tried to concentrate on the noise coming from below and not the soft rustle of fabric as she traded the bloody tunic for a clean one. Right now he should be thinking of battle strategies instead of imagining the glistening of her skin as she washed her face and hands clean of Olaf's blood.

A warrior with his attention divided was asking for death. Gideon looked around for Scim and spotted him perched on a heavy beam near the ceiling. He sent the bird diving down to the hall below so he could watch what was happening through the raptor's eyes. As always, it took him a minute to adjust to the way the world looked through the bird's vision.

Right now, Olaf was ordering some of his men to patrol the walkway along the palisade. Others were to reinforce those manning the gate. Yet a few more were to follow him back up the stairs to come after Gideon.

Find Duncan and the others. He pictured each of the warriors in his mind to make sure Scim understood. It didn't take him long. All three were mixed in with the men at the gate. He would trust them to get Kane inside.

Right now, though, he was going to have to find another way to get Merewen out of her room. If Olaf led a charge up the stairs, Gideon would have a difficult time fighting his way through them, especially trying to protect Merewen at the same time.

He ducked back inside her room and shoved a heavy trunk in front of the door. At best it would only slow the attack down, but it would buy them some time.

Merewen winced as she removed her bloody tunic and tossed it in the corner. Every move hurt. Her struggle against Olaf had left her bruised and aching, but she drew comfort from knowing all the blood shed in the brief battle had been his.

That outcome might have been far different if Gideon hadn't sent Scim as a harbinger of his own arrival. Just seeing the gyrfalcon had renewed her determination to fight, giving her the strength to hold out until Gideon found her.

She had a terrible feeling that the worst was yet to come. Things had gone too far now to turn back, not that she would even consider doing so. Someone had to put an end to Fagan's tyranny.

That didn't mean she wouldn't rather hide up here in her room. But as Gideon had reminded her, he was her champion, there to win back control of her family home. She would do her part.

"I'm ready to go. They'll be waiting."

Gideon had just shoved her trunk in front of the door. That didn't bode well. He returned to her, his strong arms snaking around her waist to pull her back against his strength for a quick hug. "I hate that we must involve you in this."

"I know, but we need to open the gate to allow Kane to join us."

Then she looked over her shoulder at him. "And I hope my presence will convince my people that the Damned are not the enemy, but allies."

He considered her words and then jerked his head in a quick nod, although still clearly not happy about the situation.

After releasing his hold on her, Gideon led her toward the balcony. "We can't risk using the stairs. I sent Scim down to spy for me, and Olaf is planning an attack. He'll be here any second, and he will not be coming alone. We'll have to climb down to the bailey."

She followed him outside, standing back out of his way while he secured the rope to the railing. A quick look over the edge left her stomach churning. Even though the distance to the ground wasn't all that far, she didn't relish yet another new adventure.

Gideon read her fear correctly. "I'll go first so that I'll be there to catch you should you fall. Merewen, you cannot afford to hesitate. That trunk will not stop Olaf for long."

With that, Gideon was over the edge and wall-walking his way down to the ground. As soon as his feet hit bottom, she clambered over the railing and tried to mimic Gideon's technique. It worked well at first. She was only about halfway down when Olaf charged out onto the balcony.

When he leaned over the edge and spotted her, he immediately reached for his knife and sawed through the rope. The last strand broke when she was a little over halfway down to the ground. Good to his promise, Gideon caught her in his powerful arms and took off running without putting her down.

Olaf shouted to the guards on the walkway above that the keep was under attack from within and that Merewen was being kidnapped. She couldn't tell if anyone was listening. Careful to keep close to the shadows, Gideon stopped just short of the front corner of the building. When he set her back down on her feet, it sounded as if they were headed straight into complete chaos.

He leaned in close to whisper, "Remain here while I scout ahead to see where the others are."

Feeling short of breath even though Gideon had been the one running, she could barely nod and say, "Hurry. Be careful."

For some reason, her comment made him smile. "I'll try."

Before leaving, he handed her a long-bladed dirk. "I hope you have no need of this, but I will feel better knowing you are armed."

She took the weapon, clutching the hilt tightly enough to make her fingers ache. He eased forward, hesitating long enough to glance back at her one last time before disappearing around the corner. With her pulse pounding in her head, it was impossible to make sense of the voices shouting in the darkness.

Was that Murdoch's deep voice? She thought it might be. Good, that meant Gideon wouldn't be facing Olaf's men alone. Where were Averel and Duncan? A dark shape swooped down from overhead. At first, she thought it was Scim, but the color and shape were all wrong. No, it was an enormous owl, no doubt another of the avatars, trained to assist its owner in battle.

Averel's dogs came skidding around the corner from the front of the keep. As soon as they spotted Merewen, they headed straight toward her and positioned themselves beside her. She was grateful for their company, but shouldn't they be with their master?

She laid her free hand on the black dog and whispered, "Where is Averel?"

The dog immediately gave a soft yip and then stared up at the walkway. Sure enough, the young warrior was up there. He waved at her before turning his attention back toward the commotion by the gate. She wished she could see more herself.

As soon as she started forward, the white dog caught her sleeve in its mouth and held on, refusing to let her move.

"I want to take a quick look. I promise not to go far."

Would they even listen to her? If Gideon was to be believed, Scim was able to take orders from his master, but he didn't mention if the avatars would respond to others.

This time the dogs let her take two steps before they protested again. At least now she had a better view of the bailey. Men scurried about with torches in hand, illuminating the night. The shadows flickered and danced, making it all but impossible to recognize anyone.

It took her several seconds to pick Murdoch out of the crowd. He stood next to the gate, arguing with one of Olaf's men. She couldn't make out what was being said, but clearly Murdoch wanted to open the gate, and Olaf's man was trying to stop him.

She looked for Averel again, finally spotting him back down on the ground heading for his friend. In an unexpected move, Murdoch gave the man-at-arms a shove, sending him stumbling backward several steps. As the two of them kept up a steady stream of angry words, Averel slipped in behind Murdoch to raise the bar on the gate.

As soon as he did, a pair of dark forms slipped through. The human one was definitely Kane, but it was his companion who left her stunned and reeling. When Gideon had warned her that no one had seen the likes of Kane's avatar, he'd been speaking nothing but the truth.

Hob was terrifying, just like his master. For the first time she truly believed that Kane was different than other men. What kind of warrior walked with a living, breathing gargoyle at his side? Hob looked as if he'd been cobbled together with bits and pieces of different animals, each more frightening than the last.

The beast moved with a serpentine grace, the scales on his skin gleaming in the flickering torchlight. As he slithered farther inside, his fearsome howl rang out through the night to terrorize all those who heard him. Although Merewen had nothing to fear, the horrific sound still sent chills straight through to her heart.

As the pair marched forth into the bailey, the next screams came from all-too-human throats.

The sounds coming from outside her window were horrific. Alina had locked her door as Merewen had suggested, but that had been some time ago. Normally, she was only too content to remain in her room with the rest of the world shut out. But whatever was going on out there, Merewen was in the thick of it.

Alina had no desire to go charging out of her sanctuary blindly, but neither would she cower in a corner without knowing what was going on. She'd grown tired of always feeling helpless and afraid.

As she paced back and forth, desperate for something to focus on besides her fear, she realized the noise was coming from outside right below her balcony. Without disturbing Magda, who dozed peacefully in the corner, blissfully unaware of the chaos thanks to her poor hearing, Alina stepped out onto the balcony.

Gods and goddesses, what had Merewen unleashed?

The clash of swords and battle cries filled the night. The fighting was vicious, far different from the weapons practice, her only other experience in watching men wielding swords. Alina clapped her hand over her mouth rather than scream and risk drawing attention to herself.

A red glow flickered and danced, coloring the bailey as if everything and everyone were awash in blood. But, no, it was fire! May the gods help them all—had anyone sounded the alarm inside the keep? Rather than wait around to see, she'd do so herself.

After unbarring her door, she lifted her skirts to scurry down the stairs. The great hall was empty, and obviously Fagan's men-at-arms were engaged in the battle outside. She headed toward the kitchen, the most likely place the servants would have taken shelter.

The door was blocked from the inside. She pounded on it with both hands. "Ellie! It's Lady Alina. Please let me in."

At first, she feared her voice wouldn't be heard over the chaos outside, but finally she heard a scraping noise. She stood back to give whoever was opening the door a clear view of her. Ellie peeked out at her, her hands shaking and her eyes worried.

She swung the door open. "Lady Alina, you shouldn't be out there while there's fighting going on! Come in before you get hurt."

Alina hardly recognized the normally calm cook. She fought against her own fear and did her best to sound far more in control of her own emotions than she really was. "Ellie, the stable is burning, and Merewen will need every able body to fight the fire. You and I will need to prepare to treat any wounded and injured."

She stepped through the door into the crowded kitchen. Pitching her voice to be heard, she drew herself up to her full height and announced, "Everyone, you know what to do. You've practiced what to do in case of fire. Lady Merewen will be counting on you to save the horses."

Her efforts were rewarded when a few hardy souls started for the outside door. Meanwhile, Ellie put water on to heat and barked orders at her assistants to fetch soap and clean linens.

When all were busy with their assigned duties, Alina approached Ellie. "Tell me what I can do to be of help."

The older woman swallowed hard, obviously fighting her own fears. "We should set up the tables and gather the medicines that Lady Merewen has made for treating burns and injuries."

Then she took one of her own aprons off a peg and held it out to Alina. "You'll need this to protect your dress."

That was the last thing she was worried about, but Alina accepted it anyway. "I'll get started scrubbing the tables clean."

Ellie, looking far calmer, nodded. "With the gods' blessing, we can do this, my lady."

On impulse, Alina gave the cook a quick hug. "Yes, we can."

Chapter 16

Gideon's men spread out across the bailey far enough apart to allow room to maneuver. Although they were outnumbered by Olaf and his men by more than four to one, the avatars would even the odds. It was the type of fight they'd been winning for centuries. Gideon's only worry was knowing that some of the men-at-arms were loyal to Lady Merewen. Their deaths would weigh heavily on her conscience.

"Hold the line."

Murdoch nodded as he moved to fill in the gap left by Gideon as he retreated to where Merewen stood in the shadows. He kept a wary eye on his opponents as he spoke to her.

"Now would be a good time to call on your father's men to lay down their weapons or stand with us."

Merewen nodded and stepped out into the edge of the light cast by the torches. She tried shouting, but it was impossible for her to be heard over the deeper male voices clamoring for attention. Gideon caught Kane's eye and flashed him a hand signal asking for Hob to once again shatter the night with his battle cry.

The gargoyle's cold, brutal challenge rang out over the keep, stunning friend and foe alike into a few seconds of silence. Merewen tried again.

"The gods themselves have sent Captain Gideon and his men here to stop the tyranny of my uncle! Those who served my father well, I ask that you offer me the same loyalty that you gave to him! Surrender now or join my champions in defense of our home."

Gideon took over. "You have this one opportunity to lay down your arms or depart. Make your choice, but know if you leave, you will not be allowed to return. Go now while the gate stands open. Once it closes, there will be no quarter given."

Two men immediately broke and ran for the gate. Duncan and Averel moved far enough apart to allow them easy passage. But when another started to lay down his weapons, Olaf charged forward shouting, "Coward! Traitor!"

With a single stroke of his sword, he slaughtered the unarmed soldier, leaving him bleeding in the dust. It was Kane who charged forward to avenge the murdered man, but several of Olaf's men immediately formed up in a ragged line, prepared to fight to the death for possession of the keep.

In a surprise maneuver, several more turned their backs to Gideon's men, falling into line beside them, declaring their allegiance to Merewen.

Olaf immediately hollered, "Take the traitorous wench prisoner!"

Gideon quickly faced off against several men determined to do exactly that. Two worked hard to hold his attention as the third tried to slip past his guard to reach Merewen. It was all Gideon could do to keep his opponents at sword's length. Rather than risk their drawing blood, he sent a mental call for his avatar while risking a quick look directly at the man he wanted the gyrfalcon to drive back.

Scim! Protect our lady!

Scim had been circling overhead. He immediately arrowed down straight at his assigned target, raking his claws over the man's face. As the injured fighter screamed and flung his arm up to knock Scim away, the bird winged his way up to stage a second attack.

To add to the chaos, Averel's dogs dashed in and out of the milling crowd, biting and snapping at the enemy. Gideon had yet to see Murdoch's mountain cat, but her scream rang out in counterpoint to Hob's. Between the two of them, it was amazing that any of the mortals stood their ground.

Slowly, Merewen's combined forces gained ground, pushing Olaf's men back until they almost had them cornered. The battle wouldn't last much longer. Gideon wounded another of his opponents badly enough to ensure he would not be rejoining the fight. Slowly, they were reducing the enemy's numbers. If they could subdue Olaf, perhaps the rest would surrender.

But as he turned all of his attention to his third opponent, a voice called out, shouting a single word that brought the fighting to a staggering halt.

"Fire!"

Had he heard the man correctly?

It came again. "Fire! The stable is on fire!"

"The horses!"

Merewen had been holding her position well out of harm's way. But as soon as she heard of the threat, she launched herself forward, diving past Gideon right into the midst of the battleground.

He managed to catch her by the arm as she flew by, intending to shove her back behind him. She clawed at his grip, clearly out of her head with the need to save her beloved horses. And no wonder. She was as closely linked to them as he was to Scim, which meant she was locked into their pain and shared their panic as if it were her own.

"Clear the way!" he shouted to his men.

As soon as they charged forward, he followed behind, barely managing to keep Merewen from outdistancing the wall of their protection. Already her people were pouring out of the buildings toward the burning stable, the fighting forgotten for the moment.

Just as they reached the front entrance, a group of mounted riders pounded past them, heading straight for the gate. The only one Gideon recognized was Olaf, but that told him enough. The bastard had deliberately set the fire as a distraction to draw everyone's attention away from their escape.

Olaf and his men bolted through the gate to disappear into the night. By the gods' will, the man would pay for his actions with his life. And if it were up to Gideon, it wouldn't be an easy passage into the afterworld. But that would have to come later.

At least the stable master had trained his people well. While some formed a line to pass buckets of water from the well to douse the flames, others were already leading the horses from the burning building.

Gideon shouted, "Guard the gate!"

Kane motioned for two of the men who had fought at their side to man the walkway. They seemed only too glad to put some distance between themselves and the warrior and his companion. Knowing Kane would ensure that the keep remained secure from outside attack, Gideon joined the parade of people in and out of the stable, hoping to get the last of the horses safely out. Flames had already spread to the roof, which would soon collapse if the fire remained unchecked for long.

He led a skittish mare out into the night air and handed her off to the nearest pair of hands before charging back into the thickening cloud of smoke. The timbers overhead creaked ominously. Once they gave way, the stable would be a death trap for anyone still inside.

His lungs struggled to draw air inside the wall of heavy smoke even as the heat burned his skin. Few of the helpers were able or willing to reenter the inferno. He didn't blame them. Only the screams of terrified horses kept Gideon going back.

As he grabbed two more animals by their halters, he prayed, *Please, gods, be merciful to any left behind.*

Before he could reach the door, one of the overhead joists gave way, falling to the floor in a crash of flames and cinders. A mortal man wouldn't have been able to hold on to the horses, but Gideon fought them back under control. The way forward was blocked by a wall of flames. He could make it clear on his own, but for Merewen's sake, he wouldn't abandon his charges.

A shout from the back caught his attention. It was Duncan. He held an axe in his hand and was madly chopping a new avenue of escape through a wooden wall. Gideon turned back with the two mares. His friend met him halfway and took charge of them.

"Have you seen Lady Merewen?" Gideon shouted over the roar of the flames.

"She was still inside the last time I saw her," Duncan hollered as he dragged the two mares toward the jagged opening in the wall.

Gideon raced back into the thick fog of smoke. "I'll look for her!"

He felt his way from stall to stall to ensure that neither horses nor their rescuers had been trapped. At the far end was a scene right out of his worst nightmares. Merewen, her face covered in black soot, struggled to calm a mare. Both were trapped on the wrong side of a fallen timber.

His heart almost burst in his chest, and he choked on the acrid stench of smoke. Merewen would never abandon the hugely pregnant mare, but he had to get her out of there before the entire building buried them all in a grave of burning wood and straw. He should do the merciful thing and put the horse down before the fire grew worse so that he could carry his lady out to safety. Would she understand or forgive his decision to choose her over a horse?

Duncan ran down the aisle shouting, "Captain, we've got to get out of here."

He skidded to a halt beside Gideon, assessing the situation with that lightning quick intelligence of his. "I'll get the axe."

Meanwhile, Gideon took a running leap to clear the downed timber to land a short distance from Merewen.

He had to get right next to her ear to be heard over the deep roar of the fire. "Get out of here while you can. I'll stay with her."

Merewen was shaking her head before he even got the words out. "She'll panic if I let go. I'm barely holding her under control now."

Stubborn woman! He wanted to rail at her for risking her precious life for one horse, even a pregnant one, but she was too locked into her connection with the mare to listen to common sense. He gave up arguing and latched onto the other side of the mare's halter as the fire crackled and popped all around them.

Even with their best efforts, the horse was giving in to panic, her eyes rolling wildly as she fought to break free of their grasp. They were wedged in such tight quarters that if the animal reared up or struck out, she could easily trample Merewen without meaning to.

Gideon stripped off his tunic and used it to cover the mare's eyes. She calmed slightly but lunged hard to the side when a shower of red hot embers cascaded down from the rafters above. Several hit Gideon's bare back, blistering his skin. He ignored the pain, concentrating instead on making sure Merewen survived long enough for him to rail at her for placing herself in such danger.

Duncan returned with Murdoch. Both men wielded their axes with all the power the gods had granted them. The timber was already half-burned through, making their job easier. Once they cut through the heavy beam, Murdoch swung his axe one last time, burying the blade deep in the thickest part of the wood. He dragged the timber back to one side, clearing a very narrow path to safety.

"Go, Merewen! I'll bring the mare!"

She didn't argue this time, instead stumbling across to where the two warriors waited. She yelped when Murdoch immediately tossed her over his shoulder and ran for the back of the stable. Gideon followed behind, dragging the terrified mare in his wake. When there was enough clearance in the aisle, Duncan took hold of the other side of her halter and threw his own weight in to keeping her moving.

Merewen was waiting for them as they broke through to clear air. She was bent over, coughing out the black smoke choking her lungs. Gideon pulled his tunic back on after two of the young stable hands took control of the pregnant mare and led her away. Just as they did, there came a loud rumble, and the ground beneath their feet shook with the impact of the stable collapsing in on itself. Sparks and flames shot high up into the night sky, casting everyone's faces in an unholy glow of red and black.

The close call had Gideon's temper looking for a handy target. If Olaf had been in reach, he would have skinned the man alive. In his absence, yelling at Merewen for risking her life would have to do. But before he'd taken one step in her direction, someone else called her name.

"Lady Merewen, it's young Edric. He was inside the stable, helping with the horses. Too much smoke, I'm guessing, because he's . . . he's not—"

It was hard to say whether the man ran out of breath or whether he couldn't bring himself to say the rest. He staggered toward her, the limp body of the young boy in his arms. Merewen immediately straightened up, her own struggles to draw a full breath obviously forgotten. She met the stable hand halfway.

"Lay him down," she ordered as she knelt on the ground beside the too-still body.

Everyone else stopped what they were doing, their faces painted with soot and stark grief.

"Edric, stay with us," Merewen pleaded as she looked around. "I need a knife."

Gideon immediately offered his. She used the blade to split the fabric of the boy's shirt. After setting the knife aside, she laid her hands on Edric's thin body and started chanting. The words tripped off her tongue in a rough whisper, her throat obviously still fighting the effects of breathing in so much smoke herself.

He recognized the flow of her magic, although this time desperation swirled in and around the chant. The longer it went on, the less likely her gift would work this time. He moved closer, wanting to help but not sure how. Finally, he simply dropped to one knee beside her, unsure what to do. If the boy didn't respond soon, Gideon would have to drag Merewen away before she burned herself out completely.

"My lady," he started to say, but she shook her head and kept chanting, her voice growing fainter.

He risked a hand on her shoulder. The connection between them surged hot as his own life force lent its strength to hers. Immediately, her words grew stronger, ringing out clearly in the night air. Her efforts were rewarded when Edric's chest moved like a bellows as he drew a gasp of air.

She paused to stare down at her patient, waiting to see if he would draw in a second breath and then a third. Already his lips looked less blue, his skin losing its deathly pallor. Then the coughing started. Merewen snaked her arm under Edric's neck, lifting him up to help him breathe more easily.

Through it all, Gideon kept his hand right there on her shoulder, savoring the connection as her magic sang and danced in celebration. He no longer doubted the beauty and the goodness of her power. Magic or not, it was truly a gift from the gods.

When she gathered the boy into her arms for a hug, Gideon finally moved back, not wanting to intrude further on the moment. After a minute, the boy protested, no doubt embarrassed by all the attention.

"Edric, don't scare me like that again," Merewen ordered as she released him. "Someone take him inside and make sure he gets something warm to drink. Then straight to bed with him."

Once she was sure the boy would be taken care of, she slowly rose to her feet and looked around. As soon as she spotted Gideon, she charged toward him and right into his arms.

He didn't remember reaching out to her, but suddenly Merewen had burrowed into his chest, hot tears streaking down her face. The last vestiges of his anger drained away as this fierce, foolishly brave woman turned to him for solace.

His centuries-long life had been filled with endless fighting and violence, leaving him feeling awkward and ill prepared for offering a woman simple comfort. He closed his eyes and stood stock-still as he held her close until she cried herself out. It didn't take long. Already he could sense Merewen pulling herself back together.

After a bit, she looked up at him, her brown eyes huge and still sparkling with tears. "I need to check on the horses and to see if any more of my people need medical care."

Murdoch spoke up. "So far as I know, only a few others were injured and none seriously in the fire. Lady Alina is seeing to them and those hurt in the fighting. She and the cook have set up inside the hall. With your permission, Captain, I'd like to assist them."

Gideon nodded over Merewen's head. "I'll help Merewen with the horses. Before you go, confer with Kane to see if he requires additional help guarding the keep. Send one of the dogs to find me if he has need of me."

"Yes, sir."

Murdoch disappeared into the milling crowd. There was nothing to do about the stable except to make sure the fire burned itself out without spreading to any of the other buildings or to the wooden palisade that surrounded Merewen's home. They couldn't risk leaving themselves open to an easy attack with so few men left to defend the keep.

The stable master had already released most of the horses into the small pasture at the back edge of the bailey. The animals huddled together on the far side of the field, calming down now that the immediate danger was over. Merewen hurried to the older man's side.

"Are many hurt? Were any lost?"

Jarod looked up from applying a thick coat of salve on a dark bay's right shoulder. "I done a rough count, and there be a few unaccounted for. I'm guessing they be the ones that fool Olaf and his brigands stole. Several of the horses got burned, but none too bad. I treated them with this."

He held up a jar. Even from where Gideon stood, he could smell the sweet, soothing scent of the salve. Although the horse flinched at the stable master's touch, the animal didn't seem to be suffering from the painful-looking injury. No doubt it was one of Merewen's special remedies.

She was still talking. "What can I do to help?"

"Nothing right now, my lady. Tomorrow you'll likely need to prepare more of the salve, but we got plenty for tonight. The only one that's worrisome is that last mare you dragged out. I'm afeard this uproar and her injuries will bring on early labor."

Merewen nodded. "I'll stay with her."

Enough was enough. Gideon would keep Merewen safe even if was from herself. "Lady Merewen, one of the stable boys can watch over the mare while you rest. Tomorrow will not be an easy day for anyone, and your people will be looking to you to take charge and reassure them that all will be well."

He pinned the stable master with a hard look. "Promise her you'll send the boy to fetch Lady Merewen at the first sign the mare is in trouble."

The old man looked from Merewen to Gideon and back again, obviously trying to decide exactly who Gideon was and what gave him the right to give orders.

"You and your men be the ones what ran off Olaf and his men?"

Gideon crossed his arms over his chest. "Yes. We're also the ones who will ensure they will not be allowed to return. Fagan, either, for that matter."

The old man gave him a gap-toothed smile. "That be good work, my lad. I'll have the boy fetch Lady Merewen, but only if she be really needed."

Gideon fought not to grin at being called a lad by a man who was centuries younger, but it lightened his heart.

"Thank you, sir," he said as he clapped the stable master gently on the shoulder.

That Merewen didn't protest the decisions being made without consulting her spoke to how exhausted she had to be. Even so, she insisted on checking on a few of the horses herself, especially the pregnant mare. When she was satisfied all was under control, she let Gideon lead her back to the gate.

There in the darkness, away from the chaos of the milling horses and people, he pulled her back into his arms. It was time for some hard truths.

"You terrify me, woman."

She blinked up at him, a questioning expression on her sweet, soot-streaked face. "I do?"

He wanted nothing more than to kiss her again, but now wasn't the time. "Yes, you do. The gods have oft charged me with serving those they deemed worthy of their protection. Never before has that someone had the fierce soul of a warrior. You charge into battles that you have no chance of winning."

Letting a little of his fear and anger show, he gripped her upper arms and gave her a small shake. "Did you even stop to think that if you'd died in that stable saving that last horse, you would have endangered all those who look to you for their livelihood and protection?"

Merewen frowned. "But caring for the horses is my duty."

"And the people who depend on you, care about you, count for naught?"

She flinched as if he'd slapped her. "Of course they count. Everything I do is for their sake. Without the horses, the duke will take back the land and let all of us starve."

His point exactly. "All the more reason for you to show common sense when it comes to your own safety. If you continue to take such risks, I will take measures to ensure it doesn't happen again. Your foolishness comes at too high a cost!"

She vibrated with temper and the vestiges of fear. "Then, Captain, you would be little better than my uncle! He would keep me prisoner, too."

This was getting nowhere. "I am nothing like Fagan, Merewen, and you well know it. I would not curtail your freedom lightly, but I will not risk my friends needlessly. If we fail to keep you safe, the gods will condemn all of us, you included, to wander for eternity, soulless and alone."

Her eyes widened in horror. "That cannot be. The

gods would never be so cruel or unfair. All you can do is your best. That is all that can be asked of any man—or woman."

"Ordinary men may concern themselves with what is fair or not, but I'm not an ordinary man, Merewen. None of the Damned is. I serve the gods as an avatar, even as Scim serves me. Our fates are all twined together for better or worse. I repeat, I will not risk the souls of my friends, not even for you."

His words hurt her, but what choice did he have? "We have yet to discern the full extent of what the gods are demanding of us this time. We suspect that regaining control of your home is only the first part of the purpose the gods have decreed."

Her eyes widened in surprise. "What do you mean?"

"You have felt the evil that roams this land yourself. You've sensed its growing presence in your uncle and his men."

He didn't wait for her to admit it. "To make sure that you are safe, we must seek out the source of that evil and stop it before it grows too strong to be contained. We know that it feeds on both innocence and blood. Unless we can contain it and soon, the people of Agathia will live, suffer, and die in darkness for eons to come.

"I fear greatly for you and your people. We need to find the root of this dark magic." He let his hands drop back down to his sides. "But I should not have started this discussion tonight when we are both tired. Tomorrow will be soon enough after you are rested."

It was far past time to see her safely to her chambers. "Let me confer with Kane briefly, and then I will walk you inside. Will you wait?"

She nodded, looking sad and weary beyond description. "I'll be here."

Ignoring his own exhaustion, Gideon jogged over to the gate. Kane stepped out of the darkness, startling him.

"Damn you—don't do that."

Kane's teeth gleamed whitely in the darkness. "After all these centuries you should be used to it. But then, I suspect the lady has your thoughts tied up in too many knots to leave you much room for clear thinking."

It was no less than the truth. That didn't mean Gideon wanted to hear it. "Any sign of Olaf and his men?"

"No. Duncan sent the owl winging after them. He returned but a short time ago. From all appearances, they are riding straight for the capital city, most likely to warn the lady's uncle that he is no longer welcome here."

Gideon had guessed as much. "That should buy us a few days to shore up the defenses."

"I have some ideas on the subject, but they can wait until tomorrow. Go. Your lady needs to seek her bed. With Olaf gone, I suspect she'll sleep more soundly than she has in a long time."

Memories of what he'd seen earlier came flooding back along with the need to avenge Merewen's honor. "The lady has had good reason to fear the night. If we'd arrived even a few minutes later, he would have—"

Kane's big hand came down on Gideon's shoulder. "But we weren't late. Be content with that for this night. We'll have our vengeance upon him soon enough."

Hob prowled by, stopping only long enough to taste the air around Gideon with a flick of his forked tongue. The beast snorted, clearly not happy with the smoky smell that clung to Gideon's skin.

For the first time in hours, Gideon smiled. "If I smell bad enough to offend a gargoyle, perhaps I should delay seeking my bed long enough to bathe."

With that, he returned to Merewen. Together they trudged wearily toward the great hall.

Chapter 17

$\mathcal{M}$urdoch carried the last of the wounded fighters over to a pallet in the corner. After he was settled on the blankets, the man gingerly stretched out his leg, wincing at the pain. His skin was ashen, but that had more to do with the stress of having the jagged gash in his upper thigh stitched closed than the severity of the wound.

It wouldn't hurt to repeat Lady Alina's instructions one last time. "Remember, if it hurts too badly, ask for more of that special brew to help you sleep. Right now, rest is what you need."

The weary man's eyes were already fluttering closed. "Yes, sir."

Satisfied he'd done all he could for the man, Murdoch headed back to where Lady Alina was tending to the last few of the injured. He stopped short of where she and the cook had set up the tables to treat those who had required more than a dash of salve or a simple bandage.

He'd already known Ellie to be a forceful woman who ran her kitchen with a strong hand. It was Lady Alina who had managed to surprise him. From the instant the first of the wounded were carried into the hall, she'd been here, there, everywhere with an encouraging word, a gentle touch, and a fierce determination to give even the lowliest of Merewen's people the best care she could offer.

Other than the one man killed outright by Olaf, no

other lives had been lost from among those loyal to
Merewen. While it was difficult to forgive Fagan's men for
setting fire to the stable, their actions may have helped
keep the deaths to a minimum. Cornered, the traitors
would have fought like trapped rats.

"Sir Murdoch!"

He straightened up at the call of his name. "Yes, Lady
Alina?"

She started for him, stopping when she was only an
arm's length away. The difference in their heights forced
her to tip her head back at an awkward angle. Her di-
minutive size and grace made him feel big and clumsy, at
the same time triggering all of his protective instincts.

"Did you need me to lift another patient?" In his
mind he added, *Or anything else I could do to help,* as he
searched for any excuse he could use to remain close to
her.

"No, I wanted to thank you for all your help with the
injured. You made our job much easier."

His manners were a bit rusty, but he managed a stiff
bow. "It was my pleasure, Lady Alina. Is there nothing
more I can do?"

She bit her lower lip as she looked around. "We need
to scrub the tables clean so that they are ready for the
first meal in the morning, but that is not work for a noble
knight such as you."

Murdoch would have scrubbed the garderobe if it had
pleased her. He kept that to himself.

"At least let me carry the tables back to where they
belong for you."

His willingness to help seemed to please her. Before
she answered, though, one of the other women called
out to her.

"Shall we boil more of the herbs in case some of the
injured need them during the night?"

When Alina turned to answer her, Murdoch noticed

she had a piece of thread in her hair; without thinking, he reached out to remove it. Or maybe he was thinking how nice it would be to touch the spun gold silk of her hair.

His reasons didn't matter; only the effect his thoughtless gesture had on Alina did. As soon as she noticed the movement of his hand out of the corner of her eye, she cried out and threw her hands up in self-defense as she lurched backward, trying to get out of his reach and ward off the perceived blow.

Murdoch's first instincts were to catch her, but one look at her too-pale face and the icy fear in her eyes froze him instantly.

Dangling the piece of thread in the air, he pitched his voice low and soothing. "My apologies. I didn't mean to startle you. I thoughtlessly reached to remove this from your hair. I would never—"

He cut himself off midsentence. The last thing Alina would want would be for him to promise never to hit her the way that bastard Fagan clearly had. Even so, she obviously knew exactly what he'd been about to say. She swallowed hard as understanding came flooding back, her cheeks flushing bright in embarrassment.

Everyone in their immediate surroundings stood in hushed silence, staring first at him in disgust for frightening her and then at Alina with what looked like pity. He didn't care what they thought of him, but Alina was a prideful, private woman. She would hate to be the object of anyone's pity. She seemed caught in a trap, unable to break free.

Someone had to take charge of the situation. "Cook, I'm sure Lady Alina would be happy to show you how to brew more of that herbal tisane for the wounded. While you do that, the rest of us will move the tables back and get them scrubbed clean."

He was well aware that any other time the cook would have come after him with one of her skewers for having hinted that she wouldn't know how to boil water and herbs together without help.

Instead, she gave him a brief nod of approval as she gently took Lady Alina by the arm and led her from the hall.

Murdoch wanted very badly to follow after them and even see Alina safely to her room. Did she believe his unspoken promise to never raise a hand to her? Now wasn't the time to question her further. It was bad enough that everyone in the household knew of her abuse. If he caused her honor to be called into question by showing too much interest in her, he would only compound the evil done by her husband.

Better that he concentrate on his duty as one of Gideon's warriors. For tonight, he'd clean tables, but come the morrow, he'd hone his sword and prepare for battle. It was all he was good for.

Merewen kept her head up, carrying herself as if she really were in charge and knew what she was doing, when all she wanted to do was crawl into a corner somewhere and hide. Yes, she was glad the keep was now firmly in possession of Gideon and his men. But right now, it was all too much.

Before everything could spin out of control, a firm hand touched the middle of her back. "Steady there, Merewen."

Just that quickly, Gideon's solid presence helped rein in the tumble of memories. "Thank you."

There was unexpected warmth in his voice. "All things considered, you've held up remarkably well. I would suggest a quick check on the injured, and then you should retreat to your room for what is left of the night. Kane and our avatars will remain on duty to make sure all stays quiet while everyone gets some rest. Nothing and no one will get by them."

"A peaceful night of sleep would be a true gift from the gods." She managed a small smile. "But not until I make sure the wounded have been seen to."

They made a quick circle around the hall, and she was pleased with the care everyone had gotten. Her last stop was the kitchen. It was no surprise to see Ellie had fresh bread baking and a pot of apples stewing for the morning meal. However, she hadn't expected to find her aunt seated on one of the benches with a mug of something hot clasped in her hands.

Alina stood up as Merewen walked in. "Niece, I'm glad to see you are well and unharmed. Sir Murdoch had said so, but it is a relief to see for myself."

For the second time since the fire, Merewen found herself wrapped in someone's arms. This time the hug was brief but still heartfelt.

"I'm fine. Tired, but fine." Merewen gave Alina one last squeeze before stepping back. She smiled at the cook. "Ellie, I appreciate what you two have done for all of the injured."

Alina shrugged her shoulders. "It's good to be useful again."

Her simple statement contained such pain. "You were more than just useful. Everyone out there was most eager to tell me of your kindness and gentle touch. They will all heal much better, thanks to the care you gave them."

That was true, but right now it was Alina herself who concerned Merewen. The woman looked as if the slightest touch would shatter her into a hundred pieces. Merewen wasn't the only one in need of sleep.

"I'm on my way to my room. Would you walk with me?"

Alina looked around, as if unsure how she'd come to be standing in the kitchen or what she needed to be doing. The cook came to the rescue.

"Both of you need to get out from underfoot. I have work to do, and you'll only be in the way."

Merewen half expected the woman to flap her apron at them the way she did the chickens and geese out in the bailey. Still, her no-nonsense attitude gave Alina the push she needed to get moving again.

Tomorrow, Merewen would ask her friend what had happened to cause Alina to look so forlorn. With Fagan banished from the keep, Merewen wouldn't have been surprised to find her aunt celebrating his absence.

Ellie followed them back out into the hall. Merewen hid a smile when the woman gave Gideon an appraising look. She sniffed the air and frowned. "I've been heating water all evening for people to use to wash up. Lady Merewen, that fancy tub of your uncle's is waiting for you in your room."

Then she pointed at Gideon. "I told your man Murdoch and his young friend that no one comes to my tables smelling of horse and burned wood. There are tubs for you and the other men set up in the room down the hall from Lady Alina's. Use them."

With that edict, she disappeared back into the kitchen, no doubt ready to terrorize her assistants into getting their chores done. Merewen couldn't help herself and let loose with a peal of laughter. The stunned look on Gideon's face was just too funny.

At first, he looked mildly irritated, but then he gave in and grinned back at her. "I can think of half a dozen battles that would've been more easily won with that woman in command."

"You should tell Ellie that sometime. It would please her."

He nodded. "But not tonight. I wouldn't dare set foot in her kitchen in this condition. I'll see you to your room and then seek out that bath she mentioned."

They started to walk away but noticed that Alina

wasn't moving. Merewen had never seen her look quite so lost. Gideon gave her a questioning look. She shrugged, unsure what to do.

Finally, Gideon stepped forward and presented his arm to Lady Alina. "I am Captain Gideon. Would you allow me the honor of escorting you from the hall, my lady?"

Her aunt finally nodded and accepted the offer, looking grateful for his support. Merewen fought down the bit of jealousy she felt at watching Gideon charm another woman. It was an unworthy emotion, especially when it was so clear that right now Alina needed his attention more than Merewen did.

As she followed in their footsteps, a movement in the far corner caught her attention. It was Murdoch, his size making it impossible to mistake him for anyone else. It wasn't just his odd behavior that had caught her attention, but the expression of raw hunger on his face as he'd watched Alina and Gideon walk across the great hall on their way to the staircase.

Granted, Alina deserved a far better husband than the one she'd been burdened with. If Fagan returned to the keep with the intent of winning back control from Gideon and his men, Alina would soon be a widow. Even if that were to happen, Murdoch would not be around long enough to take Fagan's place in Alina's life, even if her aunt was interested. The woman had little reason to trust the men in her life.

That thought brought Merewen full circle back to Captain Gideon. He was gruff, determined, and overbearing at times. Yet he'd kissed her with such tenderness and held her when she needed his comfort. Right now he was showing every kindness to a woman who had good reason to be skittish around men.

It would be all too easy to depend on him, to become accustomed to having such a man in her life. Nothing would change the gods' decree that he had so little time to walk the land before returning to the river. She needed a man who could give her strong sons and daughters to carry on her family's heritage—to face the future with her no matter what it held.

For now, the path of the Damned ran together with hers, side by side. Too soon those roads would diverge, never to cross again. A shaft of pain shot through her chest at the thought of watching Gideon and his men march back into the water, once again to sleep in the chill of the river. She stared at his back, wondering how she would bear to see that happen.

But what choice did either of them have? None.

Gideon happened to glance back at her, the touch of his gaze warming her from the inside out. He frowned, as if reading some of her thoughts in her expression.

At the top of the steps, Alina released his arm. It was a relief to hear a bit more life in her voice.

"Thank you, Captain. My quarters lie in that direction, but I can go the remaining distance on my own."

Before leaving them, she glanced in Merewen's direction. "Perhaps tomorrow you will see fit to explain to me how the good captain and his men came to be here right when we needed them the most."

"I will, Alina. I'm sorry I didn't tell you sooner."

Alina gave Gideon another considering look. "We've all had secrets we've tried to keep, Merewen. Maybe that should change. Good night to you both."

She walked away, carrying herself with such wounded dignity that it brought the sting of tears to Merewen's eyes. Her aunt had endured so much pain.

"He won't get near her again, Merewen. None of us will let that happen."

The tone of Gideon's voice made it clear that his words were more than a simple statement of fact. They were a vow, a heartfelt promise that Alina would never suffer another minute spent in Fagan's company.

"I believe you."

They'd reached her doorway. She hesitated, the memories of Olaf's attack still fresh in her mind despite everything that had happened in the interim.

"He's gone, Merewen."

She could feel the warmth of Gideon's strong body even though he stood a short distance away. Maybe it was only her imagination, but it gave her the courage she needed to cross the threshold.

As promised, an enormous tub full of steaming water sat near the fire. The servants had left another bucket of water sitting close enough to the flames to make sure she could warm the bath if it had cooled too much.

Gideon stood in the doorway. "Tomorrow I will make sure a bar is installed on your door. But for tonight, will it bother you to be alone?"

Her pulse raced. What was he asking? Or offering?

He answered her unspoken question. "Would you sleep better if your aunt or one of the servants stayed here with you?"

She tried not to show her disappointment. "No, I'll be fine. Besides, Alina needs her own rest."

Still he lingered.

"The room where Ellie had other tubs set up is down the hall to your left."

He cocked his head and listened. "I'm guessing Averel and Duncan found them first. I'd just as soon not share, not with them. They'll be done soon enough."

Again, his meaning was hidden. Was he wanting to share her bath? The images that brought forth in her mind left her tingling in places better left unnamed. Did she have the courage to invite him into her room?

It would seem so. "Then share mine."

When he didn't immediately step toward her, she wished that she could back up time long enough to retract the offer. At least he didn't laugh. Instead, the corners of his mouth kicked up in a small smile.

"Think carefully, Merewen. If I were to stay, it wouldn't be only to bathe. Your people will know."

They would. Secrets were hard to keep when people lived in such close quarters. So the question really was, did she care?

She studied the dance of the flames, remembering all too clearly how close they'd come to losing Gideon to the fire.

"I have lived in terror of my uncle, a man I have grown to hate. For months I have been waiting for him to decide what to do with me, fearing for my very life. The last night my uncle was here, he stopped Olaf from entering my room, but only because he said the duke had plans for me. Evidently, I was to remain untouched until such time as the duke was finished with me, whatever that was supposed to mean."

She could think of several options, none of them good. However, right now she didn't want to arouse Gideon's pity or even his sense of duty as her champion.

No, that was not what she wanted at all.

"Gideon, I have only ever wanted to make my own choices, my own decisions, to marry and bear children who would share my heritage. Fagan has done everything he can to prevent that from happening. In his eyes, I am little better than the broodmares out there in the pasture. Actually, not even that. The last thing Fagan wants is for me to produce a son who might have inherited the family gift. That would cost him everything."

Well aware that she was still covered in soot and smelled of smoke, she wasn't sure what to do. Her experience with men who were of her station had been severely limited, especially since her father's illness and her uncle's tyrannical rule.

She'd never learned the art of feminine discourse; she'd been too busy discussing bloodlines and breeding stock. Thanks to her work with horses, she understood the earthier side of what went on between men and women, and life within the crowded confines of the keep left little to the imagination.

But knowing Gideon had enjoyed their few kisses and embraces gave her the courage she needed. Once again, she faced him, wanting him to see her truth.

"I would choose you, Captain Gideon, if you would have me."

His pale eyes studied her for all of a heartbeat, perhaps two. "In all of my years of serving the gods, I have never once met a woman like you, Merewen. I want you so badly that my hands shake, but I won't . . . I cannot . . ."

He shook his head in frustration. "If I were a mere man, one not cursed by the gods, one who could stay, I would walk through fire to be at your side and give you those sons and daughters you crave. You deserve better than a man whose life and soul are no longer his to claim."

Once again, his honor and nobility rang clear in the small space that separated them.

It helped to know that he hungered as she hungered. "Have you already forgotten the events of this evening? You already have walked through fire for me, Gideon."

She risked a step closer to him. "We both have obligations and duties that we must honor. But for tonight and as many nights as the gods may grant us, let us find what comfort we can in each other's arms. Surely that is not too much to ask."

Then she did the bravest thing she'd ever done. She held out her hand to her champion and waited.

Chapter 18

Gideon was many things, but he was not a fool. He wanted more than anything in the world to take that single step, the one that would allow him to take Merewen's proffered hand in his. To share that steaming water, washing away the last vestiges of the night's battles against foe and flame. To lose himself in the welcome of her arms and her bed.

He was a man caught in the middle, trapped between the desires of this world and the demands of his gods.

If he refused Merewen's offer, it might wound her in ways he couldn't imagine. But if he were to accept, how would the gods weigh his actions? His poor judgment had condemned him to the river in the first place. Alone, he wouldn't hesitate to take the gift that Merewen had offered him. But he wasn't alone; he had four friends who would suffer his same fate, for good or for ill. They depended on him to make a wise decision, one that would eventually lead to the end of this false life they had all endured for too long.

Bedding her could have other consequences, ones he doubted she was prepared for.

"Merewen—"

At that sound of her name, she wilted, dropping her hand back to her side.

He hurt for her. He hurt for them both. "I'm sorry."

"No, I am, Captain. Forgive me for placing you in such an awkward position."

She kept her chin up, but he could see the sparkle of tears as they filled her eyes and then trickled down her cheeks in muddy streaks.

"Please just go, Gideon. I'll be fine, and I'm sure your men are wondering what happened to you."

Just as her words faded away, the air around her rippled with power. Gideon charged forward, reaching for his sword, ready to defend her against an invisible foe. When he reached her side, she stood frozen in place, her eyes wide and unblinking. Her breathing had been short and shallow as she'd fought against the pain he'd caused her. Now her lungs no longer drew in air.

Magic crawled along his skin, powerful enough to have his hair floating in a halo around his head. All was silent except for the ripple of water. He frowned, trying to trace the source of the sound.

The tub. It had to be.

With great trepidation, he crossed the room step by cautious step. Just as he expected, the surface of the water was covered in a series of rings that started at the center and rolled outward to lap at the sides of the tub.

He lowered his sword; it would not protect him from the forces at work. The only times he'd felt this power before was in the presence of the gods. Never before had they spoken to him except at the river's edge. What had drawn a god to this time and this place?

Placing the tip of his blade on the ground, he knelt and placed the palms of his hands on top of the pommel, one on top of the other, palm-side down. With his head bowed, he spoke.

"I am but your servant, here to do your bidding."

The temperature in the room plummeted, the chill all too familiar. He'd slept in that same cold for far too long to mistake it for anything else. He held his position though he longed to grab Merewen up in his arms and bolt for the door. But it had been his courage that had convinced the gods to let him earn his way back into their favor with his service to their cause. He would not run now.

The water churned and swirled until finally a single form rose out of the tub, feminine in shape but with no more substance than the water itself. Even so, her transparent eyes burned with terrifying power.

Her voice chimed like bells. "Captain, it has been far too long since last we spoke face-to-face."

Not nearly long enough, but he kept that thought to himself. Well, not really; after all, the gods read his thoughts as easily as they heard his words.

"Lady of the River, what do you require of your humble servant?"

The goddess's laughter rang out over the room. Her good humor remained in her voice as she chided him. "Captain, Captain. As I recall, it was precisely your lack of humility and your selfishness that led to your downfall."

"True, my lady." He risked a look to better gauge her reaction. "I have endeavored ever since to change my behavior."

"Indeed we have noted that."

The goddess passed through the side of the tub, her movements liquid and flowing with grace but leaving no trace of moisture as she passed over the stone floor. When she approached Merewen, it was all Gideon could do not to throw himself between the two women. He hadn't been given leave to rise from the floor, but he trembled with the effort to remain still.

It was too much to hope that the goddess hadn't noticed his reaction. She looked more curious than concerned.

"Interesting. In some portion this woman has usurped your loyalty to us."

"I live only to serve you, my lady."

More laughter. "Oh, Captain, are you lying to me or only to yourself? Did you think we weren't listening to your thoughts when she had you caught like a rabbit in a snare? Your desire for her glows in your very soul, enough that we had to see her for ourselves and judge her worthiness."

His blood ran cold. What game was afoot?

The goddess returned to her inspection, circling Merewen in silence. "She has great strength, this one."

She coasted to a stop in front of Merewen, her head tilted to the side. "Captain . . . Gideon, you have always served us well, and still do. Perhaps it is you who are different this time. You serve this woman's cause out of more than your duty to us. We may hold the power over your soul, but it would seem Lady Merewen has captured your heart."

She returned to Gideon's side. "Rise up, Warrior."

When he stood facing her, she reached out to touch the center of his chest with the cold chill of her hand. "By granting Lady Merewen's plea, we have set these actions in motion and cannot yet see the outcome. There is a darkness that hinders our view. We have not seen its like in an age or more." The Lady stared past him, her expression concerned. "You are correct that there is far more work to be done than regaining control of Lady Merewen's home for her. For good or for ill, your affection for this woman and hers for you have added another stream of power to the flow of events."

Gideon stated the simple truth. "I refused her offer. Lady Merewen is the innocent in this in every meaning of the word. She deserves better than me."

"We noted the nobility of your action, Captain. This is the first time you have cared more for another human being than you have cared for yourself and the four warriors who fight at your side. I foretell this is a good thing."

She passed through the side of the tub to stand once

again in the water. "When I release her, you will need to be back where you stood when she reached out to you, Captain. Listen to your heart and your honor. Then decide."

Her smile was enigmatic. "Perhaps you alone can give Lady Merewen that which she most desires."

"Freedom from her uncle?"

"That is but part of her dream, Captain. She fights not only to save her people now but also to ensure the gift she carries is passed on to the next generation."

Gideon almost dropped his sword as the impact of the goddess's words hit him. Was it true? Was his purpose in Merewen's life twofold? Not just to save her from Fagan, but also to give her a child? Would he depart from this world, this time leaving behind a son or daughter with the woman he loved? The idea stunned him, his mind whirling with images of Merewen round with child. Would she have loving words to tell the babe of his father? That he wouldn't be there himself stabbed his heart like a knife.

He didn't know what to say, so he said nothing but did as she ordered. When he was once again standing in the doorway, neither in nor out, the goddess nodded.

"All too soon we will meet again at the river's edge where once again you must stand judgment. My advice to you would be to use your time wisely, Captain."

Then with a soft splash, she poured down into the bathwater, disappearing as quickly as she'd appeared. As the ripples died away, once again the air became heavy with power. Merewen's hand slowly rose, palm up and waiting for Gideon to choose.

Then she smiled, totally unaware of all that had passed between one breath and the next. "Well?"

The goddess had allowed Gideon free will in this. If she'd disapproved, she would not have hesitated to say so. So he did as she suggested and listened to his heart

and found his answer. Nothing in his long life had felt so
right as stepping forward to take Merewen's hand in his.

"If you would have me, then I am yours for all the
days the gods may grant me."

He pressed a kiss to her hand, keeping it sweet and
gentle. His lady deserved to be treated with every civility,
which included not dragging her over to the bed in his
current filthy condition.

To make sure they were truly alone, he peeked into
the tub and detected nothing but water this time. "You
mentioned something about sharing a bath?"

Merewen nodded, her true innocence showing in the
faint bloom of color on her cheeks. "I did, didn't I?"

Gideon vowed to go slowly, to coax rather than demand. "If you'd prefer I waited in the hallway until
you're finished, I will."

She gave a small laugh. "I would prefer you stayed
right here, but I'm afraid I have no idea of how to proceed."

"I can help with that."

He started by closing the door and once again shoving the heavy trunk in front of it. Next, he doused several
of the candles, reducing the light in the room. With his
keen eyesight, he could still see each and every detail of
his lady, but she didn't need to know that. For her, the
pale glow would soften the edges, easing her journey
from innocence to becoming his lover.

She still stood in the same spot, her eyes carefully
avoiding both the bed and the tub. He approached
Merewen from behind, keeping his voice low and easy,
much in the same way she did when talking to one of her
skittish horses.

"For now, I am your lady's maid. Nothing more."

Her soft laughter pleased him. He started by unwind-
ing the leather thong from her braid. How many times
had he imagined what her red-kissed hair would look

like set free or spread out upon his pallet? When it was unbound, he worked his fingers through her hair, loosening it until it tumbled like a waterfall very nearly to her waist.

Beautiful. Dark silk, so soft to the touch.

Next, he reached around to unlace the leather jirkinet she wore over her tunic and tossed it aside. When he knelt to help her step out of her boots, she rested her hands on his shoulders for balance. Just that small touch had him hard and aching, but he hoped to hide the urgency of his desire from her for a while longer to give her time to get used to his touch.

Next, he slipped his hands up under her tunic to grasp the top of her trousers and undergarment. Her breath came in a short gasp as he quickly tugged the drawstring loose and eased them down. So far, she accepted his ministrations with little discomfiture, but then her tunic was long enough to still provide her with a degree of modesty.

Before he unlaced the back of her tunic, he paused to give her a kiss, doing his best to maintain a small distance between them. In response, her arms immediately snaked up around his neck as she pressed forward, fitting her body against his. Her eyes widened when she felt the strength of his need for her. She swallowed hard, but bravely stayed right where she was.

That pleased him, but then he'd already known of her courage. "We'll go as slowly as you need, Merewen. I don't want to scare you."

"It's not you that frightens me, Gideon. It is more that I don't know what I'm about, and I fear I will disappoint you."

"That's not possible, sweet one. Everything about you pleases me. We'll get through this together."

Deepening the kiss helped distract her as he loosened the laces on the tunic, slowly baring her elegant back to his touch. When he was done, he gently turned her around before he eased the soft cotton off her shoulders.

When the fabric slipped down beneath the curve of her breasts, it would have taken a far stronger man than he to resist testing their fit in the palms of his hands. His lady moaned as he gently kneaded them and coaxed their pretty rose tips into pebbling up. His tongue hungered to learn their taste, but that would have to wait.

Another tug sent her tunic skimming down past her waist and the curve of her hips to puddle on the floor. He immediately offered Merewen his hand to help her into the warm bathwater. To avoid giving her too much time to think, he quickly stripped off his own clothes and stepped into the tub behind her, wrapping his arms around her and drawing her back against his chest.

His lady was tense, but that was to be expected. He reached for the soap and one of the cloths the servants had left. After dipping the cloth in the water, he offered it to her.

As she started to wash her face, he told her, "I'll do your back."

He lathered up his hands. Using long, slow strokes, at first he limited his touch just to her shoulders. When he could feel her relaxing, he moved on to her arms, her neck, then her collarbone. When once again he cupped her breasts, her head kicked back against his shoulder, allowing him better access.

He turned his head into the curve of her neck, nibbling his way up to the shell of her ear. Judging by the restless movements of her legs, his lady was enjoying his attentions.

To his delight, she abruptly shifted to face him.

"My turn."

Her small hands glided over his chest, arms, hands, and face. The water was growing cooler, but it did nothing to dampen the effect she was having on him. His control began to slip, necessitating that they finish this teasing play soon.

"Let me wash your hair."

"If you allow me to return the favor."

With splashing and laughter, they managed to rid themselves of the last of the smoke and soot. Gideon reached for the pail of warm water to rinse away the soap.

He left the tub first, once again offering her his hand to support her as she stepped out onto the hearth rug. That she allowed him to dry her from top to toe showed that she was growing accustomed to his touch. It encouraged him and warmed him even further. To keep her from getting chilled, he helped her on with her robe while he wrapped a quilt around his waist.

"I will brush your hair," she insisted.

He would have never thought that such a simple thing would be so erotic. In turn, her hair took longer to untangle, but he savored each minute they spent tending to each other.

Finally, he set the brush aside. It was time to take his lady to bed and teach her the wonders of what a man and a woman could share. Her delicate build and sweetly scented skin made him feel oversized and clumsy. He wrapped his arms around her from behind, holding her close against his chest once again.

"Merewen, if anything I do displeases you, tell me."

"I cannot imagine that happening. Promise you'll teach me how to please you."

Her earnest words made him smile. "Everything you do pleases me."

She actually laughed at that. "So that was pleasure on your face when you saw me trapped with the mare in the stable?"

The memory had him squeezing her hard. "I cannot bear the thought of losing you, Merewen. Please don't scare me that badly again."

Her smile dimmed as she turned to look up at him. "I can't swear to that, Gideon, any more than you can promise that you'll not risk yourself in battle. All I can promise is that I'll be careful."

She was right; that didn't mean he liked it. The reminder that they were both caught up in dangerous times made these sweet minutes of peace so much more precious. He would cherish the gift the gods had given him.

He slowly nodded. "Then for now, for what's left of this night, the world outside that door no longer exists."

Merewen's answering smile was everything he could have hoped for, one he knew he would carry with him back into the river or even into the afterlife. It eased his very soul.

He left her side long enough to turn down the quilt on her bed and then held out his hand. Finally it was his turn to hold his breath as he waited for Merewen to twine her fingers with his.

Chapter 19

Merewen took that last step, offering Gideon far more than her hand. She was aware her skin lacked the soft smoothness that was the pride of most high-ranking ladies, but Gideon already knew she wasn't typical of her class. He obviously didn't care when he once again kissed her palm.

The tickle of his breath against her skin stoked the heat that had been simmering deep within her ever since he'd stepped across the threshold of her room. He was right. At this moment, the rest of the world had faded into insignificance, her entire focus centered on this one man and what they were about to share.

The desire that shone in his pale eyes gave her the courage she needed to tug on the quilt that Gideon still wore around his waist, letting it drop to the carpet. Her daring move pleased him if the slight smile on his handsome face was any indication. Her own robe pooled on the floor at her feet.

Now there was nothing between them, nothing holding them apart. The pale glow of the candles highlighted Gideon's powerful build and the marks several lifetimes of fighting had left upon it. She wanted to touch him, to taste him, to claim his strength for her own. But where to start? How to begin?

Gideon answered her unspoken questions. "You'll be warmer under the blankets."

She nodded and climbed into the bed that had been

hers alone. Now, for the first time she would share it with a lover. She scooted toward the far side, leaving room for Gideon to join her. He slid in beside her, the bed shifting with his weight as he tugged her into his arms for a long kiss.

He coaxed her into parting her lips, his tongue a velvet sweep across hers, even as his hand traced the curves of her body. His touch felt so good, so perfect, as if she'd awaited it her whole life. When he pressed her more firmly onto her back, she went willingly.

He pushed the covers down below her waist, but their shared warmth was blanket enough. The dark silk of his hair fell down around his shoulders as he smiled at her.

"I've been wanting to do this since first we met."

Before she realized what he was about, he kissed the tip of one breast and then the other before settling his mouth more firmly on the first, working her nipple into a stiff peak with his tongue and lips. Each tug could be felt throughout her body, but most especially in that most private of places at the juncture of her thighs. She ached for more.

Just that quickly, she couldn't remain still, her legs shifting, her hips rocking upward, asking for a touch she had no words for. But Gideon knew. As he continued to nuzzle and suckle her breasts, his hand slowly journeyed down her body. He spread his fingers out on her ribs, lingering there briefly before finally coming to rest on her belly.

Then he rose up once again to look her straight in the eye as his hand inched farther down to brush softly against her nest of curls. She couldn't think and couldn't breathe as he finally cupped her with a gentle squeeze. Gods above, she had never imagined this.

He smiled when she whimpered. Even overwhelmed as she was, it pleased her to make him happy. She suspected he'd had few enough such sweet moments over the centuries. His fingers softly parted her folds, stroking against the dampness gathering there. It was too much: the sensations, the burn, the hunger. She buried her face against his chest.

The stroking slowed but didn't stop. "Are we going too fast?"

She shook her head. "No, it's just so all unexpected, but so good."

"You can touch me, too."

Did he mean . . . ? Yes, he did, because he tugged her hand down to his shaft and taught her how best to please him. It felt like warm velvet sliding over steel. Fascinating. Entrancing. He groaned, his big body jerking in time to her tugging.

Then he intensified the rhythm of his own touches before sliding a finger past the snug entrance to her body, pausing only long enough to let her adjust to the invasion. He withdrew partway, only to thrust in deeper, this time brushing the small, sensitive nub with the pad of his thumb.

A firestorm was brewing, one that had her knees locking together as she tried to fight it off even as she trapped his wicked, wicked hand right where she wanted it most.

"Gideon! Please!"

He kissed her again. "Let it come, sweet one. It's a gift, one I want you to have."

Once again, he sped up his caresses, at the same time turning his attention back to her breasts. One touch of his tongue was all it took. Her body knew what it wanted even if she didn't. She dug her fingers into Gideon's shoulders, trying to pull him atop her, needing his weight to keep her anchored to this world.

He withdrew his hand, instead settling his body in the cradle of hers. He rocked against her, telling her without words what would come next. With the difference in their size, he should have felt heavy; he simply felt right.

She stared up into the silvery glitter of his eyes, his face stark in his efforts to hold back. She didn't want that. She wanted him.

"Take me, Gideon! Now."

"Patience, Merewen. I'm trying not to hurt you."

"You won't."

Then he thrust forward, his shaft, thick and heavy, stretching her until the sensation tiptoed on the near side of pain. At her gasp, he froze briefly and then rocked slowly until her body softened, melted, and offered him welcome. He flexed his hips to settle deep within her.

Their joining was amazing, the connection a miracle of the gods.

His skin was damp, as was hers, easing the slide of their bodies together. He finally pushed up, his thickly corded arms supporting his weight as he began working his hips in powerful strokes, letting them swing harder, faster, deeper. She wrapped her legs around his, seating him more firmly deep within her. Once again the air around them tingled with the feel of a summer storm about to break loose with lightning and thunder.

Her body grew tense, arching high off the bed as he drove them both on and on. Then his entire being went rigid, shuddering in her arms as he growled her name and pounded out his release, throwing Merewen over the edge at the same time. It was if they flew through the night sky before finally coming back to rest in her bed.

Tears trickled down her cheeks. She didn't know why she was crying, but perhaps it was in sheer wonderment at what they'd just shared. Finally, Gideon collapsed, at first lying on top of her, breathing hard and spent. Then he stared down at her with the oddest look on his face as he brushed her tears away.

"Gideon? Is something wrong?"

He rolled to the side, tucking her in next to him. For

several seconds he stared up at the canopy in silence, scaring her. At last he answered.

"No, my heart, nothing could be more right. That was the single most perfect moment in my life."

"Mine, too."

She shivered, but she doubted the blankets he pulled back up into place would do much to ward off the chill. Because while she didn't doubt the truth of his words, she just wished she knew why their most perfect moment had made him look so sad.

A few hours later, Gideon awoke to the rumble of familiar voices in the hallway. Murdoch and Duncan were arguing over which of them should knock on the door. By the sound of things, they'd already quietly searched the keep from cellar to roof looking for him. They'd narrowed his location down to one last possibility, but none of them wanted to be the one to knock on Merewen's door.

It wasn't clear if they were more worried about being wrong or right.

He would have found the whole discussion amusing if he hadn't been concerned for Merewen's reputation. Another speaker joined the discussion, followed by the sound of retreating footsteps. Gideon was already up and reaching for his clothes from the previous night. The smell of smoke and soot immediately wafted up to clog his nose, but the garments were the only ones he had handy at the moment.

As soon as he got rid of Kane, he'd let Merewen know he was leaving. He didn't want her to wake up and find him gone with no word.

Shoving the trunk aside, he winced as it scraped across the stone floor. A quick glance at the bed showed that it hadn't disturbed Merewen. Good.

He opened the door only far enough to squeeze

through. Kane stood across the hall, leaning against the wall with his arms crossed over his chest. He drew a sharp breath, his nostrils flared wide. Gideon suspected the heavy smell of smoke did little to hide the musky scent of sex that clung to his skin.

Kane's expression remained impassive, but he made his opinion of the current situation all too clear as soon as he spoke.

"I won't insult you by asking if you slept on the floor, Captain. However, I will remind you that all of us answered the call to serve the lady's best interests. From the beginning you have been drawn to Lady Merewen, but have you considered the possible consequences?"

Gideon's first inclination was to tell his friend that what had transpired between him and Merewen was none of his concern, but that wasn't true. He'd done nothing but think about all the possible consequences. His dreams had been filled with images of Merewen holding his babe close with such a loving smile on her pretty face.

His heart ached because he wouldn't be there to see it.

The door behind him opened again to reveal the lady herself. If Kane still had any doubts about how she and Gideon had spent the night, the sight of her kiss-swollen lips and faint blush on her cheeks would have dispelled them.

She didn't need to know that their private business was being discussed. "Kane, thank you for the report. I'll join you shortly to decide how best to proceed."

"Thank you, Captain. I'll look forward to it."

Then Kane looked directly toward Merewen, his pale eyes softening. "Just so you know, according to Murdoch and Duncan, Gideon slept in the same room as they did. Since I posted Hob up here to guard the hallway, it is unlikely that any of your people would have been brave enough to venture anywhere near your door."

Merewen's blush deepened, but she offered the gruff warrior a warm smile. "Thank your friends for me, Lord Kane, and thank you. And I've been meaning to tell you that I would love to meet Hob. Perhaps you'll find time to introduce us."

It wasn't often someone managed to surprise Kane, but he was clearly taken aback by Merewen's request. "He's resting in my shield now, but I will make the time, my lady. By the way, he likes sweets."

Then he pushed off the wall and walked away. Gideon waited until he was out of sight, and then a little longer to make sure he was also out of hearing.

"So does Kane—not that he'd admit it." Then Gideon smiled at her and added, "That was well done, Merewen. There aren't many brave enough to approach Hob."

"I would guess he's as scary as his owner is on the outside, but I will not let that deter me. If Hob is anything like Lord Kane, he may even act as if he enjoys scaring those he encounters. However, I suspect that makes for a lonely life."

The woman never stopped surprising Gideon with her insight and wisdom. If his men weren't waiting for him downstairs, he would have been tempted to show her how much he appreciated her kindness.

Not trusting his ability to resist the urge to revisit her bed, he stopped short of the threshold. "I regret that we woke you, but I was getting up anyway and would have wanted you to know where I was going."

"I'll get dressed and join you soon."

"Are you sure? It's still early, and you had a long night."

Her smile was sly. "As did you, I seem to recall."

True enough. Innocent though she'd been, his lady had proved to be an enthusiastic and inventive lover. Despite his relative lack of sleep, bedding her had left him feeling invigorated and ready to face the day ahead of them.

"Yes, well, I should change clothes and then find Kane. We'll either be in the hall below or out studying the fortifications."

Her smile dimmed at the reminder that this was but the calm before the storm. He lifted his hand to her face. "Always remember that the gods sent us to ensure that your people are kept safe."

What would she think if he told her of the goddess's visit or that she'd approved of their coupling? He held his tongue, though. Merewen had suffered enough shocks in the past twenty-four hours. Finding out that the Lady of the River had appeared in her quarters might prove to be too much.

Merewen nuzzled his palm, the gentle touch once again soothing his spirit. Surely he could risk a kiss without losing control.

He leaned close, at first offering a simple brush of his lips before settling them more firmly against her mouth. She turned her face up to his as a flower sought the sun, her hands finding their way around his waist.

It was good—too good. He pulled back before he gave in to the temptation to deepen the kiss or, worse yet, to drag her back into her room and slam the door.

His will was weakening, though, when she refused to let go and held him prisoner with the simple warmth of her smile. He was saved from his wavering resolve when a familiar voice spoke up.

"Captain Gideon! Merewen! What is going on here?"

They both turned to face Lady Alina, who was looking less than pleased. Gideon's first instinct was to step in front of Merewen, blocking her aunt's access. But as usual, Lady Merewen preferred to face things head-on.

She smiled at her aunt. "Why, Alina, I would have thought you would recognize a kiss when you saw one. Please come in while I dress. Gideon, I believe you had business with your men."

He took his dismissal with good grace. But as he walked away, Alina gave him a considering look that warned him she wouldn't let her question go unanswered for long. He'd rather face five men in armed combat than have that particular discussion with the lady, but neither would he act the coward.

He bowed first to Merewen and then to Alina. "Lady Merewen, we will inform you what is needed to protect the keep. Lady Alina, until later."

"I will be looking forward to it, Captain."

He was glad that one of them was. As he walked away, he could feel her gaze boring into his back. It was with some relief that he reached the room where his men had bedded down for the night and could put the stout weight of the door between himself and Merewen's lady aunt.

Chapter 20

Gideon joined his men outside near the gate. All four turned as one to face him, each of the warriors weighing and judging him according to his own beliefs.

Kane had already made his opinion clear. If Gideon's actions hurt Merewen, Kane would defend her as he saw fit. Duncan, ever the scholar, looked curious but with a hint of disapproval. Averel shifted from foot to foot, clearly uncomfortable but unsure how to react.

And then there was Murdoch. The big warrior had always served Gideon without question; yet even he was frowning. Although he understood their concern, Gideon hated being second-guessed.

"Let's walk outside the palisade."

He wanted to get far away from any prying eyes or ears within the keep. While he hoped that all those loyal to Fagan had left with Olaf, he wasn't going to count on that being the case. Not to mention he didn't want Merewen's name to be connected to his other than as the captain of the forces she'd brought in to defend her home.

They walked in silence until they reached a small rise within easy running distance of the gate. He wished it had taken longer, because he didn't know how much to tell them, not to mention that he truly hated having to justify the most meaningful experience of his life.

He stared off into the distance, for the moment seeing the past more clearly than the present.

"I hate this life we lead."

If it could be called living at all. Yes, they walked, talked, ate, and fought. But real life meant so much more. He wished he'd realized that all those centuries ago. If only he'd chosen differently just that one time, but he'd been too young, too foolish.

"It was my mistake that caught us up in this endless service for the gods. I well understand that any decision I make affects all of you."

Kane spoke first. "We've never had cause to question your decisions, Gideon. Not even the one that brought us to this point. Even now, I trust that you are thinking of more than only yourself, but we need to hear the words."

"Merewen makes me forget that I am no longer a mortal man." He looked back toward the keep. "I forget almost everything else when I am around her.

"Almost everything," he repeated with more emphasis. "But not our purpose and not the four of you. Last night I was about to walk away from the lady even though my refusal to enter her room hurt her deeply."

"But you didn't walk away." Kane spoke again, his words blunt but not angry.

"No, not after the Lady of the River spoke to me."

He held up his hand to cut off the torrent of questions and exclamations. "Looking back, it feels like a dream, but I assure you it was real. Our goddess formed out of the bathwater and moved about the room. The gods agree with what we have sensed, that this challenge is about more than simply ridding the keep of Lord Fagan and his men. But also, we are reacting differently than we have in the past. In truth, Merewen means more to me than anyone else I have been ordered to champion."

A brief silence was broken when the dark warrior murmured, "As she does to me."

Kane's admission didn't really surprise Gideon, but it

clearly shocked the others. The warrior's hand brushed the mage mark on his cheek, and he shrugged at their incredulous looks.

"She has courage enough to do one of us proud, and her first concern is always for her charges," Kane said, "whether they have four legs or two."

He stared at the ground. "That first night, she urged Gideon and me to hide while she drew her uncle's attention to her. When was the last time someone tried to protect any of us?"

No one answered. None of them had ever known much in the way of softness in their lives. That a small slip of a woman would offer herself up to pain and injury to protect Gideon and his friends was almost beyond their imagining.

Gideon saw it was time to bring this discussion to an end. "All I am going to say about the events of last night is that the goddess believes our strong connection with Merewen and others within her household is a good thing. The growing darkness means not even the gods can foretell how the future will unfold, but the goddess believes our connection to Merewen and her people has strengthened our chances of success."

He let them mull that over for a few seconds before continuing. "Duncan, how goes your search for answers in the library?"

"Several sources contain veiled hints of a dark magic that can strike at will, although I'm having trouble translating a couple of the older manuscripts. I've been comparing the various texts I've found without much success. I fear it may become necessary to search out a library with a more extensive collection if there is one within a reasonable distance."

Kane frowned. "As I told Gideon, this reminds me of the magic my grandfather studied. Even he warned it was too dangerous to be used by lesser mages. I will read over the passages Duncan has marked to see if anything resonates. I may also be able to translate some of the texts written in the older languages."

The others looked grim; Gideon didn't blame them. Access to dark magic in the wrong hands was a terrifying thought indeed. Right now they needed to address the issues they could control.

"How many men-at-arms do we have?"

Murdoch took over. "Only about ten with any real training. Another few have some rudimentary skills with simple weapons. Averel has organized a training session with them this afternoon to evaluate how best to use them should the need arise."

"Good. I'll leave you to it, then, unless you need me."

His men had all too much practice in patching together a defensive force out of half-trained men and women. That left him free to focus on other things.

"We should begin the process of clearing out what's left of the stable. These people will do better if they have something to occupy their minds other than the threat of Fagan's wrath."

It would take Olaf two to three days of hard riding to reach Fagan. Even if they set out for the keep immediately, it would take them the same amount of time to return. That gave Merewen's people a few days to catch their breath and get organized.

"All of you make sure you take time to rest, especially you, Kane, since you stood guard all night. We need to be at full strength when Fagan and Olaf return. I wish I could say that we'd routed them for good, but I do not believe that is the case. Merewen overheard her uncle telling Olaf that the duke himself has plans for her."

Duncan clenched both fists as he muttered a string of foul curses, a rarity coming from him. "The texts speak of blood sacrifices. Any blood will sustain the magic, but it will flourish with the blood of innocents, especially those who have been blessed by the gods."

Gideon's fury tasted bitter and hot. Merewen was no longer an innocent, but that did not mean she was safe.

Kane's eyes flashed red and hot. "I will look forward to teaching Fagan what happens to a man who bargains for power with his niece's life. For now, I have a few things to do before I ask the cook for something to eat and then seek my bed. Wake me at sunset."

"I will. Now, let's get to it."

Merewen wished she hadn't invited Alina into her room, because she hadn't yet come to terms with what last night meant to her. She had no regrets, but that didn't mean she wanted to talk about it. The memories were too recent, too precious.

Alina gave her only a passing glance on her way out to the balcony. Merewen changed clothes and then drifted outside after her, curious to see what she would have to say.

Finally, Alina spoke, her voice clogged tight with emotion. "This Captain Gideon, he was gentle with you?"

Of course she would want to know that. Merewen hastened to reassure her.

"He and his men are all noble warriors with all that is supposed to mean. Trust that he made last night special for me. I have no regrets."

"Where did they come from?"

How much should Merewen reveal? She settled for a partial truth. "I met them the night Fagan set the dogs after me."

Alina looked poised to say something else, but then she leaned forward to look down at the ground below with sudden interest. Merewen followed her line of sight to see what had captured her aunt's attention; she rarely looked quite so animated.

The only person in sight was Murdoch. She glanced at Alina's face and was puzzled by the expression reflected there. If she wasn't mistaken, her aunt was staring at the big warrior with the same stark desire she'd seen in Murdoch's eyes the previous night.

Interesting.

She thought he was going to pass by without looking up, but then at the last second he did. Alina flinched and stepped back. Murdoch's face, most often so stern, softened briefly and then resumed its usual impassive expression. He slowly looked around, most likely to ascertain if anyone else besides Alina and Merewen had been watching him.

He started forward again, only to stop abruptly. What was he looking at? Then she saw it. A mountain cat, a huge one, was poised at the top of the palisade.

"Alina, come watch."

Her aunt reluctantly joined her at the railing again. "What?"

She pointed toward Murdoch and then up toward the cat, which looked ready to jump down to the ground. Before Merewen could explain about the warriors and their avatars, the cat pounced.

Alina gasped, then screamed, "Murdoch, watch out!"

Murdoch whirled around to see where the attack was coming from and stepped right into the mountain cat's path. The impact sent both the warrior and his avatar tumbling to the ground in a tangle of fur and man. Shadow came out on top and took a swipe at Murdoch's face with her tongue, despite the big man's efforts to ward off the assault.

It took some effort for him to dislodge the determined feline, but he managed to roll Shadow off his chest and sit up. Despite the thoroughly disgusted look on Murdoch's face, he gave the cat a thorough scratching. As he did so, he glanced up at the balcony where the two women stood, watching in complete fascination. Then he murmured something to the cat.

Alina leaned forward, her eyes wide with wonder. "Is he truly talking to that beast?"

Merewen nodded, not sure how to answer. She settled for the truth. Alina would soon meet the other warriors as well as the avatars. "I found a text in Father's library that spoke of warriors who could be called upon to champion a cause if the gods felt it was just. That was what I was doing the night Fagan set the dogs upon my trail. Captain Gideon and his men are the warriors who serve the Lord and Lady of the River."

She paused to see how Alina reacted. Her aunt stared down at Murdoch again and then slowly nodded. "That is why your captain and Sir Murdoch have the same unusual eye color."

Merewen nodded. "All five of them do. It's a mark of their gods. Each of them is also linked to an animal, much as I am to the horses. That mountain cat is Sir Murdoch's avatar."

Before she could continue, Murdoch stood up and dusted off his clothing. He stared up at the two of them for several seconds as his cat sat quietly at his feet. She yawned, her mouth opening wide and showing her fangs to great advantage.

"Would you like to meet her?" he called up to them.

As soon as he spoke, he looked as if he regretted the offer, but it was too late.

Alina beamed in pleasure. "We would love to, wouldn't we, Merewen?"

"We'll be right down, Sir Murdoch."

Maybe he shouldn't have invited the two women down to meet Shadow, but it was too late for second guesses. He tried telling himself it was for their own good. When the next battle came, the avatars would be part of the defensive forces—an important part. There had been instances in the past where it had been one of the animals that had actually been given the assignment of guarding their petitioner.

It would be far better for the women to get used to them now rather than at the last minute. He just wished he knew whether it was the women or himself he wanted to convince of that fact.

"They're coming, Shadow. We'll both need to be on our best behavior."

The cat flashed one of her toothy smiles. Most people ran for cover when a shadow cat looked at them that way, and for good reason. Two pairs of footsteps approached, stopping some distance away. How sensible of the two women to do so. Startling a mountain cat was never wise.

He pitched his voice just far enough for them to hear, keeping it low and soothing. "You can come forward one at a time."

Although Merewen was the more adventurous of the two, it was Alina who appeared at his side. That pleased him far more than it should have.

"Lady Alina, this is Shadow."

"May I pet her?"

The big cat answered the question by prowling over to where Alina stood and brushing against her legs in much the same way a house cat would have. At first, Alina looked startled by the cat's unexpected action, but then she smiled.

It was the first time he'd ever seen the lady look truly happy. His heart twisted in his chest as he memorized her sweet beauty, knowing that image would live on in his dreams in the years to come. With a happy sigh, Alina dropped to her knees to pet the cat, totally oblivious to the dust and dirt getting on her gown. Shadow, for her part, was only too happy to soak up all the attention Alina was willing to give her.

He stood there like a stone wall, watching the two females enjoy themselves and wishing he could join in the
fun but not knowing how. Then there was the issue of Lady
Merewen looking on. As observant as she was, it was likely
that she'd noticed him staring across the hall at Alina last
night as Gideon had escorted the lady up the stairs.

He started to invite Merewen to approach, only to
find she was gone. Where had she disappeared to? He
very much feared that she'd felt as if she were intruding
on a moment meant for two. Well, three, counting the cat.
He wanted to curse Merewen's discretion but couldn't
find it in himself. What harm could enjoying these few
minutes in Alina's company do?

His conscience answered the question for him: plenty.
The lady already had endured the pitying whispers of
the people who should have protected her from that bastard Fagan. Murdoch would not give them cause for further gossip. He had to walk away.

"She's beautiful, Murdoch. How did you come to be
friends?"

Alina's soft voice pounded on his good intentions
with all the power of a smith's hammer, leaving them
shattered in pieces on the ground. Perhaps it would better if the two of them walked rather than continuing to
lurk in this deserted part of the bailey.

His decision made, he said, "If you would care to stroll
the garden with me, I'll tell you the story."

"I would enjoy that."

He offered her his arm, ignoring the surge of awareness that flooded his senses when her fingers fluttered
down to rest on his sleeve. He risked patting her hand,
settling it more firmly on his arm.

Could she feel his pulse pounding through the layers of
cloth between her fingertips and his skin? He hoped not.
It was bad enough that he could barely think through the
onslaught of attraction and desire he fought.

"Well?"

Well, what? Oh, yes, how he met Shadow. "When I first encountered Shadow, she'd been wounded."

Once he got started, the story rolled off his tongue. Even avoiding any mention of his real age or his service to the gods, he was able to keep her entertained. Shadow trailed after them for a while, but she quickly lost interest in the meandering path he was taking around the keep. She deliberately bumped into him, letting him know she had better things to do. Before disappearing, she also did another pass to rub against Lady Alina. Evidently the lady had won the cat's approval.

That both pleased and saddened him. In a more perfect world, one in which he was free to do as he chose, it would make him happy to know that the two females who mattered to him actually liked each other. But this world was far from perfect: Murdoch's life wasn't his to live as he saw fit, and Alina yet belonged to another man.

At least he could do something about that last part. Even if Fagan hadn't been targeted by the gods for their own reasons, he would have found a way to free Alina from the man's tyranny. If that cost him when he stood beside Gideon and the others at judgment time, so be it. For Alina's sake, he'd accept whatever fate the gods meted out.

Merewen watched Alina and Murdoch from the shelter of the doorway. Clearly her presence wasn't needed or even really wanted. They were adults and in no need of a chaperone. Evidently the big warrior had a talent for making her aunt smile. As uncertain as the future was right now, she wouldn't deny them the comfort of each other's company.

What should she be doing now? If any of the horses were in great distress, she would have sensed it. However, last night Jarod had mentioned they'd need more

of the burn salve. Her first stop would have to be her
workshop to make more. As she rounded the corner, she
found the bailey bustling as the men tore down the stable. It was her first view of the damage in the daylight.

Her feet wouldn't move. The devastation was heart-
breaking. Her father had overseen the construction of
the stable, doubling its original size, when she'd been a
young girl. Seeing it broken and burned struck her with
a crippling pain, as if she were losing her father all over
again.

"Don't see it as it was, my lady. See it as it will be
again."

Kane's deep voice from over her shoulder startled
her, but his words comforted her, soothing some of the
anger and sorrow. "My father designed that building."

"He did a fine job. We'll see it restored in a way that
will honor his memory."

The warrior's thoughtfulness surprised her. She turned
to face him with a smile. "Thank you, Kane. You are most
kind."

Her words clearly shocked him. "I'm not sure I've
ever been accused of that before."

She bit back a smile. "Well, we can keep it our little
secret. Now, I should start working. I need to replenish
some of my medicines."

Kane walked with her as far as the workshop. "I'm off
to get some rest, but send for me if you need anything."

"Thank you for the offer, but I should be fine."

She spotted Jarod hovering nearby, clearly waiting for
her.

"Looks as though I have my first customer of the day.
Sleep well, Lord Kane."

He bowed and walked away.

Chapter 21

A ripple of whispers drew Fagan's attention to the front of the hall. A familiar figure briefly paused at the entry but then started right for him. His throat tightened, knowing Olaf's unexpected arrival would not be to deliver good tidings.

"My lord."

Fagan stared at Olaf with disgust. It was bad enough the man had followed him to court, but at least he could have bathed before approaching him. Right now, the fool reeked of trail dust, horse sweat, and something akin to fear.

That last element was interesting, the source of the fear even more so. It pleased Fagan to let his captain suffer in worried suspense for a few seconds more. He poured himself another taste of the duke's best wine and savored the rich flavor before finally acknowledging Olaf.

"Speak. What has happened that is so drastic you would abandon your post?"

The warrior looked up with his eyes wild and sweat beaded on his skin. His face looked as if it had been raked by claws. What had happened to him? Now Fagan was at least mildly concerned. Olaf was many things, but a coward was not one of them.

"I said speak, Olaf. Don't leave me standing here playing guessing games. I'm expecting the duke to summon me anon. Rest assured it does not pay to keep him waiting. Any displeasure he expresses with my tardiness will spoil more than just my day."

Olaf jerked his head in a nod. "I regret to inform you that the keep was attacked, my lord. Those last two men you hired and that scholar who paid to use the library turned on us, as has Lady Merewen. She has been plotting against you and brought in a band of mercenaries to drive us from the keep."

Fagan forced himself to set the wine back down on the table rather than give in to the temptation to heave it against the nearest wall or, better still, at Olaf. Calm. He must remain calm. Here in the citadel, Keirthan had spies everywhere. Even something as simple as a broken crystal goblet would reveal far too much to those watching eyes.

He forced a smile, telling Olaf with his eyes to do the same. "It is a pleasant day. Let us walk outside."

"But—"

"I said outside, Olaf. I find that I'm in need of some fresh air."

Fagan quickened his steps, hoping to reach the door that opened out into a spacious garden before Olaf once again lost control of his tongue. As they stepped out into the overbright sunshine, he veered off to the left, aiming for a bench that would make it difficult for anyone to get within listening distance without being seen.

It didn't take long. He let out a slow breath, hoping to ease the tightening coil of anger in his chest. Or maybe it was fear. He watched the flitter of birds in a nearby tree that was covered in blossoms the color of fresh blood. He shuddered at the image before he could stop himself.

He turned his attention in a safe direction, the citadel itself with its plain gray stone walls. He would not let himself think on what those walls hid, especially in the labyrinth that snaked its way under the entire building.

"Compose yourself; then tell me everything. No lies. No excuses. I have neither the time nor the desire to wade through them to get at the truth. It will go better for you to admit your own mistakes as well. I have no patience with fools."

Olaf leaned forward, elbows on his knees, and stared at the ground. He looked to be hovering at the edge of exhaustion, but Fagan took no pity on him. He needed to know what had happened more than Olaf needed a bath and a bed. Lives depended on it, including Fagan's own.

"After you left, I warned Lady Merewen she was to remain in the keep and not to go wandering off by herself."

Olaf looked up briefly. "She defied me and disappeared for most of the day. When she returned, I ordered her to return to her room to await suitable punishment."

Fagan didn't call him on the lies. It would do no good; besides, he'd been unable to control her himself. If she weren't a constant source of frustration, he might even have admired her determination to thwart him at every turn.

"My niece is as she is, Olaf. I know that. Now continue."

It was if he'd lanced a boil, and all the infection poured out into the fragrant air of the garden. Olaf took him at his word and did nothing to color his description of his own role in the tragedy that had played out three nights ago.

"So let me summarize." Fagan held up his hand and counted off the significant points. "My keep has been taken over by an unknown number of men-at-arms, all sworn to serve my niece. We have no knowledge of where they came from, but you are convinced they overpowered you with magic."

He stared at the deep gouges on Olaf's face. "Oh, yes,

you were attacked by a bird while you were in my niece's bed, the one place I gave you specific orders to stay away from until we ascertain what purpose the duke has for her. Is that everything? Because, I have to say, Olaf, I'm surprised you managed to escape with your life."

His captain flinched when Fagan clenched his hand into a fist. "Care to tell me how you and a handful of my men managed to survive against these overpowering forces?"

Olaf's grimace made it clear that Fagan wasn't going to like the answer. "There were too few of us to stand against their superior numbers, so I set fire to the stables. In the confusion, we escaped through the front gate. It was the only way we could survive to bring you the news. With your permission, I will return to reclaim your home, but I will need to hire more men."

Fagan couldn't believe the man's idiocy. "You ordered the stables burned?"

It wasn't really a question, but Fagan was having a difficult time imagining such stupidity. "You do know that my family holds those lands only as long as the horses are content with their treatment. If they should decide we are too weak to protect them, they will leave. When that happens, you will no longer have a job, and I will no longer have a home, much less access to the family wealth."

"Yes, sir, I understand, but it was that or remain there to die. I felt it was necessary to ensure that at least a few of us survived to warn you of your niece's treachery. If you had returned to the keep without our warning, you would have been riding into an ambush."

True. There was that. Fine. For the moment he would let the fool live. Judging from the ripe condition of the man's clothing, he'd run from the keep with nothing but what he was wearing at the time. That was something else Fagan would have to deal with. He reached for his purse and dumped out a fair number of coins.

"Take this and find rooms for you and the men in one

of the local inns. Once you're settled, send word where you'll be. I'll let you know what my course of action will be once I've had a chance to consider all the implications."

Olaf recognized a dismissal when he heard one. He pocketed the money and rose to his feet. "Thank you, my lord. I will await your orders. I hope you will allow me to fight at your side when you are ready to retake your family home."

Then he bowed and walked away.

Undoubtedly Olaf would be part of the effort to regain control of the keep, but it was almost guaranteed he wouldn't survive the fight. If necessary, Fagan would see to it personally.

He noticed a servant hovering on the far edge of the garden, waiting to be noticed. How long had he been there? How much had he heard? It was too late to worry about it.

Fagan waved him forward and held out his hand for the paper the man held clutched in his fingers. His tension warned Fagan who had sent the note. Only Duke Keirthan inspired such fear with a simple summons.

"Thank you. You may go."

The servant bowed his head but remained rooted right where he stood. "I'm sorry, sir, but the duke made it clear that I was to escort you to his chambers."

Fagan knew where those chambers were—both of them. The duke used the one off the great hall to greet visitors, to hold court, and to render judgments. Decorated in gilt and gold, it was his public face.

It was the possibility of being summoned to the second chamber that had Fagan's knees threatening to buckle. Located one floor below the great hall, it was very near the heart of the labyrinth where the duke practiced . . . whatever dark arts he wielded.

To date, Fagan had only heard rumors. People whispered of muted screams and echoes of thunder beneath their feet, not to mention the frequent disappearances of both people and animals. As much as Fagan wanted to believe it was all rubbish, there was something different about the duke, something off, that gave all those whispers the weight of truth.

He very much feared he was about to learn the real nature of what kept the duke occupied down below for hours and sometimes days at a time. The man servant cleared his throat, a reminder that Fagan had been dithering too long. It wouldn't do to keep the duke waiting.

"Lead the way. My life is the duke's to command."

As was his death, but he tried very hard not to think about that. Trying his best to look unconcerned, he followed his guide back inside the citadel and down the winding staircase to the chambers below.

The Damned were more at home serving in the deepest shadows and darkest places. But here in the keep, all five warriors had joined the work parties, throwing their superior strength into tearing out the last of the charred and broken timbers in the stable.

Their efforts had gone a long way toward convincing Merewen's people that the warriors were on their side and not to be feared. Over the past few days, considerable progress had been made. By nightfall, they'd have the stable stripped down to bare bones. The rebuilding would begin in the morning, which should please Merewen.

On the first day after the fire, she had introduced Gideon to the carpenter, who would oversee the repairs. After discussing what would be needed for the stable, Gideon had waved Kane over to join the conversation. He'd had made a list of suggestions meant to increase the security offered by the palisade. At first, the carpenter had been understandably nervous to be in such close proximity to the mage-marked warrior.

But once he realized that Kane not only respected his skills and knowledge but also had considerable experience with carpentry himself, the man had calmed down and made a few suggestions of his own. Gideon had walked away, leaving them to it. Over the past three days, the two had become inseparable, working side by side as they reinforced the palisade that surrounded the keep.

They were almost finished with the modifications, which was a good thing. Merewen's uncle and his men could appear on the horizon at any time now. Gideon was under no illusions that Fagan would withdraw his interest in the family estate and leave his niece alone.

No, a fight was coming. He felt it in his bones.

It was the not knowing when that battle would begin that had Gideon prowling the bailey and looking for a way to burn off some of his restlessness. Maybe some weapons practice would help. He drew his sword and yelled for the guards to join him. They could all use the training, because he very much feared they would be putting it to good use all too soon.

Chapter 22

"Fagan."

The duke's voice echoed through the dark, dank passageway. It sounded raspy. Cold. Inhuman, even, but Fagan quickly squashed that thought. Approaching the duke's private domain was daunting enough without Fagan's own imagination escalating his fear. Control was important when clear thinking might mean the difference between life and death.

"Yes, my lord. I came just as you requested."

Actually "ordered" was a better description, but again Fagan settled on the cautious side of discretion. He kept walking forward. How much farther would he have to go to actually find where Keirthan was lurking in this endless tunnel? Finally, it widened out, and the light at the far end was brighter. Fagan instinctively hurried his steps even though in truth he wasn't all that eager to find the man.

All too soon he reached the point where the passage gave way to an enormous room. The ceiling vaulted high overhead, giving the impression of immense space. Torches illuminated all but the uppermost reaches of the room, their pale, flickering light barely holding back the shadows. A circular fire pit burned hot in the center of the oval-shaped room, making the temperature uncomfortably warm despite being so far underground. Some believed the afterworld for those who transgressed in this one was desolate and cold. This room, with its shades of darkness and sweltering heat, rang more true to Fagan's own beliefs.

He hated it on sight.

The duke stood behind the stone altar located in the center of the dais at the far end of the room. The altar was empty and devoid of any decoration except for the sturdy posts located at each corner. The heavy shackles that dangled from them sent a spark of fear shooting straight up Fagan's spine.

He kept moving, each step demanding more and more effort. He slowed to a stop just short of the stairs that led toward the ornately carved throne located to the right of the altar.

Keirthan finally wiped his hands on a cloth and set aside the knife he'd been polishing. "Ah, Lord Fagan, I see you have found your way to the true seat of my power, a visit that is long overdue."

Keirthan's welcoming smile was broad but not at all warm. "Don't be afraid. Come closer."

Fagan sketched a small bow before daring to tread on the first step up toward the altar. Keeping his eyes averted from both the knife and the dangling chains, he asked, "How may I be of service, my lord?"

The duke made himself comfortable on the throne. He made no offer to allow Fagan the same courtesy despite there being a small bench near where he was seated. Keirthan leaned forward to look down at him.

"My dear friend, I regret to say that just this morning I have heard some most disturbing news."

The way the duke's eyes glittered, reflecting the dancing flame of a nearby torch, had Fagan's stones drawing up tight in fear.

"News, Sire?"

"Your keep has come under attack in your absence." Keirthan shook his head in feigned sympathy. "I regret that circumstances requiring your presence here at court have left your home vulnerable."

Fagan kept his eyes focused on a spot to the right of the duke's shoulder, not wanting to make eye contact. He always had the uncanny feeling that Keirthan could see straight through to a man's soul. The last thing Fagan wanted was for the duke to go rummaging around in his.

Hoping his expression showed the right amount of concern and regret, Fagan acknowledged the truth of what the duke had heard. "I just learned of the attack myself, Sire. The captain of my personal guard rode night and day to bring me the news. I had just sent him off to rest and recuperate from his travels when I received your summons."

All of which made him wonder how the duke had found out before Fagan had. Did he have spies among the men who served the keep? Fagan thought it likely. After all, it was what he'd do if their roles were reversed.

"And your niece? What of her? Was your man able to tell you anything about her situation?"

Fagan had yet to come to terms with her treachery. He figured Olaf had exaggerated the strength of the attacking force to make himself look less the coward for surrendering the keep so quickly. Even so, where had Merewen managed to find allies willing to fight on her behalf? What had she promised them? She had nothing of value to offer except the horses—or herself.

He cut off that line of thought. If she was trading her wares for protection, the last person he wanted to learn of it was sitting right in front of him. If the truth wouldn't work, he settled for a believable lie.

"She was taken prisoner as was my own lady wife, my lord. With your permission, I will return to my keep to dislodge the usurpers as soon as my men have rested."

His fingers steepled, the duke stared down at him. The chill of his gaze left Fagan convinced his actions were being weighed and judged—and somehow he'd failed to meet the duke's expectations.

Fagan's late brother used to have the same expression on his face as he culled the herds of stallions that lacked the characteristics he wanted to breed into the next generation. A quick flick of the knife and they were gelded, all their fire and fierce nature gone. He shivered at the memory.

The duke was talking again.

"I made myself clear to you, Lord Fagan. Your favor with me depends entirely on your niece's remaining untouched until I have need of her services. As your sovereign, I claimed her as my own to use as I see fit."

Please, gods above, save him from this. A better man might worry about what Keirthan had in mind for Merewen, but right now she wasn't the one standing before the duke in his private arena.

Fagan dropped to one knee. "Since you first expressed your interest in my niece, Sire, I have refused any and all possible suitors. Before I journeyed here, I ordered my captain to restrict her movements to limit contact with anyone from outside of my own holdings. When I left home to answer your summons, Lady Merewen remained chaste. This I swear to be true."

Keirthan looked far from pleased. "I believe your intentions were good, Fagan. It's your execution of those intentions that gives me cause for concern."

Without warning, he rose to his feet and reached for the knife he'd laid upon the altar. Fagan flinched, despising himself for showing fear. He and Keirthan had much in common, including taking pleasure in watching a subordinate squirm. The difference was that Keirthan wielded a magic strong enough to burn Fagan to a crisp right where he knelt. Running would do him no good.

All he could do was remain frozen in place and pray that the duke would show mercy. A laughable idea, once he thought about it, or it would have been if he weren't the butt of the joke.

Keirthan caressed the blade of the knife with his fingers, his eyes glittering with an unholy fire. When he tested the point with a fingertip, the blade drew blood and drank it down greedily, leaving a small red streak in the metal.

Keirthan wandered closer, making his approach seem aimless when it was anything but random. When he smiled, Fagan almost pissed his pants.

"Your hand, please, Lord Fagan."

The duke held out his own, palm up, and waited for him to comply. What choice did Fagan have? None. He wiped his hand dry on his tunic before offering it up.

"We both understand that men of power must make sacrifices, don't we, Fagan?"

"Yes, my lord." He hated the quiver in his voice. It made him appear weak and only fed Keirthan's twisted pleasure.

"Listen well, then, Fagan. You will leave on the morrow with your men and a troop of my personal guard. With their help, you will regain control of your family's estate. The price for my aid in this matter is your niece and your wife to use as I see fit. Are the terms acceptable?"

"Yes, Sire. You are most generous."

"Good. I am pleased that we understand each other. However, there a couple of small details. First, you will swear to me in blood that you will succeed or die trying."

"Yes, Sire, I so swear."

"And if your niece is no longer a virgin, you will personally join her in the ceremony to bring forth my full power from the darkness."

The taste of such bitter fear was unfamiliar to Fagan. Normally, he was the one in a position of power, watching others squirm. Not this time. He fought to control the shaking in his hands and somehow found the strength to simply nod.

Keirthan shouted to the ceiling, "Let it be so sworn!"

Then in a flash of silver, he brought the knife slashing downward to lay Fagan's palm open to the bone. He screamed in pain as the blood spurted from the deep wound. The knife drank his blood before any could spill down onto the floor. The blade slowly changed from mirror bright to a dark crimson that pulsed in time to Fagan's heartbeat.

As Fagan's head grew dizzy from blood loss, Keirthan murmured words in a language that grated on the ear. He couldn't discern their dark meaning, but the wound on his palm slowly sealed shut until all that was left was a pale scar.

It did nothing to lessen his pain.

Keirthan helped Fagan to rise to his feet. "Go now, my friend. Rest and regain your strength. Tomorrow you will ride as if your life depended on it."

He smiled again, showing far too many teeth. "As indeed it does."

Clutching his aching hand to his chest, Fagan forced himself to walk with dignity as he crossed the room. The fire glowed brightly in the pit but no longer had the power to warm him, not when the chill of his fear went bone deep. He had to get out there, back to where he could breathe and collect himself.

And as Fagan made his way to the distant door, the duke's laughter chased after him. As he hurried back down the tunnel, the shadows seemed to whisper that there was no place to run where Keirthan couldn't follow.

Chapter 23

"**M**urdoch! Fetch Gideon. Kane, too."

Having issued his demands from the top of the stairs, Duncan disappeared back in the direction of the library. Averel gave Murdoch a puzzled look, but he just shrugged.

"Obviously the damned fool thinks we're his messenger boys." Murdoch smiled and tested the blade of his favorite knife for sharpness. "Ordinarily, I would show our friend Duncan what I think about that idea, but I'm guessing he's finally found something of use in all those dusty manuscripts and scrolls."

He finished the last of his wine and stood up. "You find the captain. He's usually doing weapons training with the guards about now. I'll hunt down Kane."

Averel whistled for his dogs and headed outside. They raced across the hall, tripping over each other to be the first out the door. Shadow, on the other hand, took her time standing up. She stretched, leaning back on her haunches.

Murdoch gave up waiting for the cat to get moving. She'd follow if she was so inclined. He headed toward the carpenter's workshop, figuring that was where he'd find Kane.

Sure enough, he could hear the deep rumble of his voice. When he was a short distance from the door, he called out, "Kane, Duncan has summoned us to the library."

His friend peeked out the door. "Tell him I'll be along presently. We're almost finished."

"You tell him. He wants us now."

Kane frowned. "Has he found something?"

"He didn't say, but he wouldn't call us without reason."

"I'll be right out." Kane ducked back inside.

Murdoch decided to wait. There was still no sign of Shadow. That cat was nothing but lazy unless there was a meal to be had or a fight to be fought.

As he waited, he tried to keep his eyes on the bailey, studying the changes Kane had wrought in the defenses in the short time since they'd driven Fagan's men away. Impressive, but then Kane had a real talent for strategy. The improvements would provide the maximum protection for the defenders and make it that much harder for anyone to breach the walls.

But admiring his friend's work wasn't enough to hold Murdoch's attention for long. All too quickly, he gave in to the urge to stare up at Lady Alina's window, hoping to catch a glimpse of her. His conscience bothered him fiercely because of this fixation. This driving need to see her, to talk to her, to touch her, continued to grow in strength. May the gods forgive him, but he couldn't help himself.

As he'd half hoped, Alina was up there looking back down at him. He straightened and leaned forward. Was he seeing what he thought he was? That damned animal! Shadow sat at Alina's feet, no doubt giving him one of her smug looks that he hated. How absurd was it to be jealous of his avatar? Something else he couldn't help.

"Your cat seems quite taken with Lady Alina."

Murdoch jumped and spun around, drawing his dirk. When he realized it was Kane, he blew out a breath and shoved the knife back in its sheath.

"Damn it, man, don't sneak up on me like that. You're lucky I didn't skewer you."

"I wasn't trying to be quiet, but you were too busy staring up at"—he paused to glance back toward Alina's balcony—"your, um, cat to notice me."

His friend was right. He'd been too entranced by Alina's gentle beauty to notice his surroundings. If Kane had been the enemy, Murdoch would have been dead, maybe for good this time. He had to stop this.

"I was just wondering why Shadow was up there. She normally has little use for people other than me."

He didn't add that he envied the cat for being with Alina, for being touched by Alina, and for being able to wander into the lady's bedroom at will.

Kane stared at the skeleton of the stable. "We've said before that this is all far different than our previous callings. It's not like Gideon to . . ."

He stopped again as if to pick and choose his words carefully. They all knew what was going on between their leader and Merewen, but none of them knew quite what to think about it. Murdoch figured he wasn't the only one who was worried about what effect Gideon's actions would have on them all when judgment time came around.

They'd all know soon enough. The summer solstice grew closer every day.

Finally, Kane went on. "It's not like Gideon to get so involved. In the past, we've always held ourselves aloof from the people we were called to protect. To varying degrees, none of us have remained detached this time, and I'm not sure why. Mayhap because Lady Merewen herself is not typical."

He frowned. "She asked to meet Hob."

That was almost unbelievable. "In truth? I've known Hob for centuries; yet that beast still snaps at me if I get too close."

Kane's chuckle sounded rusty. "Don't take it personally, Murdoch. He treats everyone but me that way."

So much to assimilate, but right now it was better to concentrate on his real purpose for being there. "We should go see what Duncan's found."

"Let's hope he has made some progress."

The grim note in Kane's voice hadn't been there only seconds before. Nothing ever frightened the dark warrior, but right now he was staring at the keep gate as if he saw some horror that Murdoch could not discern.

"What is it that you sense out there?"

Rather than answer Murdoch's question directly, Kane simply said, "As I said, pray Duncan has answers."

Averel and the captain stood waiting outside the library door when Murdoch arrived. Gideon shifted restlessly. "Duncan said to wait out here while he went down to the kitchen to persuade the cook to send up a tray for us. Seems he expects this to take a while."

Although some food and drink did appeal, Murdoch complained anyway. "And did he mention why we couldn't just go in and sit down?"

Gideon shrugged. "Perhaps he doesn't trust us around all the books and manuscripts he's been riffling through since we got here."

That much was probably true. Duncan took such things seriously. Personally, Murdoch had never understood the appeal of spending hours upon hours shut up inside with piles of dusty books and papers. Duncan, though, would have cheerfully given up his sword in exchange for a pen and parchment. If he hadn't chosen to follow Gideon, the man would have spent his last breath in this world with his nose in a book.

They'd all sacrificed much to stand with their captain, but sometimes Murdoch suspected Duncan had paid the highest price. Not that he ever complained. In one way or another, Gideon had saved each of them, infusing them with a sense of worth and offering his unswerving loyalty. They all owed him, but they'd followed him out of friendship, not duty.

Footsteps on the stairs announced the scholar's return. And from the curses he was muttering, Duncan wasn't alone. Sure enough, both of Averel's dogs, Shadow, and even Hob came barreling around the corner, heading straight for the library.

If there was one word all of the avatars understood, it was food. Duncan was definitely not happy about their joining the party. He stopped short of the library and glared at the animals and then at their masters.

"Can't you control these monsters? They cannot be allowed in the library."

Usually Murdoch would have enjoyed seeing the normally fastidious Duncan looking ragged around the edges. However, now wasn't the time for it.

"Shadow, make yourself scarce."

The big cat promptly plopped herself down at his side and began licking her paws while Hob wove in and out between his master and Gideon. Meanwhile, the dogs both whined and tried to sniff both the gargoyle and the cat; neither appreciated their efforts.

"Perhaps they would enjoy visiting me."

Murdoch's heart did a slow roll in his chest as they all turned to face Lady Alina. Shadow was already on her way to the lady's side. The dogs stumbled over each other, trying to be the first to get petted. Hob tasted the air in her direction before making his approach. It seemed that yet another member of the household had the power to charm the avatars.

Duncan bowed slightly. "If you're sure, my lady."

Murdoch clenched his fists. Alina was not Duncan's lady, even though Duncan had used the expression solely out of courtesy. In truth, she wasn't Murdoch's, either, which was what had him gritting his teeth.

"I would love company." She smiled down at her four-legged suitors. "Shall we, everyone?"

As she swept away, the four animals followed in her footsteps, all behaving amazingly well. Murdoch forced himself to look away, only to realize that, except for Gideon, his friends all stared after her with a certain amount of heat in their eyes. While he might be willing to share the lady with Shadow, he had no desire at all to do the same with these fools.

He moved to stand between them and Alina's small parade toward her quarters. "Duncan, you made this sound urgent."

Inside the library, Gideon shut the door and grabbed an apple off the tray Duncan had brought with him. He dropped down on a bench along the wall.

"Duncan, start by explaining to everyone what you've found."

The scholarly warrior took a long drink of water before he began. "I've concentrated my search on the oldest books and manuscripts in Merewen's father's collection. Kane translated a couple written in languages that pre-date any I was familiar with."

He stared down at the sheath of papers covered with his precise writing. "I've tried to make connections that made sense from bits and pieces and vague hints."

Averel leaned forward, rubbing the back of his neck as if it ached. "But you've found the answer, right? You know what's out there?"

"Not for certain." He shuffled through his notes until he found the one he was looking for. "Kane remembers his grandfather speaking of a magic too dangerous to be invoked by any but the strongest of mages. Even then, it would be used only for ill purpose."

The other warrior joined in. "The gift for working with magic ran deep and true in my grandfather's lineage, making them among the strongest of mages. He spoke of a power that, once set loose, would be impossible to contain."

Kane pointed at the mage mark on his left cheek. "He should know. He found a grimoire that contained the spell. The old bastard offered up his daughter—his pregnant daughter—as a sacrifice. The spell failed, but it almost killed my mother and left its mark on me. The danger of trying to wield such magic is that it will consume the one foolish enough to summon it and then move on."

Suddenly his apple had no flavor. Gideon set it aside. "So, are you saying the gods have pitted us against a force so powerful that we have no chance against it?"

Duncan stood and began to pace. "No. At least not yet. Until this darkness reaches its full strength, there's hope. If it's denied access to innocent blood, there's hope. Tainted blood sustains it but doesn't offer it new strength.

"According to the oldest texts here, just as night balances day and winter balances spring, the right kind of magic can counter the evil. However, there is nothing in these books that tells me what the right kind might be."

He ended by saying, "As I said before, it would help if I had access to a library with a more extensive collection of the old myths and histories."

Gideon had always been uncomfortable with anything to do with magic. Give him a good sword and a clear enemy, not whispers of darkness and power. Then he thought of Merewen and the sweet feel of her connection to the horses, a reminder that not all magic was tainted with evil.

All five men lapsed into silence, watching the soft shadows cast by the candles dancing on the walls. Finally,

Duncan crossed the crowded room to stand by the map he'd nailed to the wall. He pointed at a spot in the north of Agathia.

"This city bears the same name as the realm—Agathia. It's where Duke Keirthan has his court. It is doubtful I could gain access to his personal library, and I'm guessing he would have already confiscated any books of value from private collections within the city walls. Assuming he's the one behind the growing darkness, he'd want to keep the information for himself for a variety of reasons, including preventing someone from countering his efforts."

Then he put his finger on another spot located due east of the keep and some distance from the capital. "Merewen's father made mention in his journal of an abbey located somewhere near this area. Yesterday I spoke to Lady Merewen about it."

He sat back down. "All she knew was that her father had spent time at the abbey several years ago."

Gideon thought back to their previous callings, something niggling at the back of his mind. "Did she know anything about the order that runs the convent? I seem to remember one in that area that offered shelter to travelers, but that was centuries ago."

Duncan shook his head. "No, and her father didn't say much on the subject. His notes indicate only that it was located east of here and that the abbess allowed him time in the collection, but only under strict supervision. I sensed that he'd felt insulted even though she told him many of the books were exceedingly rare. She also wouldn't let him into certain areas of the library at all. He suspected they were hiding books that the previous duke had ordered destroyed."

Gideon had been pacing restlessly. "Duncan, I see no choice but for you to visit this library yourself. Do you want Averel or Murdoch to ride with you?"

Duncan didn't hesitate. "No, if the abbess is already cautious about those she lets in, she's bound to be more suspicious if we show up heavily armed and wanting access to any dark magic grimoires. Much better if I arrive looking a bit shabby and offering to earn my keep if I can study there."

Gideon didn't like his men riding off by themselves, but he saw no way around it. "Can you be ready to leave in the morning?"

Duncan was already gathering up his papers. "Yes. I'll need food for several days' travel, some clothing more appropriate for a scholar, and a mount suitable for a poor wanderer such as I."

He grinned at Gideon. "Will Lady Merewen be insulted if I request a lesser horse?"

"Probably, but ask her anyway." Then Gideon frowned. "Speaking of the lady, I thought you were going to invite her to join us."

Duncan looked up from the notes he was making. "I did. When I was down in the hall, I told one of the servants to remind her."

A sick feeling settled in Gideon's chest. "When was the last time any of you saw Merewen?"

Kane answered first. "Not since early this morning, but I've been with the carpenter all day."

Murdoch was already shaking his head. "I haven't seen her at all. I was on duty until almost sunrise, so I slept most of the morning. Averel, too."

Gideon yanked open the door and took off running with his men right behind him. He first checked the pasture to see if Merewen was working with the horses, but he didn't see her anywhere. She wasn't in her workshop, nor was she in the kitchen helping the cook.

Perhaps he'd missed seeing her go upstairs to visit with her aunt. Before he reached the stairs, though, he spotted Alina talking to Murdoch as she petted Shadow.

His friend looked toward Gideon and shook his head but made no immediate move to join him in his hunt. It wasn't the first time Gideon had seen the three of them together. It worried him, but he could hardly criticize the man for trying to find a little softness in the hard life they all lived.

Right now, though, he was more concerned about Merewen. His skin felt too tight as if it no longer fit him, the same feeling he got on the night before a battle. Back outside, he headed straight for the gate and climbed to the walkway where he could talk to the guard without shouting.

"Have you seen Lady Merewen?"

The pimply faced youth nodded but didn't say a word.

Gideon prayed for patience. "I need details. When and where did you see her?"

The idiot swallowed hard—twice—before he found the words to answer. "She rode out about midmorning, sir."

He gestured over the top of the palisade in a vaguely northerly direction. "I opened the gate just as she asked. She rode that way."

It wouldn't be fair to shove the youth off the gate for simply obeying an order from the lady of the manor, but it was tempting. "Did she mention when she would return?"

"No, sir. She said one of the mares was hurtin'. The lady didn't say what be wrong with her."

Gideon clenched his fists hard enough to crack his knuckles. "And you didn't think to tell anyone?"

The youth swallowed hard. "Nobody asked, sir, not until just now. I was told to stay right here until I was relieved, so I haven't talked to anybody."

All Gideon could do was walk away. If he stayed any longer, the youth's life might come to an unfortunate end. He didn't deserve to die when his only sin was having done exactly what he'd been told to do. Exactly. To the letter.

Later, when Gideon had tracked Merewen down and dragged her back here to the keep, he'd have a talk with Murdoch. If Merewen was going to behave in such a thick-witted way, the men needed to be trained to report to her sooner rather than later.

Her life depended on it. So did Gideon's sanity.

He charged back through the bailey toward the corrals. Kane spotted him and correctly read his mood as he fell into step with Gideon.

"What did you find out?"

"She left the keep without telling anyone except that young idiot back there."

"You're going after her."

It wasn't really a question, but he answered anyway. "I am, and then I'm going to chain her to her bed if that's what it takes to make sure she's safe."

The glint of amusement in Kane's eyes failed to improve Gideon's mood.

At least his friend helped him saddle Kestrel. "Do you want help looking for her?"

It was tempting, but one of them should stand ready to defend the keep if Fagan did show up. "I'll find her. At least the guard was able to give me her general direction."

He patted the stallion on the neck before he swung up into the saddle. "Besides, I suspect Kestrel could find her on a moonless night without any help from me."

"I'll open the gate." Kane started to walk away but turned back. "It would be wise to return before nightfall, Captain. Something is stirring out there, and I'm not the only one who has felt it. Young Averel can't stop pacing the perimeter of the keep, and everyone is tripping over those misfit dogs of his because they won't leave his side."

Gideon's mood, already grim, took a turn for the worse. "I'll return as soon as I can, and may the gods guide my footsteps. I have a bad feeling that Fagan is bringing the fight to us."

When the gate swung open, Kestrel charged forward without having to be urged, breaking into a full gallop as soon as they cleared the gate. The stallion headed in the direction the young guard had indicated but then veered off farther east.

For the moment, Gideon had no choice but to let the horse guide their way. He'd witnessed the uncanny communication between Merewen and her charges, learning to trust in it. Since the night of the fire, he was grateful to the gods who'd given her the gift, but especially right now. Without it, he would be down on the ground, trailing her on foot in the thick grass. He could do it, especially with Kane's help. But it would take hours, time they might not have.

As if sensing Gideon's thoughts, the big stallion stretched into a full run, tearing across the country in a straight line with little regard for his own safety or his rider's. Gideon held on tight and prayed they would reach her in time.

Chapter 24

"*T*here you go, little one."

It was past time to start back to the keep, but Merewen couldn't leave until she knew for certain that the foal was out of danger. Right now the mare was guiding him to his first meal. Merewen smiled when he started nursing greedily. Her work was done.

That is if she could get up off the ground. She'd charged out of the keep as soon as she'd felt the mare's distress, and it had been a near thing. Any later, she might have lost both mother and foal. As it was, the battle to save them had been hard fought, leaving her aching but relieved.

Before pushing herself up from her knees, she bowed her head and offered her thanks to the gods. They'd blessed her with a gift, one she wielded only with their help.

She washed up in the small spring hidden at the heart of a stand of tangled bushes and then returned her supplies to her specially designed bags. As she tied them behind her saddle, she noticed the entire band of mares was standing at attention as they stared off to the south.

Obviously they weren't sensing any kind of threat, but for the first time she realized how low the sun was in the sky. She hoped young Tom had thought to let someone know where she was, especially Gideon.

She tied the last knot and double-checked to make sure the foal was still feeding as she mounted up. From the vantage point of her horse's back, she spotted Kestrel heading straight for her. He wasn't alone.

What was Gideon doing out here? Surely he wouldn't be riding at such a breakneck speed over such rough ground for no reason.

She knew the instant he saw her. If anything, Kestrel sped up. They were almost within shouting distance. She knew that was true, because Gideon was definitely bellowing something at her. Although he was still too far away for her to understand his words, his dark mood was all too clear. What had happened now?

A few seconds later, he reached the small rise where she sat waiting. Before Kestrel had even come to a complete stop, Gideon was on the ground and running straight for her. He reached up to drag her down out of the saddle, his handsome face contorted in raw fury. His big hands held her prisoner, his breath a hot wind on her skin.

"What were you thinking? Riding off alone with no escort?"

Is that what this was about?

She nodded in the direction of the foal and his mother. "That sorrel mare was in distress. If I hadn't come when I did, she would have died. Her foal was breech."

He didn't even glance at the mother and her foal. "I don't give a damn about them, Merewen. It was you the gods sent me to protect! I can't do my job, not if you fight me every inch of the way. You will not do such a stupid thing again—do you hear me?"

This was getting out of hand.

"I will tell you the same thing I told my uncle and his captain, Gideon. When the horses call, I answer. Nothing—and no one—is going to change that."

She put her hands on his broad chest and shoved with all her might, not that it budged him at all. When that didn't work, she punched him in the arm. "I didn't exchange one jailer for another, Gideon. You might be my lover, but you're not my keeper!"

He flinched as if her words had bruised him where her fist had not. His face went stone cold, his voice even colder. "I never once said you shouldn't tend your horses, Lady Merewen. I ask only that you allow me to carry out the duty that my gods have ordained. I would also remind you yet again that the very souls of my friends depend on my ability to carry out that obligation."

The complete lack of emotion in his words proved how deeply she had wounded him.

"I told the guard where I was going, Gideon. Did he not relay the message?"

"That simpleton? No, he didn't. Not until I asked him, and by then, you'd already been gone for hours. If Kestrel didn't have the ability to find you quickly, I would have emptied the keep of every able man to send out search parties."

She blanched. "But that would have left my home unguarded."

"That is not my concern, Lady Merewen. You are."

The air around them grew chilly. "That's not true, Captain Gideon. I called you and your men from the river to save my home and people from my uncle and his men. That is your true mission."

"No, it is not. You said it yourself, Lady Merewen. Without you and your gift, the horses that run free on these grasslands would simply scatter. Without you, your people have nothing."

He drew a ragged breath. "If you die, I will have failed. You have no idea what that will mean to me, to you, and to the four who chose to follow me. My men have already suffered far too much because of me."

He released her and stepped back. "I betrayed them all, Merewen, out of selfishness and by neglecting my duty."

She wasn't sure if she wanted to know what he could have done to condemn himself and the others to such a hellish existence. But if he wanted her to hear his truth, she would listen. She owed him that much.

"What happened, Gideon?"

He stared past her, his face stark in its pain, as he lost himself in the past. "The five of us had ridden together for years, even young Averel, whom we took on as our squire before he earned his spurs. I assisted Murdoch's escape from the violent bastard he had been fostered with. Kane was shunned because of the mage mark he bears. Duncan's father hated his son's scholarly bent. I never owned anything that I didn't earn with my sword. The five of us became closer than most brothers."

When he didn't say more, Merewen prodded him again. "You can tell me anything, Gideon."

Another few seconds passed before he spoke again. "A local nobleman hired us to hunt down a band of brigands. They'd been robbing the trade caravans passing through Agathia, although it was known by a different name then."

Merewen sidled closer, taking his hand in hers. She gave it a soft squeeze when he glanced down at her before continuing on with his tale.

"He ordered us to ride with a caravan carrying supplies to the troops protecting the northern border, but I soon grew weary of the endless hours of eating the dust of slow-moving wagons. We had scoured the area, looking for any sign of the brigands to no avail. I was convinced the hunt was a waste of our time, that my men and I were too good to be used as simple guards. We belonged wherever real fighting was taking place.

"However, I didn't dare abandon my duties completely. One day the merchant in charge told me to send a couple of guards into a nearby town to buy fresh bread and whatever vegetables were available for purchase.

Rather than send the caravan guards, I decided we deserved a night off."

After a brief silence, he whispered, "Just one night."

She feared for what came next in the tale, but there was no stopping Gideon now. The words poured out of him as if a dam had broken.

"We had a great time eating, drinking, wenching." His strange eyes stared out at the horizon, lost in his past. "Until I met you, that was my last pleasant memory."

He shot her an embarrassed look at that last confession, but she understood. He'd been a young man in the prime of life out looking for adventure of all kinds. She leaned her head against his shoulder to show she did not judge him for something that happened in a world that no longer existed.

"Go on, Gideon."

"When we returned to the caravan, all of the guards had been slaughtered. The merchants were dead as well, their heads severed and mounted on pikes. The stench of foul magic and death hung in the air thick as wood smoke."

He shuddered as if the stench had followed after him all these centuries, his voice sounding dead. "It was obvious the men had put up no fight at all. Most had been killed right where they slept. All of the women were taken."

His pale eyes burned with remembered pain and fury. "It took us three days to track down the brigands and their prisoners at their camp near the river. The women were alive, but we didn't arrive in time to prevent—"

He stopped again, but the horror in his expression painted a clear enough picture. "Kane, Murdoch, and I attacked the brigands while Duncan and Averel circled around to lead the survivors out through the back of the camp. Even with the help of Hob and Shadow, we stood little chance against their superior numbers, especially with a mage fighting on their side. However, our honor demanded we fight to the death. I hoped, too, that the scholar and the youngest of us would survive. They weren't like the rest of us."

"But they didn't, did they?"

He shook his head. "Duncan and Averel sent the prisoners on ahead and returned to fight out of loyalty to me. Kane faced off against the mage, distracting him long enough for me to get close enough to kill the bastard with my sword. Once he was dead, we managed to destroy that nest of vipers, but all of us received grave wounds. I took one last blow to prevent Kane from being killed by the leader of the brigands, who had only pretended to be dead."

Gideon smiled briefly. "I'm not sure Kane has ever forgiven me for dying in his place."

At those words, Merewen needed to reassure herself that her lover was alive. She wrapped her arms around his waist and snuggled against his chest, taking comfort from the steady beat of his heart.

"As I lay dying, I prayed to the gods to save my men and the prisoners, pleading that no one else should suffer for my foolishness.

"The gods were listening. The Lady of the River appeared before me and offered me the chance to redeem my honor. If I would pledge my soul to the gods, to fight for them for as long as they commanded it, they would ease the wounds caused by my selfishness. I didn't hesitate. The women were healed and returned to their homes. Beyond that, I know not what became of them."

His chin came to rest on the top of her head. "My friends chose to join me as avatars of the gods, to become the Damned. I argued against it, but none would leave me. The Lady of the River accepted their decision and allowed our animal friends to fight at our side. I sometimes fear my friends will never know peace because of me. If I disappoint the gods, we will all suffer until the last of the ages pass away. I cannot afford the luxury of failing, not even once."

That confession had clearly cost him, so much so that her heart ached for him and the men who served him still. "Gideon, you have to believe that I never meant to worry you. Next time I am called, I will tell you or at least one of your men, and I promise I will not ride out again unescorted. But know this much, too. I will do what I must to protect the welfare of the horses."

He looked only slightly happier. "We need to return to the keep. Kane senses the great evil at work in this land is growing in strength, and the danger now moves toward us."

They'd known the peace of the past few days wouldn't last. "Do you think it is Fagan?"

"If it were only him, I'm not sure Kane would sense his presence. Yet we all know your uncle will attempt to retake the keep. Fagan's pride will demand that much of him. But there's something more—a dark magic that stirs Kane's mage mark. It calls to him."

"Does this dark magic have the power to harm Kane?"

Gideon's eyes narrowed. "Why don't you ask what you really want to know?"

He was already angry, so she did. "If this magic calls too strongly to him, will he answer?"

"No."

"But—"

Gideon stopped her by putting his fingers across her lips. "You've known Kane for only a short time. He has been not only my ally but my friend for centuries, and at a terrible cost to himself. That he bears the mark of dark magic was not of his choosing. He is the strongest man I've ever known, and his honor defines him. There is no one I trust more at my side when the fighting starts—no one. What's more, if I were to fall, I would trust him to keep you safe. If this magic is powerful enough to destroy Kane, then none of us will withstand its power."

His mouth was but a straight slash when he repeated, "None of us."

The impact of his words left her shivering in the late-afternoon sun. She was overwhelmed with the need to get back to the shelter of the palisade. Out on the open grasslands they were both too exposed—vulnerable.

Gideon seemed to be waiting for an answer, although he hadn't asked a question. He was right. Her heart knew that Kane would not betray them. "I apologize. This is no excuse, but everything that's happening is so frightening, and I let my fear talk. I have faith in your honor and in that of your friends."

He looked mollified. "Let me give you a boost back up in the saddle. Time runs short."

"I know, but there is still time for this."

She captured his worried face in her hands and tugged him down for a kiss. His arms snapped tight around her, pulling her in close to his body.

She'd meant it as a peace offering, a reminder of what they shared when they were alone in her room, the door shutting out the world. But then his tongue swept past her lips, flavored with the hot spice of a claiming that promised far more than a simple kiss. Her body had already learned how to respond to his touch and craved the way they fit together with a sweet heat that was theirs alone.

His hands found their way down past the curve of her waist to cup her bottom, lifting her higher with a not-so-gentle squeeze. She could feel the bulge of his manhood against her belly. Oh gods, yes. Her inner core softened and dampened, wanting more than this press of bodies with far too many layers of clothing between them. She moaned and wrapped her leg around his, rocking against the hard ridge that strained against his trews.

"Merewen!"

His voice was little better than a deep growl, more suited to Hob. She loved it.

"If you don't stop me, Merewen, I'm going to take you right here in the grass. We need to return before they come hunting for us."

He punctuated each statement with a kiss. There was nothing in the way he held her that hinted that he'd let her go even if she wanted him to. She was not that foolish.

"We don't have time for this," he murmured.

She tangled her fingers in his dark hair. "Can we not make time?"

This was pure madness. He'd always been known for his focus and determination, but with one kiss this woman had stripped him of all control and rational thought. His body was on fire, demanding to be on her, in her, and staking his claim in a wave of pulsing heat.

But where?

"We can't, not out here in the open."

Merewen pointed down the hillside toward a stand of bushes. "There's a small clearing inside. We'll be out of sight."

Still clutching her in his arms, Gideon carried her down the slope and through the thicket. There he sank to his knees in the soft grass with Merewen straddling his thighs.

She deserved a gentle touch, a soft bed, not to mention a man who could stay in her life. But right now she wanted him, and he wouldn't disappoint. Shifting his hold on her, he pressed Merewen back onto the ground, the bright green of the grass contrasting with the dark red highlights in her hair.

He wouldn't have been surprised if the heat they were generating set the grasslands afire. He loosened the ties on her trousers and worked them down her legs. The scent of her desire perfumed the air as he tossed her clothes to the side. She smiled up at him, watching as he cursed the stubborn laces on his own trews.

Finally, his fumbling fingers managed the simple task, and he shoved them down just far enough to free himself from their confines. Merewen's eyes widened at the sight of him looming over her. How did he look at the moment with this craving, this compulsion, driving him so hard? Then she smiled and held out her arms in welcome.

There was so much he should tell her, so many ways he should show her that she mattered. Right now, the need to mate with her left him without words and without gentleness. He would apologize later. Right now, all he could do was take her hard and fast.

He rocked against her honey-slick folds several times, fanning the flames and frustrating them both at the same time.

Merewen glowered up at him. "Now, Gideon!"

A man should never argue with a woman, especially when she was right. Her hips arched up and her hand gently wrapped around his shaft to guide him home.

"Hold on, my lady," he warned her just before he plunged into her welcoming heat.

When he was seated deep and tight, he withdrew partway and waited for her to look up at him. "Do you want this?"

She licked her lower lip and nodded. That was all the encouragement he needed. He lifted her legs up over his thighs and drove deep again, his hips working hard and fast. Just that quickly, Merewen crooned her approval with each stroke.

It wasn't going to take long, not with the storm building in his flesh and bones as his lover's body grew tight. Still he drove them both on. Finally, the first ripple of her pleasure gripped him, slowing his pace only slightly. He slipped his hand between them, parting her folds to caress the swollen nub hidden there with the pad of his thumb.

A few soft circles were all it took to have her keening out her release in the warm afternoon sunshine. As she shuddered in his arms, his own body reached its limits, and he lost what little control he'd had. On and on he went. At last he roared as his own pleasure pulsated deep within her body, stealing away the last of his strength. He collapsed with his face buried in the side of her neck, drawing in deep breaths of Merewen-scented air.

When the world slowly righted itself, he kissed her, gently this time. She encircled his neck with her arms, their legs still tangled, their bodies joined, and their hearts pounding hard.

He'd never given way to such desperation with a woman and had to ask, "Did I hurt you?"

Her smile warmed his heart and soothed away his worry even as she brushed his hair back from his face. "I'm fine, but I think you mentioned something about needing to hurry."

She was right even if he hated it. He rolled to the side and reached for Merewen's clothes. "This wasn't the smartest thing we could have done, love, but I can't find it within me to regret it."

"Nor I. But as you said, we should go. I'd hate for anyone else to worry enough to come looking for us, especially right now."

She eyed his still-unfastened ties with an impish smile. If Kane or one of the others had taken it upon themselves to come help him search, he'd never live this down. He quickly righted his clothes and then gave Merewen the boost back up into her saddle that he'd promised earlier.

She waited until he caught Kestrel and swung up into the saddle. Then as one, they set off for the keep at a slow gallop. The sun now hovered a short distance above the horizon, but with luck they'd reach the gates before dark.

The thought of night's approach had him urging Kestrel into a faster pace. Just as Gideon and his men were at their strongest under the cover of darkness, that was likely also true of the evil approaching. It wouldn't do to be caught out on the plains once the sun set.

If Merewen wondered about his rush, she didn't ask. But one look at the worry on her face, and he knew she was feeling the same way. With a heartfelt prayer to the gods for her safety, he rode with one eye on the horizon and a hand on his sword.

Chapter 25

*F*agan's men rode clustered close to him. He'd like to think it was out of personal loyalty, but he knew better. In truth, none of them, not even he himself, felt comfortable around the men who rode in formation behind them.

Besides the unavoidable creak of saddle leather and the occasional snort from one of the horses, thirty of Duke Keirthan's men rode in absolute silence. Another thirty were infantry, marching behind the mounted troops. They had been walking for hours without a single one complaining about the torturous pace set by their captain.

In fact, as far as Fagan could tell, not one of them had said a single word since leaving the city of Agathia two days ago. They set up camp in silence, ate in silence, patrolled in silence. It was eerie and off-putting to say the least.

The only one who spoke at all was their leader, Captain Terrick, whom Keirthan had put in charge. In as few words as possible, the man announced when everyone should mount up, when they should make camp, and when they should pack up and leave the next morning. Fagan wondered if they even slept, but he'd been too afraid to actually stick his head out of his tent at night to check.

No doubt they would fight on command, but what had Keirthan done to them? It was as if they had been stripped of all but the most basic of functions. Their pale faces lacked all expression, the only sign of life their relentless walking and breathing. He tore his gaze away from the unsettling sight.

For the moment, all Fagan could do was ride and think about the upcoming battle. He had no desire to lead the charge. True, he had a well-deserved reputation with a sword. That didn't mean he relished putting his own life on the line. However, he couldn't avoid being embroiled in the upcoming fight, not without being seen as weak and a coward. Even if his own men could forgive such behavior, which was by no means a given, the duke's troops would report him to their master.

Keirthan had little use for anyone unwilling to sacrifice everything to further his cause. Keirthan's cause. Right now, all Fagan longed to do was regain control of his family home—and his niece.

While Fagan wasn't willing to offer up any more of his own blood to the duke, he would cheerfully lash Merewen to the back of a horse and drag her back to the capital city—anything to deflect Keirthan's attention away from Fagan himself. He'd even take Alina along to keep his niece company as the two of them faced whatever plans Keirthan had for them.

After Merewen's betrayal, if Fagan never saw either of the two women again, that was fine with him. Then he'd round up all the horses and sell them to the highest bidder. He'd already learned that even the strongest fences couldn't hold that cursed black stallion and his mares.

But before any of that could happen, he had to survive the upcoming fight. He'd already suggested to Captain Terrick that they rest for the night and attack at first light when the guards on the palisade were more likely to be tired and slow to respond. Besides, fighting at night made it that much harder to tell friend from foe.

However, Captain Terrick was adamant the battle be fought under the cover of darkness—the duke's orders, or so he'd claimed.

So despite having been on the move since just after dawn, leaving both the men and horses tired and hungry, they were to form up to attack as soon as they got within sight of the keep. It was insanity, but Fagan had no choice but to go along with the plan.

For now, he shoved all thought of the fight out of his head and concentrated on what lovely punishments he could devise for his wife when he dragged her to his bed one last time. His body stirred at the thought—not the most comfortable way to ride, but even that was better than dwelling on things he'd rather not think about.

Like his chances of surviving the night.

Murdoch had been pacing the great hall for the past hour. It was getting to be late in the day with no sign of either Gideon or his lady. Something had to be done.

He headed up the stairs to find Duncan, who had once again buried himself in the library. Without bothering to knock, Murdoch barged in. To his surprise, Kane and Averel were also there.

"Duncan, send Kiva out to check on Gideon. He and Lady Merewen have yet to return."

Duncan didn't hesitate. "Of course, but this room lacks a window. Perhaps Lady Alina wouldn't mind if I used hers."

Murdoch blocked the way. "Give the bird his marching orders, and I'll send him aloft. You have enough to do to get ready to leave."

Which did not include a visit to Lady Alina's private quarters across the hall. Duncan gave him a considering look, but he didn't argue. Instead, he rested his hand on his avatar's head and communicated what they needed Kiva to do.

When he was finished, Murdoch offered his arm to the huge owl and carried him out of the library and toward Alina's door, cursing himself for a fool three times over. Not only was he once again putting himself within temptation's reach, but he'd only confirmed his friends' suspicions about his feelings for the lady.

He knocked at her door, hoping her maid would be the one to answer. But no, the gods seemed to be conspiring to throw the two of them together. Alina cracked open the door to peek out. As soon as she spotted Kiva, her face lit up with a smile.

"Is this another guest for me?"

The owl nibbled gently at her fingers as she reached out to stroke his chest feathers with the back of her hand. "He's a handsome fellow."

Watching the sensuous pleasure she took in petting the bird had Murdoch picturing all too clearly what it would be like to have those same hands caressing him. The effect on his body was both predictable and painful in its intensity. When he abruptly shifted to ease the pressure, Alina jerked back out of reach and flung her arms up to protect her face.

The sudden movement startled Kiva, who flapped his wings in protest. Murdoch muttered a curse and pushed his way into the room to fling the damned owl out the window.

When Kiva was safely winging his way out into the gathering darkness, Murdoch eased closer to where Alina now stood, her hands covering her face.

"Alina, I'm sorry. I didn't mean to scare you again."

Her shoulders shook as she fought to hide her tears from him. It broke his heart to see her in such pain. What could he say to make things better? Nothing came to mind, but then he'd never been a man of words, only of actions.

He did the only thing he could think of. He wrapped

her in his arms and held on tight while she cried herself out.

Finally, she sniffed a few times and raised her tearstained face up to look at him. "It is I who need to apologize. I overreacted. You would never be so cruel. Not like Fagan, and I know that. I'm so sorry."

He caught her chin with a crooked finger. "You have nothing to apologize for. All you need do is remember that bastard will never lay a hand on you again."

At his touch, her eyes widened, framed by long, damp lashes as she stared at his mouth for the longest time. Then she raised herself up just far enough so that their breath mingled, their lips separated only by his conscience. He wanted her so badly, but he would not take advantage of her in this moment of weakness.

But neither would he let her think he was rejecting her. He let his hands drop to her waist and took a step back. Her disappointment quickly turned to embarrassment. When she tried to turn away, he stopped her.

"Alina, I would promise you something else. When the day comes that you are free of your marriage vows, if you desire me, then nothing short of the gods themselves will keep me away."

He touched her cheek with his fingertips. "Understand?" When she nodded, he added, "Now, I should to get back to work."

She gave him a soft shove. "Go. I'll be fine."

Before he reached the door, she called his name one last time. "Murdoch?"

He glanced back. "Yes?"

Her eyes flickered toward the curtained bed in the corner and then back to him. "Thank you for your patience with me."

"You are most welcome, my lady."

Then he executed a bow that would've done Duncan proud and softly closed the door on his way out. He managed to make it all the way back to the library without tripping over his feet. Even more important, he succeeded in wiping the big smile off his face before rejoining his friends.

An hour later, all four men had lapsed into silence, watching the soft shadows cast by the candles dancing on the walls. The entire meal had been subdued as everyone awaited the return of the captain and Merewen. If they didn't arrive soon, Murdoch would have little choice but to send out search parties, especially if Kiva didn't return.

Duncan had started to pour himself another drink of wine when he dropped the pitcher and grabbed his head with both hands.

"Kiva! Quieter. Hurting me."

The grimace on the scholar's face gradually eased, but his eyes were still wide with horror. What was that damned owl showing him?

Kane moved to catch Duncan when the warrior suddenly slumped. The owl had obviously released his mind, but the connection had left Duncan struggling to talk.

Finally, he looked around as if having to reacquaint himself with his surroundings.

"Gideon and Merewen are approaching, but so is an armed force coming from the direction of the capital city. It has to be Fagan returning with reinforcements."

He drew a ragged breath. "From what I could see, it's unlikely the captain is aware of the other riders. If he and Merewen don't hurry, they'll ride right into them."

Murdoch stood up. "I'll sound the alarm and send the guards up to the walkway armed and ready to fight."

As they all headed for the door, he started issuing orders. "Averel, tell Lady Alina that she and the cook need to prepare for possible wounded. Duncan, send

Kiva back out to warn the captain. Kane, you and Hob ride out to meet them. Between the two of you, you should be able to fight your way through to the gate if necessary."

Kane caught the younger knight by the arm before he left. "Averel, be waiting to open the gate when we return. There's a good chance we'll be only seconds ahead of pursuit. We'll need to get in quickly."

With that, they all went their separate ways. Murdoch waited by the gate as Kane and Hob prepared to ride out. As he looked around to make sure everyone was doing as they'd been told, he spotted Alina heading straight for them.

"Return to the hall, Lady Alina."

"I will, but know that I will be praying the gods keep you and the others safe. Please send word about Merewen as soon as you know anything, or if there is something I can do to be of help."

"I will."

Then she eased closer to the other warrior and his horror of an avatar. "Lord Kane, I know you will keep my niece safe, but have a care for yourself and the captain. And Hob here, too."

Kane's rough voice was surprisingly gentle. "I will do my best, Lady Alina."

"I know you will."

As she spoke, Murdoch drew her to the side as he opened the gate.

Rogue immediately reared up, pawing the air as Kane shouted, "Hob, to the captain!"

When the gate slammed shut behind the hard-riding warrior, Murdoch watched to make sure Alina made it back to the hall safely before he joined the others on the walkway above. His hand gripped and released the pommel of his sword over and over, his blood running hot with battle fever.

He had no doubt the upcoming fight wouldn't be the last in this campaign; they would have to face the real evil out there before it was over. But this night would be the last time they would have to face Fagan, and that was a worthy-enough goal for him.

Chapter 26

Kiva swooped down a second time, appearing out of the growing darkness with his amber eyes aglow and flying close enough to ruffle Gideon's hair. He held out his arm to offer the bird a perch, but the owl was already winging his way back toward the keep and his owner.

Gideon figured the first trip had been Duncan wanting to know where Gideon was, which meant the second one had been meant as a warning. Something was wrong. That was all Gideon needed to know. He rose up in his saddle, attempting to see far enough ahead in the darkness to discern the danger. Nothing. He closed his eyes and listened to the night as he drew a long slow breath, tasting the scent of the wind.

Horses. Nothing unusual about that, given the herds that wandered these grasslands. No, it was the taint of unwashed men and the faint creak of leather that had his pulse racing. He reached for his shield and called out the words that would bring forth Scim. The brief flash of light might reveal their location, but right now Gideon needed the gyrfalcon's eyes to scout ahead to see what they were riding into. It would take several seconds for the bird to position himself over the approaching threat.

Gideon pitched his voice just loud enough to carry back to Merewen. "That was Duncan's avatar warning us we're not alone out here."

She brought her horse abreast with Kestrel. Shortly after they'd started for the keep, her mare had picked up a stone and developed a limp. Merewen had bound the horse's right foreleg. From that point on they'd kept to a slow walk to avoid causing the horse any further injury.

"How is the mare doing?"

Merewen closed her eyes and leaned forward to rest her hand on the horse's neck. After a few seconds, she straightened up. "Her foreleg is better but definitely not up to full strength. She'll be able to maintain a short burst of speed but not much more. Beyond that, we'd be risking permanent damage to that leg."

Right now Gideon was more worried about getting Merewen back to the keep safely than he was concerned about the horse. He kept that opinion to himself, knowing how Merewen would feel about it.

"We need to move faster."

He led the way but made sure she stayed close behind him. Trusting Kestrel to keep them moving in the right direction, he closed his eyes to connect with Scim soaring overhead. As usual, the first few seconds left him feeling queasy until his inner eye adjusted to the bird's view of the surrounding area.

The grasslands rolled on into the distance, but the land closer to the keep itself was filled with rocky outcroppings. They'd serve to slow down Fagan's men, about the only thing playing in Gideon's favor right now.

Almost immediately, Gideon broke off the connection. At this slow pace, the approaching forces would overtake them before they could reach the gate. At least he'd also spotted Kane and Hob heading straight for them. Good.

"Merewen, switch horses with me. You stand a better chance of reaching the keep safely on Kestrel."

He dismounted before she could argue. Still, she hesitated. "I can call for another horse to come."

Gideon held his hands out to her. "Hurry. There's no time for that."

She climbed down and traded reins with him. "What did you see?"

There was no hiding the truth from her and no good to be gained by trying. He cupped his hands to toss her up onto Kestrel's broad back. "I would guess that your uncle is back, and he has a number of men-at-arms riding with him. Hasten now or we'll never make it to the gate before they get into position to attack. Kane's on his way toward us with Hob, so we won't be alone."

He mounted the mare. "Ride, Merewen, and don't look back. I'll be right behind you."

Or he would be as long as the mare held up. With one last look back at Gideon, Merewen gave Kestrel his head. The mare did her best to follow, but her uneven gait made it unlikely Gideon would reach the gate at all. Realizing he couldn't protect Merewen from this point on, he prayed to the gods to watch over her and keep her safe from harm.

All too quickly she was out of sight. He connected with Scim long enough to send him after her. The bird would warn Gideon if she ran into trouble. He kicked the mare into a slow gallop, hoping to stay within reach of Merewen without disabling the horse completely.

It worked for a short time, but soon the mare was limping hard enough to almost throw him from the saddle. He gave up and dismounted. Using his knife, he cut the cinch and shoved the saddle off onto the ground.

"Go with the gods," he whispered to the mare, and slapped her on the rear. Sword in hand, Gideon followed after Kestrel on foot, hoping that Kane would reach Merewen in time to escort her safely back to the keep.

There was no way Gideon himself would make it that far before the enemy forces did. Rather than try, he looked for the best place to make a stand and buy Merewen the time she needed.

Sharing Scim's view, it appeared the approaching

forces would be funneled through a rocky area that would slow them down. If he could block the near end, he could further delay their progress. He took off running, his legs pumping hard as he strained for every bit of speed he could muster. By the time he reached the narrow passage, his muscles burned with fatigue. He hid behind a cluster of boulders and stood ready to attack.

Scim silently circled overhead, still watching Merewen's progress. Gideon drew comfort from his avatar's presence but as always worried about what would happen to Scim if Gideon didn't survive the upcoming fight. Their spirit bond had been created by the gods. Did that mean the two of them would remain partnered together in the afterlife? He hoped so.

At the same time, he grieved over the thought he might have kissed Merewen for the last time—that he might never again know her touch, never again feel her shudder in his arms as they both reached completion. Might he have given her a son or daughter?

But for now, he and Scim would join forces to fight. From where he stood, he couldn't see anything. Laying his hand on the big rock to his right, he felt for the vibrations that would herald the enemy's approach. He felt only a slight buzz, not nearly enough for the number of riders he'd counted through Scim's eyes.

That could mean only one thing: Kane was coming. Damn the man; he was supposed to stay and protect Merewen. Instead, he was about to charge right into the path of the fight.

Gideon ordered Scim to lead the dark warrior to where he was hiding. With luck or maybe the guidance of the gods, the two of them could ride double on Rogue long enough to buy them some time. He watched as Scim banked off to the south and then abruptly dove down. Judging by the steep angle, Kane wasn't far away.

In the end, it was Hob who arrived first, his fangs already dripping venom. Kane appeared out of the darkness right behind him, his sword drawn and ready to fight. Gideon had never been so glad to see his friend, despite his worries about Merewen.

"Did she make it back safely?"

Kane nodded. "She was nearly to the gate when I passed her. She promised to send Kestrel back for you."

Kane's eyes glittered in the darkness, his excitement at the prospect of a battle all too clear. His need for violence was a constant companion, one he could suppress for only so long.

"Do we run or make a stand?"

Rogue pawed the ground, picking up on his rider's restless nature. Kane controlled him easily, but the stallion wasn't happy about it. Clearly the horse and his rider were both in the mood for a good fight.

Still, he started to say, "Rogue can bear us double if you want to—"

Before Kane could finish the offer, Hob screeched a warning. Out of the darkness charged the first handful of foot soldiers. Gideon vaulted over the boulders to meet their charge as Kane fought from horseback. Scim dove down from above to attack with talons and beak, drawing blood before climbing back to the sky for another attack.

Gideon lined up against three of Fagan's men with his shield on his left arm and his sword in his right hand. He swung hard, hitting the first fighter's sword with enough force to send the man stumbling to his knees. Another blow removed him from the fight permanently.

The second warrior took his place, this time making room for the third one to join him in the lethal dance. From somewhere behind Gideon's right shoulder, he could hear Kane taunting the enemy, his deep voice echoing through the night.

In past battles, facing the Damned and their avatars was enough to send most human soldiers into a panic.

These, however, fought in grim silence. Even when Gideon slashed open his current opponent's leg to the bone, the warrior continued to fight without even a whimper until his leg gave out completely.

Something to ponder later. Right now, it was all Gideon could do to keep from being surrounded as more of the enemy swarmed into the clearing on horseback. Kane joined him on the ground, assuming his usual position at Gideon's back while Hob and Scim harried their enemies from above and below.

Even Rogue joined in the fighting, using his weight to knock other horses aside. If he succeeded in unseating the rider, his hooves ensured the man didn't get back up.

The rocky terrain at that part of the trail limited how many of the enemy could approach at once. If they found a way to circumvent the narrow passage and come up from behind, things could go badly for the two warriors.

Gideon prayed Kestrel would arrive soon. Even their god-enhanced strength wouldn't hold up forever against this many opponents. He bellowed out his rage, laughing when Kane screamed out his battle cry, his words rough and grating on the ear. Hob joined the chorus as he darted in and out of the mass of panicky horses and their oddly quiet riders.

It was getting difficult to move without tripping over the dead and dying. Gideon had suffered a few nicks but no major injuries. He blocked a blow from a mounted fighter and then pulled him from the saddle. After finishing him off, he backed away, hoping to gain a few seconds to catch his breath.

In the moment of stillness, he noticed the ground beneath his feet shook with the vibration of pounding hooves. If it was Kestrel, he'd brought company. If it wasn't, then both Gideon and Kane would be surrounded; eventually someone would get in a lucky swing and take them both down.

Rogue reared up again, bugling a challenge, as a band of riderless horses appeared in the clearing with Kestrel leading the charge.

Once again, Kane's battle cry split the night as Rogue and Kestrel formed up side by side to challenge the enemy's horses. It was instant chaos as the two stallions forced the others to retreat. Several panicked and unseated their riders before bolting into the night as the rest of Kestrel's band did their best to block the relentless approach of more of Fagan's forces.

The chaos gave Gideon and Kane just enough time to mount up again. Neither stallion needed to be told to run full tilt for the keep, with Kestrel's band following close behind. When they were clear of the fray, the mares and bachelor stallions veered off the trail and headed back toward the mountains, leaving the enemy behind to retreat and regroup.

The first skirmish was over, and they'd survived.

Kestrel barely slowed down enough for Merewen to jump off outside the gate before he cut away from her to tear back off into the night. She landed awkwardly and went down to her knees hard. She wasn't about to complain, not if Kestrel's speed meant getting Gideon to safety that much faster.

While the stallion was carrying her toward the keep, she'd sensed the mare's increasing pain and knew exactly when Gideon had been left afoot. Knowing he was back there alone to face off against who knew how many men sent Merewen's fear soaring to new heights. Only the knowledge that she would've been more hindrance than help had kept her from turning back.

At least she'd been able to convince Kane that her cause would be best served by his going after his captain. In truth, it hadn't taken much persuasion on her part. As he and Hob had charged back out into the darkness, she sent heartfelt prayers flying up to the night sky for their safekeeping.

She pushed herself up to her feet and was dusting the bits of dirt and gravel off her knees as the gate swung open. Murdoch and Duncan caught her by the arms and dragged her into the safety of the keep.

Murdoch grabbed a nearby torch and held it close to her. "I smell blood. Are you hurt?"

"I fell after getting off Kestrel and scraped my knees. I'll be fine."

She leaned against the palisade, grateful for its support as the effect of everything hit her all at once. She needed to sit down—now, before she fell again. What she really wanted to do was climb to the walkway overhead and watch for Gideon and Kane, but when she tried to take a step forward, her legs buckled and refused to support her.

Duncan swooped in to catch her. Her head lolled back against his shoulder as the stars above her spun in circles. She closed her eyes, hoping to stop the dizziness, but it didn't help all that much.

She was dimly aware of the transition from the outdoors into the warmth of the hall where she was unceremoniously laid out on a tabletop. The worried murmur of voices surrounded her as someone—Duncan?—started issuing orders. Something about food or drink or wet rags. Nothing made sense. She didn't need their attention.

No, they should all be outside watching for Gideon—or, better yet, riding to his rescue. She fought to sit up, but a strong pair of hands pushed her shoulders back down against the table.

"I'm thinking you've gone too long without food and drink, so stay still until they bring you something to eat, Lady Merewen. I'll return when we have word about the captain."

Then a calloused hand took hold of hers. "Squeeze

my hand if you understand. We're going to need you at full strength before long."

She must have conveyed her agreement, because the male voice disappeared, to be replaced by Alina's. "I'm going to hold you up so you can sip this broth. It's cool enough to drink, but take it slow."

She worked her arm under Merewen's neck and lifted her head far enough so that Merewen could sip the warm liquid without choking.

"That's enough for now. Let's see how that settles before I give you more."

For the next few minutes, they repeated the process until Alina declared Merewen's color much improved.

"I need to sit up."

Her aunt helped her, standing in front of her to prevent her from toppling forward onto the floor. "Fine, but let's go slowly. Sir Duncan isn't here to catch you this time."

When Merewen was upright, she reached for the cheese and bread that one of the servants had brought out. Nibble by nibble, she finished it and started on a second piece. The shaking had stopped, and the waves of nauseating dizziness were tapering off.

She eased off the edge of the table and was relieved that this time her legs supported her weight. "I must return to the gate."

Alina blocked her way. "Duncan promised to send word."

Merewen stepped to the side, intending to go around her aunt. "I cannot remain here and do nothing."

"You'll only be in the way, Merewen. The men won't be able to concentrate on defending themselves if they are worried about protecting you."

True enough, but right now that didn't matter. She had to be there when the gate opened to let Gideon back in. Nothing less would do.

She raised her eyes to meet her aunt's. "I'll leave the gate when Captain Gideon and Kane are back, but not until then. I can't."

The tears started then. "What if he doesn't return? What if they've killed him already? My mare went lame, and he sent me back on Kestrel. He was left to face that bastard Fagan and his men on foot!"

Alina flinched at the mention of her husband's name. "Have faith, niece. At his best, my husband is no match for your captain. I have faith he and Kane will return. You'll see."

Merewen gave her aunt a hard hug as an unspoken apology. She couldn't help how she felt about her uncle, but the path he'd chosen to follow was hardly his young wife's fault.

"As soon as Captain Gideon rides through the gate, I'll retire to my workshop to prepare the medicines we'll be needing."

The other woman nodded and stepped back. "I'll pray for the captain, Merewen, and the others who will defend the keep tonight. With the gods' blessing, the enemy will be vanquished. I have great faith in Sir Murdoch . . . and in the others, too, of course."

Alina must have felt torn apart, with her hated husband preparing to attack, and the man who had obviously captured her heart defending the keep. They both knew Fagan had brought this upon himself with his greed and cruelty. For the moment, all they could do was brace themselves for the worst.

With that happy thought, Merewen started for the door with leaden feet to await word of her lover—no, not merely her lover, but the man she loved.

Chapter 27

Kestrel and Rogue ran through the night with Hob keeping pace off to the side. The night was far from over, and the enemy forces were but minutes behind them. There was no point in looking back. Either they reached the keep in time or they didn't. Such was the life the two of them had been living for centuries and even before they'd taken up the cause of the gods.

But it had all led them to this one moment. Gideon had never waged a more important battle in all his long years of fighting. The fight against the evil in this land would start this night. Too long Fagan and his minions had been allowed to go unchecked, and Gideon would put a stop to it before it spread any further. He wouldn't hesitate to sacrifice himself and even his men if it meant that Merewen and her people would live in peace. His love for her would accept no less.

Yet Fagan was only part of the trouble they faced. They needed to survive this battle in a much larger war. It would be better to capture Fagan and pry answers from him, but Gideon knew this battle would end in one of two ways—with Fagan's death or his own.

Even with Kestrel's great heart and stamina, the stallion was gradually slowing, and Rogue was falling farther and farther behind. Gideon would not leave Kane to face the enemy alone. He pulled back on Kestrel's reins, fighting against the horse's instincts to charge forward to safety. The faint sound of other horses carried on the night air.

It was going to be close, but at long last the palisade loomed up ahead. The gods were with them.

Or were they?

From out of the darkness charged a line of mounted fighters. Gideon recognized the one in front immediately— Olaf, which meant the man riding slightly behind him was most likely Fagan.

With the enemy behind them and this new threat in front, he and Kane were surrounded. Gideon didn't even hesitate. Drawing his sword, he cursed the enemy and called down the gods' fury on them. He might not survive the night, but he wouldn't be alone in the long darkness of the afterworld. His enemies, broken and bleeding, would ride beside him.

Kane drew up nearby, his curved swords flashing in a glint of moonlight, his voice harsh with hatred and determination. The mage-cursed warriors behind them continued forward, but the human ones in front fell back in confusion as Kane and his avatar charged into their midst.

Gideon yanked hard on Kestrel's reins and spun the stallion to face the menace approaching from behind. He and Kane had thinned the enemy's numbers, but they were still seriously outnumbered. At best, he could only hope to whittle them down enough so Murdoch and the others could finish the job from within the safety of the keep.

As his sword connected with the first of the silent soldiers, he remembered the sweet feel of Merewen in his arms. For the first time he had something to live for—no, some*one* to live for. But if he had to die to keep her safe, so be it.

He screamed in challenge, waded into the enemy, and made them bleed.

Murdoch cursed under his breath. He'd known it was a mistake to allow Lady Merewen to join the men on the walkway despite her promise to return to the hall as soon as the captain returned.

Well, Gideon had returned, but right now he was trapped outside the gates and fighting against over-whelming odds. Both men were on foot. Even with Kane at Gideon's back, they stood little chance against the two forces closing ranks around them.

Merewen looked up at him with stark fear in her eyes and tears streaming down her face. "Murdoch, do some-thing. Ride to his aid."

That was exactly what he wanted to do, but his pri-mary duty was to protect the keep and those within. If he and the other Damned rode out to join the fight, who would protect Merewen? And Alina? Never before in his long life had Murdoch felt so torn in his duty.

Duncan joined him, the same need to shed enemy blood gleaming in his eyes. "Well?"

That single word held a world of questions in it. They had all sworn to serve the gods, but their oath of fealty to Gideon predated that. Without Gideon, Murdoch would never have survived the abuse of his foster father. Duncan had his own horror stories; so did Averel.

Without Gideon, they were nothing.

So in the end, the answer was just that simple. "We fight."

Together they ran down the stairs from the walkway. Averel must have guessed what Murdoch's decision would be, because he was already mounted and leading two other horses to where the guards stood ready to open the gate.

Murdoch blocked Averel's way. "One of us has to stay to protect the keep."

The young warrior tried to shove his way past. "Gideon is my friend, too, Murdoch."

He understood exactly how his friend felt. Before he could argue the point, Merewen charged down the steps and caught his arm to get his attention one last time. "Let him fight, Murdoch. If the five of you fall, we have lost anyway. Go, but come back. All of you."

Murdoch smiled down at her. "If the gods ordain it."

The gate swung open, and the three rode out. If this was to be their last battle, at least the Damned would go down fighting together.

Gideon heard their battle cries long before he saw his friends. He should have known they'd never stand by and watch him and Kane die without throwing themselves into the fray. While he wanted to curse the idiocy of leaving Merewen and the others unprotected, he couldn't help but be proud of his friends, his brothers-in-arms, for their loyalty.

Shadow and the two dogs acted as harbingers for their human companions. Even Kiva had joined in the battle, the huge owl startling the horses and drawing blood with his claws. Sensing his own avatar's near exhaustion, Gideon had already sent Scim back to the keep to rest and keep an eye on Merewen for him. That made the reinforcements even more appreciated.

Kane dripped blood from several wounds but continued to fight. Another of the silent soldiers dropped to the ground. No time to count the victories, not when the battle still waged on.

Rogue played rearguard for them, forcing the enemy to come straight at them rather than from their blind side. Kestrel bolted in and out of sight, challenging the enemy mounts to fight or surrender. Several had reared up over and over until they unseated their riders. Once free of their burdens, they disappeared into the darkness.

Afoot, the enemy was less of a challenge. Shadow launched herself at another rider. He tried to wheel his horse out of her path, but the cat adjusted her attack in midair, sinking her fangs into his arm and dragging him to the ground. His dying scream ended on a bloody gurgle.

Finally, Murdoch and Duncan broke through the enemy lines with Averel only slightly behind them. In seconds, they joined Kane and Gideon on the ground, forming up beside them, swords already bloody. For the first time since the fighting started, Gideon smiled.

The evil that stalked this land was about to meet its first major defeat. Each of the five gave voice to their challenge to the enemy. As one, they stepped forward, ready to meet death head-on if that was what the gods demanded of them.

Slash and stab. Two steps forward, one step back. Again and again. Gideon risked one glance in the direction of the keep. Even from a distance he savored the sweet taste of Merewen's love. For her, he would fight to the last breath in his body. For her, he would fight harder. For her, he would send her enemies straight into the darkness of the afterlife to be weighed and found wanting by the gods.

Slash and stab. Another step, each harder won than the previous. Yet they made progress. The enemy lines were thinner now, but the Damned still stood shoulder to shoulder and grimly dealt out death and pain to those who dared oppose them.

Slash and stab. If he survived the night, Gideon would tell Merewen that he loved her with every breath he took and even beyond the day the gods called him to face their judgment for the last time.

It hurt to breathe. It hurt to stand, and his hands were slick with blood. His or his enemy's? He didn't know and wouldn't slow to find out. All that mattered was to keep pushing forward until they reached the keep.

Slash and stab. Slash and stab. One step closer to Merewen, one dead opponent at a time.

*   *   *

Merewen couldn't remember how to breathe much less how to think. All she could do was look on in horror as she watched Gideon and his men fight for their lives—for her life, too, and that of everyone who claimed the keep and the surrounding land as home.

The clang of metal against metal and the whimpers of the wounded combined with the eerie cries of the avatars in a melody of horror. Men were dying out there. Had they chosen to fight for her uncle's cause, or had they been forced to side with him against Gideon and his men?

Regardless of how they came to be there, she prayed for their departing souls even as she begged the gods to spare the lives of her champions. Had she known this would have been the outcome of her calling them from the river, would she still have chanted those words?

Yes. Her people had needed Gideon and the others to fight for their freedom.

"How bad is it?"

Merewen tore her eyes away from the fighting long enough to glance at Alina. "Bad enough."

Alina put a tentative arm around Merewen's shoulders, pulling her close. Merewen leaned against Alina, wishing they could do more than support each other. One way or the other, eventually the battle would be decided. Until then, all they could do was wait.

A movement at the bottom of the wall outside the gate caught her attention. Someone was attempting to force the gate open from the outside. No, not just someone. She would recognize that brute anyplace, anytime.

Olaf was attempting to sneak back into the keep. It was just like him to leave his men to do the dying. To her horror, someone on this side of the gate had already raised the bar. So they hadn't rooted out all of the traitors after all.

She yelled out a warning to the remaining guards,

who quickly subdued Olaf's confederate and then faced off against Olaf, their former captain. There had to be something more she could do! At the least, she could close the gate.

Alina latched onto her arm, holding her back. "No, Merewen! You will only be in the way!"

Her aunt was right, even if she didn't want to hear it. The warriors were closing in on the keep, but she wasn't sure they'd make it in time to save her men. The scream of a raptor split the night as help arrived in the shape of a gyrfalcon in a steep dive. Scim!

Next, Shadow slipped through the open gate, followed closely by Hob. Even the dogs returned to the keep. Merewen's men recognized them as allies and fell back, letting the swooping bird and snarling gargoyle force Olaf into retreating until he was pinned in a corner. He continued to brandish his sword and shout threats, but his efforts were futile against the avatars.

She checked on the progress outside the walls. Without Olaf to lead them, the rest of Fagan's men broke and ran. The last flurry of fighting was bloody and brutal, but finally Gideon and his men ran for the gate. As much as she wanted to be there to greet him, common sense ruled. Until Olaf was ... what? Captured? Dead? And where was her uncle? She hadn't seen him, but that didn't mean he wasn't still alive.

Gideon strode through the gate, his bearing almost regal. Duncan came next, supporting Kane who was limping badly. Averel entered unassisted, but his shirt was soaked with blood. Gideon called off the avatars to face Olaf with his men spread out beside him in a ragged circle.

"Surrender?"

Merewen held her breath as they waited for Olaf's answer. It wasn't long in coming. He charged toward Duncan and Kane, mistaking them for the weak link. Kane straightened up to face off against the desperate man. Even wounded and bleeding, he made quick work of Olaf.

"Where is Murdoch?" There was no mistaking the fear in Alina's voice. "I don't see him!"

Merewen could barely bring herself to tear her eyes away from the drama unfolding below, but she understood her aunt's fear.

She peered out into the night, only just then realizing the darkness was already giving way to early morning. It wasn't hard to spot the big warrior. He lay sprawled in the dirt just outside the gate with two men wearing the duke's livery dead at his feet. Obviously he'd warded off one last attack on his way into the keep.

With a horrified gasp, Alina went charging down the steps, leaving Merewen no choice but to follow. Her aunt reached Murdoch's side, kneeling down to lift his head into her lap. His eyes fluttered open when she brushed the hair back from his face.

"Murdoch, don't you dare die! We have plans, you and I."

"My lady," he whispered with a faint smile. "Nothing will keep me from you."

"No! She belongs to me!"

To Merewen's horror, Fagan appeared out of nowhere, his appearance so changed that it took her a heartbeat or two to even recognize him. His face was a twisted mask of insanity; his normally immaculate clothing was torn and filthy. Another of Duke Keirthan's men was at his side.

Fagan sneered at Murdoch, who struggled to get up. "She's mine, you lowbred scum! Not that the slattern is worth having. I have promised her to the duke to use as he will. The same with my niece. He'll kill me in their place if I don't deliver them."

Wild-eyed, he raised his sword, ready to plunge it down into Murdoch's chest.

Merewen screamed as her aunt flung herself over Murdoch's body, trying to protect the wounded warrior. As Fagan thrust downward, his silent companion shouted, "Hold!" and threw himself between the two women and her uncle. The blow meant for Murdoch bit deep into the stranger's chest.

It plunged straight into the medallion he wore on a chain around his neck, releasing a blinding burst of light and a crack of thunder. The unknown man screamed in agony and collapsed on the ground in a boneless heap. Fagan stepped over him, once again raising his sword. Before he could start the downward swing, he was jerked backward and tossed several feet away.

Gideon.

Keeping his eyes on Fagan, he asked, "Did he hurt either of you?"

Merewen shook her head. "Sir Murdoch was already down, but Alina and I are fine."

She pointed at the man on the ground. "He tried to save us."

"Take care of Murdoch." Gideon followed Fagan, who scrambled backward, trying to get away from the specter of death stalking toward him.

Despite everything, Gideon gave him a choice. "Which will it be—surrender or fight?"

Her uncle, his eyes wild, looked around, only now re-alizing that he was alone, his men dead or deserted. When he spoke, it was with resignation.

"I'm a dead man either way, and at least you'll make it quick and clean."

"Merewen, take Murdoch and go. Averel, help them."

The younger warrior appeared next to them. While she wanted to argue with Gideon, she understood he was still trying to protect her and her aunt. She left only be-cause Alina didn't need to witness her husband's execu-tion.

The two women and Averel half carried, half dragged Murdoch back inside the gate. As soon as they stepped into the bailey, she heard the clash of steel. The battle didn't last long.

Her uncle's dying scream greeted the sunrise.

Chapter 28

*I*t was midmorning on the third day after the battle. Gideon sat astride Kestrel, watching Duncan disappear into the distance. He hated to see him go, but it was the best hope they had for finding some answers.

The previous two days had been spent recuperating and burying the dead. Merewen had chosen to lay her uncle to rest near her father, saying she'd done it in memory of the man he used to be.

Alina seemed to have taken Fagan's loss with a mix of emotions, relief probably being chief among them. Luckily, caring for Sir Murdoch and the other wounded gave the new widow something to keep her hands and mind occupied.

It was impossible to know how many of Keirthan's men had escaped, but Kane and Hob had gone hunting during the past two nights and eliminated a handful. If any had gotten past him, the duke would soon know Fagan's efforts to regain the keep had failed. It was unlikely the man would take defeat well.

They'd taken but one prisoner: the man who had stopped Fagan from killing Murdoch and Lady Alina. He'd yet to regain consciousness, so they knew nothing of him or his motivations other than, judging by his uniform, he'd been a high-ranking officer in the duke's service.

Gideon doubted they'd done the soldier any favors by letting him live, knowing the low tolerance the man's former master had for failure. However, he might yet prove useful to their cause.

For certain, eventually the duke would make another move against them. Perhaps being denied both Merewen and Alina for use as sacrifices would weaken him for a while, but Gideon had no doubt that the man would find some way to strike back at them.

The question was how best to prepare for that possibility. To Gideon's surprise, the previous evening a pair of warriors had approached the gate. They represented several of the neighboring estates.

It would seem that there was growing concern throughout the outlying areas of Agathia. People had gone missing; entire homesteads had been found vacant with no sign of what had happened to the residents. The visitors were seeking out others willing to band together to provide a defense against the mysterious attacks.

The sound of another rider approaching had Kestrel stirring restlessly, but Gideon only smiled.

"You are thinking too hard."

Gideon kept his gaze on the horizon but held his hand out to Merewen, entwining his fingers with hers as her mare came to a stop next to the black stallion.

"There's much to consider."

She followed his line of sight out to where Duncan was approaching a distant rise. "Our visitors are asking if we will join forces with the others or if we'll at least meet with their liege lords."

"If you think they can be trusted, it would make sense to do so even if they aren't ready to believe that it is the duke himself behind the attacks. There is greater safety in numbers."

It was several seconds before Merewen responded. "I've sold horses to several of the men they mentioned, and they've dealt fairly with me. They also treat their horses well, which I take as a sign of good character."

Finding some trustworthy allies would be a true gift from the gods, especially with Gideon's own forces divided. "If you agree, I'd like to invite them to hold the discussions here where I can better control the situation. The duke already knows that at least we stand against him, so there's nothing to be gained by going elsewhere."

"Do as you see fit, Gideon."

There was one more thing. "Kane approached me with an idea today that I'm still considering. He thinks we would do well to place a spy close to the duke, specifically him. Since Keirthan is practicing magic of the darkest kind, he wouldn't question someone who bears a mage mark being drawn to his side. He might even take it as a validation of his supremacy."

He glanced at Merewen to see how she was reacting to the idea. She frowned but didn't reject it out of hand.

"What if some of Keirthan's men make it back to the city and Kane is recognized?"

"We've considered that. They wouldn't question his being a mercenary who would sell his sword and loyalty to the highest bidder."

Merewen looked back toward the keep where Kane was prowling along the walkway at the top of the palisade. "I hate for him to be exposed to such evil, especially when you say this dark magic calls to his blood. Alone, it could go hard on him."

Her concern for his friend warmed Gideon's soul. "I agree, which is why I'll send Averel with him. They will separate, with Averel traveling as a troubadour. He'll seek work in the city where he can keep in touch with Kane."

Gideon hated this whole situation. "Merewen, we are sworn to protect you, but it would seem that we would best serve you by scattering our forces. If that worries you, I'll keep Kane and Averel here, but we'll be fighting blind."

"I trust your judgment, Gideon. If we don't oppose the duke, then no one will remain safe for long."

And the sands of time were running. "Let's ride."

They rode side by side all the way to the clearing by the river. It was the same spot where the two of them had walked together and then shared their first kiss.

Gideon dismounted first and then held his arms up to Merewen. He removed the pack he'd secured to the back of Kestrel's saddle and set it on the ground. "I plan to be here awhile, so let's unsaddle the horses and let them graze in comfort."

Merewen let him lead her down to the water's edge where he spread out a blanket and set down the meal he'd had Ellie prepare for the two of them.

"Shall we sit?"

She joined him on the blanket. He leaned against a log for support while she curled up at his side, her head upon his chest. For the longest time, they were content to enjoy the warmth of the sun.

But finally, his lady asked, "Gideon, what is on your mind?"

He listened to the rippling water, wishing he found it soothing. Where to start? "Our time is speeding by, and we must make each day count. This evil must be stopped. All too soon, my men and I must return to the river. Before that happens, I need to know that you will be safe."

He felt Merewen shiver and wrapped his arm around her, pulling her closer. She turned to look up at him, her dark eyes so sad. "I hate that for all of you. Haven't you done enough to atone for your mistakes?"

He tried to smile. "It isn't our place to question the gods, Merewen. We freely swore to serve their cause. Our honor demands we fulfill that vow."

He stared up at the sun, loving its warmth on his skin

and loving the woman in his arms. "Each time we face judgment, I pray my friends will be released from their vows, that we've finally balanced the scales. This time will be that much harder for all of us because we have let ourselves care about your people."

Her soft hand cupped the side of his face, forcing him to look down into her eyes. "Just my people?"

She deserved his truth. "No, not just your people. I love you with every breath I have in me. I believe the goddess herself has blessed our mating, and that means something. But until we know how this battle will unfold, all we have is each day the gods give us. In that, we are no different than anyone else who faces the evil the duke has unleashed upon this land."

He brushed his lips across hers. "I will understand if that is not enough."

Her eyes carried a sheen of tears, but her smile was strong for all that. "I cherish each moment that you are in my life, Gideon. What time the gods give us will be enough to fill both my heart and my soul."

She pulled away and sat up. He watched as she tugged the ribbon from her braid to let the dark silk of her hair spill down around her shoulders. Next, her hands went to work on the lacings of her tunic, revealing all that velvet smooth skin.

"Merewen—"

He had no words—none at all.

Fortunately, his lady knew the right ones. Her smile was all temptation and desire. "You said something about making each day count. I suggest we start with this one."

When she melted into his embrace, he found the right words after all.

"I love you, Merewen. Now and for always."

Read on for a special preview of
the next book in Alexis Morgan's
Warriors of the Mist series,

Her Knight's Quest

Coming in March 2013 from Signet Eclipse

*T*he mirror-smooth surface shattered, sending a sudden surge of cold water gushing over the side of the bowl to soak the skirt of Lavinia's dress. Despite her best efforts to impose her will over the unruly liquid, it continued to ripple and refused to come back into focus, a clear reflection of Lavinia's own agitation.

When her third attempt failed, she snatched up the bowl and tossed its contents toward the roses in her private garden. Maybe the water would do more good for the plants than it had for her. The simple truth was that she'd learn nothing until she controlled her emotions, especially her fear.

"Shall I fetch a fresh pitcher of water?"

Lavinia forced a more pleasant expression onto her face before turning to face Sarra, who hovered a short distance away. The young girl practically vibrated with the need to be of service.

Lord and Lady, had she ever been that earnest and innocent herself? All things considered, it didn't seem likely.

Injecting a soothing note into her voice, Lavinia shook her head. "No, my child. I will do so myself. The walk will help clear my head."

Then her smile became more genuine. "Besides, Sarra, I do believe it is time for your music lesson. Sister Joetta will be waiting for you."

Sarra's face lit up as she immediately bolted toward

the door that led back inside the abbey. About halfway there, she froze and slowly turned back, her eyes wide with chagrin. "I'm sorry, my lady. I forgot."

Then she dropped into a low curtsey with her eyes trained on the floor. "May I be excused?"

Lavinia crossed to where the girl remained frozen in position. She gently raised Sarra's face and then smiled at her with a wink. "All these rules and procedures take a while to master, don't they? Go. Seek out Sister Joetta. Tell her that you don't need to report back to me until after the midday meal."

Sarra immediately straightened up and surprised Lavinia with a quick hug before continuing on her headlong charge toward the door. "Don't worry, my lady. I'll do my best for Sister Joetta."

"I know you will, little one."

Once she was alone again, Lavinia sank down on the bench and rested her eyes. She'd been up since before dawn searching for answers among the forbidden texts. All her efforts had garnered her were a headache and more questions with no answers.

She'd hoped her gift for scrying would prove more useful, but it had failed her as well. Perhaps that walk she'd mentioned to young Sarra would actually help. As much as Lavinia loved the sanctuary of her private garden, sometimes the high walls closed in on her. She glanced up at the narrow slice of blue sky overhead.

How long had it been since she'd last ventured beyond the abbey's thick walls and out into the real world?

It didn't bear thinking about. Even if she didn't have responsibilities that kept her firmly anchored where she was, the world outside was far too dangerous a place for her right now. Not all predators that prowled the world walked on four legs.

As tempting as it was to sit there in the warmth of the sun until the midday meal, she couldn't. Too much was at stake to pretend everything was all right. She picked up the pitcher and walked back inside, cutting through her office to the hallway that ran through the heart of the abbey. The thick rugs muted the sound of her footsteps as she made her way through the building to the courtyard that surrounded the well.

After filling her pitcher, she savored a ladle of the cool, sweet water before returning to her garden. This time, she moved slowly as she sought to quiet her spirit. She carefully filled the scrying bowl again and set the pitcher aside. Lacing her fingers together, she closed her eyes and concentrated on her breathing.

Slowly Lavinia centered herself, consciously shutting out the distractions of the world beyond the abbey walls. Next, she shut out the muted sounds of the other sisters going about their daily lives and duties. Finally, she shut out her own fearful thoughts and worry. That was the hardest part.

When at last she opened her eyes, the water in her bowl was mirror smooth and still. At last! She shuffled a half step closer and stared down into the shallow depths of the water. At first, she saw nothing but the rich green of the glass, but then, piece by piece, a narrow strip of road came into focus.

It was impossible to gauge its exact location, but judging from the terrain, it had to be the trade route that led caravans through the Sojourn Valley and past the abbey. Odd, though, there was no line of wagons anywhere in sight. Why would the goddess show her a stretch of empty road? She started to step back when a small movement at the edge of the water caught her attention.

Ah, so the road wasn't empty after all. A solitary horse and rider trotted into sight heading in the direction of the abbey. The image was too small for her to pick out any detail, so she closed her eyes again and concentrated on asking for more information.

When she looked again, the image had changed. This time the horse was grazing, and the rider was sitting cross-legged next to a small campfire. She leaned closer to the water, hoping to get a better look at the man, hoping to pick out enough details so that she'd recognize him if she were to meet him in person. In truth, not *if* but *when* she met him. He would not appear in her vision if there wasn't a connection to be forged between them.

This vision appeared to be a warning that the traveler would find his way to the abbey. That wasn't unusual in itself. There weren't many places to stop along the route between Agathia and the lands beyond. Most travelers stopped at the abbey to enjoy a night's hospitality among the sisters.

The only oddity was that few were either brave enough or reckless enough to travel alone. Times were too dangerous, yet this man didn't seem concerned. A more prudent traveler wouldn't have kept a campfire burning out in the open, knowing the light might draw unwanted company.

As she watched, the focus abruptly plunged down like a hawk diving after prey. Her stomach lurched with the sudden change. The man jumped to his feet, his sword appearing in his hand as if by magic. His head spun in all directions as if to defend himself from an imminent attack.

Finally, he looked straight up, his strangely pale eyes staring right into Lavinia's. The power of the connection shattered her hard-won calm. She stumbled back from the bowl. What had just happened?

Her heart pounded in her chest, and the air in the garden had grown too thin to breathe. Never in all of her years of scrying had such a thing happened. Her mentor, the prior abbess, had never mentioned the possibility of the mirror of the water working in both directions.

Rather than risk another look, Lavinia averted her

eyes as she carefully covered the bowl with a black cloth. After whispering a short prayer of thanks to the goddess for the gift of the vision and asking for the wisdom to understand it, she left the garden.

The gong sounded, summoning everyone to the dining hall. Right now, she was too unsettled to be hungry, but rituals and routines were important. If nothing else, they provided a sense of order in a world that had long since become dark and dangerous. Maybe later she would let herself think about the mysterious stranger who was wending his way toward the abbey. Until he actually arrived, there was no way to know if his purpose was for good or for ill.

With that unsettling thought, she fell into line with the other sisters and let their loving presence comfort her.

Duncan thanked the gods that his friends weren't there to witness him jumping at shadows. Murdoch would never let him forget it. After one last look around, Duncan sheathed his sword and sat back down by the fire. He fed another log to the flames and watched the sparks fly up into the night sky.

That had been the second time in one day that he'd experienced the strangest sensation that he was being watched. The first time happened as he had been riding along the trail, his thoughts drifting with the breeze. Between one breath and the next, his mare had snorted and sidestepped, almost unseating him. He'd managed to stay in the saddle, but it had been a close call.

He'd looked everywhere trying to determine what had startled the horse. When nothing obvious presented itself, they'd continued on, but he'd found himself looking back over his shoulder for some distance afterward.

Then he'd been staring into the fire, waiting for Kiva to finish his nightly hunt. At first he'd thought it was the owl swooping back to their makeshift camp that had disturbed him, but then that same powerful sensation had washed over him.

He'd reacted instinctively, jumping to his feet, sword in hand, ready to ward off an attack. One that never came. The night was silent; nothing stirred, the only threat the uncanny feeling that someone was out there watching Duncan's every move.

After checking in all directions, he started to relax when he happened to look up. For the briefest instant, the image of a woman, one with worried eyes and a lush mouth set in a deep frown, had superimposed itself over the gibbous moon. Her face had appeared and then disappeared so quickly that he knew he had to be imagining things.

Even so, he could still see her face in his mind with disturbing clarity. She'd been lovely, with the kind of beauty that could haunt a man's dreams. Duncan shifted uncomfortably, his body reacting in a way it hadn't in a long time. Centuries, in fact.

It was definitely time to seek his pallet. At first light, he would resume his trek to the abbey.

AVAILABLE NOW FROM

Virginia Henley

THE DARK EARL

It's love at first sight for Lady Harriet Hamilton—love with Thomas Anson's ancestral home, that is. Thomas' father, the Earl of Lichfield, has gambled away the family's honor, and now it's cost them everything at Shugborough Hall. The estate sale is shameful enough without some little brat sneaking around his property—but young Harry has caught him sneaking around as well…

When they meet again, years later, neither Harry nor Viscount Thomas has forgotten their encounter. While he's grown into the exact opposite of his reprobate father, Harry is outspoken, audacious, and now, Thomas must admit, quite a beauty. But he's committed to restoring the family holdings, not chasing after a wife. If only she wasn't hurling herself against his principles—and having such a good time doing it…

New York Times bestselling author

BERTRICE SMALL

The Border Vixen

This novel in the Border Chronicles
series "reaffirms her standing as a
historical romance stalwart."*

Aware of the covetous interest in his land, the laird of
Brae Aisir announces that any man who can outrun,
outride, and outfight his headstrong granddaughter
"Mad Maggie" will have her as a wife—along with her
inheritance. His proposition causes more chaos than
resolution, especially when King James II sends his
cousin, Fingal Stewart, to compete for Maggie's hand.
The competition brings out the fire in both of them, and
it doesn't take long for the rivals to become lovers. But
there are those who will do anything to gain control of
Maggie's inheritance—even if it means getting rid of
Fingal Stewart and his border vixen.

*Publishers Weekly

**Available wherever books are sold or at
penguin.com**